PETER VOSSLER

The Seventh Chamber

PETER VOSSLER

THE SEVENTH CHAMBER

A Phantastic Novel

Sebastian Münster, *Tree of Paradise*, in: *Cosmographia,* Basel, 1544

Translated into English by the author
Typesetting, cover design, and illustrations, unless otherwise indicated: Peter Voßler

Set in Bembo® MT by Monotype,
Remsen Script™ by Three Island Press,
American Scribe™ by Three Island Press,
ITC Benguiat® by ITC,
IM FELL Double Pica by Igino Marini.
"The Fell Types are digitally reproduced by Igino Marini, www.iginomarini.com."

Initials by Hans Holbein, from *Imagines Mortis* (Public Domain).

Published via Kindle Direct Publishing (KDP).

ISBN: 978-3-9826918-4-8

CONTENTS

"I approached the confines of death,
and, treading on the threshold of Proserpine,
returned therefrom,
being borne through all the elements.
At midnight I saw the sun
shining with a splendid light;
and I approached the gods beneath
and the gods above,
and adored them face to face."

Apuleius, METAMORPHOSES (XI, 23)

CHAPTER I.
HÔTEL LA PORTE NOIRE

Paris 1831

The rain drummed upon the gleaming, rain-washed cobblestones, which, cleansed of the gutter's filth, shone like black obsidian beneath the sun. Shopkeepers hastily shut their doors, while shadowy, pallid faces peered out from beneath awnings and overhangs, their features distorted, offering only meager refuge against the tempestuous downpour. Long rows of towering Lombardy poplars, their slender trunks bending from their pedantic alignment, swayed like drunken men beneath the oppressive, leaden weight of the sky. Dark puddles flooded the gutters, their surfaces marked by concentric ripples reflecting the towering facades of the buildings above.

Leaning into the wind, clad in a dark, high-buttoned frock coat, a stranger carved his way through the vertical deluge. His umbrella, stretched to its limits, its metal spokes fencing in ceaseless, flashing parries against the gales, at last succumbed to the relentless onslaught. Discarding it, he pressed his hat lower over his brow, gripping a suitcase in one hand while tucking the ruined umbrella under his arm, striding forward against wind and rain. He followed a branching street on his left, a serpentine artery winding through gray, steep-gabled houses, their roofs, dormers, and overburdened gutters disgorging torrents of water upon the cobbled main road and the mire of side alleys.

His path led toward an imposing building at the end of a labyrinthine alley, flanked by ungainly, time-worn houses that had long since settled into asymmetry. Its ornate gable sliced through an expansive mass of clouds, which, like a foam-capped tidal wave, loomed over the violet-gray horizon before spiraling downward into a distant, churning maelstrom. Hand-hewn beams, dark and furrowed like bog oak, with peculiarly carved embellishments, framed the water-stained plaster, which in many places had eroded to reveal the underlying masonry. Symmetrical rows of tall, mullioned windows stretched like the gun ports of a man-of-war across the skeletal timber framework. On either side of the structure, dented downspouts, corroded with holes, snaked in bizarre curves toward the roof, casting erratic fountains of water in all directions.

Above a direct stairway, amidst stone foundation walls that rose like the ramparts of a fortress, lay a spacious portal, approached by a decrepit, rust-eaten railing that emerged from the weathered steps. Yellow-tinged iron oxide had gathered in the recesses and streaked downward, forming long rivulets that ran like tears over the stone. The immense door, set in iron hinges, bore a blackened bronze relief, its surface adorned with cryptic inscriptions and enigmatic symbols. *Hôtel La Porte Noire* was emblazoned in elegant script upon a porcelain plaque affixed, seemingly in recent times, to one of the stone pillars supporting the entrance.

The stranger set down his suitcase. His strong hand grasped a sculpted door knocker, shaped like the sinuous, scaled body of a serpent rising from the dark wood. The blows rang out, reverberating through the towering stone walls, just as the rain suddenly ceased, and the sun, in a final defiant surge, cast its rays through the mist-laden veil. These beams multiplied a thousandfold upon windowpanes, scattering into a dazzling spectacle of radiant halos, striking flagpoles and door handles, glistening upon the rain-saturated slate, and breaking upon the leaded domes, dormers, and cornices of the surrounding buildings. He raised a shielding hand toward the heavens, lest he be blinded by the brilliance of the celestial display.

After what felt like an eternity, a staccato of dull footsteps echoed upon stone, then the door swung inward with a discordant overtone. The sunlight, emerging from the mist, hungrily illuminated the space beyond, revealing a towering figure clad in the livery of a late-seventeenth-century servant, who suddenly loomed before him like a wall. The stranger removed his hat, wiped the rain from his face with one hand, and returned the murmured greeting, thick with an unfamiliar accent. Hair black as coal framed his pale, youthful face—he must have been nearing thirty—upon which capricious fate had etched its traces. His blue, dreamlike eyes held a depth that seemed incongruous with his age.

As he followed the hulking figure toward a long oak counter, his gaze flickered across the space in a fraction of a second. The dim light of the entrance hall barely reached the high ceiling, upheld by massive oak beams. Iron wall sconces, their flames fed with oil, cast flickering shadows upon faded murals depicting nature scenes and biblical motifs. For a fleeting moment, he thought he had glimpsed a vision of paradise, yet the creatures portrayed were of a kind he had never encountered—neither in any zoo, be it here in Paris'

Jardin des Plantes, nor in Vienna or London, nor even during his travels through the Near East or any other forsaken corner of the map he had set foot upon. A simian hybrid with a grotesque skull, an armadillo of bovine stature, and a Nubian lion with a nightmarish maw stared at him in eerie stillness from faded pigments.

In the center of the spacious reception hall, a staircase flanked by column-like balustrades ascended into the dimness of the upper floors. Old carpets, seemingly Oriental or perhaps Caucasian in origin, interwoven with strange patterns, trailed from his vantage point over the stone steps, disappearing into the dimly illuminated corridors, where the meager light reflected only faintly upon the nameplates affixed to distant doors. The spiral staircase, seemingly anchored by unseen supports within the space, evidently extended into the lower recesses of the building as well. His gaze rested upon the darkness gathered before those unseen depths, yet his eyes could not pierce its obscurity. He thought, however, that he perceived the sound of rushing water, echoing ominously upward from the twilight realm of its Piranesian architecture.

The hôtel seemed ancient, far older than London's *Grand Hotel* in *Covent Garden* or the *Royal Clarence* in Exeter. Even the inn from which it must have originally evolved bore no resemblance to medieval lodging houses. And for some inexplicable reason, an unshakable unease settled over him, a heavy weight of oppression for which he could not provide a rational cause. "Monsieur!"—the porter's voice tore him from his trance—"Would you be so kind to tell me your name?" He looked up in surprise at the giant's face, which, in its attempt at a smile, only seemed all the more ominous.

Only now did he become fully aware of the unnatural silence enveloping every sound like an intruder. The hôtel seemed utterly abandoned; the reception hall stood empty, and even in the hallways, as far as he could see, the usual bustling activity had given way to an eerie stillness. A cough from the expectantly staring giant before him finally scattered his disjointed thoughts. "Camill," he answered in a thick voice, and, as the oak-paneled reception seemed to swallow his words, he repeated more firmly: "My name is Phineas Camill. I require a room for several days." The porter scrawled the name with a fountain pen that, in his enormous hands, resembled a tiny gilded embroidery needle, into a leather-bound ledger. Phineas wondered how such a slim volume could possibly suffice for what he had expected to be a heavily booked establishment. "Are the number of guests usually so few?" he asked, his tone uncertain as he gazed up at the mountainous figure before him.

"Without invitation, you not can sleep here," the porter muttered in his thick, slurred accent. Rather than pressing the question, Phineas found himself wondering whether the man had even understood it at all. Then, without the slightest unnecessary movement, the giant handed him a key and gestured vaguely toward the upper floors. "Room forty-two," the massive mouth intoned. Phineas gathered his leather suitcase, reinforced with brass corners and wooden slats, along with his rain-sodden umbrella and hat, and ascended the vast spiral staircase toward that room whose number rang forth from the dusk of the lobby like an oracle's utterance. He steadied himself against the stone railing, which seemed to narrow endlessly as it climbed toward the unseen heights. The carved surface, worn smooth over time, felt cool beneath his palm as he trudged upward, each step an exertion against the weight of his exhaustion.

A faint glimmer of light seeped in from outside, filtering through the cracks in the heavy, curtain-draped windows. Dust motes sparkled like will-o'-the-wisps within the cathedral-like beams. Instead of gaslights, oil lamps flickered throughout the corridor, their glow converging in the distance into a dim, golden haze, barely illuminating the brass nameplates upon the doors. After some time, he found his assigned room. Releasing several bolts, he turned the key with a metallic click, and the heavy door creaked inward, the sound accompanied by an eerie discordance. A stale, musty odor met him, as though the chamber had been left untouched for months. Utterly exhausted, he set his suitcase and umbrella down, where they immediately formed a small puddle upon the wooden floor. Casting his drenched hat and coat over the back of a chair, he unlaced his boots and collapsed onto an imposing wrought-iron bed. The door swung shut behind him with an unsettling finality, leaving him in utter darkness. With his feet, aided by the edge of the bed, he slipped off his boots, then discarded his damp clothing in a heap upon the floor. Within moments, he plunged into a deep, dreamless sleep.

At some unknown hour of the night, he awoke. With stiff fingers, he fumbled for a sulfur match in the darkness. The first snapped under his clumsy grip; cursing under his breath, he struck another, bringing the cotton wick of an oil lamp to life. The burgeoning glow flickered over the wooden paneling, illuminating strange inscriptions—ornate hieroglyphs, an indecipherable sequence of Phoenician consonants, and stylized depictions of gods reminiscent of ancient Egyptian iconography, their forms imbued with an almost cosmic significance. Still dazed with sleep, he turned away from the strange engravings, hoisted his suitcase onto the bed, and began unpacking, placing his belongings into one of the large wooden armoires.

Among his shirts lay a portrait of Eireen. He picked it up reverently, tracing his thumb over the delicate, gold-leafed surface of the frame. His eyes gleamed, as if a thin sheet of ice had formed over them. When he blinked, tiny, glistening pearls clung to his lashes. The corners of his mouth quivered ever so slightly. He savored the moment—it had an almost ritualistic quality—for when he suffered, he felt alive once more. And this suffering, strange as it seemed, tethered him to existence. His grief, inexplicable yet profound, imbued his life with a deeper meaning, as though it rendered him worthy of some higher form of communion, as though this affliction itself bore a purpose beyond his understanding.

Lost in such thoughts, he was jolted from his lethargy by a loud scraping and creaking, leading him to suspect that these noises had been the cause of his earlier disturbance. The strange sounds seemed to emanate from the room adjacent to his own. He strained his senses, narrowing his eyes and tilting his head toward the opposite wall, but no further activity could be discerned. After a time, the unsettling noise resumed—something heavy shifting across stone and sand. He wondered what kind of fool would be dragging furniture about at this hour but refrained from investigating, as his mind quickly supplied several rational explanations for the nocturnal disturbance. The most plausible seemed to be that some sluggish servant, having finally stirred from his stupor, was clumsily hauling travelers' luggage up to one of the upper floors. He sat up, pressed his ear to the wall, and listened, but once again, the same unnatural silence enveloped him—the same eerie quiet that had seemed to settle over the hôtel the moment he crossed its threshold, as if he had stepped into an oubliette.

Minutes passed. Reclining on the bed, his gaze drifting aimlessly along the ceiling, he slipped back into a drowsy reverie. Then, once more, the inexplicable noise erupted—deeper, more resonant, and this time accompanied by a tremor that seemed to shake the entire structure. Flecks of plaster crumbled from a gap in the ornately framed ceiling moldings. It seemed to him that stone was splintering, yet in some unplaceable way, the sound was distant, muted—far removed from the force of the tremor itself, as if the deafening collapse of a dam or a mountainside landslide were reaching him only as a faint echo from some remote abyss. With a frozen expression, he stepped into the hallway. Pausing unnaturally before the neighboring door, he listened once more. A dull, low frequency rumbled, then the door suddenly jolted within its wooden frame, as if a gust of wind had torn through an open window inside. Fine dust swirled in the dim light, drifting sluggishly toward the floor through the gap beneath the door. And then—as if the room beyond belonged to another world—voices arose. First a whisper, low and indistinct, a murmuring filled with eerie words, a susurration spiraling up from the depths of lost ages, monotonous incantations of an unanswered liturgy. Then, without warning—screams, shrill and piercing, filled with madness and despair, as though someone were gazing into the abyss of hell itself. At once, the voices resumed, but now with reproach, chastising someone unseen, before dissolving into the whimpering of a frightened child, fraught with an internal torment impossible to reconcile.

Phineas was just about to turn away when a bolt from within slid back, and the door swung open so suddenly that he recoiled several steps in alarm. A gaunt old man, peculiarly dressed in an antiquated robe adorned with mystic-spiritual symbols and an equally adorned headdress, its archaic design evoking both theatrical grandeur and the wisdom of ancient rites steeped in incense, stumbled into the corridor. Pale, parchment-thin skin, mottled with age spots, stretched over his skeletal visage, from which a sparse, wispy beard spilled down his deeply furrowed cheeks. His pallid hand, long and bony, with gnarled veins snaking beneath its surface, seized Phineas's shirt with unexpected strength, his tendons standing out like the prongs of a rake. His hollowed eyes, now locked with Phineas's at close range, radiated a terrible knowledge—a vast understanding overshadowed by the unmistakable madness of one who had beheld something beyond human comprehension, some vision too immense for mortal senses to grasp.

Strange, foreign words, meaningless fragments of speech in a chaotic cascade of multiple tongues, many of them likely long forgotten, an unsettling string of cryptic *nomina barbara* swelling into dark incantations and hymns, poured forth in a monotonous rhythm from his stammering lips. Time and again, he burst into curses and imprecations in French, only to spiral into such a frenzy of meaningless delirium that, as his cries weakened to nothing more than a hoarse whisper, it seemed as though he were expelling the very last remnants of his untainted soul. Phineas understood little of the dreadful utterances spilling from that accursed mouth. Beyond the monotonous, seemingly endless repetition of obscure and foreign-sounding names—ones that might well have belonged to angels or their infernal counterparts in the deepest reaches of hell—one word stood out with distinct clarity amidst the absurd litany of Hebrew, Latin, French, and something altogether unrecognizable: "Misraim." He heard it multiple times but could make little sense of its meaning.

A few distant doors along the vast corridors briefly opened and shut again, leading Phineas to conclude that he and the deranged old man were not the only guests in this unsettling place. At the peak of his frenzied outburst, the old man suddenly fell silent. His gaze cleared, and for a fleeting moment, he seemed to regain his senses—only to lapse almost immediately into an unnatural, vacant apathy. He stared blankly at the towering porter who had seemingly materialized out of nowhere before him, allowing himself to be led wordlessly back into his chamber. The door slammed shut behind him with the finality of an asylum cell, and for a time, only the muffled, indistinct murmur of the porter's voice seeped through the thick wood, as though he were attempting to reason with the senile guest.

Phineas withdrew to his own room, carefully bolting the door behind him. Yet, contrary to his expectations, no further sounds emanated from the adjoining room that night—nor from anywhere else within the ancient building. Resuming his previous task, he finished stowing away his clothing and a few personal effects in the wardrobe. From his writing desk, Eireen's gold-ornamented portrait smiled serenely at him as he drifted into a restless, uneasy sleep.

Phineas dreams of Eireen, watching the sunken, narrow features of her face and the emaciated body, marked by spasms, writhing beneath the damp-stained linen, growing weaker with each passing hour. He brushes the sweat-soaked strands of hair from her pallid face, dark rivulets spreading across her skin like ink. His trembling hand rests against her cheek as he gazes into her eyes, now lifeless, nothing more than empty, dark chasms.

Through tear-filled eyes, he stares as though through mist at her strangely altered visage—her head tilted back, washed in the bloodless pallor of the grave; her hollowed temples; the taut and parched skin of her brow; her nose, sharp and finely upturned; her mouth, slightly parted, its final breath dissolving in a wretched sigh; her leaden flesh, no longer held firm by the sinews of her form, collapsing in upon itself; and her once loving gaze, now sunk into the abyss of a lightless void.

He stands over her lifeless body, motionless upon the catafalque, an image of sanctity sculpted in marble, severed from time, yearning beyond the veil. He buries her in the family crypt. "Too much grief is a sin!" admonishes the priest, William Frye, yet though Phineas is certain that Eireen rests in Abraham's bosom, he cannot overcome the weight of his sorrow, the deep and abiding grief that clings to him like a shadow.

He awakens at the break of dawn, feeling surprisingly rested despite his interrupted slumber and the haunting visions of his dreams. He washes himself in the clear water of a copper basin, drying the droplets from his finely cut features with a cotton towel. For the first time, he takes a careful look around the room in which he has spent the night, his fingers gliding over the wooden paneling, tracing the sharp contours of its peculiar carvings. A vast secco mural, spanning the entire wall, had eluded his notice the evening before, obscured by dim lighting and faded pigments. Now, he beholds its imagery—a paradisiacal garden, teeming with wondrous beasts, rendered in an ethereal perfection untouched by decay.

He unfastens the aged, fogged window to let in the morning air, hoping to glimpse the street he had so hastily traversed the night before. To his disappointment, his view is obstructed by a crumbling, salt-encrusted wall some distance away. The cool morning air sweeps into the chamber, raising goosebumps upon his skin. He leans outward, tilting his head skyward, his gaze resting upon the cloudless expanse where unreachable sunbeams fracture against a leaded roof edge, their nascent radiance unfurling far above him. He discerns additional floors rising overhead and notes that his room occupies a secluded wing of the building.

Kneeling on the wooden floor, his limbs stiff with the chill, he recites one of the prayers the priest had once instilled in him with patient severity. The words fall from his lips with mechanical precision, practiced and rote, as though he were reading from a *materia medica*, dutifully repeating the prescription of a remedy. Though he considers himself, at his core, beholden to a Christian worldview and faith, his prayers are more the product of a vague sentimentality—an adherence to traditions ingrained in the deepest strata of his being, something that might best be called conscience. He cannot cast them aside without feeling a hollow unease, an unsettling sense of incompletion. And so, bound to this inherited piety and its nebulous impressions, he utters his prayers with unwavering regularity, though they lack the fervor of true devotion—for the longing of his heart had long since fallen silent.

"O Lord Almighty, God of our fathers, Abraham, Isaac, and Jacob, and of their righteous offspring, who made heaven and earth and all that is within them, who bound the sea by Your command and shut up the deep and sealed it by Your fearsome and glorious name..." His

thoughts drifted to the unsettling image of the old man raving in madness. "*... that all may tremble before You and fear Your great power! ...*" Then, to the vision of the hôtel's sharp gable, rising like the nave of a cathedral from cataclysmic floods. "*... You, O Lord, have, according to Your great goodness, promised repentance for the forgiveness of sins. But I have sinned, and my sins are more numerous than the sands of the sea, and I walk bowed down in heavy iron fetters, finding no rest, for I have provoked Your wrath and done much evil before You...*" His mind wandered again—to his dream, to Eireen, to her final, pain-stricken struggle and the last farewell. To the cruel fact that he had not returned in time, that his final words of love had reached her only in the haze of fevered delirium. It seemed to him an unforgivable sin. He gathered himself and forced his mind back to the prayer. "*... But now I bend the knees of my heart and implore You, O Lord, for mercy. Do not let me perish in my sins, nor let Your punishment remain upon me, but be gracious to me, unworthy as I am, according to Your great mercy; and so will I praise You all the days of my life. For the whole host of heaven sings Your praise, and Yours is the glory forever and ever. Amen.*"

While he was still kneeling on the floor, a loud knock sounded at the door. As he unlatched it, the giant stood before him, a tray balanced in one hand, a package tucked under his muscled arm, and a grumbled "Breakfast ready!" escaping his lips. The stone arch of the doorway seemed to hover over his massive shoulders like a yoke.

"Is there no dining hall in this establishment?" Phineas asked, puzzled.

The servant hunched his head slightly as he stepped inside, set the tray and the package on the table, muttered his mantra once more—"Breakfast ready!"—and then squeezed his enormous bull-like neck back through the archway before slamming the door shut behind him.

The meal was simple, yet after the tribulations of the previous day, it tasted exquisite. As he sipped his *café au lait* and broke off pieces from a golden round loaf of bread that the French call *boule*, its crust crisp beneath his fingers, he found his thoughts drifting to Monsieur Lameth, his benefactor and soon-to-be employer, who had summoned him to Paris on business and recommended this peculiar hôtel—of which he also appeared to be the proprietor. It was Lameth who had taken him under his wing after those fateful days. By his own account, he had been a friend of Phineas's long-deceased parents and had possessed the foresight to recognize the potential slumbering beneath the bloodshot, directionless eyes and the unkempt exterior.

He unwrapped the parcel, neatly enclosed in firm paper and secured with a cord, and retrieved several books—evidently sent by Lameth, as confirmed by a small card that slipped out upon removing them. Lameth had yet to reveal the precise nature of his employment, having only provided him with a reading list to study in advance—a task Phineas had undertaken with initial enthusiasm, though his dedication had soon waned. The selection consisted largely of dense material: ancient and medieval metaphysics; Pythagorean, Jewish, and Christian numerology, replete with bewildering intricacies; the teachings of the Greco-Roman mystery schools; Old Testament Merkabah mysticism—many of the texts being unpublished translations of ancient Hebrew manuscripts, with Lameth himself credited as the translator. There were also writings by Clement of Alexandria and other Church Fathers on Gnosticism, along with a manuscript illustrated with geometric diagrams, reportedly acquired by a Scottish scholar from some nameless tomb in Thebes, near the mortuary temple of Ramesses III, which Lameth claimed to have copied and translated from Coptic. Additionally, the collection included Hermetic philosophy rooted in ancient Egyptian thought, such as the 'Corpus Hermeticum'; Kabbalistic-alchemical works like Welling's 'Opus Mago-Cabbalisticum et Theosophicum', Agrippa's 'De Occulta Philosophia', and Paracelsus's 'Aurora Philosophorum'; a German edition of the 'Egyptian Great Revelations' of the Jew Abraham von Worms; and various medieval grimoires that, in Phineas's opinion, no Christian should read without reluctance.

"Magic, my dear Phineas," Lameth had remarked in response, "is by no means a reprehensible practice. *The Three Magi*, as they are commonly known, were well-versed in its arts, and it was their privilege to behold the coming of the Lord." Yet Phineas had noticed a subtle tightening of Lameth's expression as he uttered the latter part of his sentence, as though the specter of impending judgment loomed before him. He wondered whether Lameth was truly so devout that he feared the return of the Redeemer and the divine reckoning for his sins. Lost in thought, Phineas absently turned the pages of Lenglet du Fresnoy's 'Histoire de la Philosophie Hermétique', until a passage seemed to press itself upon his attention:

"The cogitations of their earliest founders far surpass all that has ever been discerned since the creation of the world. They are destined to restore the universe in its entirety. They are subject neither to hunger nor thirst, nor to the ravages of age or any other natural afflictions. Through direct revelation, they discern who is worthy of admission into their society. They are able to live in every epoch as

though they had existed since the dawn of creation and were fated to endure until the end of the ages. They are capable of subduing the mightiest spirits and demons and rendering them subservient."

As he read these lines, he earnestly began to wonder what it was that Lameth might expect to gain from the study of such blasphemous flights of fancy, and his well-founded doubts multiplied—whether that man truly intended to employ him for the earning of his bread, or merely to keep him occupied with some trivial pursuit in honor of his deceased parents, to have nurtured a fool within him, or, perhaps simply out of refined ennui, to share with him his own interest in mystical and magical literature. He also wondered what knowledge Lameth might be hoarding in his country house, situated south of Colchester in England, for he had, if only fleetingly, caught sight of ancient, half-decayed codices and scrolls—primarily inscribed on parchment or papyrus—from epochs long past, which appeared as though Lameth himself had wrested them from the desert. They were stored within his home either in dark glass display cases or as bound volumes on towering, meter-high shelves.

After the taciturn porter had delivered his midday repast to his room and cleared away the remnants of breakfast, he subjected himself—lying upon his bed—to interminable accounts of mysteries and obscure initiation rites. As the text repeatedly threatened to lull him into slumber, he alternated between reading while seated at the table, standing, and even on the windowsill. Yet the room unsettled him in an inexplicable way, as though at any moment the veil might be lifted, revealing something ineffable, something ancient, lurking behind the white paint—now gray and faded, peeling away in many places. He rose and strained to extract any useful information from the cryptic pictorial narratives adorning the paneling, and to decipher that strange script as well—both endeavors proving futile. Counseling deities, mysterious astronomical symbols and star maps, a Sumerian–Akkadian stepped temple of titanic proportions replete with countless annotations, and cherubim guarding its gates all gazed at him in mute, secretive portent from the dark wood.

At length, he closed the books with a look of discontent and massaged the burgeoning headache at his temples. He opened the window, sat cross-legged on the floor, and endeavored to rid himself of the ceaseless thoughts that swirled within his mind. During his travels through India, a bald, lizard-faced monk—who dwelled in Bodhgaya near the ruins of the *Mahabodhi Temple* beneath a tree—had attempted to instruct him to visualize a heap of earth before his inner eye for so long that his very powers of consciousness might be elevated to the point of extinguishing all sensory activity and attaining a kind of enlightenment. In his youth, the prospect of decades of purification—which the emaciated ascetic claimed he required to reach perfection—seemed unattainable, and the sacrifice of a lifetime did not appear sufficiently desirable; hence, in due course, he practiced this knowledge merely as an exercise in relaxation.

Within the cyclical rise and fall of his abdomen, he drew in the cool air, acutely aware of the life-force surging through his lungs; he gathered his unbridled thoughts only to release them anon, until nothing remained but a complete, fulfilling void. Suddenly, the room appeared subdued and otherworldly—as if he had lost a part of his hearing or were submerged beneath water. His consciousness expanded in an instant, as though he were leaping over centuries of arduous practice.

He perceived a tremendous intensification of all his senses, which transported him to a remote, unattainable plane of awareness. Enlightenment seemed tantalizingly near. Despite his closed eyes, he could discern the wall before him with a clarity surpassing that of his natural sight. His body appeared to diminish, shrinking at a dizzying pace, while the surrounding architecture swelled disproportionately into unfathomable dimensions, until he was nothing more than a grain of sand within the cosmic tapestry—insignificant, apprehensive, and utterly lost in the endless space unfurling before him. The wall transformed, curving multidimensionally, as if obeying a non-Euclidean geometry. Then, as though a fissure had appeared in its very fabric, dazzling light escaped—a light that blazed like fire and was accompanied by sounds for which there existed no counterpart in his world. At length, his soul, along with all his yearning and senses, lay exposed before the probing gaze of eternity.

CHAPTER II.
MONSIEUR LAMETH

Phineas awoke, lying on the floor, stirred by the monotonous tapping of the porter. Still somewhat dazed, he rose, opened the door, and accepted from Monsieur Lameth a letter—one that the latter had undoubtedly deposited at the reception earlier that day. The few, hastily inscribed lines, rendered in an ornate, curling script, declared that he was to meet with him for dinner later that evening at a certain establishment; beneath these words, a fleeting sketch of the locale had been lightly drawn.

Since his glance at the clock afforded no thorough assessment of his mental state and the accompanying delusions, Phineas dismissed the disconcerting waking dream as the product of his overtaxed mind and resolved henceforth to take better care of himself. Donning his frock coat, he stepped boldly into the corridor. As he meticulously secured his door, he noted that the adjacent room stood open, its interior displaying a remarkably tidy and orderly aspect. The nocturnal malefactor now appeared to have long since departed. To his astonishment, the room was devoid of any furnishings—precluding any possibility that such an extraordinary clamor could have been produced by their shifting during the night—which only reinforced his belief that his room neighbor, equally disturbed by those uncanny sounds, had ventured into the corridor, thereby partly explaining his own perplexity.

A chambermaid—youthful and unassuming yet pleasing in manner, clad in the somber fabric of an antiquated servant's uniform, a vestige of once resplendent days—was busy filling one of the innumerable candelabra with lamp oil while towing behind her a small cart laden with bottles and polishing cloths. The wheels glided with a faint, mournful squeak across the dark, lustrously polished parquet, as if the very act of motion itself were rebelling. A wisp of petroleum lingered in the air, intermingling with the distinctive mélange of beeswax, timeworn furniture, and the muted moldiness of dust-laden draperies. When she perceived Phineas, she paused. With a polite, almost coquettish bow and a shyly inclined head, she greeted him. Her gaze—both dreamy and tentative—peeked out from beneath her long, dark lashes. A slight squint—a delicate, nearly imperceptible flaw—imparted to that wistful glance a curious lopsidedness. Instinctively, Phineas offered a gesture of a bow—a gesture as out of place here as a velvet drapery in a seedy tavern—which prompted the chambermaid to conceal the onset of a hysterical laugh behind her hand, and then swiftly lower her gaze, as though wishing to dissolve into the gleam of the floorboards.

He descended the massive spiral staircase toward the hall—shaking his head—with the obliquely streaming midday light now rendering it less gloomy than the previous day, though it had lost none of its impressive grandeur. On his way down he encountered only two guests: one Oriental, who regarded him condescendingly with lips drawn downward, and an overbearing gentleman, attired in a flawlessly fitted dark suit, complemented by a dandyish cravat and a silk top hat, who was reproofing his bashfully demure servant in English with the aid of his walking stick. Phineas greeted courteously as he passed, only to be halted by the gentleman's outstretched stick. "With whom do I have the honour of making your acquaintance?" the gentleman inquired in an affected tone. Meanwhile, the servant straightened up and, seizing the opportunity, absconded with several trunks.

"I overheard from your conversation that you are a fellow countryman. I myself hail from Suffolk, if you wish to know precisely." Phineas extended his hand, but the gentleman seemed not to notice his gesture, withdrawing arrogantly with a smile—still clutching his stick and adjusting his gloves. "Phineas Camill is my name," Phineas managed, endeavoring to complete his reply as required.

"Delighted indeed—Serpentarius Stroude is mine. What brings you from this blessed region of the Empire to this abhorrently stinking metropolis?" the gentleman declared.

"Business; I am here in Paris by the orders of Monsieur Lameth," replied Phineas.

"Ah, Lameth! He already informed me that he would welcome a guest. It pleases me, for a change, to encounter someone with English blood. Although Lameth crossed the Channel half a century ago—as though he possessed an uncanny nose for what might flourish among the aristocracy in this damnable country—that does not make him an Englishman, does it?"

Mister Stroude stared at him so penetratingly during their conversation that Phineas, feeling visibly uneasy in his presence, descended several steps as they spoke. He could not shake the feeling that those ominously fixed eyes were capable of probing his most secret thoughts. "Quite so, I suppose. But I must now be on my way; Monsieur Lameth and I are scheduled to dine," replied Phineas.

"Of course—I do not wish to detain you. Something tells me that we shall meet again."

Phineas bade farewell—with a queasy sensation in his stomach—to the man of the strange name. Upon entering the spacious vestibule, he found the eerie giant once again stationed behind his counter, watching him with a suspicious air as he passed by. Nimbly, Phineas descended the well-worn steps and soon became lost in the bustling throng of the great city. A myriad of impressions crashed into his consciousness like a wild sea, stirring within him a deep longing to leave behind the confines of his known world forever. Casting one more glance over his shoulder, he beheld the stately building, resting upon massive blocks and rising majestically toward the heavens like a cathedral.

He then proceeded in a southeasterly direction and crossed a generously planned, octagonal square which, despite the monotonous symmetry of the surrounding edifices, exerted a peculiar fascination upon him. Rigidly aligned dormers—sometimes elongated, sometimes squat—seemed to peer over the two-storied, pilaster-divided facades as if through a hundred watchful eyes; uniform ground floors, punctuated by arched openings in bossed masonry; and amid it all, a colossal triumphal column, stripped of its imperial effigy after the fall of the Empire, now standing in orderly, lavishly proportioned monumentality, a testimony to absence and faded glory. He turned onto the venerable *Rue Saint Honoré*, passing the parish church of *Saint-Roch*, whose columned façade still bore, despite numerous repairs, the marks of cannonball impacts from the Royalist uprising.

Through a side street, he caught sight of the *Louvre*—adjoining the *Palais des Tuileries*—which, in all its majesty and splendor, rose prominently above the silhouettes of secular city houses. He briefly considered taking a carriage, but then resolved to reach the appointed meeting place on foot. Arriving at the *Palais Royal*, he wandered absentmindedly around the lavish edifice; then, to resume his journey, he turned right into a side street and entered a bustling market. In the shelter of the Gothic buttresses of *Saint-Eustache*—the church of merchants—stretched out the halls of Paris, which the inhabitants respectfully called, in memory of the former cemetery, the "Market of the Innocents."

Phineas strolled leisurely through the colonnades of the shops along *Rue de la Tonnellerie*—directly opposite the market halls—and allowed himself to be swept along by the densely packed crowd that swayed like an endless sea between the wooden arcades and the imposing, meter-high columns of the storefronts. He ambled through the colorful, bustling scene of earnest bread-making, pleasure, and idleness, passing by bakeries and patisseries exuding delectable aromas, cozy cafés, and picturesque street restaurants. Squeezing his way through a tangle of human bodies, baskets, porters, and handcarts, he made his way toward the pavilions, whose square-arranged wooden roofs, supported by hundreds of pillars, entirely encircled the impressive square in which the *Fontaine des Innocents* rose like an oversized monstrance at its very center.

That market exuded every odor and fragrance within the dazzling spectrum of the human sense of smell: the dull, musty stench of fish waste, the sharp, briny aroma of shellfish and crustaceans, the delightful, sonorous sweetness of ripe fruits, and the heady bouquet of blossoms heavy with nectar; the rich, crackling sizzle of fried fare, steaming onion soup, and freshly baked loaves drawn from ovens with crisp crusts; as well as the cheese in all its olfactory variations—secured through the artful coagulation of milk, ranging from the youthful, milky mildness to that austere intensity achieved only through long aging—that ancient alchemy of rustic craft. The heavy aromas of essential oils and sharply invigorating odoriferous salts, confined within tiny phials, mingled with the biting sweat of the laboring masses, the inescapable reek of narrow alleys, and the heavy, almost narcotizing scent of perfume—this invention of laboratories and salons that poured over the place in every nuance, from delicate floral notes to sultry animality. And above it all, surging and overwhelming with a staggering force, came the clamour of innumerable voices—screaming and haggling, laughing and bickering in a mélange of foreign and familiar tongues—mingled with the barking of dogs, the constant, trembling peal of distant bells in the air, the muted thunder of hooves and wheels on uneven cobblestones, the shrill howling of playing children, and the echo of an exuberant celebration, whose music—borne by gentle breezes—dissipated into the labyrinthine alleys.

In the shadow of the roofwork before him stood a market stall whose display table offered a veritable necropolis of expertly minced fragments of some indefinable pair-hooved creatures to the uninitiated. Suspended from a framework above, a variety of animals—neatly arranged in a regular pattern of multicoloured pelts—hung in orderly fashion. A little further on, alongside a row of rabbits with bared incisors and soulless eyes gazing dimly, the larger animals occupied the full height of the stall. A skinned, blood-veined calf's head, complete with a ghastly hook for a nose, glared down from above with a fractured expression. Separated from it by a vertical oak beam was another framework on which hung long-tailed male pheasants—greenish-purple and copper-hued with a head flushed red—alongside their less vain females; nearby, squat, grey-plumed partridges with red-brown patterned wings and speckled breasts; speckled hazel chickens; exotic, pitch-black turkeys; ordinary pigeons; fattened ducks; an entire assemblage of delicate songbirds; and an intricately plucked pheasant, left with its tail feathers, wings, and head intact, which resembled a naked woman with slender thighs and a monstrous torso. Beneath it, alongside a heap of plucked chickens, lay a whole row of fat geese, repeatedly stacked with their heads dangling over the table's edge like a white-skirted Saxon infantry regiment.

He circled a tower of stacked wooden cages from which all manner of live fowl thrust forth their wildly twitching, clucking heads as if they could scarce wait to be relieved. He drifted aside for a spell, pausing before a cart laden with vegetable refuse, then pressed his way through a tangle of baskets, crates, and sacks, past bent-over laboring women slurping soup—who had clustered about a steaming kettle and a woman crouched on the ground wielding a large ladle—and thereafter traversed an avenue of towering plane trees, beneath whose shade citizens rested from their labours upon cast-iron benches, smoked pipes, or conversed animatedly. Tattered, grimy street children frolicked on the cobbles, shrieking in high-pitched voices, playing with stones, sticks, or discarded detritus, and openly relieving themselves before all onlookers.

He passed by the wine merchant's shop, which exuded such a penetrating aroma of wine that it rendered unnecessary the gilded sign suspended above its massive stone columns; he heard the muted clamor of the tavern's drinkers—forced through clumsy arched windows—then exited the market via a narrow side alley, and, directing his gaze upward toward the stone tablets and iron plaques of the street signage, collided with a drunken man who assailed him with a torrent of vulgar curses. At length, he arrived at the *Place du Châtelet*, where once the mighty bulwark of the *Grand Châtelet* had sheltered the *Pont au Change* from the north with its round towers—a fortification now reduced to a flat, expansive square amid soaring city edifices—from which, like a solitary tooth jutting from an aged mouth, a column adorned with palm fronds and set upon a mighty pedestal rose from a fountain, upon which a bare-breasted Victoria brandished two victory wreaths above the Napoleonic eagle.

He crossed the *Pont au Change* and wandered, utterly forgetting time, through the *Île de la Cité*, surveying the *Palais de Justice* and the *Conciergerie* to the west, whose appearance—though stripped of the terror of the Revolutionary tribunal and the carts laden with guillotine victims—still evoked a strange, indefinable disquiet, as if one were entering the catacombs of an enchanted edifice. As dusk slowly descended, he beheld with wonder the ethereal arches of *Notre-Dame* and the sculptural embellishments of its portals, which had been severely marred by the barbarity of the Revolution; yet, overwhelmed by the manifold impressions of the day, he soon grew weary of Gothic excess and, at length, crossed the *Pont Saint-Michel* to the southern bank of the *Seine*.

He strolled along the *Seine*, entranced by the city's pulsating rhythm, by the ebb and flow of the waves against the quay walls, and by the multitude of lights that burst forth from the grand urban edifices, reflecting upon the dark, undulating water like a parallel universe. In the twilight of silent, dark trees and soaring rows of buildings, he suddenly felt as though he perceived a menacing aura—a presence that, despite the euphoria of the moment, weighed upon his spirit like a foreboding omen, causing him to regard every approaching soul with a measure of suspicion. At one moment in the dim light, he fancied he saw a large figure cloaked in a dark coat, appearing to follow or observe him—a notion that, in the end, proved to be nothing more than an illusion. He continued on in thoughtful silence for some time, attributing these sensations to his tense mood, yet soon he felt his premonitions confirmed.

"Ho there! You're new here in town, aren't you?" a rough voice called out with feigned interest, as a wily-looking street rogue emerged from the dark shadow of an unlit side alley. "Is it all right if I ask for a little alms, seeing as you're out alone tonight?" The ragged fellow tilted his head conspicuously as he spoke—as though expecting other silent listeners in that very alley—while Phineas was quite certain that some unsupervised riffraff was lurking there. He drew a five-*centime* piece from his waistcoat pocket with two fingers and flicked it toward the man. The scoundrel bent down, picked up the copper coin, and examined it serenely from all sides. "Just a paltry *sou*!" the man feigned offense. "How condescending, to bestow charity upon me like a beggar. As if I were in need, eh? That noble fellow must fancy himself as something better." He spat on the ground. "Wouldn't you rather check if there's any silver coin in your waistcoat? I'd be happy to help you with that, if you please."

As if on cue, several figures emerged from the darkness and stepped into the dim light of the gas lanterns. Their long shadows reached out toward him with greedy arms, merging in the distance with the dark silhouette of a warehouse. The rogue before him laughed hoarsely and drew an imaginary knife along his throat. Phineas twisted his head in desperate search of an escape route, then frantically groped his upper body in the vain hope that, unbeknownst to him, some weapon might be concealed there—or that he had absent-mindedly tucked away his carving knife at luncheon. His pulse pounded like the chimes of *Saint-Jacques*.

Then his well-trained reflexes and instinct for self-preservation took over. His step traced a semicircular path; after briefly assessing the meager prospects, he turned away at once and quickened his pace. The footsteps of his pursuers grew louder—first tentative, then hastening. Steel flashed treacherously. Whispered orders and shouts from alcohol-drenched throats rang out, then suddenly screams erupted—gurgling, guttural sounds culminating in smacking, wet, gasping cries, the ripping of fabric and even skin so terrible that Phineas dared not look away—followed by a plaintive lament and sheer terror, all articulated in one ghastly scream, as though one of the henchmen had gazed into the fiery maw of Hell. Within moments, the pursuers, one after another, struck the cobblestones with dull thuds. A nocturnal creature let out its cry from one of the tall alley trees, and then, as if the very earth trembled before the horror of that night, silence fell.

He eventually dared to halt and turn about. Only the questioner—who had likewise slowed his pace—stood solitary like a statue against the night sky, and when he cast his gaze back to behold all his accomplices lying motionless, the scornful grin vanished from his countenance. That man then fled, leaving his dumbfounded, gaping victim behind. In the distance, a figure clad in black emerged from the dark shadow of a treetop. *How could one solitary man have slain so many attackers at once?* He had heard no gunshots, and even the silent arrow of the Java poison tree—used by savages in the accursed Malaysian rainforests or the tropical inferno of Sumatra—would scarcely be capable of dispatching several foes in full flight. Yet his rescuer had no intention of revealing himself; instead, he abruptly turned away and vanished, shrouded in the blackness of the night with a billowing cloak.

Phineas felt his tension ebb and the adrenaline drain from his body. With cautious curiosity, he approached one of the fallen. The corpse lay in the gutter's filth, its limbs unnaturally contorted and its eyes grotesquely dilated—as though its soul had been wrenched away at the mere sight of some unspeakable horror. With the clinical detachment of a physician, he inspected the body, whose throat—severed in a half-circular arc from one earlobe to the other—appeared as though it housed a second, ghastly mouth, from which an unceasing dark stream now poured onto the uneven cobblestones. He did not linger to scrutinize the other corpses; rather, he hurried along the street flanked by somber warehouses, crossed a sprawling tannery whose peculiar, repulsive odor of tanned hides had already assaulted his nostrils on the breeze, lost his bearings, inquired after directions, and finally arrived at his destination with an acceptable delay.

A warm, golden light filtered through the elliptical arches of the squat window fronts onto the cobblestones—bathed in gold—before the *L'Auberge du Géant*. Colorful, lead-framed glass insets cast kaleidoscopic patterns upon the throng of people, who appeared to be largely of higher society. A wrought-iron tavern sign—a stylized, fire-breathing giant in the crest—projected its long shadow like a protective emblem over the building's façade, constructed of pitted, dark-grey limestone and sloping unevenly forward upon sunken foundations.

He pressed his way through a throng of people into the overcrowded entrance hall. Warmth, the aroma of food, and a clamor of voices assaulted him like a surging tide, while above all, a dense cloud of tobacco smoke drifted overhead. Several eager waiters directed vast arrays of crockery through the teeming room and its scarcely centimeter-wide gaps between tables, chairs, and hesitant guests—almost as if, in defiance of all physical laws, they could contort their limbs like the snake-men of Bhubaneswar in East India.

He strained his gaze over the heads of the assembled guests in search of Monsieur Lameth. At a table right before him, an aristocrat—engorged by sumptuous indulgence and languid luxury—was dining, with rivulets of sweat streaming abundantly down his bloated face and through his tightly buttoned collar, while a strikingly attired lady, gaudily made-up with lips painted a vivid red that jutted like a smeared blot upon her lead-white complexion, sat at his side and pressed in on him, her presence hardly distracting the gluttonous feast before her. Nearby, several tipsy ladies in high-necked dresses with scarcely flushed cheeks fanned themselves coquettishly with graceful, brightly ruffled fans and chattered excitedly about the latest gossip that was so much the talk of Paris. A refined company of gentlemen smoked cigars, drank red wine to excess, and engaged in heated debates over politics and world affairs—at least, Phineas could catch fragments of their conversation, predominantly concerning the cholera epidemic, the defeat of the Poles at Ostrolenka, or the fabled wealth of the *Citizen King*. A young man, utterly plastered and resigned in countenance, was being assailed by a woman brimming with gossip; as Phineas drew nearer, he overheard that she was unleashing a highly emotional torrent of accusations—alleging either an unwanted pregnancy, adultery, or perhaps both.

At last, his eyes fell upon Monsieur Lameth, who had taken solitary seat at a table at the far end of the room. He knew not his full name, for Lameth had ever spoken to him only by that one family name, and all his correspondence bore that sole signature. The man immediately noticed Phineas and, with a nod, indicated an unoccupied chair. A candle in a modest tin holder illuminated his expressive features—his gracefully curved Roman nose bestowing upon him a classical air, high cheekbones, and a narrow, sharply defined mouth set above an angular chin that jutted forth as boldly as the steel beard of a *cuirassier*. An indefinable aura of distant realms, legends, and myths enveloped him, and his dark, penetrating eyes spoke of a keen intellect and the profound erudition of a scholar. He was clean-shaven, sporting short grey hair that might once have been as black as Phineas's own. Although he bore a Mediterranean mien, his naturally darker skin—accentuated by bluish stubble—appeared remarkably pale, as if he habitually shunned the sunlight. Countless wrinkles cloaked his face like the brittle leather of an ancient tome, hinting at an age which, despite his robust physique, defied logic—so much so that Phineas felt, in a manner utterly absurd, that the experience and fate etched into that visage mirrored the physiognomy of the centuries.

Lameth rose with an exuberant greeting. He towered over Phineas—who would hardly describe himself as small—by several centimeters. His handshake was like that of a vise, a fact Phineas found exceedingly odd, especially since he employed a considerable retinue of servants, lackeys, footmen, and maids who dutifully attended to every task for him. He appeared to attach fastidious importance to his attire, even though his style was decidedly archaic. Thus, contrary to prevailing fashions, he wore tight, black breeches paired with high riding boots that reached to the knees, a long-sleeved dark doublet adorned with delicate filigree patterns and a high collar, and—following the customs of the English landed gentry—a black, nearly floor-length *Garrick* coat. Prominently displayed over his clothing hung a striking amulet, which looked like a curious heirloom from a centuries-old family legacy. On his powerful hands shone lavish rings, such that one would be well-advised not to venture out alone at night if one wished to return home with all one's fingers intact. The entire extravagant ornamentation was crafted in a most peculiar fashion, replete with marvelous symbols and inscriptions from bygone eras. One striking ring, which Phineas often stole a furtive glance at, bore a mysterious inscription and, curiously, the very same symbol of a serpent—or perhaps a dragon—devouring itself in a closed circle, the counterpart of which appeared on the dark portal of the hôtel in that picturesque door knocker.

At times, Lameth's eyes were dreadful to behold, emerging beneath his bushy brows with a severity that could freeze the blood in one's veins. His servants avoided meeting his gaze, as though he bore the head of Medusa, and the moment he entered a room, all conversation fell silent; the assembled throng transformed into bowed, speechless figures, diligently attending to their daily tasks with lowered eyes. Yet on some—albeit rare—days, his eyes appeared introspective and overcome by an extraordinary weariness, as if he dwelled in an indeterminate past or existed beyond the fixed confines of space and time. In such moments he seemed almost fragile, despite his tall and imposing stature, and Phineas fancied that he beheld an old man sustained by a fantastical elixir—much as if one had reanimated one of those mummies, which in those days were exhibited for amusement, with a wondrous alchemical concoction. Even in that inward, vulnerable state, however, those around him kept their distance, for he was capable of effecting a transformation within mere moments—as if he shed a mask or concealed himself beneath it, though one could never be entirely sure which was the case.

There was, however, another state in which he customarily presented himself to Phineas—a state in which he was exceedingly sensitive and highly attuned to every emotional nuance of his counterpart, acting as a mentor and fatherly friend whose eyes would gleam with unbridled enthusiasm whenever he recounted long-hidden secrets and wondrous happenings, with a fluidity and expansiveness and an extraordinary knack for details that he seemed to read between the lines—or even to fabricate anew—as if he had been present at those fantastic events himself. And then, from time to time, his stern eyes would fill with a barely perceptible glimmer of moisture, and emotions would rise in defiance against the relentless will that encased his body like a steel corset. A tremor would run through his staggering frame, and

Phineas felt for him a pity he could not fully define; Lameth appeared to him as a lost soul, bound by some unspeakable fate to linger in the earthly spheres for an indeterminate time, until, exhausted and spent, it might at last ascend to heaven or some other realm.

Although, in light of the remarkable diversity of his character and the mercurial nature of his mannerisms, his mind did not appear confused or subject to any delusions—unlike the pitiable inmates of *Bedlam* in Southwark who eked out their miserable existence—but was instead exceedingly layered, multifaceted, and, in a manner of speaking, inscrutable in its intentions; a being that seemed to adhere to its own, unspoken rules, shaped by bizarre and enigmatic twists of fate and founded upon singular experiences along extraordinary paths that had formed him into who he was. At times one might read a man's character in his face as one reads a book, yet Lameth's features defied any interpretation, and any attempt to pigeonhole him alongside his contemporaries or to classify him within any conventional pattern of behavior was destined to prove illusory.

Lameth, who—by his own account—had arrived at the appointed place but a few minutes earlier, inquired in a low, resonant voice after Phineas's state of health, to which the latter proceeded to recount in meticulous detail the strange occurrences that had befallen him since their last encounter. Lameth listened attentively, interjecting here and there with probing questions to discern the full meaning behind the vivid, at times almost overly animated, narrative. When Phineas, endeavoring to provide a sober, mitigating explanation for his peculiar daydream and subsequent fainting spell by offering several possible interpretations, related his experience,

Lameth appeared both attentive and intrigued, his sinewy hand composedly tucking itself into the tablecloth.

While they conversed, a serving girl presented an opulent repast—a meal which Lameth, in contrast to Phineas, who after the day's ordeals felt as though he were on the brink of starvation, did not so much as disturb—whereas Phineas delighted in a steaming plate of *coq au vin*, its tender morsels nestled amid a dark, wine-infused sauce and an assortment of vegetables, accompanied by rustic bread and quenched his thirst with a robust, ruddy *Pinot noir*. After finishing his meal, he puffed out his cheeks and let out a breath with raised brows, then settled back against the rough wood of his chair, his gaze drifting lost about the room, whilst Lameth—who had sat all the while with his eyes stoically fixed upon his glass—resumed the conversation. "Man is indeed a most singular creature, unparalleled in his simplicity!" declared Lameth with the impassive mien of a clerk. "It is quite astonishing that people so willingly succumb to that which even the Jacobins, with their unspeakable terror, could never attain. Did you observe the adulterer at the next table? Or the glutton immediately behind you? What you behold here, as the clergy so aptly term them, are the *deadly sins*; for, like beasts, men behave as such once they have renounced all faith in the divine."

"But even during the darkest hours of the Revolution, men venerated the *Culte de l'Être suprême*, and for seventeen years now the Holy Father has again reigned upon the *Papal Throne* in Rome," countered Phineas drowsily, as he languidly rubbed his belly.

"The sickness of the soul is godlessness!" Lameth intoned, as though reciting a sacred quotation. Then he leaned forward, drawing his bushy brows together until they nearly met. "It

requireth no golden calf to cause the forgetting of the Creator. Nor would even the blood-stained priests of Bel-Marduk and Nergal, nor all the idols of the Babylonians, Canaanites, Ammonites, or Philistines, have endured such scorn—though the lascivious youths and temple harlots were by no means unacquainted with that very piety." He laughed scornfully, and Phineas, visibly abashed by the final remark, averted his gaze; at which moment, in mere seconds, Lameth shifted the subject. "Have you read the books I had sent for you?"

"I have been in Paris for only a day," replied Phineas truthfully.

Lameth clicked his tongue softly. "Of course—do pardon the impatience of an old man. I sometimes feel...—how might I aptly express it?—that my years seem to be slipping away, and that I have lived more days than may yet lie ahead. Let us leave it at that."

Gathering all his courage, Phineas posed the question that had long been on his lips. "What is with that maddening babble of the old fellow? And what do you know of the name 'Misraim'?"

Lameth appeared lost in thought. His brow furrowed, the candlelight glinting upon it as if upon craggy rock. "My dear friend, it is my earnest desire to quench your thirst for knowledge, and together we shall, in due course, discuss all your queries," he suddenly broke out after several reflective seconds. "'Misraim' is the Hebrew name for Egypt. Furthermore, 'Misraim' designates a person—in truth, one of Ham's sons, who was himself one of Noah's three sons, the very man who built the Ark to rescue his family and a considerable number of creatures from the death-bringing waters of the Flood."

"And further?"

"Noah cursed his son Ham for his impertinent conduct—having seen him naked and inebriated by the fruits of his vineyard, lying in his tent—and related it to his brothers, Shem and Japheth. Strangely enough, that curse is pronounced upon Canaan—one of his sons—rather than upon Ham himself or his other sons, Cush, Misraim, and Put; a not insignificant inaccuracy in that biblical account, for which I beg your indulgence should I now refrain from offering a more precise interpretation. But let us proceed. Have you, perchance, read what Ibn 'Abd al-Hakam and other scholars have written concerning the pyramids and the Deluge?"

"Are you suggesting that the pyramids were erected by a primeval race before the Flood?" Phineas replied timidly.

"Yea, even this was my meaning. 'Misraim' is, as I have already spoken, the Hebrew name for Egypt; and Misraim—so some do assert—was he who laid claim to that secret knowledge, which, concealed within the great pyramids and inscribed upon hidden places, did endure even the floodwaters, and which, in ages long past, was first brought forth by a fallen race. Manethos's 'Aegyptiaca' doth provide us with a most comprehensive account of this matter of utmost intrigue. Remind me, in due course, to send you the 'Chronicle' of Eusebius of Caesarea! This knowledge, verily, may be found in sundry other sources, though oft in a form much altered. According to Paracelsus's 'Aurora Philosophorum'—a volume I have had delivered unto your chamber—Adam, who after the Fall retained as much knowledge of all things as afore, did prophesy that the world should be destroyed by water; and his descendants did engrave this most ancient wisdom, in secret characters they named hieroglyphs, upon two stone tablets. Flavius Josephus, moreover, doth recount that Adam's grandsons, the sons of Seth, did inscribe this wisdom upon two pillars—one of brick, should fire consume the earth, and one of stone, should the floodwaters rise. The stone pillar, it is said, endured the Deluge and may yet be seen in Syria, though, I must note in passing, this is not a claim that withstandeth scrutiny. But in the end, it was Nimrod—a descendant of his brother Cush—who laid hold upon this pre-diluvian knowledge and made it his own. 'Misraim'—if one be willing to name a thing of such singular import in such fashion—thus doth stand as a symbol of the secret wisdom of the world before the waters came. This, my dear Phineas, must suffice thee for now." Lameth leaned back and folded his arms.

Phineas gazed at him, mouth slightly agape, prompting Lameth to recite, as an addendum, a passage from an unspecified scripture:

"And in the twenty-ninth jubilee, in the first week, at its beginning, Arpachshad took a wife named Rasueja, the daughter of Susan, the daughter of Elam. And she bore him a son in the third year of this week, and he called his name Kainam. And the boy grew, and his father taught him writing. And he went forth to seek a place where he might establish a city. And he found an inscription which the forefathers had engraved upon a rock. And he read what was written upon it and translated it, and he found that it contained the knowledge which the Watchers had taught..."

Phineas still stared at him in disbelief. "Surely, you do not mean to claim that there is even a grain of truth in such old wives' tales?"

"Do you believe in the Bible?" Lameth countered with a question of his own. Phineas nodded hastily. "Tell me then,"

Lameth continued, a faint smile playing upon his lips, "is it easier for you to believe that a man was swallowed by a whale and survived three days within its crimson entrails, amidst the all-consuming gastric juices, a thousand meters below the surface? Or that a man might grant sight where blindness had reigned? Or even that one who was dead did descend from the cross and live again?" Lameth had spoken these last words so loudly and piercingly that several guests turned with reproachful shakes of their heads—though, intimidated by the severity of his gaze, they promptly averted their eyes.

"But the first is merely a pious fable," Phineas objected, regaining his composure, "at best an allegory of resurrection. And who is to say it could not have happened? I once saw a fin whale in the Mediterranean, easily twenty meters long—it could have swallowed an elephant whole. As for the power of the Son of God, of which you speak, it is not to be compared with the faculties that dwell within us, for His divinity places Him beyond mortal bounds. Nor is every biblical miracle subject to rational explanation. Is that not so?"

"When one is indoctrinated from childhood, a thing seems familiar and plausible. And if, on the surface, it appears within the realm of possibility, it is rarely questioned. But should one dare to question it—ah, then one suddenly finds oneself facing an atheist." Lameth laughed with quiet derision. "But let us leave the great fish to his lead role in this farce and turn instead to the second matter. Arnobius the Elder once wrote of a debate he held with an Egyptian priest, a man who, with deepest conviction, asserted that Jesus was but a sorcerer—that all His miracles were wrought by means of secret arts, through the sacred names of mighty angels, and that this knowledge He had stolen from the shrines of the Egyptians."

Their conversation, which weighed heavily upon Phineas, was interrupted by a larger crowd pressing into the establishment from outside. "It seems the *séance* is about to commence!" remarked Lameth, who had regained his composure and now exuded his usual measured calm. Phineas could not shake the feeling that Lameth had allowed himself to divulge more on the matter than he had originally intended. His gaze fell upon a flyer resting at the side of the table, its grandiloquent announcement of the *séance* printed in *Egyptienne* type. The medium was listed as the apparently internationally renowned Madame Darcie Morrígu—of whom Phineas had never heard. Someone extinguished the overhead light, and a murmur rippled through the gathering as a dim, flickering glow was kindled at the front of the hall, where a piano had been pushed aside to make space. The feeble illumination barely revealed a covered dining table and two wooden chairs. Darcie Morrígu entered the room through a side door, followed closely by a broad-shouldered, bear-like Siberian, clad in Mongolian attire, who took position behind her with arms crossed over his chest. Madame Morrígu was a woman of middling years, her face pale, her mouth—painted dark—small yet sensual, while her immense, kohl-darkened eyes peered out like inscrutable wells of shadow. Her long, raven-black hair cascaded freely beneath a peculiar tiara, lending her the aspect of a high priestess.

A volunteer from the audience was invited to step forward. It was none other than the corpulent aristocrat who, now that he had devoured his meal and his paid companion had evidently transferred her attentions to a more willing patron, seemed already overcome with boredom. Madame Morrígu fell into an ecstatic trance while the shaman at her back began a disturbing overtone chant, drumming upon a flat ceremonial tambour like a man possessed. After some time, the rotund gentleman was granted the opportunity to pose a question regarding a deceased ancestor, which he did, receiving in return a relatively innocuous answer—yet the medium delivered it with such conviction, her voice altered to an eerie, resonant depth, that even Phineas, who harbored little patience for such matters, felt a chill run down his spine. To heighten the illusion, the gaslight flickered erratically for a moment before the ceiling lamps were reignited. The crowd rewarded the phantasmagoria with thunderous applause, while the volunteer, puffed up with pride, waved and strode back toward his table, receiving approving pats on the shoulder from his fellow guests.

Madame Morrígu, seemingly still entranced, let her gaze sweep across the room. A few guests reacted feverishly when her eyes fell upon them. Phineas, however, kept his attention on Lameth, who, with lowered gaze, sipped indifferently at his wine, as though he were enduring some tiresome birthday gathering. Yet once again, his hands betrayed him.

Lost in thought, Phineas brooded over Lameth's confounding statements, until he became abruptly aware—through the sudden silence that had settled over the hall—that something had shifted in the room. His eyes darted about, and with a flush of embarrassment, he realized that all were now staring at him. His gaze lifted, bewildered, to Madame Morrígu, who loomed above the assembly like a goddess of fate, rigid as stone, her arm outstretched, her brows arched high, pointing at him with an air of inexorable judgment. Some guests whispered furtively behind their hands to their neighbors; others murmured their disappointment at not having been chosen. Here and there, voices rose in encouragement from the crowd.

Phineas, utterly taken aback, found himself reluctantly rising, staggering forward toward the table. As the lights dimmed once more, the drumming intensified into a frenzied clamor. It was now for Phineas to ask a question, yet he stood motionless, entranced by the infernal pounding of the drum and the piercing gaze of those black-rimmed eyes beneath their strange headdress. There were a thousand things he longed to ask Eireen—had the occasion not been such a disquieting, sacrilegious abomination, a mockery of all holy prophets and apostles. *"If any soul turneth to mediums and necromancers, I will set my face against that soul, and will cut him off from among his people,"* he murmured, his voice taut with Scripture, his expression set in grim defiance against the temptation.

He gasped for air, drenched in sweat, but Madame Morrígu took his hand with deliberate gentleness, as though it belonged to a frightened, simple-minded child. Overcome by the orgiastic rhythm of the drum and the abyssal depth of her dark-rimmed eyes, he found himself powerless to resist. He surrendered, plunging into the darkness, as a thought—unspoken yet resounding in some subtle, etheric realm—shattered the barrier like a wave crashing against an unseen shore.

Before his inner eye, an image began to form: a veil of swirling mist disturbed the very fabric of the aether, and from within it, Eireen emerged—ensnared in a luminous vortex of white light, drawn inexorably toward him. He reached out his hand, and tears of purest joy—tears he felt no shame in shedding—ran freely down his cheeks. It seemed as though Eireen would reach for him in turn, would greet him with an outstretched hand, yet the closer they drifted toward one another, the clearer he saw that she lingered in a posture of refusal. She gestured frantically, shaking her head, struggling against unseen forces that held her fast. Her face was twisted with sorrow, an agony beyond words. "No, dearest Phineas!" The voice, though not heard with his ears, reverberated in some deeper, more spiritual sense. Madame Morrígu, whose monotone voice echoed those very same words, convulsed as though seized by electric currents. "Phineas, let me go!" the voice pleaded again.

Eireen, fighting desperately, begging to be released, shone as a radiant, pure light within that pulsing aura of unmanifested energy, while Madame Morrígu, in contrast, took on the semblance of a gray raincloud, sagging downward, disintegrating as if she were dissolving into nothingness. Yet close at hand, a yawning chasm opened. Darkness coiled and surged forth in a twisting, spiraling tide, growing ever larger, devouring the space around it until it filled the entire room. Phineas writhed, struggling against the hypnotic thrall. He bid Eireen farewell, told her that he loved her. With a jolt like the tremor of an earthquake, the hallucinatory illusion shattered into a fractal explosion of countless light-particles, and Madame Morrígu collapsed onto the table with a ghastly scream upon her lips.

CHAPTER III.
JAHDIS

The twin-faced moon cast its luminous sorcery upon the gentle hills of Herndún and the tree-lined avenues of Thuriasàn, its argent glow caressing the desolate cratered peaks of Neèbh, which plunged into the shadowed valley of Amoneáth, shimmering through the labyrinthine depths and winding caverns of Kartham, before resuming its celestial course over boundless fields of green, undulating like a vast and whispering sea, only to unveil, in full and dazzling splendor, its resplendent retinue amid the vaulted radiance of the Thousand Lights of Erydin. That most sacred of temples, marvel of the elder world, and long-echoed longing of the Athalanian peoples, stood defiant against the many-hued evening sky, its form stark against the firmament. Leaden light drifted across the star-forged dome of bronze and translucent glass, a thing of titanic heights, perched high upon the Holy Mount, safe from the capricious world-sea and the brooding tides. Towering trees, swaying in the burgeoning dusk, framed a white wall, its ancient stones entwined with ivy and wild vine, encircling the mountain's breadth. Wrought from cyclopean blocks by hands long forgotten, it crowned the jagged crags—a bastion of bygone might, weathered by ages untold. At the southern slope of the mountain, upon a crystalline ledge of ore-bound rock, stood Jahdis—barefoot amidst a grove of slender, wind-swayed trees, their whispering branches shifting in the hush of twilight. Her gaze, dream-laden, followed the twin moons as they now unfurled their silent wisdom beyond the dark lacework of interwoven boughs, for above all celestial bodies, the people of this world ascribed to them the gift of foresight.

She was clad in the white vestments of the Temple of Erydin, her long stola of gossamer fabric clinging to the elegant lines of her form. Low-set, sweeping brows framed her large, contemplative eyes, ever cast toward distant horizons. Their interplay with the fullness of her lips and the defined curve of her delicate chin lent her an air of quiet defiance—an assumption she would effortlessly dispel with the radiance of her laughter. A diadem of exquisitely wrought filigree crowned her russet, glistening tresses, casting an ethereal sheen upon her brow. So perfect were her features in that moment that she seemed the very echo of The Eldren—those august forbearers whose solemn visages, wrought in gold and shadow, watched in eternal silence from their venerated frames, where they had lingered for uncounted ages along the soaring walls of the colonnade.

Her thoughts, long since mastered through diligent discipline, soared upward, threading the far-reaching corridors of memory, rattling at doors long sealed. She summoned forth the visions of her childhood: the exhilarating excursions beneath the shadow of the towering, cloud-piercing trees, which had seemed to her then as titanic pillars upholding the firmament itself; the mirthful, carefree games amid the hundred fountains of the grandiose cascade that formed the entrance to the labyrinthine gardens; the heedless, reckless scaling of steep stairways and jagged rock ledges, which her small yet unwavering steps had once ascended without fear; the arduous, day-long ascent along the narrow path, winding over riven chasms and unfathomable abysses, toward the *Gates of Alharion*—a slender plateau framed by overhanging cliffs at the loftiest heights of the mountain—where she had first beheld the sacred, awe-inspiring vista of the surrounding realms of Vilarien. Yet all that lay before that fateful moment, when she had gazed, her eyes veiled in tears, upon the hallowed, crown-like summit, and was thereafter borne aloft by compassionate hands into unfathomable heights and entrusted to the care of the White Mountain City, was now shrouded in the mists of memory. And so, above all else, she hungered for that knowledge.

Chirion, Master of Secrets, Guardian of the Glass-Lit Dome, Keeper of the *Citadel of Knowledge* and all its concealed wonders and mysteries, had taken her under his charge, so that from that day forth she dwelt in his house and was raised in kindness beneath his tutelage. The consecrated ones found in her an ardent, unyielding pupil, and when she had but just come into womanhood, they crowned her with the diadem and initiated her into the boundless wisdom of the Holy Mountain, where her clear, fathomless gaze fell upon the faded pages of books written in the Elder Tongue—volumes still hidden from the eyes of ordinary men.

Jahdis cast her gaze from the dizzying parapet, peering through the parting mists into the depths below. In the lowlands of the mountain, at a safe distance from the coast, lay the city of Vilarien, where its people dwelled within towering, stone-roofed houses—structures that reached toward the heavens, built centuries ago upon the remnants of an even older foundation. Far below the white mountain city, upon a storm-lashed cliff, stood a solitary door, forged from the dark ore of the mountain itself—an entrance the consecrated ones had long shunned. To approach it, one had to descend a treacherous slope, a path hewn in some forgotten age with coarse strokes into the jagged rock, perilously close to the primordial tides that roared in the abyss below. That door led into a vaulted chamber, from which an unfathomable labyrinth of halls and passageways branched forth, burrowing deep into the mountain's very roots like the hollowed lair of some entombed worm of the underworld.

Yet the consecrated ones feared the descent not for the perilous path nor the raging sea that ceaselessly besieged the green-clad cliffs, but for the sake of those strangers who, in some long-forgotten age, had emerged from that passage and heralded an era of darkness. No army had marched at their heels to lay waste to the land, for their numbers were few, yet it was their teachings, and the unspeakable acts wrought in their wake, that had brought war upon the realm—war that had ravaged the land and left the great city in ruin, so that only its oldest foundations remained to whisper of its former grandeur.

Within the 'Chronicles of Nemiáh,' a vast and ever-growing account meticulously recorded since the first emergence of those travelers, lay a grim testament to their ways. Jahdis had read much of it in fascination—of the first gatherings, the learning of tongues, the generous exchange of knowledge, and the rise of a newcomer to the throne; of oaths sworn in secret, hidden from all eyes; of shrines and altars raised upon the plains, their carved effigies depicting alien gods; of sorcery, its forbidden rites so ancient and abhorrent that they filled her heart with a terror beyond words; of a dreadful man, whose thirst, it was whispered, could only be slaked by the blood of his victims; of abominable revels, unbridled excesses, and deeds so heinous that the chronicler found no words to describe them; of the mines in Amoneáth, of new weapons and great wars, and of suffering so vast and boundless that no tongue could rightly speak of it.

At last, Jahdis had closed those books and abandoned them to the merciful oblivion of their dust-ridden existence, for what she had read had weighed upon her spirit beyond measure, haunting even her nights with dreadful visions. And yet, despite all, there remained something in those visitors that fascinated her in ways she could not name, and often did she question Chirion concerning them. But he, ever guarded, would answer in veiled utterances and cryptic allusions, his words as shrouded in secrecy as the past he seemed so unwilling to unveil.

Since those events recorded in the Nemiáhian Chronicles—events that culminated in the tyrant's hasty flight through the forbidden passage, shaking the mountain's very foundations on that fateful day—a watch had stood ever-vigilant before that door. And more dreadful still than the foam-flecked wrath of the surging tides were, at times, the furious blows that came from deep within the mountain, yet on the highest decree, they remained unanswered—and so they would remain forevermore, for the black door stood closed. But scarcely two decades past—so it was whispered in hushed and fearful voices—those ominous visitors had been sighted once more in various parts of Vilarien. And those who bore tidings of such sightings spoke in unshakable accord, describing the same strange garb, the same unnatural mannerisms, the same alien tongue, so that no doubt could linger. What errand had brought them hither none could say, but it could be nothing of good omen. The iron-bound door had been found wrenched from its hinges, and those whose duty it was to stand watch that day had vanished—never to be seen again—and fear began to spread among the peaceable folk of Vilarien.

Since that day, tales of wonder and dread had multiplied throughout the land, and the rumor persisted—tenacious, unyielding—that the strangers had returned to complete what once they had begun. Some declared, with unwavering conviction, that loyal devotees of the fallen despot yet lived unseen among the people, blind zealots willing to fulfill any command their master might issue—but for such claims they received naught but scorn or pitying glances. A lone wanderer swore he had seen smoke rising from the deep mines and tunnels, those same gouged and gaping wounds that still marred the reaches of Neèbh and the valley of Amoneáth. And among the younger folk, there were those who looked back upon those bygone days with a strange and wistful admiration, calling them a Golden Age, as though they themselves had lived within its vanished glories. Some even dared to claim that the visitors had borne no blame for the war—that, in truth, they had brought prosperity and advancements unknown before to the land.

In that time, it came to pass that Jahdis was found before the shattered door, and at first, the dwellers of the Holy Mountain ascribed this cruel deed to the frenzied mind of some grief-stricken mother, driven to madness by the unearthly events of those days. Then, peace returned once more, and the door was sealed anew—this time reinforced by all the cunning craft of the Master of Secrets. With his own hand, he etched strange sigils upon its inner surface, while upon the outer face, he inscribed words of command in the characters of the common tongue—words whose meaning none who read them could grasp. And it was decreed, under pain of punishment, that they should never be spoken beyond the vigil of the watch, nor should any record of them be set to parchment. Yet in secret, he instructed his most trusted confidants that such measures were necessary, for in some distant hour, a righteous traveler must one day pass through the threshold from the other side—as had been revealed to him upon the stone plateau where, in ages past, Alharion himself had hearkened to the words of eternity.

Jahdis cast aside her somber musings and allowed herself to smile, thinking of all the goodness that life in this blessed corner of Vilarien had bestowed upon her. She glanced upward through a vertical cleft between the tree trunks, toward the glass-lit dome, where the firmament was reflected in flawless symmetry. There, the men of science and the men of faith wrestled with the same eternal questions, each contributing, from his own station, a fragment of the great and boundless mystery that surrounded them all. A faint growl in her stomach reminded her that it was, perhaps, time for the evening meal. With a fluid motion, she leaned gracefully against one of the towering trees, as though it were a partner in some silent dance, steadying her as she moved. She felt the warmth of its rough bark against the bare skin of her arms, sensed the indomitable strength thrumming through its mighty trunk. Closing her eyes, she drew in the cool, aromatic breath of a passing wind, laden with the fragrance of trees and shrubs.

Then, bidding the radiant heavens farewell, as one might grant a living being a gentle goodnight, she sent forth a prayer to the Creator-God, who had ever watched over her and blessed her with all things good.

Jahdis moved with light and effortless steps through the moonlit darkness, ascending the winding path toward her dwelling. Her bare feet glided smoothly, the soles rolling gently over the time-worn, polished stone. From small windows set within the closely clustered facades—walls pierced by balconies and jutting alcoves—warm yellow light spilled onto the steep alleyway, which coiled like a fortress rampart upon both sides of her ascent. The night thrummed with voices, interwoven with the sharp barking of dogs. She passed by the birthing house, where she had spent the morning tending to her duties, and from within its walls came the heart-rending wails of newborns. A smile stole across her lips as she thought of those helpless little creatures, whose demands were proclaimed to the world with such fierce insistence, their tiny faces flushed with the fervor of their own existence. Softly, carried on unseen voices drifting like mist through the nighted lanes, there rose a song—ancient, woven into walls and shadow, sung each night as tradition ordained. At first it whispered, tentative as dusk, then swelled, many-voiced, rising from the yellow mouths of windows set in the clustered façades; verses murmuring of the primal light when darkness itself was young, of that first radiance that pierced the night and, even upon one's final journey, might yet shine with gentle benediction upon all mortal souls.

As the close-walled alley at last gave way to an open square, Chirion's house loomed before her, seated in solitary majesty at the end of the winding path. The massive stone blocks of its walls bore silent witness to a distant past, a kingdom long since forgotten, for they, like the outer ring wall itself, had been hewn from the mountain's flanks and raised into a monumental edifice. Jahdis unlatched the imposing, column-framed door and stepped across the threshold, absent-mindedly humming the melody still lingering in her thoughts.

A long, fantastically shaped shadow loomed against the wall, stretching greedily toward the high ceiling before it collapsed in a billowing cascade of shimmering white and silver feathers. Something sharp and curved, like a beak, prodded her cheek with delicate insistence, expelling a soft breath against her skin, so that her hair lifted in the sudden warmth, as though she stood upon a wind-swept cliff. Jahdis, laughing helplessly, crouched on the floor, pressing her hands against a vast, taloned paw that had settled upon her midriff, pinning her breathless. "Xerxes, you disobedient little beast! Have I not taught you patience, to wait until I am inside? Get off me at once, or you'll ruin my dress!" The strange creature withdrew, stepping backward with careful, deliberate grace, moving with a lightness wholly unexpected of its formidable form. Then, with a fluid arc, it settled itself upon a great straw-laden resting place. Jahdis rose, brushing down her gown with a stern, chastising glance—but her pretense of severity could not last, and laughter overtook her as she flung herself against the creature, embracing it with fierce affection. Though reclining, it still loomed a full head taller than her. She buried her face in its glistening plumage, inhaling its warmth as she moved against it, and Xerxes answered her caresses with a low, affectionate rumble. When at last she withdrew, a veil of stardust clung to her face, as though she had sneezed into a miller's trove of flour.

Xerxes fixed her with a long, profound gaze, his eyes vast as moonlit pools, and on some finer, more ephemeral plane of perception, she understood the silent speech he wove between them. She felt his longing to race through the halls beside her, the dull ache of his empty stomach, and beyond these—deeper, more primal—a creature's unclouded affection, purer and fiercer than that of many men. She sensed, too, his yearning for the open sky, for the caress of the wind that rippled through every feather upon his plumage and rustled the down of his fur-clad underbelly. He longed to plunge headlong into the bottomless vastness, to skim the jagged cliffs in reckless descent, to hunt his prey—some scurrying morsel clad in grey fur—upon the boundless plains, to find, at last, communion with his own kind… "Poor Xerxes," she murmured. "You are just as lonely as I am." She took the great head in both hands and brought her face near, until the tip of her nose brushed against the mighty beak. "First, let me fetch you something to eat, my friend. I shall return in but a moment," she said with a smile, before taking her leave.

She hastened through the soaring arcades that encircled an open courtyard, their slender vaults upheld by an architecture so exquisitely wrought that despite their weight, they seemed delicate, near weightless, as though they hung by some unseen artifice. From the ceiling's central rib, long filigreed chandeliers descended, glistening like star clusters set adrift in an unfathomable void. No tapestries adorned the walls, no ornaments nor needless embellishment, for this house had been fashioned, in some distant age, as a sanctuary for the High Clerisy, and thus was consecrated to humility and the unending pursuit of wisdom. Beneath her feet stretched a floor of dark, ancient wood, its grain so timeworn, its surface so rugged and deeply grained, that it evoked the rough-hewn planks of some primordial vessel, adrift upon the boundless seas of history. Everywhere small glass-shielded lanterns burned with quiet radiance; thick carpets and inviting cushions beckoned the weary to rest, while towering shelves along the walls bore a formidable trove of well-thumbed tomes. Chirion had little regard for wealth or worldly possessions, having gathered, within the vast Library of the *Citadel of Knowledge*, the intellectual treasures of all lands—far dearer to him than all the hoards of kings. And indeed, that radiant dome, wherein understanding took form and blossomed into revelation, was to him of greater worth than the finest gold, the rarest gems, the most dazzling of jewels. He was ever mindful of his station as MASTER OF SECRETS, and so had shaped his dwelling not in the likeness of some ancient tyrant's accursed throne-room, but as the modest study of a monastic scholar. Yet despite his every effort, the grandeur of these halls—once the seat of the temple's supreme authority—could never be fully concealed.

Jahdis made her way toward the chambers beyond the great dining hall, where the preparation and storage of food was overseen. These vast kitchens, though once meant to serve an entire household, now seemed far too expansive for herself and Chirion, whose own children had long since outgrown his home. Only a small portion of the quarters was maintained, with the aid of a handful of attendants. It was here, rounding a corner too swiftly, that she nearly collided with Chirion himself. He set down a sheaf of papers and several broad tomes upon one of the dark shelves, then, without hesitation, embraced her warmly, with the unfailing affection of a father. Jahdis deftly slipped from his grasp, pressing a swift, affectionate kiss to his stubbled cheek before darting away in playful retreat. "Has my daughter once again no time for me?" he asked, feigning disappointment.

"Your daughter, above all, is starving!" Jahdis quipped as she stepped into the dining hall, while Chirion, gathering up his documents once more, followed in her wake. She stood by the sideboard, finishing what remained of an evening meal, and he watched her with quiet amusement as he entered the room. Though he was nearly a head shorter than Jahdis, he possessed a frame of immense, stocky build. Age had left parts of his head bare, and what hair remained—like the long, tapering beard that framed his jaw—had faded to an ashen silver. The skin of his face was a parched riverbed, etched with furrows and crevices deep as time itself, yet his grasp remained unyielding, his blue eyes flashed with a vigor that defied the slow ruin of his years.

His robe, though plain and unadorned save for an elaborate embroidery at the collar, fell freely about his form. Upon his massive hands gleamed a single, unassuming ring—an heirloom passed down through the centuries, from one Keeper to the next, since the days before any visitor had ever crossed the threshold of the Passage. Though his features bore the weight of advancing age, they retained an austere nobility, and Jahdis often wondered how he might have looked in his youth.

"No secret has ever been unraveled through mere zeal," he remarked, quoting an oft-repeated maxim.

"And whoever lingers in idleness shall renounce wisdom," Jahdis countered, answering with a well-known verse.

"I have not seen you all day," he continued, his tone half-curious, half-reproving. "Where, pray, have you been loitering?"

"I was tending my duties at the birthing-house, assisting those little troublemakers as they arrived wailing into the world, only to place them moments later into the trembling arms of their mothers—who, despite the torments they had just endured, clutched those wrinkled, squalling things as though they had been granted the greatest joy upon this earth."

"I expect you will understand such joy yourself, when the time comes."

"I would rather make the climb to Alharion's Gates ten times over and back again than suffer so, only to emerge from it half-mad with bliss," Jahdis declared, though she barely finished the words before bursting into a fit of coughing, having spoken too hastily through a mouthful of food.

Chirion regarded his ward with quiet affection, undeterred by her impudence. He knew, from the many praises that often reached his ears, that her heart was vast enough to cradle the joys and sorrows of a hundred such wild-eyed, enraptured mothers, whose reason had fled in the wake of newborn love. "Your duties ended by midday. Were you at the Citadel, by chance? And tell me—did poor Niahl once again forfeit his midday meal on your account?"

"It is hardly my fault that he refuses to let me be in the crypt unsupervised. He follows me incessantly, watching my every move, as though doubting my ability to turn a page without assistance. If I do not go to eat, he would sooner fast an entire day than leave me alone with the books for even a moment. Oh, forgive me, I forgot—apparently, they are his books."

Chirion let out a hearty laugh. "I hope you are aware that never, since the days of The Eldren and likely long before, has such a precocious wretch as yourself been granted insight into such matters. Niahl had to be coaxed with the tongues of angels to permit it. And truth be told, he seems as wedded to his books as those mothers you spoke of are to their newborns." Both laughed heartily, and for a brief moment, a most unsettling image formed in Jahdis's mind—Niahl, cradling and nursing an infant, a vision that, given his remarkable corpulence, did not seem entirely beyond the realm of possibility.

"I spent the entire afternoon in the southern grove," Jahdis answered truthfully, striving to banish the ghastly thought from her mind.

"You have always been drawn to that place. When you were but a child, your nurse would always find you there at last, lying on your back amidst the trees, searching the heavens with your eyes. In the beginning, we all fretted over you, you may be certain of that, and save for the strangers who once stepped through the black door, there was no other matter that ever so unstrung your nurse. But in time, we abandoned all attempts to master your talent for vanishing."

"Today, once more, those unanswered questions tormented me," she confessed suddenly, a wistful tremor in her voice, stirred by the memory of that sacred place that for so many years had been her silent refuge, the wellspring of her strength—a sanctuary where she had felt as though cradled in the warm embrace of a mother she had never known. A single tear traced its way down her cheek, a glimmering crystal upon her skin. "And though no words can contain my happiness, there is a longing in my heart for distant things, and I know not whence it comes, nor why it burdens me so."

Chirion grew silent, his gaze dropping to the ground, burdened with sorrow. The muscles of his face twitched, as though he wrestled with an inner compulsion—to bring to light what was long kept hidden, to offer her tormented questions some measure of solace. He sighed deeply, then wrapped his foster daughter in a firm embrace, and she, having no strength left to resist, wept freely against his broad chest. Xerxes approached from behind, his movement soundless, and nudged her gently in the side with the curve of his bowed head. "Xerxes, my dear one, I completely forgot your meal," she sobbed, noisily drawing up her breath.

"His meal? It has been barely an hour since I last fed him," Chirion said with a chuckle. "It defies belief, what that glutton devours in a single day." Jahdis pulled away from him, wiping the tears from her eyes. Chirion reached into a vessel, retrieved a bone as long as a man's forearm—rich with red meat marbled with fine veins of fat—and handed it to the winged beast, who accepted it carefully with the side of his mighty beak before tearing into it, pinning the bone down with one of his razor-sharp talons. Jahdis sensed his gratitude, not only for the treat but for his silent sympathy; he had come not merely in hunger but because he, too, suffered with her. As Xerxes devoured his meal, the crack of splintering bone filling the chamber, Jahdis made her way to her quarters, where she prepared for the night and lay herself down to rest. She called for Chirion, who came and seated himself at her bedside, brushing a stray lock from her face before pressing a tender kiss to her forehead. Then he spoke a prayer, invoking the Creator's blessing and entrusting her to His divine protection. Jahdis, lulled by the soothing cadence of his deep, resonant voice, drifted swiftly into slumber. Beneath the white linen of her bed, her body rose and fell in the tranquil rhythm of even breathing. Chirion watched her as she slept, his weathered hand lingering a moment in her unruly hair before gently tucking the covers over her shoulders, an act she acknowledged in unconscious contentment with a soft, drowsy murmur. He rose, extinguished the lamp's flame, and strode toward the door. But at the threshold, he turned once more, gazing upon her with a shadowed expression—one of deep worry, though he himself might not yet have grasped its cause. A muffled sound, unnatural in the quiet of the night, tore him suddenly from his thoughts. For a few seconds, he stood frozen, his senses sharpening, straining to discern its origin. Then it came again. Shrieks—sharp, unrelenting—cut through the night's serenity, clashing against the ceaseless murmur of the waves and the rhythmic chirr of the insects. His brow furrowed. He inclined his head slightly forward, listening with intent. The clamor swelled, cascading like an oncoming tide; more voices joined the first, calling out in panic, in warning. Then came a furious pounding against the great door.

Chirion flung the door open. Standing at the threshold was a tall man he recognized as a resident of one of the houses beneath the Citadel. His pallid face was contorted with fear. It took some time, and a great deal of coaxing, before he could gather from him any coherent account of what had happened. By then, Jahdis, roused from her sleep, had emerged as well, her eyes still heavy with drowsy confusion. Behind her loomed Xerxes, a vast shadow in the dim light, his talons scraping softly against the stone floor. "Death," the man stammered, his breath coming in ragged gasps. "Death—everywhere! The Citadel… the gate—it has been broken open!" He wheezed, struggling to regain his breath. "Who… in God's name… would do such a thing?"

Chirion placed a steadying hand upon his shoulder. With a meaningful glance, he bade Jahdis see to the shaken man's needs, then turned on his heel and set out at once toward the Citadel, lifting the hem of his robe to keep from stumbling. As he strode forth, his voice rang out in sharp commands, issuing swift, decisive orders to those still gathered in the streets. He called for order, urged the frightened townsfolk back to their homes, and exhorted them to remain calm. Beyond the great Dome of Light, its argent sheen gleaming beneath the stars, rose the *Citadel of Knowledge*, its own lesser dome cast in sharp relief against the night's darkness. Though the hour was late, the stronghold blazed with light, its glow reflecting against the rooftops of the clustered houses below, rendering them no more than diminutive silhouettes before its towering presence. Chirion climbed the steep stairway with swift, purposeful strides, ascending the final steps before passing beneath the sacred archways of the Temple's heart.

The towering walls, pierced with arcades, bore mighty buttresses upon which rested a vaulted ceiling, curving upward to a central apex left open to the sky—a feat of such vast proportions that, whether one entered this hallowed place for the first time or returned after long absence, it never failed to instill a sense of profound humility. He could discern a cluster of figures huddled behind a colonnade, bent over something that his view was yet denied. A strange, resonant wailing, amplified by the vast architecture, swelled like a mournful choir of lost souls through the vaults. As he strode forward with purpose, the gathered onlookers parted, their eyes filled with silent entreaty. A woman, her face ravaged by grief, bit into the knuckles of her clenched fist as though to stifle a scream. Someone made a sign of warding. Without acknowledging these gestures, Chirion pressed onward, stopping abruptly as his gaze fell upon the sight unveiled before him. A young adept—she who had but recently received the diadem from his own hand—lay in an unnatural contortion, her throat slit, in a dark pool that slowly spread across the stone-laid floor.

Moving through the labyrinthine corridors—lined with statues and echoing with every footfall—he came, by degrees, to apprehend the full extent of the calamity. Again and again he came upon the dead, whose final breath had, in like manner, vanished into the cold blackness of the marble. That baleful trail wound its way through a debris-field of shattered relics, their origins long since blurred between cataloguing error and occult legend—a sedimented archive of forgotten artefacts: splintered shrines of ancient knowledge, ruined instruments of dark provenance, tattered folios strewn far and wide—book-bodies outstretched like corpses—until it came at last to a secret recess, hidden beneath the main tract of the monumental edifice, once sealed by a perforated grille of heavy iron, now standing wide to the dark. His heart pounded as he stepped over the threshold of the crypt—the heart of his stewardship. Summoning a guard, he stationed him at the entrance before advancing deeper into the chamber. At the far end, slumped against a wall, lay the corpulent form of a man who had seen better days. "Niahl, old friend," he murmured, his expression dark with concern. He cradled the wounded scholar's head, laying it upon the nearest tome—an ornate manuscript of untold value, which, in this moment, seemed a mere trifle. Tearing strips from his own robe, he bound the grievous wounds upon the man's arms and torso.

"They have taken it!" Niahl gasped, lifting a trembling hand toward an empty alcove in the rear of the crypt. The iron plating that had once reinforced it lay torn from its hinges, twisted and battered as though wrenched apart by an inhuman force, now crumpled and useless, like a shattered shield cast upon the dust-covered floor. Chirion's breath caught in his throat as he stared into the hollow void where once an artifact of unspeakable significance had rested. His hands trembled, the weight of the revelation pressing upon him like an iron yoke. Niahl clutched at his sleeve with surprising strength. "It is gone!" he cried, his voice quivering with despair. A pallor overtook Chirion's features. The visitors of old had left behind something of immeasurable value in their hasty retreat—an object upon which all their aspirations had once fixated. Now, it seemed, those who followed in their footsteps had reclaimed it. Chirion sent for one of his trusted aides, instructing him to visit the Black Door and those who stood watch there, so that he might ascertain whether all was already lost.

CHAPTER IV.
THE THRICE-GREAT HERMES

A merciful faintness stole over Phineas, granting him a fleeting reprieve from the world's disarray. He was caught in the steadfast arms of Monsieur Lameth, who had made his way to the stage as the spectacle drew to a close, and under his firm grasp, he was guided back to their table, where a draught of brandy was unceremoniously pressed to his lips to summon him from his stupor. Through the dim haze of his vision, still blurred by the veil of unconsciousness, Phineas discerned the shaman shaking Madame Morrígu, whose form lay draped across the table, giving no sign of life. He seized her shoulders, gave her a rough jolt, then, failing to elicit a response, struck her pale cheek in a gesture more of urgency than of cruelty, while that peculiar headdress she had worn now spun aimlessly upon the floor, tracing erratic circles upon the dust-laden boards.

Oppressed by the stifling heat of the overcrowded room and the potency of the brandy, which burned through his senses with slow insistence, Phineas entreated Lameth to take him outside. The cool breath of the evening brushed against his fevered brow, dispelling the mist that had gathered in his mind, as though a fogged windowpane had been wiped clear.

"It would seem, perhaps, that this was all rather too much," remarked Lameth, his voice tempered with the faintest trace of amusement.

"Too much indeed! Too much of everything!" Phineas exhaled, his tone laced with incredulity. "A night of horrors within that accursed hôtel, these unfathomable murders in whose shadow I feel myself complicit, your blasphemous accounts of ancient terrors, and, at last, this—this grotesque *séance* that trespasses upon the boundaries of the world! Tell me, Monsieur, do these things truly transpire, or am I slipping, inch by inch, into madness?" A passing couple, strolling beneath the golden glow of the gas lamps, cast wary glances in his direction, having caught the frantic cadence of his speech. At this, Phineas lowered his voice, his gaze flitting over his shoulder, as if fearing unseen ears lay in wait amid the nocturnal hush.

Lameth, however, chose not to answer, nor did he offer any reassurance to his companion's mounting distress. With deft efficiency, he summoned a carriage and ushered Phineas within, for the young man's senses had become a tempest of incoherence—at times launching into breathless tirades, at others lapsing into a leaden silence, his thoughts lost in some ungraspable abyss. Upon their arrival at the hôtel, Lameth saw to the fare with his customary indifference and, citing an obligation of pressing import, departed forthwith, leaving Phineas to navigate his way alone. No sooner had he stepped across the threshold of the lobby than he was met by a flurry of apologies from the staff. The portly concierge, wringing his hands in evident distress, informed him that, due to circumstances beyond their control, he was to be relocated to another room. There was no avenue for protest—for his belongings had already been removed, his valise and personal effects transferred without so much as a by-your-leave. Yet Phineas, finding himself in no condition to debate the matter with so obtuse an adversary, resigned himself to the arrangement with uncharacteristic indifference. If truth be told, the events of the previous night had tainted his lodgings with a pall of unease, and this unforeseen change, rather than a cause for grievance, seemed instead a fortuitous stroke of fate. Whatever misgivings he might have harbored about the hôtel's structural integrity, he dismissed with a shrug—choosing, in an unanticipated flourish of optimism, to regard this unwelcome disruption as an improvement upon his circumstances.

The climb to his new lodgings led him up yet more breath-stealing flights of stairs. The porter, expressionless, placed the key into his hand, gestured vaguely toward the door, and watched him ascend from his place at the foot of the staircase, as though to ensure that Phineas did indeed seek out the correct chamber. The number "6" was inscribed in delicate engraving upon a brass plate, and Phineas could not help but wonder whether the craftsman responsible for the numbering had suffered from some inability to count, had assigned the figures in sheer caprice, or had adhered to some unfathomable internal logic known only to the proprietors of this singular establishment.

He pushed open the door and stepped across the threshold. A lamp, already kindled, cast its muted glow across the chamber, which bore such resemblance to his former quarters that it might have been its twin, were it not for one notable difference—there was no proper window to speak of, save for a narrow aperture set high into the wall, which, he presumed, admitted light during the day but allowed no glimpse of the world beyond. A small wooden-latticed opening in the wall proved itself to be nothing more than a ventilation shaft, for upon drawing it open, he was met with the disheartening sight of a second wall set at an offset angle behind it. A worm-eaten table, attended by two antiquated chairs; a spacious wardrobe; a bookshelf with bowed, burdened planks that spoke of once-weighty tomes now long removed; and a great iron bedstead—all these proclaimed that nothing he might require for his stay had been omitted. And yet, despite the room's apparent adequacy, he could not rid himself of that gnawing unease, that instinctive wariness toward this house and all it contained, toward the lurking shadows that gathered in the deep grooves of the blackened ceiling beams, along the uneven plaster of soot-darkened walls, and—most ominously of all—within the yawning void of the chimney shaft, where the darkness seemed to coil and pulse with a sentience of its own.

Once more, sections of the walls bore wooden panels, upon which scenes of figures had been rendered in exquisite detail—scenes that bore a striking resemblance to those he had glimpsed in his former quarters. It was as if they had been conceived as part of some vast and continuous pictorial narrative, spanning chamber upon chamber, unfolding in silent procession through the very walls of the building. He wondered if some scholarly treatise had been dedicated to this evidently significant, meticulously wrought mythological tableau—if somewhere there existed lithographs documenting its full expanse, its strange pantheon, its cryptic cosmogony. With this thought in mind, he reached for a sheet of paper from a neat stack laid upon the table in the corner, placed it carefully against a chosen section of the relief, and with a stick of graphite, made a rubbing of the accompanying inscription. The task required several overlapping sheets to capture the full extent of the text. His intent was clear—he would present these to Lameth and entreat his knowledge in deciphering the meaning of this enigma that now surrounded him, silent and omnipresent, in the very fabric of the place.

One of the walls, as before, was adorned with a masterfully executed yet faded landscape mural, whose aged pigments and melancholic composition suggested the artist had labored under some deep despondency. Unlike the previous scene, this one depicted a barren and desolate terrain—an accursed garden where twisted, gnarled trees, their trunks split and deformed, clung to life upon arid soil and jagged rocks, choked with brambles and thorns beneath a merciless sun. The few animals that populated this wasteland seemed seized by an all-pervasive dread, their postures rigid with terror, their expressions—rendered with uncanny skill—betraying the imminence of death. A lifeless bird lay upon the withered grass beneath the stump of a dead tree. A viper slithered forth from its lair, its forked tongue tasting the air for unseen prey. Some unidentifiable beast—no creature of this world, surely!—clamped its jagged maw around the bloodied remnants of a carcass, its merciless fangs gleaming. The stark ribs of a lamb, torn open by some brutal force, jutted white and naked from the gaping wound in its flank, while a swarm of grotesquely detailed carrion beetles feasted upon the raw flesh. A monstrous bird, standing knee-deep in the stagnant waters of a weed-choked pool, picked at rotting carrion, and upon a desolate clearing lay a malformed beast, bearing two heads.

Never before had Phineas beheld such a harrowing and unflinching depiction of the enmity that reigned among the creatures of the world, nor had he imagined that an artist's brush could capture death and decay with such terrifying vividness. Both appalled and fascinated, he tore his gaze away and turned instead to his belongings, which had been neatly arranged—his clothes hanging once more within the armoire, his personal effects laid out with meticulous care beside his trunk. The books Lameth had entrusted to his study had likewise been brought up. Placing Eireen's portrait within sight of his bed, he discarded his outer garments and knelt in prayer upon the cold floorboards. The lateness of the hour and the turmoil of his mind compelled him to brevity, yet he strove to form his supplications in his own words, rather than resorting to hollow repetition. At last, he extinguished the lamp, burrowed into his bed, kneading the pillow as though shaping a loaf of dough, and lay shifting drowsily from side to side, until the weight of exhaustion overtook him, and he succumbed to a deep and dreamless slumber.

Once more, Phineas dreams of Eireen. She approaches him, her countenance radiant with exultant joy, her being suffused with profound gratitude for her deliverance from the fetters of Madame Morrígu, which had bound her so cruelly. She ascends swiftly, eager to pass into that world of purest light that awaits her. Yet, for a fleeting moment, she lingers—her lips forming a silent farewell, a knowing smile gracing her face, bearing the luminous imprint of a wisdom forever denied to mortal understanding. Light of a preternatural brilliance enfolds her, a radiance surpassing all conceivable intensity, before which even the most scorching noonday sun pales to a dim and smoke-veiled flicker, the dying ember of an extinguished wick. And under harmonies of such celestial grandeur—symphonies that cast the loftiest compositions of human genius into discordant cacophony, that render the greatest oratorios and all attempts to enshrine sublimity in sound to mere jarring dissonance, as of unskilled hands striking the keys of an ill-tuned piano—she is borne away into those blissful realms of unfathomable splendor, ungraspable to mortal sight.

Phineas drifts weightlessly through the abyssal void of an uncreated, formless, and lightless cosmos, until an immense force seizes him, drawing him forth with ineffable speed, his very form dissolving into the maelstrom, until suddenly—his journey ends. Before him unfolds a churning vortex of primordial matter, shaped and wrought over eons unreckoned—ages immeasurable by human time, which here unspool like fleeting instants—by beings of ineffable majesty, timeless architects of creation. And with the sight of his spirit, he beholds the archetypes of all things, clothed at last in substance. Then, drawn downward, he passes through chaotic deluges, through chasms of searing flame and torrents of blackened ash, until at last he halts before a garden—a garden beyond the reach of mortal dreaming, whose beauty no earthly tongue may hope to utter.

There he witnesses the weaving of forms, the intermingling of essences, the conjoining of harmonies—each thing fashioned after its nature, each according to its kind. He beholds how the bodies of all living things are conceived and shaped, molded in imitation of the First Man. And he sees how the soul, divine and radiant, is enshrined within the prison of the flesh. Beneath the shade of a tree of surpassing majesty, he beholds a man and a woman entwined in loving embrace—beings of unblemished grace, of beauty unparalleled. Their forms are fashioned in accordance with the sacred numbers, each limb wrought to perfection, their countenances bearing the divine symmetry that, in the dawn of creation, pervades all things, as does the ineffable splendor of the garden in which they walk.

And then, he perceives a figure of purest light—a presence at once foreign and hauntingly familiar, whose sight rends his very soul. But as he gazes, a shadow slithers forth, and the luminous presence vanishes. He beholds the woman, lingering in contemplation amidst the unspoiled glories of the paradise of beasts and trees. A being moves near to her—serpentine, walking upright upon two legs, of stature exceeding that of man, its form clad in gleaming scales, patterned and burnished like an armor of living metal. It coils beside her, its long limbs outstretched, its hissing whisper a venomous intermingling of falsehood and truth—not by its own will, for its will remains ever subject to the Most High. And Phineas beholds as the woman, under the spell of the Serpent-Formed, plucks and eats of the tree's fruit—and proffers it, in turn, to the man beside her.

Phineas awoke with a start, his eyes fluttering open to the angled shaft of light that streamed through the narrow upper window, its golden beam streaked with drifting motes of dust. The hour was already advanced. Upon the table, a breakfast tray stood waiting—a silent testament to the fact that he had failed to bolt his door and had slumbered so soundly that he had not stirred at the intruder's presence. He reached for his garments, only to recoil in sudden shock at the sight of a figure standing in the farthest corner of the room, half-obscured by shadow. The girl's head was bowed, her hands wringing one another in nervous agitation, arms drawn awkwardly downward as though weighed by unseen fetters. It was the old-fashioned chambermaid with the pretty, unsettling eyes—the same he had observed replenishing the oil lamps in the corridors on his first night. She made no attempt to speak. Instead, her gaze remained averted, fixed upon the worn leather of her shoes, and her teeth nibbled fretfully at her lower lip.

It was Phineas who first broke the silence. "I see that breakfast has been set," he remarked, his voice measured yet inquisitive as he pulled the shirt over his broad shoulders, the fabric grazing the pale scars that marred his flesh—souvenirs of a disastrous hunting accident. Still, the girl said nothing. "Can I be of some assistance to you?"

No response. Only silence, thick and weighty, as she gnawed at her lip with increasing fervor. Then, as though some inner dam had burst, her cheeks flushed crimson in an instant, as if every drop of blood in her body had surged to her face. "You must leave at once!" she blurted, her voice trembling yet urgent. And once the words had begun, they tumbled forth in a desperate, breathless cascade. "You must leave! You are not safe here!"

Phineas arched a skeptical brow, the mounting incredulity of the past days hardening his tone. "And why, pray, should I not be safe, you foolish girl?"

"You wouldn't understand—you couldn't," she pleaded. "You must only believe me."

"I was summoned here by Monsieur Lameth, my employer," Phineas countered, his voice even but firm. "I cannot simply vanish into the night without knowing the reason." The moment he spoke Lameth's name, he saw the girl shudder—a visible tremor that ran through her slight frame like the rippling of a wind-stirred leaf.

"*Mon Dieu!* I cannot explain—it is too complicated."

"What is too complicated?"

"He is not the man you take him for, and he means you no good. Wherever he treads, misfortune follows. Once, I listened in the hush outside his chamber, and what I perceived..."

Their conversation was abruptly interrupted by the heavy clatter of boots upon the stairwell below. She flinched, her shoulders tensing, then darted toward the door—yet, just as swiftly, she hesitated, turned back, and with tear-brimmed eyes, pressed a desperate, wordless kiss upon his lips before fleeing the room in haste. "What is your name?" Phineas called after her, his voice hoarse with astonishment.

"Farah," she whispered, her brows drawn high, her head bowed forward. Then, with a resolute motion, she pressed a finger against her lips, bidding him to silence, before vanishing into the labyrinthine corridors and stairwells. Phineas stood for a long while, staring after her in bewilderment. From one of the lower floors, he heard hurried steps and the sharp reprimand of an unseen voice—no doubt meant for her. What he had just heard unsettled him to his very core, for through all the upheavals since his arrival, and even in the bitterest years of his life, Lameth had been a steadfast pillar upon which he had leaned. He splashed his face with the cool water from a pewter jug, smoothing back the unruly strands of hair that clung in disheveled locks to his temples, then regarded his own distorted reflection in the rippling surface of the washbasin with a pensive, wary gaze. Once dried and composed, he turned his full attention to the meal before him—though, judging by the stark confirmation of his pocket watch, it was far closer to midday than morning.

As he pored over the books Lameth had sent him the previous evening, his thoughts drifted inexorably toward the dream—the haunting vision whose vivid impressions, moment by moment, seemed to fade, as though his mind were incapable of holding onto such things for long. He thought back to the instant of waking, when, stepping into the clarity of day, he had felt the immutable certainty that he had gazed into the unveiled heavens and glimpsed the mysteries of eternity. And yet, scarcely an hour later, he could no longer grasp its fullness, nor summon even the faintest echo of the awe that had gripped him as he beheld the genesis of all things and the hand of its Creator.

His breakfast was cleared away rather late, as though the staff had, with indulgent resignation, resigned themselves to the irregularities of his daily routine. To his great disappointment, it was not Farah who entered his room, but instead the wretched porter once more—a man whose very presence inspired distaste. He set down a well-prepared midday meal before him and, in his usual gruff manner, announced that a bath would be drawn for him in the evening, a prospect Phineas accepted with gratitude. Without lifting his gaze from the task at hand—gnawing with both hands at a roasted *confit de canard*, every so often punctuating his meal with a satisfied murmur—he offhandedly inquired after the man's name. "Obed," came the reply, delivered through a gap-toothed, vaguely unnerving grin.

As the man turned to leave, he seemed to recall something, for he halted mid-step, retraced his path, and wordlessly handed Phineas a letter from Monsieur Lameth. The note bore an invitation for supper at a specific hour that evening. Phineas set it aside, where, under his grease-slicked fingers, half-transparent stains swiftly blossomed upon the paper's surface. He then speared a neglected potato with his fork, carried it absentmindedly to his mouth, and wiped his hands upon a napkin. Picking at his teeth with a fingernail, he cast a lingering glance toward the bed, debating whether to succumb to idle repose—only to recall his duties. With a sigh, he returned to his books, completing one in its entirety, before continuing his graphite rubbings of the wall panel inscriptions. His thoughts drifted first to Eireen, then to the sweet, fleeting kiss of that mysterious girl and the youthful, untroubled ease she carried about her. He felt, in a way both inexplicable and strangely familiar, drawn to her; yet, that did not deter him from dismissing her warning outright—regarding it as nothing more than a flight of girlish fancy, or else the lovesick musings of a child desperate for attention.

Hours later, the ever-phlegmatic house-servant appeared once again, guiding him down several flights of stairs to a secluded bathing chamber. Beside an ancient rope winch stood an array of buckets, their pooled contents betraying the arduous labor of carrying water to this upper floor. The bathhouse itself was of considerable age, faintly reminiscent of a Roman thermae. The floor was laid with polished stone, while the walls were adorned with dark, turquoise-glazed tiles, broken at intervals by relief carvings and intricate ornamental patterns. The chamber did not appear to be in frequent use—this was evident from the thin film of dust that coated the furnishings and the horizontal ledges—but someone had at least made a half-hearted attempt at cleaning. The area in which he now stood had been freshly mopped, and a stack of crisp, neatly folded towels awaited him.

Upon brass-colored trays rested gleaming carafes and an assortment of vessels, each containing precious soaps, oils, and balms of exotic origin. A misty vapor curled over the rim of the richly ornamented bathtub, lending the chamber a dreamlike obscurity. Phineas unfastened his shirt, drawing it over his head with both hands before continuing his undressing until he stood wholly bare upon the cold stone slabs in the vast expanse of the room. Despite the season, a shiver passed over him, and he crossed his gooseﬂeshed arms over his chest, his gaze drifting absently through the chamber's dim haze. He dipped the shaving brush into the ivory-colored foam, which, under his measured strokes, blossomed into a fragrant cloud. Drawing the razor in slow, deliberate sweeps across his skin, he shaved with practiced precision before sinking at last into the waiting embrace of the copper tub. His fingers sought a slender glass vial capped with gold; a single drop of the amber-hued oil dissolved in the steaming water, releasing the deep, woody essence of sandalwood, mingled with the bright sharpness of bergamot. The mingled scents wreathed the air, weaving a heady spell that softened the weight of the world beyond the vaporous walls of the chamber. He submerged himself beneath the water's surface, indulging in a few moments of profound silence—until, unbidden, those visions, defying all natural law, surged once more into his consciousness: those strange, timeless reveries glimpsed in his meditations. Alarmed, he abruptly resurfaced. He did not leave the bath until the water had long since grown tepid, his fingers and toes furrowed with the telltale ridges of time spent in idle contemplation. Dressing with unhurried care, he gathered his papers—the graphite impressions of the carvings from his chamber—intending to elicit some useful explanation from Lameth.

By the time Phineas arrived, Lameth was already seated in the spacious receiving hall, reclining in one of the inviting armchairs arranged in a half-circle. A haze of pungent smoke coiled about him as he languidly drew upon some foul-smelling herb, its acrid scent unearthing in Phineas an unwelcome memory—of a filth-ridden hut in Haiti, packed to the rafters with mummified creatures and grotesque fetishes, the dwelling of a deranged *bocor priest* whose sorcery had reeked of madness. "Anything of note today?" Lameth inquired with an air of idle concern.

"Thank you for your inquiry. It is, in fact, quite remarkable—nothing has yet occurred today that could be described solely with the superlatives of a negative lexicon. Rather unusual for this particular stay," Phineas quipped, settling himself into one of the plush leather armchairs opposite Lameth. "I had the pleasure of indulging in a most agreeable bathhouse today."

"I instructed Obed to prepare one for you. Last night, at *L'Auberge du Géant*, you seemed to me… how shall I put it? You appeared somewhat beside yourself." Lameth regarded him with a piercing gaze, the smoke from his cigar coiling in a thin column towards the ceiling.

"One ought to let the dead rest," Phineas replied, struggling for composure, without so much as acknowledging the wordplay.

"Ah, indeed, how right you are! And I see you have brought me something," Lameth noted, gesturing toward the crumpled sheaf of papers clenched in Phineas's hand. "You have taken an interest in the wood paneling. Most impressive, do you not think?"

"Indeed, most impressive! Though I must admit, I have gleaned little from it," Phineas responded, placing the stack of papers upon the hammered brass-inlaid smoking table before him. "I have come to the conclusion that it is a Renaissance-era fantasy, devised in a spirit of intellectual pastiche. Nothing about it coheres. The text in the upper section appears to be some early consonantal script—my best estimation is Phoenician-Punic. The depictions bear an undeniable resemblance to an archaic, likely Egyptian hieroglyphic style, yet the script below seems as though someone had merely traced those same hieroglyphs with a brush."

Lameth retrieved one of the sheets and studied it with an appraising eye. "It is unmistakably Ancient Egyptian. The text, however, is in Hieratic—the script of the priesthood. The author, therefore, is Thoth. Here, in the upper portion, some explanatory notes have been appended in an early form of Aramaic, for the sake of clarity."

"Explanations? And whom, pray tell, does it benefit to provide explanations in a language equally as dead as the one it seeks to elucidate?" Phineas remarked, perplexed.

"The early travelers were not of this part of the world. I should also not neglect to mention that this is a replica—I commissioned it myself to lend the chambers a certain… how shall I phrase it… authenticity. The original is hewn into stone, and of an age beyond reckoning. The artisan who wrought it was extraordinarily skilled, capable of carving stone with such effortless precision as though he were inscribing upon parchment."

"But surely, the hôtel cannot be as ancient as you suggest. It lies far beyond the *Île de la Cité* or the original city walls of Philip II."

Lameth exhaled a slow, curling plume of smoke before replying. "Paris has swallowed us whole. In those days, when the Parisii first founded Lutetia, it was little more than a shrine atop a vast, labyrinthine cavern. In a manner of speaking, we have merely ascended from the depths into the light of day—though, I might add, such exposure is far less conducive to one's health."

He turned back to the manuscript and studied the text with solemn gravity. The ash of his cigar crumbled onto the paper, and as he began to read, his voice deep and resonant, the wisps of smoke drifting from his lips, it seemed to Phineas as though a tragedian had stepped forth upon the stage, emerging through a swirling haze of paraffin fog to deliver his lines. Phineas listened intently, arms and legs crossed, watching Lameth as though he were witnessing the unfurling of some great and dreadful revelation.

"It is true, without falsehood, certain and most true:

That which is below is like unto that which is above, and that which is above is like unto that which is below, to accomplish the wonders of the One.

And as all things proceed from the One, through a single thought of the One, so have all things come forth from this one cause by adaptation.

The Sun is its father, the Moon its mother. The Wind has carried it in its womb. The Earth is its nurse.

This thing is the source of all perfection in the whole world.

Its power is most complete when it has once more returned to the Earth.

Separate then the Earth from the Fire, the subtle from the dense, with great skill and utmost care.

From the Earth it ascends to Heaven, and from Heaven it descends again to the Earth, to receive the power of the Above and the Below..."

Lameth tilted the paper slightly against the light, as the graphite rubbing had grown faint.

"In this way, thou shalt attain the glory of the whole world, and all darkness shall flee from thee.

This is the strong power of all powers, which binds together all subtle things and penetrates all that is solid.

Thus was the world created.

Wondrous things may be wrought if it be done in this manner."

Phineas could not discern whether Lameth was translating from the Hieratic script or from Ancient Aramaic. He read the text as though he knew it by heart, never faltering over a word nor pausing to correct himself. He even managed to render the sentences with such nuance and solemnity that the words flowed like a sacred recitation. "I was aware that you were versed in the ancient tongues, but I did not know that you could read across the centuries as though it were poetry," Phineas said, his eyes glistening.

"I must confess, this was no particularly arduous task, for the text in question is one of those well-known writings attributed to Hermes Trismegistus, that mythical author and keeper of secret knowledge. Legend holds that the text was engraved upon two tablets of emerald, which he clasped in his lifeless hands within a hidden burial chamber beneath the *Great Pyramid of Cheops*."

"Are you suggesting that all these inscriptions belong to the same hermetic tradition?"

"By no means. But Hermes Trismegistus, as is well attested, is none other than Thoth—the very one who, it is said, inscribed his wisdom upon stelae in hieroglyphic script before the Deluge. And much of what the scholars of the Ptolemaic era devised under the influence of Platonic natural philosophy and the Stoics draws upon that ancient knowledge, for Alexander the Great plundered all from Macedonia to the westernmost reaches of the Himalayas, seizing even the accumulated wisdom of the old Orient."

"But was it not Isaac Casaubon who, as early as 1614, thoroughly discredited such claims, demonstrating beyond doubt that these writings were nothing more than Hellenistic treatises composed during the Roman Imperial era?"

"Casaubon? That damned Huguenot! Have you not read what has been written of the Library of Alexandria? Do you grasp the unfathomable wealth of knowledge cultivated by the civilizations of Sumer, Akkad, Egypt, and Babylon, which was then fused with the learned treasures of Greece? To dwell amidst the accumulated wisdom of Mesopotamia, a legacy spanning millennia, and to find in all of it nothing that transcends, nothing that hails from those blessed ages when man still breathed in the pure, uncorrupted truth—why, it would be easier to march through a dense forest carrying a five-ell-long beam without so much as grazing a tree!"

"Seven hundred thousand scrolls—the memory of mankind in that age!" Phineas intoned reverently. "Of course, I have read of it. But did not the Romans put Alexandria to the torch in 47 B.C., and did not the Muslims under 'Umar ibn al-Khattāb complete that ruin in 642 A.D.? It is said that for six months, Caliph Umar fed the fires of the city's bathhouses with those very books."

Lameth's nostrils flared, almost imperceptibly. "I can assure you, much of what has been written on this matter is pure invention. And you neglected to mention the part that Christian zealots played in that devastation. Seleucus spoke of twenty thousand, Manetho of thirty-six thousand five hundred and twenty-five Hermetic books that contained the entire philosophy of the Egyptians. A great portion of that knowledge was forever erased from the face of the earth. But not all. Some of what lay upon those dust-laden shelves was preserved and endured, carried forth through the toil of unnumbered scribes—through copies of copies, handed down across the centuries."

"To speak plainly, I had hoped you might enlighten me as to whether there exists any scholarly treatise upon such matters, which linger here, unremarked and wholly withdrawn from public scrutiny, upon the walls of this very establishment—yet now you name for me so renowned a subject! But what, pray, do these nebulous words signify? It seemed to me they were utterly devoid of meaning."

"Did not Pico della Mirandola describe it most aptly, when he observed that the Egyptians adorned all their temples with sculptures of the Sphinx, signifying that divine knowledge—if indeed entrusted to the written word at all—must be shrouded in veils of mystery and clothed in poetic obscurity? And did not Imhotep, whom the Greeks venerated as Asclepius, cite his teacher Thoth—who is none other than Hermes himself—saying that those who peruse his writings might find their expression simple and clear, when in truth they are riddled with mystery, their meaning concealed? That the very nature of the Egyptian mother tongue, the loftiness and power of its utterance, preserved within itself that which was conveyed, so that its truth was direct, precise, and bound to the reality it sought to express? And that, should the Greeks later render those words into their own tongue, they would become wholly unintelligible, distorted beyond recognition, for their manner of speech, with which they sought to translate, was naught but an empty, overblown, and feeble clamor?"

"As for the inscriptions upon the wooden panels, I should not neglect to mention that little of what you have here transcribed through the pressure of graphite has ever been revealed to the eyes of common men. It was mere fortune that the first passage you presented allowed me to find an immediate reference. But this page here..."—he indicated one of the rubbed impressions—"...this is a matter for which I must entreat you to exercise patience until such time as I am permitted to unveil its contents—far more wondrous in nature than you might conceive. You thirst, and I assure you, soon you shall drink from the very source of all knowledge. Moreover, have you not taken notice of how few guests are in residence here, despite the establishment's prime location and ample accommodations? To pass a night in these halls, and thereby catch even the faintest glimpse of those mysteries concealed within, one must first present a letter of recommendation of the highest order."

"Your porter alluded to as much," Phineas admitted, "but I could make little sense of his words."

Lameth reached once more into the stack of papers. "Let us examine the next page. The translation of this passage, too, I must withhold for the time being. This one, however, belongs to another section—this here, to be precise. Here we have something most intriguing: a depiction of Moses's initiation at the Pharaoh's court into the Egyptian sciences, which were conveyed through symbols. And here, upon this paper, an instruction on how one must proceed when facing the guardians of the seven palaces. In due time, I shall instruct you in these matters. This next rubbing is but a fragment—it appears to be a warning, yet the text is incomplete."

"I simply ran out of paper. I take it this so-called letter of recommendation came from you?"

"Yes, quite so, otherwise Obed would have seen to it that you were promptly cast back onto the streets. Though, in truth, his intervention is seldom required. There is a certain...

how shall I phrase it… an aura about this establishment. It takes souls of the most profound desperation to willingly cross its threshold."

"And what, pray, qualifies one to receive such a letter of recommendation?"

Lameth leaned back slightly, exhaling a slow stream of smoke, his gaze distant, contemplative. "You see, our number dwindles with each passing year…" He paused for a moment, as though weighing something in his mind. "And let us not forget the tribulations we suffered in this godforsaken country at the hands of the Revolution. Simjael, a most loyal companion and a highly esteemed member of our *secret and learned society*, found himself upon the scaffold during the days of the Terror—and this without having committed the slightest offense. Even my far-reaching influence was not enough to wrest him from the clutches of those roaring fanatics or the executioner's blade. Ah, give me the tranquil countryside of East Anglia, where aristocrats may still be bribed with ease."

"And?" Phineas could barely conceal his impatience and inwardly cursed the rhetorical pauses Lameth so deliberately employed.

"The criteria are manifold, and were I to enumerate them all here and now, I fear I would only weary you. From what I gather, you have already made the acquaintance of some of the other guests. Serpentarius informed me that he was most delighted to meet a true countryman here on the Continent. Baldassare, too, arrived yesterday at the same hour as yourself."

"Yes, we exchanged a few passing words," Phineas replied, resigning himself to the futility of pressing Lameth further on the matter. "How did you come by such a towering house-servant? A peculiar fellow, as it seems to me."

Lameth coughed and nearly choked on his cigar. "Obed?" he scoffed, derisively. "I fished him from a pond after his own mother had attempted to drown him. He owes me his life and is bound to my service. Moreover, he is astoundingly dim-witted, as you have no doubt observed by now. But he is strong as an ox, which rather exhausts the list of his talents." Phineas cast a pitying glance toward Obed, whose moonlike visage loomed behind the counter. The man met his gaze with an exaggerated grin, revealing darkened gums and exposed tooth-roots that sent an involuntary shudder through Phineas. "Come, let us sup. The cuisine here is exquisite," Lameth declared, still eying Obed with disdain. The servant lowered his gaze and turned away, not unlike a chastised hound.

Together, they descended to the spacious dining hall, situated several floors below the entrance hall and connected to it by a winding staircase. Above them loomed a ribbed vault of exposed stonework, upheld by massive columns and deep-set abutments hewn into the very rock. Were it not for the long rows of wooden tables and benches, Phineas might have mistaken the chamber for the lightless dungeon of a medieval fortress. This section of the building appeared markedly older than the levels above—one could discern as much from the varying degrees of decay in the masonry, as though each step downward carried them further through the centuries, tracing the ascent of this structure from the chthonic depths of some nameless and ancient cult to the light of the present day.

They seemed to be the only guests dining there, and indeed, throughout the course of the evening, not another soul joined them. A gaunt, hollow-cheeked attendant, flitting back and forth between a dimly visible kitchen area and the dining hall with the restless energy of a spider, bore forth a profusion of cold dishes. Yet Lameth seemed scarcely inclined to eat, offering only a few desultory remarks to Phineas. Once more, he was impenetrably reserved, withdrawn into the citadel of his own thoughts, and on this night, Phineas found himself entirely unable to extract any further knowledge from him.

CHAPTER V.
THE CITADEL OF KNOWLEDGE

Heartening news reached Chirion from the lips of a harried messenger, his garments drenched in sea spray, who hastened through the night toward the Citadel, breathless yet bearing glad tidings. The Black Door remained unscathed, and no soul had dared attempt to cross the forbidden threshold. Without delay, Chirion commanded the watch to be doubled and summoned additional forces to lend aid to the gatewardens, who, though steadfast, awaited the dawn with troubled hearts.

With the first light of morning, he convened the Inner Council—a gathering of a handful of venerable men and women, whose countenances bore the weight of the ages, their hair silvered by wisdom rather than time. They assembled in solemn procession around a great circular table in one of the upper chambers of the Citadel. At the entrance, flanking the high, twin-winged doors, the sentinels stood in rigid formation, clad in polished breastplates sculpted in the likeness of the human form. Their plumed silvered helms caught the morning's radiance, muskets with slender multi-barreled muzzles slung across their shoulders, their long trousers tucked neatly into high boots. With chins lifted in unwavering discipline and visages unmoved by aught save duty, they saluted each council member in turn. Beyond the lofty, arched windows, the serrated peaks of a titan-born mountain range unfurled into the mist-laden horizon. The sun, still low, spilled its blinding light over the heights, casting long, golden rays across the frost-kissed stone.

Not far from the table, upon a hastily prepared cot, lay a most curious sight—a mass of bandages wrapped around a figure of such considerable bulk that he seemed more a mummified ox than a man. Niahl had refused to heed the healers' orders and would not be dissuaded from attending the council. He was, indeed, in a wretched state, though his wounds had been tended by skilled hands, which he deemed sufficient cause to resume his duties. With every slight movement, dark stains bled through the linen wrappings, spreading in slow, ominous blooms. The council members exchanged glances, shaking their heads, yet none spoke against his folly, well aware of his legendary obstinacy.

A hush of reverence fell upon the chamber as Chirion entered, striding through the towering columns and past the solemn grandeur of the vaulted hall, making his way toward the silver-gleaming council table. His entrance was met with a ceremonial greeting, a rite bound in tradition. To each member he gave his formal reverence, then, casting aside all rigid protocols, embraced them with the warmth of deep-rooted kinship. At Niahl's bedside, he hesitated briefly, uncertain where to place his hand without causing further injury. Settling at last upon the man's thick, bull-like neck, he pressed his forehead against Niahl's own and whispered a string of sharp yet affectionate reprimands. The room resounded with the deep rumbling of Niahl's laughter as Chirion finally took his place among the gathered elders, setting his strong hands upon the massive wooden table—its surface inlaid with gleaming intarsia, depicting the sun, the twin moons, the wandering planets, and their celestial configurations, interwoven with glyphs of the lost tongue, a script pristine and unaltered since the dawn of all things.

"O you, most noble ones, the hour is dire!" Chirion declared, his voice steady yet heavy with burden. "We mourn the loss of twelve lives, and this sorrow lies heavily upon my soul. Yet graver still is the knowledge that, after so many years of peace, one has dared to commit such a sacrilegious crime upon this sacred mount—an act most heinous, whose perpetrator remains veiled in shadow. We must act with the utmost haste to unearth the culprits and reclaim that perilous artifact which, through means most sinister, has been stolen. It is not beyond reason to suspect that the murderer, or murderers, still dwell among us. No sign was found along the walls that might suggest a trespasser entered or departed unseen. Nor did the Black Door yield any trace of disturbance, no hint that one had sought to set foot upon that path which is, by sacred decree, forever forbidden."

"To slay an innocent maiden, then butcher every soul that stands in one's way like cattle to the slaughter … Whoever is capable of such an inhuman deed must suffer from a madness most wretched, a sickness of the mind beyond all reason," spoke one of the councilors, his voice weighted with emotion. His features, sculpted with such noble majesty, might well have led one to mistake him for the High Lord of the Sacred Mountain.

"I thank you for your words, O Cynfar, venerable son of the White City. And yet, it seems you do not fully grasp the gravity of this calamity. This assault was not the act of a deranged lunatic. The scroll has been taken from the crypt, and the fate of Vilarien—nay, perhaps of all who dwell within the far-reaching constellations—may one day be bound to it." As Chirion spoke, his hand traced a slow, deliberate arc over the delicate intarsia upon the polished wood of the council table, its gleaming symbols speaking in silent discourse.

"If none have entered the Temple Mount, nor fled unseen, then the object of which we speak in hushed secrecy must still remain among us. But in the Creator's name, who could seek to gain from it, without intent to traverse the forbidden passage? And who could possess knowledge of such matters, so closely guarded?" Cynfar's arms were bent, his hands outstretched in a gesture of invocation, emerging from the voluminous sleeves of his richly woven robes. His features, sculpted with an almost divine gravitas, commanded the silent assent of his listeners.

Then another spoke, one who stood a head taller than all others, his deep voice like the measured toll of a temple bell. "O Cynfar, and you, O noble Chirion, warden of the Storm-Clad Coast, your far-seeing eyes cannot have failed to discern this: the chronicles speak of a great number of survivors, all of them sworn vassals of the Tyrant, who neither fled through the Black Door nor perished by the sword. On that fateful day, when the mountain's very foundation trembled, only those bound closest to him made their escape. The rest were made to stand trial before a tribunal which—if the records are to be believed—judged with clemency and leniency, rejoicing in their victory rather than striking at the root of the evil, to sever it for all time."

"Meekness is nobler than victory upon the battlefield!" Chirion responded, invoking the wisdom of the sacred texts. "The judges had grown weary of death and destruction, O Myrgil, Most Exalted One, and the accused seemed more like the deluded—those bound by the iron will of that tyrant, following his every command in blind obedience—than men who acted out of their own malicious intent."

"They were all instruments of his power," Myrgil replied. "As the Chronicles recount, he favored certain of the old families, placed them in positions of great influence, and thus bound them to his yoke, ensuring their support. These, in turn, reaped the benefits of his rule, strengthening their own claims and expanding their reach. Others basked in his favor, enjoying privileges far beyond their former station—not for their own merit, but solely for their unwavering obedience, their cold-hearted willingness to carry out his every command, no matter how cruel, without question or pause. Some embraced his wickedness entirely, seeing in those dark times an opportunity to indulge their basest appetites unchecked. No doubt, many were merely followers—weak souls, devoid of conscience, who, whether driven by fear or bound by secret oaths, executed his every bidding.

However their roles may have differed, I have no doubt that some among them—those who feigned repentance to escape judgment—spent the rest of their lives spreading their ruinous teachings, ensuring that their corruption would endure to this day. From time immemorial, our kind has possessed too great a mildness of temper to answer such transgressions—even under inward protest—with the severity required, and thus to serve a just cause more truly than overflowing love and well-intentioned mildness have ever seemed able to do."

The tall figure let his gaze sweep over the assembly, seeking silent affirmation from each of those present.

"Myrgil speaks truly!" declared one of the venerable women, who until now had remained silent, following the discourse in solemn contemplation. Her voice was clear and melodious, like the mountain streams cascading from the Holy Mount into the lowlands below. Her back, despite the weight of age, remained upright with unyielding dignity, and her chin was lifted in quiet pride—neither haughty nor overbearing. Her thick white hair, coiled and bound with golden rings and ribbons, was wound like a serpent ascending to the heavens. "We have, in our folly, abandoned the very institutions that were meant to safeguard us amidst this fallen world, yielding them up in pursuit of a romanticized vision of peace. For too long, we have shut our eyes to what transpires beyond these high walls, so that we have lulled ourselves into the belief that we yet dwelt in a paradise. A most grievous illusion, as it now proves to be. But I, for one, have walked the lands beyond our sheltered domain, and I tell you this: the wicked seed, thought long eradicated after the Great War, has sprouted anew like weeds, taking root not only in the minds of common folk. It would have done us well—or rather, it would have served us well in times past—to cast our gaze beyond the narrow bounds of our governance, which deceived us into believing that, shielded from the outer world, all would continue to unfold in our favor. A perilous misconception indeed.

As I reported before this very council many years ago, there exists beyond our self-fashioned idyll a distorted view of the events that once plunged this world into ruin. A veiled and secretive cult, not unlike the one we once vanquished, has now grown bold enough to lay hands upon our most sacred stronghold—a place we, in our blindness, failed to defend. And does not history, in its cruel and unwavering wisdom, teach us that there are times when violence is the only means by which peace may be preserved? That to forsake it breeds only a feeble and cowering generation—like a beast declawed and toothless, forced to look on helplessly as its kin are slain in agony? Perhaps it is not peace-loving gentleness, but rather the unyielding enforcement of a firm and merciless law, that best secures the order we so cherish. And now, as it is beyond all doubt that we find ourselves in the very predicament I foresaw so many years ago, should not my counsel bear greater weight than it did in times past?

Let us, then, summon forth all our strength to reclaim what was lost through our own failure. Let us restore the ancient protocols that once made us formidable. Reinstate the tribunals and the full powers we, in our recklessness, so thoughtlessly curtailed. Let us call forth a levy of those of fighting age, increasing our standing forces to a number befitting our security. Let us revise the punishments for transgression to the severity of old, and take up once more the methods of inquiry that—against my most earnest counsel—we so foolishly outlawed. Excessive leniency is but weakness, and the yearning for an ideal world, mere folly. Are not suffering, death, and ruin the bitter harvest of such neglect?" The other members nodded in solemn accord, moved by the clarity and resonance of her words.

"Restore to me my old office, and I swear to you that the transgressors shall be seized in the shortest time, and that which was lost shall soon be returned to our custody!" declared Myrgil. "We are the direct descendants of the ancient families, those to whom the Creator granted long life and blessed above all others with access to the untainted wisdom of the ages. It is our solemn duty to take the necessary measures to avert harm and to prevent such trespasses in the future."

"You have spoken wisely," replied Chirion, "and yet I believe it would be premature to respond to an intrusion into our library with such a sweeping curtailment of rights—even if it was accompanied by heinous murders and the theft of so perilous an object. Would this not be precisely what the adherents of that tyrant would have wished for? What could be more ruinous than to witness the very power entrusted to us exceeding its rightful bounds, no longer heeding a higher order? A lawless autocracy—unshackled from its moral and legal restraints—would, in its excesses, pave the way for an unjust ruler's rise to tyranny far more readily than under our present system of governance, which remains carefully bridled by divine law and our own solemn self-restraint. Even in the darkest of days, we must not forget the blessings that a system founded upon the highest and most immutable principles of divine justice and eternal order bestows upon our land." Myrgil bowed reverently before Chirion, paying due respect to his words, though his expression remained grim and troubled. It seemed as though an inner struggle waged within him, one that visibly tore at his spirit.

"In essence, I share the views of Yaelyn and Myrgil," spoke Cynfar, his voice imbued with the same warmth and understanding that so often compelled those who heard it to nod in assent before they even realized it. "By no means, however, would I counsel rash action. As you may well recall, crimes have occurred before in Vilarien and in the lands beyond, though I must concede that here upon the Holy Mountain, we have been spared such disturbances and have pursued our labors undisturbed. If indeed there remain those who still pay homage to the Tyrant, then it would seem that at least one among them has lingered unseen within these walls for some time. In some manner, they have learned of that wondrous artifact and its resting place, and they have bided their time, waiting patiently until the moment arose to seize it. Their next move may well be to spirit it beyond the walls of the Watch or, perhaps, to take the Passage themselves—to deliver it into the hands of the Tyrant, or to that Unhallowed One ... provided, of course, that either of them yet lives."

"The days of suffering lie more than a thousand years behind us! No mortal is granted such a span of life—not even we bear within us the fullness of the gift once bestowed upon The Eldren," countered Myrgil. "But allow me to direct your gaze to a far more immediate truth. Save for ourselves, only Chirion's ward and an exceedingly small number of trusted brethren have ever been entrusted with knowledge of these hidden matters. Of these, none remain save that half-mummified fool lying over there and a feeble old man whose time has long since passed. We must not close our minds to what is most evident—however much our hearts may recoil from the thought, and however grievous the possibility may seem to us."

"What precisely do you mean by that?" Chirion asked sharply.

"I mean that we must also consider the possibility that Jahdis herself is in some way entangled in this affair, however absurd that thought may seem—and however well known it is that she is your foster daughter. After all, she was found upon the very threshold of that accursed vault, and is she not, by consequence, one born of the worlds beyond the forbidden Passage? Why would any leave such a child there unless for a purpose? And as for Niahl—he alone has emerged from this calamity alive, which compels us to ask whether his—admittedly grave—wounds were not inflicted as a veil to shroud some greater secret."

At this, Niahl erupted into a fit of indignant rage upon his cot, thrashing so violently that he nearly tumbled off entirely. None in the chamber could help but feel relieved that he remained so tightly bound in his wrappings that he was as helpless as an infant—though this did not prevent any from discreetly increasing their distance from him. Chirion met the piercing gaze of the towering figure with quiet, unwavering resolve. "Myrgil, I hold your wisdom in the highest esteem, and it is right to question that which may elude our well-meaning yet oft-clouded sight. But I shall place my hand into the fire for my librarian and my foster daughter alike, for I have tested the hearts of both and found them steadfast. And in this, too, is wisdom."

"I alone saw the attacker and lived to tell of it," Niahl croaked from his cot. "Does it not strike you as odd that, despite my present indisposition, I still drag myself to endure this tiresome council meeting? Had they simply hacked off a proper chunk of me, instead of merely carving these infernally painful gashes, I might at least fit into my breeches a little more comfortably in the morning." Chirion smirked, while the other council members exchanged glances of sheer disbelief. "For all your supposed wisdom, you are dreadfully slow-witted—and might I add, entirely humorless!" Niahl observed dryly. His bald head flushed a deep crimson, as though scorched by the sun. "The attacker was no ordinary man, and most certainly no woman. And unless any of you can explain how I might wield a knife in such a manner as to stab myself squarely in the back—when I can scarce manage to scratch myself there as it is—then I suggest you abandon such asinine notions altogether."

"Speak!" Myrgil commanded, his voice sharp with suspicion. He, for his part, was not so easily convinced, and several others in the assembly murmured their assent, aligning themselves with his stance. Stepping forward, he loomed over Niahl like a prosecutor before the accused, while much of the gathering drew in behind him, forming a silent wall of judgment.

"I was sitting in the crypt, sorting through some of the old manuscripts—and, as usual, doing a bit of reading on the side, because when you've got such a fascinating thing in your hands, it's damn hard to just set it aside—when all of a sudden, hell breaks loose upstairs, and the blasted door explodes off its hinges with a deafening crash. Then in storms some hooded bastard, waving a blackened dagger in my face like he's done nothing else in his life, stabbing away like a maddened hornet from all sides, and looking downright puzzled when I don't just keel over dead—on account of the fact that his cursed blade can't quite reach my life-sustaining organs. Now, the reasons for that should be obvious, and I'm sure you lot can figure it out. But he just doesn't let up—keeps at it like a man possessed—until I bring a book down on his skull, which, strangely enough, seems to have no effect on him whatsoever. Which is odd, when you think about it, because that book was damn heavy. I could've felled an ox with it, but no—he hardly even flinched! So there I am, bashing him with the book, keeping him at arm's length, and he lunges at me again—only this time, his bloody dagger gets stuck right in the binding, skewering the first chapter clean through. And let me tell you, that's a real tragedy, because it was a rare book—no, scratch that, a unique book—and in excellent condition... well, up until now, anyway. And the best part? It was a copy of 'Trismalion's Herbarium', and the first chapter was all about the healing properties of scorch-thorn henbane. You ever cut yourself on the leaves of scorch-thorn henbane? Stings like hell, I tell you! Anyway, next thing I know, I get something cracked over my skull, and when I come to, I see the iron door to the Adyton has been torn clean off its hinges, the chamber beyond is empty, and I think to myself—well, that'll shut Chirion up for once. And sure enough, the next thing I know, he's standing over me, looking at me like he's seen a ghost."

As Niahl's rambling account unfolded, Myrgil's expression darkened perceptibly. "Worthy Niahl, we thank you for your most detailed account of what transpired in the crypt, but—"

"I reckon there were at least two attackers, perhaps more," Niahl interrupted with a degree of impertinence, "for while I held one at bay, another struck me down from behind. Has the dagger been examined yet? It might yield some useful insights into exactly who we're dealing with."

"The crypt has been sealed. We shall tend to it in due course," Chirion replied with quiet authority. "For now, let us seek out Misraihl. That seems to me the most pressing matter at hand. I wonder if his faded eyes will still recognize me."

"You will count yourself fortunate if any of his dwindling senses still take heed of you," Niahl remarked dryly, his gaze still locked in a narrow-eyed stare upon Myrgil, whose face had taken on a distinct shade of red. "He is nearly as old as your kind—and that without the gift of long years. What do you hope to gain from visiting my master? He has not set foot in the crypt in over fifty years, not since I took up his charge."

"It is self-evident," Myrgil admonished him, "that if Jahdis and yourself, as you so adamantly proclaim, are untainted by these events, then only one other remains in question—unless, of course, a member of this esteemed council saw fit to betray the whereabouts of the scroll." The gathered councilors stared at him in open shock, as though he had uttered blasphemy of the highest order, as though the mere suggestion that one among them could be capable of such a sacrilege was itself an unpardonable affront.

"I believe we have spoken enough!" Chirion declared, drawing the assembly to a close. "Honored Myrgil, would you see to it that the dagger in the crypt is secured? Moreover, I wish to know how the guards were so effortlessly subdued, and how, in but a few fleeting moments, those gates—of which I was assured nothing in all creation could breach—were forced open. And you, gracious Yaelyn, might I impose upon you and a select few among us to restore order within these halls? Honor the fallen, and see to their preparation for the passage beyond. Tend to the bereaved. I require an exact accounting of all we have lost—be it in names of the dead, or in the mere wreckage of what once stood. Above all, ensure that nothing else of worth has been stolen, particularly from within the crypt. And as for you, Niahl—get yourself to bed at once. I do not wish to lay eyes upon you again until your ruddy flesh is kept in place without the aid of those bandages!"

Once each had departed to attend to their appointed tasks, Chirion climbed into a carriage accompanied by two attendants, and they set forth through a labyrinth of narrow alleys that wound their way out of the city. They traveled along a heavily fortified road that skirted the edge of a wooded precipice, then crossed a covered, many-arched bridge spanning a dark and forbidding gorge, before the path resumed its course on the other side, mirroring the first. In time, even this road came to an end. On a vast, leveled plateau, a throng of single- and multi-horse carts, carriages, wagons, and handcarts mingled with their owners and passengers. Artisans and merchants busied themselves amidst the ceaseless industry of their respective trades. Their driver reined in the horses, and after instructing him to remain until their return, Chirion and his two companions continued the rest of the way on foot.

They descended steeply hewn steps and followed a narrow, nearly level path until they came to a halt before a sheer, looming cliff face. Here, at the base of this towering escarpment, lay Misraihl's dwelling. A rectangular structure, crowned by a monolithic architrave, framed the entrance to his abode. An innumerable host of similar dwellings, their inner chambers hewn backward into the raw stone of the cliffside, sheltered by façades of massive quarried blocks, ascended the escarpment in irregular succession, linked by staircases that led ever higher. From this vantage, one might believe the sheer rock face—its perspective narrowing as it soared ever upward, piercing the clouds at vertiginous heights—would extend into infinity, as though one need only follow the narrow steps carved into the jagged stone long enough to ascend into that otherworldly realm, which, enthroned beyond mortal sight, reigned in ineffable spheres above.

A heavy sense of foreboding crept over Chirion as they approached the door, which stood ajar, swaying on its hinges with the wind—knocking against the stone frame in rhythmic intervals, only to swing back again without ever closing. His knees trembled as he stepped across the threshold into the forehall, where shards of broken pottery, scattered garments, and other belongings lay half-buried beneath overturned furniture, already proclaiming the atrocity that had transpired. He entered a chamber, its rough-hewn stone walls punctuated by long, narrow windows that resembled arrow slits, and there he beheld Misraihl's lifeless form—bound against a cabinet as though affixed to a torture stake. His mouth, forced open in an eternal grimace, was stuffed with a crude gag. Dark blood had pooled beneath him, spreading in thin rivulets through the seams of the stone floor. Sinister, crimson stains—twisting trails of droplets and long streaks, as if clawed by desperate fingers—marred the ground and continued in grotesque patterns upon the walls and ceiling, leaving behind the faintest, fragmented impression of the torment that had taken place, though the full, unspeakable horror of it remained mercifully veiled from those who beheld the aftermath.

"Misraihl, old friend... death has eluded you for so long, only to claim you at last with a cruelty unmatched by anything this fallen world could devise," Chirion whispered, his face ashen. With careful hands, he removed the vile rag from the dead man's mouth, gently closed his clouded eyes, and then bid his attendants help him free the body from its bindings—a task that took several strained attempts. Once Misraihl had been laid upon the ground, Chirion dismissed them with an imperious tone, sending them to fetch the undertaker—his true motive being that he could no longer endure the shame of hiding his tears. Alone at last, he sank to his knees beside the lifeless form, clutching the cold, bloodied hand between his own as though he could still offer comfort, even in death. And there he wept. When at last his tears subsided, grief gave way to anger, and the words of Yaelyn and Myrgil—so readily dismissed only hours before—now rang with a wisdom he could no longer deny. Rising, he nearly lost his footing in the slick pool of blood, catching himself against the cabinet to steady his stance. Just then, an unexpected shaft of light pierced through one of the narrow windows, casting an ethereal glow upon the site of Misraihl's martyrdom. For a fleeting moment, Chirion thought he glimpsed the old man's soul ascending, carried upon the countless dust motes that danced in the golden beam.

Something on the floor struck him as peculiar, as though the slanting light had revealed a subtle, calculated uniformity amidst the dried bloodstains—the final traces of suffering, exacted from a ravaged body in fatal measure. He stepped closer, scrutinizing the patterns with a wary gaze, until—when once again the sun's rays pierced through a gap in the clouds—the dim glow cast upon the ground unveiled a familiar arrangement. What at first seemed the chaotic smears of a dying struggle took on a discernible order; upon closer inspection, they resolved into written symbols, scrawled in the victim's own blood before he had yielded his life upon that wretched, repurposed wooden cabinet. At first, the grotesque shapes seemed devoid of meaning, a frantic distortion of script in the throes of agony—until Chirion discerned the language. It was the tongue of the Arrivals from beyond the Black Door, known to the sages alone, a language long dead and forsaken in Vilarien. "In secret toil they who have sworn the unholy oath," he deciphered, recognizing the passage from the Nemiáhian Chronicles. Beneath it, crudely yet unmistakably rendered, was the outline of a sigil—hastily drawn, yet strikingly evocative of one of the noble emblems of old.

Like an ancient pictograph daubed in ochre upon the walls of a primordial cave, the stylized image of a clawed, rearing wolf emerged from the cold stone slabs—a symbol none other than Myrgil's ancestral crest. For long moments, Chirion regarded the message in silence. Then, with the sleeve of his robe, he wiped it away into oblivion, obscuring its traces from prying eyes. Yet he locked the knowledge within his heart and resolved to await the unfolding of events.

CHAPTER VI.
LINGUA ADAMICA

In the days that followed, Phineas found himself meeting more and more frequently with Monsieur Lameth, whose demeanor, for reasons wholly indiscernible, grew increasingly restless with each passing hour. It was as though some unseen force urged him to hasten Phineas's progress, to press him forward with relentless fervor, compelling him to immerse himself ever deeper in the labyrinthine mysteries of those ancient tomes he so ceaselessly procured. The books he provided, once merely esoteric, now burgeoned in complexity, their contents at once more cryptic and impenetrable, their language an archaic echo from the vaults of forgotten time. Before long, entire crates of volumes were brought forth, crowding the walls and furniture with long, unbroken rows of venerable books, their leather-bound spines embossed with titles in faded gold, their bindings thick and rounded, their covers adorned with intricate brass clasps or curious, arcane fastenings. Within their yellowed and foxed pages, penned in the painstaking hand of long-dead scribes, lay the accumulated wisdom of the ages—texts inscribed in Greek and Latin, Hebrew and Arabic, Coptic and Syriac, alongside those in the newer tongues of German, French,

Italian, Spanish, and English, all of which seemed to harbor within them the guarded knowledge of centuries, as though they alone might hold the lost secrets of mankind.

Yet though Lameth proved an instructor of unparalleled depth—one who not only broadened Phineas's linguistic prowess, but who could, with uncanny vividness, conjure before his mind's eye the very epochs that had given birth to these languages, as though he himself had stood among the towering ziggurats of Sumer when the first empires rose from the cradle of the world, or had beheld with his own eyes the barbarian hordes setting forth to conquer the lands of Europe—Phineas nonetheless struggled with the peculiar idiosyncrasies of those ancient scripts, their letters more like whispered incantations than mere marks upon parchment. Seeing his pupil's frustration, Lameth, whenever possible, procured translations to ease his burden. Once, Phineas held in his hands a book whose title page bore, beneath the name of the work and that of its author, a most curious inscription—one that named Lameth himself as its translator. The crisp scent of fresh ink, the sharp tang of paper and binding glue betrayed its recent birth, and Phineas, struck by the thought, could not help but wonder if Lameth had, in the long and sleepless hours of the night, labored at great cost—both in time and gold—to bring forth this volume for his eyes alone.

The greater portion of these tomes contained texts of the most singular nature, revealing their arcane knowledge only in veiled allusions and cryptic parables. Phineas wrestled with descriptions of the transcendent, of the soul's journey through celestial realms and divine palaces, of secret passwords and sigils, of the soul's ascent and the ecstatic hymns that accompanied the vision of God's majesty upon His throne.

He read of shadowed legends and forgotten cults, of esoteric rites and enigmatic incantations, prayers, and invocations. Some passages struck him as oddly familiar, as though he were perusing the primordial text of an Old Testament scripture or one of those apocryphal writings that bore the cadence and spirit of ancient days. He marveled at how Lameth had come into possession of such rare and precious manuscripts.

"They are not, in truth, of any singular worth—mere degenerate abridgments of a greater wisdom—but they shall aid you in fixing your mind upon the object of our inquiry," Lameth demurred when Phineas, with some trepidation, inquired whether he had harbored no misgivings about transporting such venerable volumes across the Channel. Then, quite suddenly, something transpired—some occurrence, subtle yet unmistakable, that weighed heavily upon Lameth's mind. From that moment forth, he pursued their studies with uncharacteristic urgency, as though pressed by an unseen hand, driven by a matter of utmost import. Whatever this concern may have been, it was a thing of profound significance to him, a quest upon which he had expended the waning years of his existence. Yet, for all Phineas's persistence, he could extract no further particulars from him, no matter how often he pressed the matter.

The following day, he was once again required to relocate to another chamber—just as before, and, once more, without any plausible explanation. Obed, who seemed visibly crestfallen, handed him the new key with a litany of apologies, mumbling something about unforeseen circumstances, that the master had so decreed, and that the new accommodations were, moreover, far more agreeable. He then personally escorted Phineas up the stairs to his new quarters. It appeared to be among the highest rooms in the establishment, for the staircase terminated abruptly at its threshold. Yet, beyond, a narrow corridor extended into darkness, its course flanked by a series of small, arched stone doorways, leading, he presumed, to the attic or some other unseen recess of the building.

The gentle glow of the wall sconces skimmed across the polished surface of the doorplate, glancing off the sharp edges of its diagonals, crossbars, and serifs, revealing a delicately wrought inscription—once again, following the same obscure system of designation as before. The number "72" emerged from the interplay of light and shadow, its etched grooves standing in stark contrast against the gleaming ridges. He had half a mind to question Obed about this absurd, ceaseless shifting of his quarters, but the man bore such an expression of melancholy, his head bowed in silent dejection, that Phineas, well aware of his dull-witted nature, deemed it futile to inquire further. The likelihood of extracting anything useful from him seemed altogether remote.

The chamber into which he was now quartered was of extraordinary spaciousness, and a tall, mullioned window—so high that no neighboring house could possibly afford a glimpse within—offered a view stretching far beyond the *Mur des Fermiers généraux*, across a labyrinth of crooked rooftops, their ridges smothered in lichen and moss, all the way to that wild, forsaken strip of ramshackle settlements, which sprawled at the city's edge like a festering blight upon its borders. The furnishings, in essence, were much the same as those of the rooms he had previously occupied, yet in this instance, every detail was wrought with a finer, more opulent hand. Once again, the wooden paneling bore a sequence of figurative images, a pictorial cycle whose arcane significance eluded him.

Lameth had, over the past days, endeavored to instruct him in the reading of hieroglyphs and their hieratic counterparts—an enterprise that, owing to the sheer abundance of signs, the absence of vowels and punctuation, and the complexity of the grammar, was all but doomed to failure. Phineas had therefore resorted to intuition, attempting, however precariously, to unravel some fragmentary meaning from these esoteric tableaux. The sequence of images depicted a colossal step-temple, its vast structure occupying the entire span of the composition, as well as a labyrinthine network of chambers and corridors, their convoluted windings resembling not so much a perspective illusion as a deliberate assault upon the very notion of spatial logic. These passages meandered through planetary alignments and open gates, yet all converged upon a final barrier—rendered in the manner of the temple veil before the Sanctum Sanctorum of Herod's Temple—stirring within him a recollection of an illustration from 'Hortus Deliciarum', that exquisite medieval compendium, which, in his own time, lay housed in the district library of Strasbourg.

This dividing curtain, adorned with striking symbols and suspended from richly ornamented pillars, had been composed in such a manner that it concealed, in part, a veiled world beyond—a realm suffused with radiant beams of light, which converged upon a solitary, exalted throne. The few textual fragments he had managed, however tenuously, to correlate with the accompanying imagery seemed to speak of an ascent into a celestial sanctuary. Yet he was unable to discern who it was that undertook such a journey, nor to whom the throne, bathed in its luminous effulgence, was rightfully owed. Unlike his previous quarters, no mural adorned the whitewashed walls, though in places the crumbling plaster had begun to yield to the slow erosion of time. It seemed, however, that one section had been recently restored, for several bands of wallpaper—its delicate floral motifs and light, playful *rocaille embellishments* strikingly at odds with the room's otherwise somber, religiously charged decor—stood out, not least for their unblemished state, against the surrounding surfaces.

Someone had transferred his luggage and the many books to the new room, arranging everything with meticulous care. Upon the writing desk lay a parcel, wrapped with utmost precision and adorned with a small card, once more bearing Lameth's name as the sender. Within, Phineas found a heavy tome, bound in tooled leather, its surface worn and cracked from extensive handling. Accompanying it was a letter in which Lameth urged him to set aside his other studies for the time being and instead devote himself entirely to this new volume. The dark brown leather, richly craquelured and embossed with intricate, ornamental designs, bore the unmistakable signs of great age. Several missing portions had—presumably in the course of a later restoration—been reinforced with patches of fresh leather, and the spine itself appeared to have been entirely rebound in more recent years. Across the title label, in gold-stamped Antiqua lettering, ran the words 'lingua adamica', and Phineas found himself wondering whether he was once again holding one of Lameth's pseudepigraphic books of magic, to which the man seemed so inordinately devoted.

He lifted the heavy, well-thumbed cover and, flipping rapidly through entire chapters with his left hand, bent the book forward toward the light, examining it at an oblique angle. With the tips of his fingers, he traced the faint, uniform indentations upon the surface of the parchment—

guidelines scored by the scribe's sharp stylus before the text had been meticulously inscribed in two parallel columns. Occasional blank pages and half-heartedly executed illustrations, interruptions in the text, and passages compressed onto the narrowest of spaces all suggested that the work was a manuscript copy of an original scroll, transcribed into *folio* form. The characters of the first column bore a distant resemblance to Hieratic—at least insofar as Lameth had taught him—or to some other cursive variation of the hieroglyphic script. The second column, composed in Latin and evidently a translation of the adjacent text, varied significantly in length, carrying annotations, strikethroughs, and handwritten additions. A third layer had been introduced—a flowing, handwritten French commentary, expanding upon the Latin text in the generous outer margins. This latter addition, given its distinct hand, seemed likely to have been penned by Lameth himself.

He pored over the Latin text for the entirety of the afternoon, striving to grasp some intuitive sense of what he assumed—lacking any explanatory literature—must be an early form of Egyptian. He studied Lameth's handwritten annotations, yet the peculiar nature of the content remained utterly impenetrable. Now and then, his gaze drifted from the page, and he leaned back against his chair, pressing a hand against the ache in his neck. Eventually, exhaustion dulled his concentration, and he found himself idly leafing through the worn pages, his mind adrift. Beyond the cryptic urtext and its Latin translation—whose abstruse and, at times, entirely unfathomable commentaries attempted to outline the principles of a universal grammar—the book contained a wealth of illustrations sprawling across multiple folios: alien diagrams and geometric sigils encircled by strange, indecipherable inscriptions; an intricate, near-maddening heptagram set within concentric wheels brimming with enigmatic letters; portentous ideograms; page upon page of tables and formulas; extensive lists of a mysterious alphabet, expressed symbolically through numbers and glyphs; charts of encoded numerals and mystical ciphers; planetary characters and alchemical emblems; and, again and again, exemplary passages inscribed in the sacred script of hieroglyphs, accompanied by their sprawling, unsettling correspondences. The sequence of bewildering symbols unfolded before him in a dizzying cascade of wonder and incomprehension.

By late afternoon, he met once more with Monsieur Lameth in the hôtel's antechamber, where the latter—lounging in one of the high-backed chairs, a cigar smouldering between his fingers—had evidently been awaiting him with impatience. As soon as Phineas arrived, Lameth inquired, with formal politeness, after his well-being, though he did not afford him the time to furnish a thorough response. His true concern, it seemed, was the progress Phineas had made with his new studies.

"Pray, enlighten me regarding that which we now discuss," Phineas entreated, shifting his weight forward in his seat and resting his chin upon his bent arm. "Never before have I encountered the notion that there exists some primeval tongue—some linguistic urtext from which all other systems of speech are derived—and yet this *lingua adamica* appears to be precisely that. Has such a language ever been discovered, let alone deciphered? Is it merely another of those constructed languages that rest upon the scaffolding of our known tongues? Or does it resemble the universal language of a Leibniz, the divine speech of a Böhme or Van Helmont, or the pasigraphy of a Maimieux?"

"And God taught Adam to speak according to His manner; and He formed from the dust of the earth all the fishes of the sea, the beasts of the land, and every winged creature under heaven, and He bade them come before Adam, that He might behold how he would name each living thing. And whatsoever name Adam bestowed upon each living creature, so was it called. And Adam gave a name to all the fishes of the sea, to every beast upon the land, and to the birds beneath the heavens, and he made them subject unto him. And in like manner, he gave name also to all other things that surrounded him within the Garden of Eden," Lameth recited solemnly from the First Book of Moses.

Phineas stared at him in open bewilderment. "I must confess, I do not quite grasp what you are attempting to convey."

"Nominatio rerum," Lameth intoned with quiet gravity. "The Adamic tongue, the primeval speech Adam learned within the Garden of Eden—the very language with which he named all things—bore within it an ineffable power, for it alone could express, with unerring immediacy, the true nature of all creation. The perfect knowledge of all things was inherent in its utterance. And by the mere sound of his voice, Adam wielded dominion over all existence, bending the living world to his will. By the aid of the book you now possess, and through certain fortuitous alignments, it has been granted me to recover fragments of this lost tongue, to preserve them unto this very age."

Phineas looked visibly perplexed. "I am not unfamiliar with such linguistic and philosophical speculations, and I have already mentioned Böhme's 'Aurora, oder Morgenröthe im Aufgang'. And if you have indeed accomplished the master-stroke of reconstructing this so-called *lingua adamica*, then you are surely a scholar of unparalleled renown—worthy of being counted among the likes of John Dee. But what I still fail to grasp is why a language, no matter how extraordinary, should possess the power to grant an individual dominion over all things. For your own words suggest that you are not merely speaking of the power of rhetoric, nor of persuasion—the subtle manipulations by which an astute mind may, through carefully chosen and deliberate words, bring another to his cause. Nor, I presume, do you refer to the kind of grandiloquent oratory that can stir the passions of the masses with invocations of fatherland and victory. And certainly not to that gentle, lulling murmur by which one might soothe an agitated beast. Am I mistaken in this assumption?"

"Not in the slightest," Lameth replied, his voice touched with an almost imperceptible amusement. "Nothing could be further from my purpose than to weary you with such mundane trifles. Did not Philo of Alexandria, in 'De Opificio Mundi', write that God led all the creatures before Adam, whose privilege—by virtue of his wisdom and kingly dignity—it was to name them? And that, with an intellect unclouded by frailty, affliction, or passion, his soul beheld the purest essence of all things and assigned to each its fitting name? That in the naming of a thing, its very nature could be discerned? Adam was wise, not by the instruction of men, but by the very hand of his Maker. And he was also a king, for God had appointed him as regent and sovereign over all living things, and it fell to him to bestow names upon each of his subjects."

"As fantastic as that may sound, let us suppose, for argument's sake, that you are correct," Phineas answered cautiously.

"This peculiar lexicon you have given me contains an odd grammar, one that utterly eludes my comprehension. Nor does it seem to contain any sort of glossary, at least not in the Latin translation of whatever Urtext this is—if indeed these endless expositions are translations at all. And I cannot, for the life of me, discern the purpose of the illustrations, whose figures resemble necromantic diagrams from some *grimoire* of ill repute."

Lameth smiled with understanding. "*Lingua adamica* cannot be recorded in an ordinary lexicon, as you would conceive it, nor do the divine names with which Adam named all beings resemble the names that fallen man has assigned to things in his feeble tongue. And even if one were to entertain such a foolish endeavor, it could only be through the figurative language of poetry—an attempt, however inadequate, to approach the perfection of the first tongue, to grasp the ineffable with frail words and the meager instruments of our known speech. But Adam beheld all things in their absolute and most veritable essence. The language of Paradise is the language of pure knowledge, the vessel of the hidden, primordial divine idea—the archetypal forms of all things, which, in the ur-original sphere of unshaped conceptions, were brought into being and are ever in the process of becoming."

Phineas looked at him, perplexed, struggling to grasp this strange and profoundly bewildering notion. "I do not even remotely understand what you are trying to tell me," he admitted at last, defeated after several attempts to make sense of it.

"You are not listening!" Lameth rebuked him impatiently, as though explaining the most elementary principles of the natural sciences to an obstinate and ignorant pupil. "Do you not see? To every existent, sensibly perceptible being, there must correspond a divine name. In his glorious, paradisiacal state, subject neither to illness, suffering, nor death, Adam completed creation by calling forth the spiritual archetypes of all earthly things from the sphere of unshaped ideas. He then perceived, in perfect clarity, the true nature of all things—their essence, their inner meaning, which points back to the archetypes, to the primordial seeds of creation—and he translated the nameless into name. Thus, he bestowed upon each thing not merely an appellation, but its spiritual identity, its hidden, intrinsic mystery—the creative word of the original divine act of making, which slumbers within all things. There is, therefore, a mirroring between language, thought, and the fundamental nature of all existence."

"If this were true: does not the Bible teach us that this first of all languages was confused at the moment when men sought to build a tower to reach the heavens?" Phineas spoke more to himself than to Lameth, not looking up as he did so. "By that reasoning, we must assume that even the wicked peoples who lived before the Flood, and Cain, the brother-slayer himself, would have been fluent in this divine tongue—if, indeed, it ever existed. To be quite frank, that strikes me as highly improbable." By the time he reached the end of his sentence, his voice had grown firmer, as though the act of speaking had, in turn, convinced him of his own argument.

"The tongue that I once spoke has long since vanished from the earth, even before the peoples of Nimrod set forth upon their impossible task," Lameth replied.

"Did you just quote Dante?"

"Indeed, I did. And rightly so. Mankind already spoke many tongues when the biblical tale of the Tower took place.

Read the Scriptures more carefully! Noah's sons dispersed across the face of the earth, and each bore his own language."

"Then when was the *lingua adamica* withdrawn from the world? And what, then, are we to make of the biblical account of the Tower? For without the one tongue that all men shared, what sense remains in Babel's confusion? And without that—well, it seems there was no tower at all, whose pinnacle was meant to reach the heavens, by which those thus confounded sought to make themselves a name."

Lameth leaned forward, and the oil lamp's flickering glow cast wavering shadows across his features, as though he had spoken to Phineas from the embers of some primordial past. "I cannot but observe," he began, "that the biblical account tells only half the truth, as you, perhaps, have already suspected. Allow me, then, to answer the latter part of your question first. Nimrod—if I recall correctly—was a name I had already mentioned to you once before. He was the first man after the Flood upon whom the mantle of kingship was bestowed. He founded a mighty dominion and ruled the land between the Euphrates and Tigris. The beginnings of his kingdom were the cities of Babel, Erech, Akkad, and Calneh, in the land then called Shinar. From there, he set forth to subdue the city of Asshur and expand his dominion, building the cities of Nineveh, Rehoboth-Ir, Calah, and Resen.

His capital, Babylon, lay upon the banks of the Euphrates, encircled by mighty, towering ramparts, crowned with battlements, pierced with arrow slits, and guarded by a hundred gates of copper, their colossal bars wrought from iron. Nimrod was formidable in stature, a leader to whom his subjects looked up with awe. He instructed his people in the means by which they might liberate themselves from the dominion of heaven, casting off the naive traditions of their forefathers and the futile hope of some distant salvation—a hope that, as he claimed, merely servėd to abase them in the dust and shackle them in submission. Instead, he revealed to them the path by which, through the sheer force of their will, they might seize control of their own destiny and turn away from the rule of a paternalistic god.

Thus did Nimrod—just as Flavius Josephus most accurately recounted in 'Antiquitates Judaicae'—undertake the construction of a tower, one so lofty that, should God once again trouble the earth with a deluge, its waters would not overcome it, thereby exacting vengeance for the destruction of his forebears. And the people, persuaded by his words, followed him eagerly, for they deemed it cowardice to continue their obedience to God. Yet by no means was Nimrod's tower intended to reach heaven by mere physical height. Such a notion is, with all due respect, a wholly misguided interpretation of the matter and an astonishingly naïve reading of the account. The truth, however, is that Nimrod—the very one whom Epiphanius Scholasticus, among others, named as the inventor of magic and astrology—sought to behold the God of Abraham and thereby unseal one of the gateways between worlds, a passage by which he might ascend into heaven—that is, the realm beyond. And therein lies the key to the name Babylon, which in Akkadian means *Gate of the Gods*. For, as its very etymology attests, Nimrod sought not merely dominion over men but to raise himself to the stature of the divine. And in Babylon, within his own domain, he and his diviners and sorcerers discovered one of those sacred junctions where heaven, earth, and the underworld converge, where the veil between realms grows thin, and passage between them might be made possible."

"You mean a passage such as the one described in 'Amduat'?"

"Ah, so you have read my translation of the 'Book of the Hidden Chamber'?" Lameth's lips curled into a smile, sharp and unsettling. "Ha! Those fools, wrapped in pitch and linen, thinking their tombs might conceal what the gods had long since abandoned to oblivion!" He gave Phineas a nod that sent a shiver down his spine before continuing, his expression now solemn. "Nimrod was a man bold enough to seize his fate and demand what he desired, through a ritual both secret and arcane, a knowledge unearthed from the ruins of the ancient sanctuaries—ruins that had withstood even the fury of the Deluge. And so, to return to the first part of your inquiry. As I have already explained, the *lingua adamica* had long vanished from the face of the earth by the time Ham's descendants undertook the building of their infamous tower. Yet, though it was taken from the world with the Fall, a remnant of its primordial divinity lingered in the tongues that followed—fragments of power, scattered and imperfect, concealed within the sacred letters, those vestiges of sorcery, unfathomable words of enchantment from the unfathomable presence of the original Names, veiled beneath the weight of alien meanings.

And just as the Creator destroyed the fallen peoples in the waters of the Flood, and thereafter decreed in his immutable will that he would never again scourge the earth with water, so too did he remove from the world those words of power—the last remnants of the primeval tongue, whose pictorial words, by the force of a natural and immediate relationship with the world, had been transmuted through graphic alchemy into those hidden sigils, enduring beyond the reach of time. Thus did he thwart Nimrod, preventing him from uttering the words and crossing the threshold. How ingenious!" Lameth added with a scornful chuckle. "For indeed, had the purpose been merely to halt the hands of laborers, who toiled by the thousands beneath the scorching sun to complete the edifice, then God need not have confounded their speech—for beneath the lash of their taskmasters, they would have labored still, whether they understood their commands or not." Lameth paused, his lips curling into a grim smile, as though savoring some long-buried memory. " *'Why was their language confounded?'* it is written in the book of 'Zohar', *'Because they all spoke in the Holy Tongue, which granted them a power beyond their station. And in this manner, they were able to call upon a force greater than themselves to aid them in their construction. Therefore, their language was confounded, lest their will might prevail through the sacred tongue.'*

It is the same principle, even though its original meaning has been lost over the centuries, as I have already explained. But, deprived of those words of power, Nimrod could no longer accomplish what he had originally intended—to pass through the *Gate of God* himself and partake of the fruit of the *Tree of Life*. For Nimrod sought to overcome death without offering the sacrifice that a life of submission would have required. Nor had he any desire to linger for centuries in the dark prisons of damnation, only to be subjected thereafter to a stern and merciless judgment."

Phineas stared in disbelief as images of an unthinkable antiquity passed before his mind's eye. Lameth had recounted the tale with such conviction that Phineas could not help but wonder whether, deep down, he harbored some secret admiration for that despotic ruler of old—if, indeed, he sympathized with his rebellion against God and even found within it an understanding that did not seem, in the least, to contradict his own faith. Phineas had always held to the simple notion that the world was best divided into atheists and believers—the latter free to practice their faith as they saw fit, much as the medieval mind had found no contradiction between New Testament charity and the tribunals of the Inquisition. Yet, here was something entirely different: an unshakable belief in the divine, coupled with defiance and enmity toward it. It struck him as a second Fall, as though one could possess an absolute certainty of God's presence and yet strive against Him. He hesitated to voice this thought aloud, fearing he might offend Lameth.

"That was a most excellent tale," Phineas conceded at last. "And thanks to your vivid narration, I found myself transported to the Mesopotamia of the earliest kingdoms. And yet, I must admit—though the purpose of this Babylonian portal, or the mysterious truth veiled within this allegory, remains wholly beyond my grasp—that the idea of a language imbued with such formidable power is a most exalted thought. To decipher it would indeed be a pursuit worthy of your noble endeavors. But suppose, for a moment, that everything you have said is true—what, then, would one do with such knowledge?"

Lameth smiled, and the rings on his fingers glimmered treacherously in the light of the oil lamps. "Consider this," he intoned. "If man were to master this pure, primordial tongue—the language of creation itself—by which Adam not only named all things, but by which God Himself formed the primal elements and commanded them into being, then man would attain dominion not only over nature, but over the vast infinity of the universe itself. Yea, he would make himself equal to God. Thus, the knowledge of the *lingua adamica* grants the true seeker access to divinity, to the realms of glory and their manifold wonders, in accordance with the station once held by man in paradise."

"Did you not say earlier," Phineas interjected, his voice tinged with uncertainty, "that you had already managed to reconstruct parts of this language with the aid of this book? Then how can I be of any use to you? And surely, you must recall what a fruitless struggle I have had with this peculiar text. I do not wish to disappoint you—not after all you have done for me—but I fear I cannot be of any assistance in this matter."

Lameth regarded him with a gentle gaze, free of resentment, then gestured with his chin for him to hand over the book, which Phineas had set aside upon a small round table. Taking it into his lap—for the tome was large and weighty—he turned to a particular page, then opened it fully and began explaining sections of its enigmatic contents, as though he had not heard a single word of Phineas's protestations. It seemed—as if for reasons of pedagogy—that he had selected a few of the more comprehensible figures, and he proceeded to discuss with him several pages of the book's intricate diagrams, filled with wondrous hieroglyphs, whose mastery, he claimed, had cost him an eternity in human reckoning. And strangely, as Phineas listened, he could not shake the eerie suspicion that there was, indeed, a glimmer of truth in that extravagant assertion.

With a patience as boundless as the heavens, Lameth guided him gently over the precipices of that bewildering grammar, explaining in meticulous detail how he was to interpret and apply its underlying mechanisms. He unveiled for him the esoteric meaning of the diagrams and the encrypted symbols of that hieroglyphic tongue—the language of the gods. And then, after imparting but a fragment of that strange knowledge, making it clear that Phineas had scarcely scratched the gilded, diamondine surface of that towering mountain of mysteries, he made an attempt. He spoke one of those sorcerous words—no more than a single utterance drawn from that ineffable book—yet in its primordial essence, measured by the wondrous, forgotten standards of that celestial tongue, it had not yet formed syllables, lingering instead in an embryonic state of ideality, nearer to the realm of archetypes than the loftiest poetry could ever aspire to reach. It was a speech akin to the language of ecstatic glossolalia, still bound in a state tethered to the earthly sphere.

From Lameth's lips, the word sounded jagged and coarse, as though he were speaking a rough and distorted dialect. It was a corrupted, tainted language, a pandæmonic perversion of that paradisiacal *forma locutionis*—akin to the speech of the fallen angels. The air in the room trembled, as if some vast, resonant mechanism had been set into motion—one whose misaligned cogs ground against each other with an agonized strain, groaning as though it might shatter. Lameth seemed to grow in stature, as though the very utterance of that tongue displaced the dimensions of space. His shadow, at first weakly cast by the oil lamp's glow, now unfurled to the high ceiling and stretched into the furthest corners of the room, as though it were devouring the very light from the air.

Phineas could scarcely endure the sound of it, so profoundly did it unsettle him. When Lameth, perceiving his unease, fell silent, he regarded him for several moments with lips that trembled faintly. "Only the man of pure heart can perceive the essence of things and name them rightly. It would seem that long ago, I lost this gift." Phineas opened his mouth to protest, but Lameth raised a hand, as though some overwhelming humility, some deeply attuned conscience, restrained him from invoking the atoning blood of the Savior for what must surely be the slightest transgressions—wrongs committed either in the frailty of his youth or the long passage of his days. Moved beyond words, Phineas at last consented to aid him in mastering that wondrous and fearsome language.

They conversed idly for a while longer, making no further mention of their previous discussion. But as the hour had grown late, Lameth took his leave, though not before accompanying Phineas—despite the arduous ascent of the many stairs—all the way to his chamber, where he left him alone with the peculiar book, in the oppressive solitude of the room. "Persevere in your studies! You will do well to approach its contents in small portions. The progress may be slow, but wisdom is ever found in patience," he counseled him, before stepping beneath the rounded arch of the door and vanishing into the darkness beyond.

The climb and the chill clinging to his chamber had roused Phineas enough that, before retiring, he knelt for a moment and sought reassurance from the heavens. He washed his face, then absentmindedly tended to his teeth. Frothy toothpaste powder swirled in a pool of bubbling water atop the basin, from which his leprous reflection shimmered back at him. He opened the window and drew deep breaths of the cool night air. Gazing upon the portrait of Eireen, he felt the sorrow in his heart dissolve, as though the painting's soft hues cast a healing spell over his soul. His thoughts drifted, and he found himself thinking of Farah—whom he had not seen since her unexpected declaration of love. A sudden, overwhelming fatigue settled over him, and scarcely had he lain upon the bed before he slipped into a dream-laden sleep.

At first, he believes himself to be dreaming of Eireen, standing with her back to him, silhouetted like a cut-out against the moonlit night sky. But as his vision shifts in a slow, circular movement of disembodied perception, he becomes aware that this woman is unknown to him, and yet, in some strange and ineffable way, profoundly familiar. She stands with youthful ease, barefoot upon the stone ledge of a towering mountain, encircled by colossal trees that creak and sway in the wind's unseen grasp. White fabric, delicate as drifting veils of mist, caresses the marble pallor of her form in the picturesque folds of an ancient garment. Upon her brow, a strange and artful circlet gleams in the moonlight, its craftsmanship evoking the celestial smithy of Hephaestus, while the deep red of her hair glows like a crown of living fire.

He watches as she gazes into the distance, across the vast and heaving blackness of a nocturnal sea, its cresting waves illuminated by a narrow, wavering band of silver light, as though beyond the horizon lay something for which her heart burns with an unquenchable longing. And then, as though the dream were untethered from the strictures of time, he beholds her lying upon the soft grass, her searching eyes lifted to the alien constellations above.

All at once, the vision shifts, and he finds himself standing in a glade, witnessing a pair of figures, adorned in garments of forgotten symbols, their hands clasped in the solemn gesture of dextrarum iunctio, like an image lifted from an ancient icon. And in that instant, he knows with immutable certainty that he himself is one of them, and before him stands the maiden he had seen but moments ago, for he perceives the vision not merely as an observer, but from within its depths, seeing through the very eyes of his dreamlike counterpart. And her name is made known to him, and the fullness of her life unfurls before his sight, even as she, in that single, timeless instant, perceives his own entire being as though traversing the breadth of his soul.

And suddenly, it seems to him that his senses have been sharpened beyond all mortal measure, so that he becomes one with the surrounding nature and with the universal force that pervades all things. And all is revealed to them—past, present, and that which is yet to come—and their longing, their yearning, is pure and untainted, a flame without shadow, a desire without deception. And he speaks one of those wondrous words, and all creation falls into breathless silence; and for a fleeting moment, the very elements pause, as though time itself had ceased its ceaseless march. Then, as his word fades, the universe stirs anew, and a single, piercing tone resounds, filling the boundless reaches of the cosmos, rising in exaltation toward an ecstatic crescendo.

And the heavens are rent asunder, and a pillar of light bursts forth from the darkness of the night between the stars. And from the light, a path emerges, unerring in its course, ascending straight into the radiance that pours down from above, its farthest reaches dissolving into a golden luminescence, enfolding them both like the leaf-gilded halo of a saintly icon. And they ascend the steps, passing through gates that open wide, while the watchers stand aside and yield the way, so that they press forward, unhindered by any force that would delay them. And in the far distance, a final barrier rises, and beyond it, a resplendent throne, before which wondrous beings are gathered, their unspeakable words of praise and adoration interwoven with music composed in a notation never before beheld by mortal eyes.

CHAPTER VII.
STEPPING INTO THE LIGHT

When Phineas awoke the next morning, fragments of his dream still clung to him, drifting like delicate strands of mist in the pale light of dawn. Throughout the morning, his thoughts lingered upon the girl he had seen—a stranger, and yet, in some ineffable way, intimately familiar. Even as Obed entered his chamber and set the tray down with a clatter, Phineas remained so deeply lost in reverie that he failed to take note of the sorrowful gloom clouding the servant's face—a melancholy as heavy and impenetrable as a rain-sodden sky, bereft of sun.

Having completed his morning ablutions, devoured his breakfast with ravenous haste, and retrieved a letter from Monsieur Lameth—its envelope damp and curling at the edges from the puddle of spilled coffee in which it had been left—he seated himself upon the window ledge and resumed his study of the enigmatic book. Now that Lameth's elucidations had paved a path toward understanding, the text enthralled him in such a manner that, had it not been for the rhythmic intrusion of meals, silently brought and just as silently removed by the house servant, he would scarcely have noticed the passage of time. It was as though the mere act of beholding the book, of letting his gaze dwell upon the marvels therein described, had severed him from the mundane laws of space and duration.

Though much of its content still eluded him—if only due to its immense breadth and unfathomable depth—he sensed, at first imperceptibly, then with increasing clarity, the germination of a nascent comprehension. It was fragile, indistinct, veiled—like a text missing entire passages, further obscured by a compositor's errant hand that had scattered its letters into a cipher without key. He could not have articulated his thoughts, nor shaped them into any form intelligible to a patient listener, for they remained incomplete, mere shadows cast upon the threshold of understanding. Yet he was aware of a seedling of knowledge, awaiting its first rain before it might take root and unfurl its leaves in the loamy soil of his mind. A thought, as yet without branches or tendrils, beyond his capacity to grasp, as though some dull and leaden weight—ordained at the moment of his birth by the unseen hand of divine decree—pressed upon his faculties, blinding his perception and veiling the nascent realization that stirred within him. He longed to be freed from the fetters of his own limitation, to be, like the prophets and holy men of old, rapt in ecstasy, touched by the spirit, or otherwise liberated from the narrow confines of mortal understanding. But such was not his fate. And thus, throughout that entire day, he felt like an utterly unlettered man, straining to follow the discourse of a learned scholar—one who spoke in the grave and weighty language of science, a tongue too heavy for his mind to grasp, though its meaning loomed just beyond his reach.

The days hastened by, and at last, the eve of the day Lameth had named in his letter began to dawn. That evening, Phineas retired early, for his host had announced that their practice would commence at the break of day—though he had offered not the slightest hint as to what this practice might entail. Lying beneath a white linen coverlet, his head slightly elevated upon two stacked feather pillows, Phineas lay as though he had been laid out in state, gazing somberly into the darkness, watching the oblique moonlight slanting in from without, casting a band of silver-blue silence upon the walls. He strained to recall the girl from his dream, nurturing the dubious hope that his coming visions might seamlessly continue where the last had left off, that he might once again behold that beloved countenance, or perhaps even be granted the fortune of ascending with her once more toward that luminous realm without darkness. But his mind felt shrouded, as though one of his senses had been stripped from him, and the exalted emotions that had once stirred him now seemed but a faded whisper of a dream long since dissipated.

At some point, he must have drifted into sleep, for he awoke to the insistent sound of knocking at his door—though his slumber had been empty, devoid of those wondrous landscapes he had so yearned to revisit. Instead, his mind had been troubled by the most meaningless fragments of an utterly chaotic, yet tediously mundane dream, a jumble of incoherent recollections, as if his subconscious had, in its cruelest irony, chosen to present him with the most trivial absurdities in stark contrast to the sacred grandeur of his former vision. He rose sluggishly, stretching his stiff limbs, and caught a fleeting glimpse of his own reflection in the dim, vignetted mirror that framed his sleepworn appearance in its half-blind glass. As he unlatched the door and opened it, he found a tray of breakfast set alone upon the wooden floor. Its bearer had already departed—evidently Obed, as the sound of heavy, clattering footsteps retreating down the stairwell echoed through the hollow vastness of the house.

After completing his morning ablutions, he partook of his breakfast, which, to his astonishment, was so pitifully meager that he already dreaded what awaited him beyond this frugal repast. He dressed, seized by a peculiar restlessness, and in his distraction, forgot both his morning prayer and the thought that it was not some idle romantic fancy, but rather a divine spark that had ignited his visions—the dream of the girl, the celestial spectacle that had unfolded before him. Just as he was about to descend to the reception hall, there came another knock at the door. He opened it abruptly, and there stood Monsieur Lameth, looming from the dimly veiled corridor like some specter risen from the very depths of hell, his form expanding beneath the stone archway of the door.

Lameth greeted him with exuberance, wished him good morning, and—before even stepping inside—immediately inquired about his progress with the new language. His eyes, once more set in that terrible gaze, fixed upon Phineas with such grim determination that he seemed on the verge of committing some unspeakable act. "And where shall we conduct this undertaking?" Phineas asked hesitantly after answering all of Lameth's questions with patient diligence.

"Exercise but a moment's patience," Lameth replied with feigned ease, as though attempting to mask his own excitement—though even his remarkable self-control now seemed tested to its very limits. "These very chambers, I believe, will prove sufficient for our beginning."

He took one of the heavy chairs from the corner of the room and dragged it noisily across the floor to the center. His gaze swept seemingly idly over the pictorial paneling, and Phineas thought he noticed a faint shudder ripple through Lameth's carefully composed façade for but the briefest, almost imperceptible moment. Lameth seated himself astride the chair, leaning forward, and with a motion as fluid as a conjurer's sleight of hand, produced a leather-bound book from within his coat. It appeared, once again, to be one of his own transcriptions—faithfully copied from rare and ancient manuscripts—for Phineas could, with some certainty, recognize the binding as belonging to Lameth's extensive library. Brushing a few articles of clothing from the back of a chair, Phineas seated himself across from him. "Shall we return to the study of the Adamic tongue? Or have you once more wrested something from oblivion—some hidden treasure of knowledge that has eluded the dreams of scholars for centuries?"

Lameth seemed visibly flattered, though he chose not to acknowledge the remark. "To answer the first part of your question: We have far weightier and more urgent matters to attend to today. We shall bring your studies to a fitting and worthy conclusion." He opened the book and skimmed a few pages, as if to confirm he had selected the right volume. A fleeting smile crossed his lips—not one of mirth, but of satisfaction—before he closed the book once more and, with a solemn air, presented it to Phineas. Phineas, sensing the gravity of the moment, accepted it with due reverence. The title, JANNES ET JAMBRES, embossed in gold, spread across the leather cover in the imposing majuscules of a baroque Antiqua.

"A book about the sorcerers who opposed Moses," Phineas quoted from the Second Epistle to Timothy.

"It is not the apocryphal text on Jannes and Jambres mentioned by Origen," Lameth corrected him, "but rather the work cited by John of Nikiu in his 'Chronicle of the World'—a text said to have been inscribed by Jannes and Jambres themselves—more properly Johanai and Mamre—chief among the Chaldeans. With their own hands they set down this knowledge, the very knowledge with which Pharaoh established his dominion, a compendium of arcane wisdom containing fragments of the lost magic of that fallen kingdom, and even the arts of the antediluvian ages."

As Lameth spoke, Phineas opened the book at its midpoint, pressing his thumbs firmly into the binding, and with his left hand, he skipped whole chapters at a time, rifling through the well-thumbed pages before letting them flutter rapidly beneath his fingers. Stirred by Lameth's tantalizing words, he sought to grasp the nature of the tome's contents. The volume contained a French translation of some cryptic primal text—one that, judging by Lameth's singular gift for resurrecting the obscure, had likely been transcribed from one of the countless manuscripts hoarded in his English estate. The pages bore intricate woodcuts—figurative depictions executed in flat relief and symbolic perspective—cosmological diagrams, and ominous cryptographic sigils. Every leaf was thick with accounts of blasphemous miracles, arcane rites, and the oldest superstitions known to man. It was a book of unspeakable darkness, a relic of a time so remote that its sorceries seemed to rise like desert wraiths from the sands of Libya, bearing a knowledge so dreadful that it outstripped even the most audacious claims of the darkest medieval mystics. Phineas could barely endure what he read. And yet, despite the text's baleful nature—its unmasked horrors, its forbidden secrets—he turned its pages with an almost hypnotic fascination. Occasionally, he came upon marginalia in Lameth's flowing, elaborate script, annotations in which the Englishman had amended, supplemented, and, in some instances, provided practical commentary on the rituals, formulas, and invocations contained within.

"I transcribed the text from that brittle hieratic papyrus," Lameth remarked with measured nonchalance. "Translated it into a more contemporary tongue and prepared this and other copies for everyday use. After all, one reads far more comfortably from a *quarto* volume than from one of those unwieldy scrolls—especially when they have a lamentable tendency to crumble into the dust of centuries at the slightest touch."

Disturbed, Phineas looked up at Lameth, who regarded him with a patronizing gaze—like a proud father watching his child take its first faltering steps. "I cannot in the least discern what you intend to accomplish with this most peculiar text, which fairly drips with Simonian self-aggrandizement," he expressed his irritation with perfect candor.

"Nimrod's Gateway of the Gods was not the only one of its kind," Lameth replied with a knowing smile.

For several seconds, Phineas stared at him, mouth agape, before shaking his head in bemusement. "Are you suggesting that Nimrod built another such gateway in his time?"

Lameth let out a resonant laugh, though his expression quickly sobered. "Nimrod could not have built such a gateway, not even with all the sorcery that seethed within his vast dominion. I should perhaps mention that, at this very moment, you find yourself standing upon just such a place."

"This hôtel?" Phineas asked incredulously, leaning forward with his hands twisting in apprehension. "It seems to me a most unsuitable site for something of such extraordinary nature."

"I have already told you that long before Paris was founded, this was a sacred place—one of those liminal junctures that have existed since the beginning of time. And since we are travelers—Celestial travelers, to be precise—what could have been more fitting than to raise an inn upon it? A most peculiar inn, to be sure." Lameth laughed once more, and it seemed as though a thousand recollections stirred within him—memories of events that had transpired within these walls in some distant age. "Have you never sensed that this hôtel is unlike any other? Have you not, since the moment you arrived, questioned whether all within these walls truly proceeds by natural order? Of course you have! By your own account, you can verify the truth of my words for yourself. Is that not so?"

"Do you truly believe such things to be possible?" Phineas stammered. "What manner of gateway could this be, and how could it have remained hidden from the world for so long? And why should anyone desire to tread such a path? Is it not the fate of man that his years are numbered, and that he may, when his time is done, hope for salvation—without resorting to so grave a transgression? And do we not all—if that is indeed your concern—have a rightful claim to grace, even if our journey has been fraught with doubt and sin?"

"Who would not wish, forsaking all that is human, scorning the gifts of fortune, and casting aside the needs of the body, to become a guest among the gods even in this life? Who would not long to be seized by those Socratic raptures that Plato extols in 'Phaedrus', that he might, with winged feet, take swift flight from this world, which is founded upon evil, and in a frenzied ascent be borne to the

heavenly Jerusalem?" Lameth's voice rang out with sonorous clarity as he recited from Pico della Mirandola's 'De hominis dignitate'.

"How could anyone dare to tread a path that the Creator Himself, according to Scripture, has condemned?" Phineas countered.

"That Nimrod, driven by vengeance and ambition, sought to exalt himself above God does not mean that we are forbidden to seek what lies beyond those gates. Was it not the very pursuit of all holy men and great mystics—to fathom those secrets guarded in the darkness of ancient sanctuaries, to lift the veil from priestly and mystical allegories, to embark upon the celestial journey even before death, to descend through the seven chambers, the palaces of the angels, to behold the heavenly throne and taste of ineffable bliss? Who would not be enraptured by the thought of hearing the unspeakable words, of casting himself before the Majesty of God in the *Chamber of Glory*, and offering adoration? Tell me, then—why should it be forbidden to enter the ziggurat and pass through the unseen threshold that separates time and space? The great mystery of all the sacred teachings of the past millennia points to one singular truth: that man is a mortal god, and the gods are immortal men. The arcane exists for no other purpose than to conceal complete knowledge from the profane. Did not Jesus Himself declare in the Scriptures that the sacred must not be cast before dogs, nor pearls before swine?"

Lameth's voice was soft and melodic, weaving its way through the air with such compelling and persuasive cadence that, though Phineas recoiled at first, he found himself unable to resist the gradual erosion of his own misgivings. With every word spoken, his objections seemed to him increasingly feeble, their contradictions more glaring, until he felt himself like a wayward, obstinate child—while Lameth's discourse, measured and wise, bore the weight of undeniable reason. The act of acquiescence carried an almost soothing relief, whereas resistance became a nearly physical torment. Such tremendous force of will was required to maintain his stance that, before long, his defiance dissolved, leaving him only to seek refuge in feeble justifications for his own inadequacies.

"In Nubia, south of Meroë, I once witnessed an exceedingly instructive incident," Lameth recounted. "I observed a man, a Nilote… Yes, I saw this man who had gone to the river to fetch water, only to be so overcome with fear at the sight of a group of ravenous crocodiles lying in wait that he dropped his bucket and stood there, paralyzed, staring at them, unable to move. And then, in his place, a child came, scooped the water from the very same spot without the slightest hesitation, and calmly returned home to give his family to drink."

"Yes, and?" Phineas looked at him blankly.

"Perhaps I should draw your attention to the fate of the man," Lameth continued. "At that very spot where he had stood, transfixed by fear, marveling at the child's courage, some hippopotamuses were grazing. One of them broke away, crept up on him unseen, and tore him apart. The others followed suit, trampling his remains into the mud of the riverbank until nothing of him was ever seen or heard of again."

"I think I understand what you're implying," Phineas murmured, subdued. "But why me? What qualifies me, in your eyes, for such a task?"

"Some whim of nature brings forth the old in irregular intervals. A cosmic cycle, beyond any order known to us, engenders a mysterious atavism, one that conjures the likeness of a particular ancestor—a bearer of hereditary substance in astonishing fidelity, just as Seth resembled Adam, an identical twin though separated from him by centuries, yet bound to his soul through the unfathomable pathways of providence. Do not ask me how I know this, for not all that I perceive is fit to be spoken of in the light of day. But of one thing you may be certain: You possess attributes that emerge only once every few millennia, and the Ancient One himself seems to have been the mold from which your being was cast. This task demands a man of courage and exceptional ability. That is where you come in, my esteemed Phineas. I must therefore ask you—will you make yourself available for such an undertaking?"

"What supposed talent do you see in me that has thus far eluded my own recognition? And how, indeed, is such an astounding endeavor even to be accomplished? Surely, I am not merely to turn a handle and open a passage of such cosmic magnitude."

You must be patient. There is one thing, however, that I may already entrust to you at this time: The language of the first man is the key, and the instructions for its use lie within your hands. *'The people of Israel inherited what Egypt lost,'* as Karl von Eckartshausen so aptly put it. But what is that inheritance, truly? 'THE GREAT IN VISION' and 'HE WHO BEHOLDS THE MYSTERY OF HEAVEN'—such vain epithets did the high priest of Heliopolis bear. And the Jewish mystics of old did not see with mortal eyes that which awaits beyond the gates of flame. They spent their lifetimes extracting secret names and passwords from the *Torah*, devising feeble incantations by which they hoped to gain entry. These simple fools then bent themselves to the earth, burying their heads between their knees, languishing for untold hours in unimaginable torment as they fasted and chanted their monotonous hymns and psalms. After countless years of suffering, some of them at last attained such refinement that they became clairvoyant, reaching that state in which they could sever soul from body and thus embark upon the journey. In this manner, they could gaze into the innermost chambers of the seven palaces as though they stood there with their own eyes. Yet even in this rapturous state, what they beheld could bring ruin upon their body and soul, for they could not endure what was revealed to them, or else the gatekeepers, perceiving their unworthiness, would afflict their minds and torment their spirits until they descended into madness. Jannes and Jambres, however, possessed the secret knowledge by which they passed through the gates in their own flesh, and with their potent amulets, they could not be denied. According to legend, they withstood even Michael and Gabriel, until Metatron, in the fifth heaven, tore their amulets from them, rendering them vulnerable.

Never before has a seeker been granted such manifold possibilities as those now presented to us in this place, nor has the knowledge of any single man ever been greater. But first, you must do what those before you have done, before you may undertake this journey in corporeal form. You must practice! Practice how to separate the spirit from the fabric of the body. Practice how it feels to traverse the astral fluid of the otherworldly realms in your etheric body. But fear not—we shall proceed with safeguards, following an ancient, well-tested method once undertaken in the temples of the White City. And I possess certain means by which this process may be hastened, so that you need not spend the next fifty years as a hermit in some desolate wilderness. Before we begin, however, I must ask you a few questions."

Lameth, in a manner resembling a formal interrogation, sought to ascertain that Phineas's motives were pure and, above all else, entirely selfless. And after Phineas had answered each question truthfully—though not without displaying a general bewilderment—Lameth administered an oath, binding him never to disclose what had been entrusted to him, nor to reveal under any circumstances the experiences of the initiatory rites. More bewildered than convinced, Phineas consented, and throughout the entire exchange, he could not shake the impression that Lameth's primary concern lay less in probing his moral integrity than in observing the proper formalities, as though he were merely following a prescribed protocol rather than earnestly weighing his worthiness. Indeed, Lameth barely seemed to listen to his answers, brusquely interrupting him whenever he expressed self-doubt instead of responding directly to a question, attempted to engage in discussion regarding its meaning, or, worse still, sought to embark upon a theological discourse on the reasonableness of what was asked. Lameth's words swarmed in his mind like a hive of bees, and a sense of inadequacy vied against a sudden euphoric elevation, which seemed to deceive him into believing that the future held something grand in store for him—that through some providential design, a particular destiny was beginning to reveal itself in his being. These conflicting sensations struggled against each other, at first evenly matched, until at last, the notion of some special election yielded, and a deep disquiet took hold. The spell of Lameth's words was broken, and Phineas could not help but feel that whatever it was the older man imagined he saw within him, it was naught but a product of an idealized affection—an illusion cast upon him through sentiment rather than truth.

Thereafter, Lameth bade him follow to one of the deeper chambers, where he was clothed in a garment of peculiar cut. Catching his reflection in a mirror, Phineas was seized by the disquieting notion that he beheld, staring back at him, the very same mad old man who had so terrorized him on that dreadful night. Turning to Lameth, he inquired as to the necessity of such attire. "It is, in truth, more a matter of tradition than of any genuine effect upon the matters which lie before you," came Lameth's reply from behind the dividing screen. "Already in Memphis, and in Nineveh before it, and even in the ages preceding, the priests wore linen at their initiation. If it unsettles you, then discard it! Though such things hold profound symbolism for those who possess understanding, they bear little actual weight upon your success."

Phineas chose to wear the garment over his customary clothing and followed Lameth with purposeful strides down the winding staircase, which descended yet another considerable distance, burrowing into the rocky foundations beneath the estate like a colossal corkscrew. The massive stone blocks lining the curved walls seemed to age with every step they took toward the depths, until at last, they merged seamlessly with the bedrock itself. Moisture clung to the walls, trickling in thin rivulets over the surface, crusted with white efflorescence, pooling at times in patches of blackish moss that, in the flickering glow of the oil lamps and the shifting shadows of their own bodies, seemed to take on a life of its own—coalescing, in Phineas's fevered imagination, into grotesque shapes of disquieting entities. A handful of sparsely placed wall sconces, affixed to the damp stone with iron nails, provided a meager illumination, until the light failed altogether, swallowed by the abyssal darkness ahead.

Lameth reached into a niche veiled in glistening cobwebs and retrieved a single oil lamp left there for this purpose, lighting it with a steady hand before continuing his descent without hesitation. Phineas followed, though his steps were uncertain. The stone stairs, ancient beyond reckoning, grew ever more worn as they descended—their edges rounded, their time-worn surfaces eroded to a perilous steepness, coated in a slick, treacherous dampness that caused him to stumble more than once. A vile, moldering stench thickened the air the further they ventured into the cylindrical abyss. The grandly carved balustrade of the upper noble halls had long since given way to a crude iron railing, its coarse-forged fastenings having, over the centuries, worked themselves loose—like splinters festering from an ancient wound—so that now, rusted nails jutted halfway free from the cavernous rock, leaving the once-solid ironwork in a state of dubious reliability. Still, they pressed onward, downward, toward what felt like a bottomless chasm, and with every step, the oppressive atmosphere grew denser, bearing down upon them with an unrelenting force, as though they neared the lair of some primordial cult lost to time.

After what felt like an eternity, they finally reached the end of the staircase—or rather, the terminus of what would later emerge as the winding descent above. Here, the neatly hewn stone blocks had vanished entirely, giving way to naturally formed rock, glistening with multicolored mineral deposits and a slick film of moisture. Lameth led Phineas toward a narrow passage, sealed by an iron-bound, half-rotted door, which he now noisily unlatched. The door swung inward with a dreadful groan, revealing a vast, shadowed chamber, its ceiling vanishing into darkness beneath the heavy spans of ribbed vaulting that rested upon pillars. The feeble glow of the oil lamp, held aloft in Lameth's gnarled hand, barely illuminated the cavern's entrance, leaving the rest swallowed in oppressive obscurity. A miasma of decay, dampness, and long-forgotten rot lingered in the dust that coated every surface.

For some time, they wandered through the suffocating gloom, until suddenly, the wavering lamplight illuminated a circular stone table hewn from the living rock. In its very center, Phineas now discerned, stood an unassuming chalice, caught in the filaments of a slanting cobweb. Arriving before it, Lameth set down the flickering lamp and, with reverent hands, took up the vessel. He wiped its outer surface clean, blew the dust from its hollow, then produced a small silver phial, hidden until now within his breast pocket. Unsealing it with quiet deliberation, he let the liquid within trickle slowly into the chalice. Without a word, he extended the cup toward Phineas, his head bowed, his furrowed brow casting deep shadows across his face. Phineas trembled with anticipation so violently that he feared his limbs might betray him. "What… what do you intend for me to do?" he asked in a voice barely above a whisper, his throat dry with apprehension.

"At last," Lameth intoned, his voice heavy with omen, his face—caught in the erratic flicker of the lamplight—twisting into something almost demonic, "your purpose begins to unfold. This draught will help you transcend the narrow confines of your present state of consciousness. Wander the vast expanse of eternal night and face the trials that await you there! Know yourself—clearly, without illusion! Cast off the sluggish shell of flesh and don the luminous raiment of fire! Behold the mysteries of the Land of Light! And when your journey is complete, emerge reborn into the radiance of day!"

Phineas still hesitated, unwilling—indeed, unable—to drink a potion that seemed to promise the very forfeiture of his life, even if he supposed that Lameth spoke only in metaphor. The ancient figure perceived his reluctance and sighed. "The written word is barren when left to itself. There are things that cannot be grasped merely by burying oneself in a book. Before the primordial elements took form within the life-giving sphere of the world, we wandered clad in eternal flame. Now, you must cast off your earthly shell, so that with unveiled sight, you may gaze upon the secrets of creation—see with unclouded vision the divine mechanisms that govern the universe and guide it along its appointed paths, and hear the mighty words by which the elements are compelled."

Lameth's countenance flickered in and out of sight, momentarily illuminated by the wavering flames of the oil lamp—like a will-o'-the-wisp in the darkness. Phineas, overwhelmed with apprehension at the unknown trial before him, could scarcely comprehend the words spoken to him. He raised the vessel to his lips, took a hesitant sip of the inky, viscous liquid streaked with strange iridescent swirls, and then—fighting back his revulsion—drained it in one swift motion. The taste was vile, and he struggled not to retch. Lameth carefully lifted the glass cover of his lamp and, with a piece of tinder plucked from the refuse-strewn floor, ignited a tiny Roman oil lamp, which he handed to Phineas like a farewell token. "The bitterness is but a gatekeeper standing before the world of deeper mysteries. Your path now veers from the well-trodden roads of this mortal realm. Press on, undaunted, with courage and resolve," he urged one final time before turning away. Phineas saw only the narrow halo of Lameth's lamp, hovering in the gloom like a willful specter, before it diminished into nothingness. Then came the creak of the great oaken door being drawn shut, the unmistakable sound of the lock sliding into place, and silence—total, absolute, and crushing.

Only now did he fully grasp the necessity of the fragile clay lamp in his grasp. Its meager flame cast a feeble glow, illuminating but a few paces ahead. For a time, his light flickered against the yawning maw of a sloping shaft, its sickly gleam stretching just far enough to reveal the curve of a brick-lined archway that loomed above like the gaping threshold of the underworld. *Descensus ad inferos*, the phrase surfaced in his mind as he steeled himself and stepped forward through the dreadful portal. Roughly hewn half-columns, barely two meters high and covered in unknown inscriptions, lined the cavern walls on either side. Their grotesquely contorted capitals pressed upward into thick, squat pillars that seemed to strain under the weight of the encroaching ceiling. The passageway grew steadily narrower, its walls pressing ever closer until he was forced to stoop. Further still, the path constricted, forsaking its procession of stone sentinels altogether, until he found himself before a jagged opening barely wide enough for his frame. With no alternative, he wedged himself through, pushing the lamp forward with his hands as he crawled—clinging to the faint hope that the passage would lead him back into some vaster, more forgiving expanse of architecture.

The dampness that saturated the rock floor and walls seeped into his clothes at the knees and hands. At some point, with a final, feeble flicker, the tiny lamp expired, leaving him crawling blind, bereft of all hope, suspended in the desolation of a lightless corridor. "Lameth has led you into a trap!" The voice rang out suddenly, echoing with such gleeful malice that anger and despair seized him in equal measure. "Turn back while the passage is still wide enough! Or do you wish to be buried alive?"

"Who speaks?" he cried, his voice laced with rising panic.

"A friend. Don't be a fool—go back!" The words came at him from unseen apertures in the stone, shifting with an unsettling, spectral quality. "There is much worth living for!"

Now he was utterly certain—he would die down here if he did not turn back at once. Without the feeble glow of the earthen lamp, he would never find the path ahead. He would wander aimlessly in the abyssal dark until hunger or thirst overtook him. Or worse—perhaps he would stumble into some nameless chasm, an end that, in this moment, seemed not the worst fate to befall him. He began to crawl backward through the narrow passage. The jagged rock tore at his robe and shirt at the shoulders, the raw stone drinking his blood as it seeped into the tattered fabric. He shivered uncontrollably, his body wracked with convulsive tremors. Cold sweat burst from every pore, drenching the garment beneath the strange robe until it clung to his chest in clammy folds. As he struggled against the suffocating embrace of the rock, Lameth's warning rang in his mind. *This is a test!* The realization struck him like a flash of lightning. *Lameth seeks to know whether I am truly resolute, whether I am worthy, or if I shall falter and turn back.* And why, he reasoned, would someone carve these subterranean corridors and bid him traverse them, if not for some profound, hidden purpose? "Without wisdom, life is without value!" he cried aloud and, with renewed resolve, dragged himself forward once more, toward his original goal.

He suddenly thought he could hear drums—underlaid with rhythmic chants and invocations—but dismissed it as a trick of his overstimulated mind, the hammering of blood in his temples, or the effects of the draught Lameth had given him earlier. Yet the pounding of the drums swelled with increasing urgency, the incantations became more insistent, more commanding, and he thought he saw a glimmer of light in the distance. His lacerated fingers clawed at the stone, nails cracking as he pulled himself forward with the last remnants of his strength, crawling through the last agonizing meters until the passage finally widened and emptied into a vast, cavernous stairwell. He stumbled forward, propelled by the sudden, disorienting expansion of space—like a newborn cast from the womb of its mother. Dim light filtered in through several vertical shafts, faintly illuminating the towering, right-angled walls that stretched upward into unfathomable heights. After allowing his limbs a brief moment of respite, he struck flint and iron together, igniting a torch from a bundle of them stacked in a recess of the wall. Under the lingering echo of those eerie chants and the rolling thunder of the drums, he ascended the massive stone stairway, which spanned a yawning, unseen abyss before branching into a labyrinth of corridors and chambers. This place—woven with illusory stone doors and cunningly devised passageways—was an architectural simulacrum of the underworld, and the sheer ingenuity of its design both unsettled and fascinated him. He pressed forward into the darkness, where the torch's golden light spread beneath a vast canopy of inky blackness, wandering without any sense of time through the subterranean maze. First climbing, then descending into unimaginable depths, he at last reached a most remarkable chamber.

The entire room was a furnace. Flames leapt toward the high, column-borne ceiling, their tongues writhing against the soot-darkened vaults. The floor was formed of a vast iron grate, glowing red-hot beneath his feet. The walls were lined with enormous iron pipes, feeding strange contraptions whose mechanisms were beyond his understanding, while towering brick chimneys vented thick smoke into unseen heights. The heat was so immense that he turned away, searching in vain for another passage, only to return moments later, lingering in wonder before the raging fire. The walls and pillars were blackened with soot, while smoke billowed in dense, curling columns from the searing tongues of flame. Yet as he observed more closely, he noticed something—one section of the room had remained untouched by the fire's stain. Even beneath the glowing grate, the red and yellow embers seemed to lose their strength at this one particular spot. Summoning his resolve, he stepped forward, shielding his face with his hands, and strode through the fire at that very point—where, impossibly, the inferno lost its consuming grasp. Emerging almost unscathed, his clothes smoking and his hair singed, he reached the other side.

After he had walked on for some time, he began to hear the muffled rush of water, echoing ominously through the vast expanse of the passage ahead. With every step, the sound swelled, growing into a deafening roar, until he finally stood before a torrent of swiftly flowing water. Its gurgling current howled with such force that, in this shadowed underworld, it reverberated as though the entire vault might collapse in upon itself. Once more, his careful deliberation guided him to a solution, and as he left his torch in an iron bracket, he reached beneath the waterline, running his hands along the moss-covered walls of the channel. There, embedded in the stone, he found iron grips that afforded him enough purchase to hazard the depths of that Stygian stream. Plunging into the foam-laced darkness, he made his way across, emerging safely on the other side. Dripping wet, he wrung the moisture from his garments before stepping forward, traversing a long corridor that opened into a vast, light-filled hall. Pillars adorned with elaborate cube capitals structured the space, and after the long confinement of the narrow passageways, the sheer openness of it seemed to him as though he had stepped into paradise. An eternal radiance issued from hammered bronze basins, which sat atop great candelabra, their flickering glow casting restless shadows upon the walls—walls hewn from the living rock, covered in inscribed hieroglyphs and depictions of the underworld, as if this titanic columned hall had risen from the sands of Giza itself. Fragrant smoke coiled upward in delicate spirals, and the splendor and magnificence of that chamber lay beyond all description. The ritual chants had now reached their climax. The throbbing drums, now joined by the elongated notes of horns, seemed to speak of those dark dominions that had slumbered for aeons upon the face of a nascent world.

A knight in a gleaming suit of armor stood watch in silence, gripping a wavy-edged sword that shimmered in the light like pure fire. Upon his head, a helm shaped in the likeness of an animal mask, with a lowered visor that rendered his face inscrutable; atop it, a crest sculpted in the very image of the jackal-headed god of Egypt, giving him the unsettling appearance of Anubis himself. High upon a gallery, enfolded by colossal pillars covered in hieroglyphs and gilded ornaments—labyrinthine colonnades whose shadows crept across the floor like thresholds to sanctuaries long since sunken into oblivion—there sat enthroned a priest, his aspect recalling those painted masks of mummies, the insignia—amulets, pectorals, priestly staffs—and the statues of Egyptian servants of the gods, such as Phineas, half in shadow, half reflected in glass, had once glimpsed gleaming within the dust-shrouded cases of the *British Museum*. And in the background, partly lost in a golden haze, a host of flower-crowned celebrants moved in a solemn round-dance, their procession bearing the unmistakable stamp of an age no longer remembered by the mind of man. It was only as he drew closer that Phineas recognized the priest to be none other than Mister Stroude, who had exchanged his rakish attire for priestly vestments and now fixed him with a piercing gaze, as if attempting to ensnare him in some hypnotic spell. At last, he recognized the voice—the same voice that had sought to dissuade him in the labyrinth, urging him to turn back. "The first trial has been passed," Stroude intoned, his expression marked by a thinly veiled disappointment. "And it would have been my pleasure to guide you through the rest. However, to my deepest regret, Monsieur Lameth insists on abbreviating your training." Phineas dared not imagine what such an omission had spared him.

His counterpart, assuming the role of Hierophant, led him behind the veiled partition, where he imposed upon him oaths whose violation would incur the most dreadful consequences. Then, in a trembling voice, he whispered to him the secret of secrets—mysteries so profound that even Lameth had not dared entrust them to his silent, timeworn pages. Mister Stroude frequently interrupted his instruction, hesitating at every turn, so that at first Phineas believed he was simply overcome by the sanctity and majesty of the revelation, trembling in awe before its solemn grandeur. But after some time, a suspicion crept over him—that the man was, in truth, afraid, as though one might force the Devil himself to recite the *Apostles' Creed*.

When Mister Stroude had finally concluded his discourse, and Phineas was just on the verge of comprehending what he had heard—struggling to grasp it in thought, to shape it in the theater of his mind, an endeavor made all the more impossible by the fully unleashed effects of the draught—he was clad in a new robe, and a golden wreath, its leaves fanning outward like sunrays upon the circlet, was placed upon his brow. Then food and drink were set before him, accompanied by the solemn pronouncement that by partaking of them, he would *"join the company of the gods."* Mister Stroude's words grew increasingly frenzied, until at last, with wild conviction, he urged him to recline within the *"body of the celestial goddess"*—an anthropoid stone sarcophagus, which, for the sake of comfort, had been outfitted with a frilly white pillow, a detail that did little to enhance its appeal as a resting place. Phineas, however, so utterly weakened and drained by the harrowing journey through the catacombs and the intoxicating weight of the potion, found himself too weary to resist. Without protest, he surrendered himself to that strange and solemn bed. *"I will birth you anew, in rejuvenation,"* Mister Stroude intoned. *"I have spread myself over you; I have reborn you as a god."*

Disturbingly, he perceived new, unfamiliar sensations and impressions, though his vision remained veiled and indistinct, as if he were peering through the thick bottom of a beer glass. Mister Stroude, who had suddenly appeared within Phineas's limited field of vision, still clad in his priestly vestments and busily occupied with something above him, was swallowed, all at once, by a wave of darkness. It was then that Phineas realized, with mounting horror, that the man had sealed the sarcophagus with something. He pounded against the smooth stone of the lid until his limbs ached. *Buried alive!* The thought struck him with maddening intensity. *Who in their right mind would so foolishly, so willingly, lay themselves to rest in their own tomb before their time?* His breathing grew rapid and shallow, broken into short, desperate gasps. *How could I have allowed myself to be drawn into this madness, to come to Paris only to yield to the morbid whims of this old fool?* The draught had taken full effect, for his limbs began to stiffen, as if the potion were draining the very life from him.

Phineas was no longer aware of the moment when his breath ceased and his consciousness slipped into that liminal state between existence and oblivion, for his perception was not extinguished but, rather, sharpened a hundredfold—his senses heightened in the most uncanny manner. He considered the possibility that this was no more than a delusion—must be a delusion—for even in this strange place, what he now saw and experienced could not possibly be real. With an awareness wholly unbound from physical sight, he first beheld the reddish porphyry sarcophagus in which his body lay in what seemed a peaceful slumber. Then, he saw Mister Stroude moving toward a concealed doorway that led into an adjoining chamber. Even in his disembodied state, Phineas sensed that the man's treacherous eyes had somehow detected him, as though Stroude possessed an expanded sense of vision.

All at once, Stroude turned, swiped his hand through the air as if attempting to catch an insect, and, raising his brows with an awkward, upward-glancing scrutiny of the chamber, his gaze sweeping the unseen, he revealed a knowing, triumphant smile.

Phineas beheld Obed, slumped despondently on a stool in the lobby, as well as other guests and servants who moved about the building; then Farah, curled up in a small, windowless room, her face wet with tears as she lay upon a wooden cot. For a brief moment, he felt compelled to approach her, to understand her distress, but the onslaught of impressions was so overwhelming, so utterly breathtaking, that the thought was cast aside in an instant, eclipsed by the grandeur of the scene before him. He saw Lameth, seated at a writing desk, composing a document—and in that very moment, Lameth saw him as well. Lameth rose to his feet, and with a mere motion of his hand, a force unfurled from him, sending darkness spiraling upward like a tempest unleashed. And in that unshrouded revelation, a terror beyond all reckoning was laid bare, subjecting Phineas's disembodied soul to a torment so excruciating that, with every inch the figure drew nearer, he recoiled in agony. Lameth fixed him with a terrible gaze—eyes so fearsome that even the treacherous stare of Serpentarius Stroude seemed, by comparison, as guileless as that of a child. And from the depths of the darkness, a voice rang out—a cry in the old, forgotten tongue of the young world. Yet the pronunciation was crude and corrupted, the speaker devoid of the majesty that once belonged to those who had wielded it. The words, however, did not fail in their purpose! A blackness darker than the void gathered, towering before Lameth like a storm of titanic proportion.

Phineas, too, called upon that ancient speech. And as words of boundless, now-unfettered understanding came to him, the barrier before him was cleaved apart. For the briefest of moments, he saw it—a being of unfathomable age and power, driven by boundless ambition and seething with malice, yet burdened also with despair, sorrow, and an inner void so abyssal that it would have plunged any mortal mind into the depths of despair, if not obliterated it entirely. Hatred flared as the Lameth-being realized that its facade had been lifted, if only for an instant. A wave of force surged forth, striking Phineas with the force of a thunderclap, hurling him backward. Had he withstood that dreadful onslaught for even a moment longer, it might well have shattered his very soul. He withdrew—retreating to the realm he was permitted to traverse—and at once, that presence relinquished its grasp upon him.

At first, he lingered within the subterranean halls, sensing the immense currents of energy coursing through the hôtel with such unfathomable force, as if an entire ocean were being forced through the eye of a needle. Then he learned to fix his mind upon a single thought, and in the very same instant, he was carried there. He traversed inconceivable expanses, gazed down from heights beyond measure, and descended into depths that lay far outside the bounds of human comprehension. The confinement of space around him dissolved, unveiling a world unseen, unfamiliar, and utterly inconceivable by human standards. Space and time—foolish notions of an evolving, yet primitive life form—faded before the grandeur of that unveiled reality. And just as a retreating curtain of rain unveils the horizon, he beheld with unclouded sight, and in the delirium of convulsively unfolding planes of being, he listened to the revelations of that ethereal realm, which laid bare a celestial mechanism—akin to a Flammarion cosmic clockwork—that bound the universe to the divine word and immutable laws, holding it within its ordained limits.

Twisting and labyrinthine corridors, following a geometry unknown to the earthly mind—narrowing and, in the very same instant, multiplying kaleidoscopically—arched through the infinity of space, ascending toward a glorious, ineffable light that surpassed all understanding. A staircase—if one might venture to name this marvel of radiant dust and fire-light in the crude language of the world—linked celestial wonders to one another, and at each threshold stood mighty beings, filled with knowledge and dreadful holiness. Phineas, recalling the words of passage, beheld and heard the unspeakable—things that could neither be uttered nor written down.

CHAPTER VIII.
MAJESTAS DOMINI

He awoke to a throbbing head and aching limbs, but an immense relief flooded through him at the sight of the burning lamp, at the realization that the heavy stone lid of the sarcophagus had been removed. Mister Stroude was gone. In his place, looming beside him, was a dark silhouette—beginning with a half-bald head and plunging downward in a rapid descent over terraced folds of flesh, cascading into a chest of colossal proportions. Only now did he grasp that he was back in his own room, lying in his own bed. He was dressed in a nightshirt, and his wounds had been expertly tended. "You awake!" Obed declared with remarkable astuteness. "I help you get up. Slow, slow, eh? Most take long time before head is right again." His enormous hands were unexpectedly gentle as he helped Phineas sit upright.

"How long have I slept?"

"Today is second day, since you go down to... under-room."

"Where is Monsieur Lameth?"

"The master, he must go. Very urgent, no wait. Important business. He tell me say you—" Obed's forehead furrowed as he searched for the right words. "You keep study, do what he say."

Phineas's thoughts drifted to the visions of his out-of-body experience, though he could not discern whether they had been mere hallucinations, the delirious phantasmagoria of a drugged mind, or if indeed everything had transpired as it seemed. He struggled to recollect what he had seen. "Tell me, I beg you—what has become of the maid, Farah?"

Obed hesitated, his massive eyes rolling in their sockets, his lips trembling as if he were choking back tears. "She... she gone." His voice was barely more than a whisper.

"No," Phineas protested, his voice sharpening. "She is not gone. I saw her, lying on a pallet in a narrow, windowless chamber. She was in distress—she needed help."

For a fleeting instant, Obed's face lit up, as though some small ember of hope had been rekindled within him—only to dull again into a heavy, vacant stare. Then, all at once, something within him shifted, as if his first thought had only just arrived at the right junction of his sluggishly firing mind. He leapt up, his arms flailing wildly. "I think—I think I know that room!" he burst out and bolted for the door. Phineas attempted to rise and follow, but the throbbing in his skull was so punishing that he was confined to the bed's edge for some time, unable to do more than sit. It was only after another long while that he managed, with some effort, to stand.

"What are you keeping from me, Obed?" Phineas asked, standing before the window like a wind-warped tree, bracing his weakened frame against a piece of furniture.

"I cannot talk 'bout these things," Obed answered. "Just follow, quick!"

Phineas relieved himself into a chamber pot, hastily pulled his trousers over his nightshirt, threw his frock coat over his shoulders, and stumbled barefoot onto the hallway. Dim light crept through the exposed cracks of curtained windows as they hurried down the worn stone staircase. They reached a narrow corridor, situated halfway between the lobby and those deeper cellar levels Phineas had explored with Lameth in the preceding days. They passed through a succession of storage rooms, cluttered with spider-laced bric-a-brac, until at last they stopped before a door where Obed suspected Farah to be kept. He fumbled with a bundle of keys—countless in number, all strung together in a ring—and after several attempts, managed to find the right one. Yet even as the lock yielded, the door would not open. A thick chain had been threaded through an iron loop and secured with a heavy, oversized padlock.

"Farah, you in there?" Obed banged his fists against the oak planks. At first, only silence greeted them. Then, after a long moment, a faint whimper seeped through the warped doorframe, barely audible. While Obed hammered at the wood, Phineas cast about for something with which to break the lock by force. But before he could even begin his search, Obed hurled his massive body against the planks, then, finding them unyielding, seized the iron chain in a fit of desperation, yanking at it as though he possessed the strength of Hercules. Phineas, hurrying down a dim passage in search of a suitable tool, found, beneath a row of soot-streaked, wrought-iron grates—likely belonging to the mansion's heating system—a large fire poker, half-buried in the shadows of a soot-patterned wall. Returning at once, he offered it to the giant, who sat slumped on the floor, massaging his shoulder with a pained expression. Like a trophy, Phineas held it out to him.

With their combined strength, they managed to pry the hasp from the wall and force the door open. The room was narrow and tall, much smaller than Phineas remembered from the vantage point of his disembodied state. A thick layer of dust covered the scant furniture. Cobwebs stretched across every corner, and the air was so thick with damp decay that one instinctively raised a hand to the face. In the farthest corner of the chamber, upon a wooden cot affixed to the wall with rusted iron brackets, lay Farah. Someone had gagged her, and rough flaxen ropes coiled around her wrists and ankles, wound as tightly as mooring lines upon a harbor post. She was frightfully emaciated, her frilled servant's dress hanging from her shoulders like an oversized nightgown. Her eyes, red and swollen from long-unheeded weeping, had dried at last, as though despair had left no more tears to shed. Yet now, as she gazed up in fearful bewilderment, a flicker of hope softened her wan features. Phineas carefully pulled the filthy rag from between her teeth while Obed set to work untying her bonds.

Holding her gently in his arms, Phineas ran a hand through her tangled hair. Her frail body trembled, wracked with relief and silent joy at her impossible deliverance. As he cradled her thus, her fingers sought Obed's hand, reaching out blindly until they found it where he sat beside them, mute and unmoving. Her delicate fingers rested within his palm, as small and weightless as a porcelain doll's hand in the massive grasp of some hulking beast. Phineas rose and surrendered her quivering form into the safety of Obed's powerful arms. Obed let out a broken sob. "I— I didn't know..." he stammered, struggling for words, as though he himself bore the guilt of her suffering.

Phineas ascended to the kitchen adjoining the dining hall, where he first had to shoo away the gaunt servant who eyed him with wary suspicion. He then returned below with a loaf of bread and a jug of water, taking care not to make a public affair of his discovery, uncertain who among the staff was loyal to Lameth. Farah sipped from the jug in small, delicate swallows, bird-like in her movements, and it was some time before she found her voice. "Is… HE near?" she whispered, her voice thin with dread, her eyes flicking toward the door.

"Don't trouble yourself over Lameth," Phineas assured her. "He's gone away." Obed nodded gravely in agreement.

"We gotta be careful no one sees," Obed said, rising to his feet, holding the girl in his arms with such effortless ease it was as though he were laying down a tablecloth. He peered into the corridor, and when he was certain they were unobserved, he carried Farah up a creaking, spiraling staircase, a passageway constructed for the use of the servants. From there, he slipped through a narrow side hallway until they arrived at a spacious yet peculiarly furnished chamber. A plain, oversized bed—nearly the size of a hay cart—with a straw-stuffed sack for a mattress suggested that this must be Obed's sleeping quarters, unless Lameth had another giant in his employ. Obed carefully laid Farah upon the rumpled bed linens while Phineas let his gaze wander across the room. Were it not for the enormous furniture, one might have mistaken it for a child's chamber—so unkempt, so chaotic, so unmistakably youthful was its atmosphere. A threadbare, crudely stitched doll, its single remaining eye gleaming like a cyclopean orb, stared down from a pile of colorful drawings. In the far corner of the room, a makeshift shelf of warped wood cradled a collection of small treasures: polished pebbles, seashells, shards of colored glass, and driftwood plucked from the banks of the Seine. Alongside them lay an assortment of trinkets, the sort peddled in the labyrinthine arcades of the *Rue de la Tonnellerie*. Another piece of furniture held further discoveries—broken pastel crayons and scattered sheets filled with vibrant drawings. "All mine!" Obed declared with unmistakable pride when he caught Phineas's astonished expression.

Phineas examined a few of the paper sheets, moving aside a bowl of candied fruits and caramelized sweets—an act Obed observed with barely concealed reluctance. Yet what astonished Phineas was not so much the quality of the drawings, most of them rendered in pastels with an undeniable yet self-taught skill, but the consistency of their theme: a low-hanging sun over a storm-swept desert, its dunes rolling like waves, dotted with grazing herds, birds of splendid plumage perched upon scattered trees, caravans winding through the sands, camels, humble clusters of dwellings that resembled Bedouin encampments, children at play, women draped in black veils, and men clad in flowing robes and towering turbans of brilliant hues. Setting aside the first stack, he took up another. He noticed that in most of the colored sketches, a dark shadow stretched eerily across portions of the composition—yet there was no visible obstacle to cast it. It encroached upon the scene, swallowing patches of its vibrant world in its gloom. And yet, unfailingly, the brilliant saffron glow of the sun prevailed over the dunes, valiantly resisting the gray oppression of shadow—much like the golden-hued oranges atop the sideboard in van Eyck's 'Arnolfini Portrait.'

After Farah had somewhat regained her strength, Phineas deemed it necessary to demand an explanation from them both. "What is happening here? Farah, why in the world were you imprisoned?" He glanced at Obed's face and saw that something was stirring behind his broad brow, but the man remained silent, as if either too simple to articulate himself or simply unwilling to speak.

Farah was the first to find her voice again. "I warned you about Lameth, and somehow, it reached his ears."

"Who in the devil's name is Lameth truly? What wretched being hides behind the deceitful mask of his whitewashed façade? I saw a dreadful vision when I was in the lower chambers, and I do not believe he intended for me to glimpse beyond the boundaries he had set. But something—some higher force—tore through the veil he had woven around himself and granted me a sight of something that filled me with terror. He attacked me—not in body, but in spirit—and the powers he summoned, or that are in his service, lay beyond all description. I thought for a moment that I would be annihilated, in both body and mind. I cannot fathom that any ordinary man in this life could wield such power."

"I prayed for you," whispered Farah, her voice frail, "and my heart found peace."

"You must tell me everything you know about Lameth and this hôtel."

"Lameth is evil," Farah said. "Everyone here is terrified of him an' what he can do. No one knows where he came from or how long he has been here. My nurse—*que Dieu la bénisse!*—whispered on 'er deathbed that he 'ad scarcely aged since she first entered service 'ere in her youth, as if he'd cheated death itself. Only for a time, when the Revolution was at its worst, did he leave for some years—until it was all over, all the killings an' executions an' all that. He keeps another estate, somewhere on the British Isles."

"I must obey the master, but I watch over Farah. I promised," Obed spoke up, though his words had little to do with the conversation. Judging by the expression on his face, he was wrestling with some inner conflict that seemed to weigh heavily on his conscience.

"They say that in olden times, many men an' women came here an' stayed at the hôtel," Farah resumed her account, "but for years now, only few come—an' they're all cruel, unfriendly folk, real bad sorts. You were different, nothin' like the others—so handsome, so kind an' well-dressed."

Phineas lowered his head in embarrassment, and Farah smiled so innocently, so radiantly, as though the horrors of the past days, her captivity, were but a distant and long-forgotten memory. "What business do these people have at the hôtel?"

"They've sworn secret oaths—not a word of what they do ever reaches the outside world. But I know they perform some sort of ritual in the catacombs beneath the house. At night, strange noises can be heard. Some of the servants swear they've witnessed eerie gatherings; others claim to have heard chants an' invocations—or even screams. Some of the guests just appear, all of a sudden, in one of the rooms, like they walked right through the walls. Others, it's like the hôtel itself drives them mad—but no doctor is ever called, an' after that, you never see those poor souls again." She lowered her voice, almost to a whisper: "Lameth seems to consort with a frightful being. At times, voices came from his chamber—sounds that bore no human quality, no cry that any earthly throat could have produced. When he steps out afterward, his face pale and trembling, his eyes hollow, as if he had gazed into abysses no mortal can endure to see, the weight of uncounted years seems suddenly to rest upon him. For days he remains shut away, until, as if some strange power had breathed new life into him, he returns—imperious and distant as ever—punishin' every mistake, every smallest lapse, harshly and without mercy. Even the wicked folk who come here—they fear him, deep down, though they won't say it aloud." She held still for a moment, as if listening, and added softly: "The strangest thing of all is: he takes no food for days, goes only seldom out to eat. Somehow he found out that I warned you—as if even the walls of this cursed place had eyes and ears. He swore he'd kill me—*au nom du ciel!*—but then he said maybe I'd still be useful to him. He locked me in that room. A woman was with him, one that arrived a few days ago—she beat me, over an' over, 'til he told her to stop."

"He's been tellin' everyone in the hôtel you ran off," Obed added. "Said you took up with some man from *Faubourg Saint Marceau*." At those words, Farah let out a quiet sob, as if the memory of her ordeal and all that had transpired in the hôtel were clawing at her anew. Phineas gently lifted her chin, brushed his fingers along her tear-streaked cheek, and pressed a tender kiss to her salt-touched lips. Farah sniffled, then met his gaze with swollen, questioning eyes.

"I believe I owed you an answer," he murmured with a smile.

"We gotta go—can't stay here!" Obed warned, his massive arms tensed, his thick brow furrowed in disapproval. The sight of such carefree affection in their dire circumstances plainly did not sit well with him.

"Obed's right," Phineas conceded. "When was the last time anyone saw you?"

"Sometimes round midday, that awful woman came an' brought me water an' some bread. I keep thinkin' she musta taken it from the rubbish just to be cruel—bread ain't supposed to taste that foul."

Obed's face darkened, his lips pressed into a thin line. Then, as if stirred by some unspoken resolve, he reached for his cherished bowl of confections and stared long at its contents, like a dragon reluctant to part with his hoard. After a moment's hesitation, he held it out to Farah. She plucked a sticky piece between two fingers, popped it into her mouth, and sucked at it with evident delight. Obed, watching her, broke into a wide, gap-toothed grin.

"We need answers first," Phineas said firmly. "Where has Lameth gone?"

"Don't know. The master don't speak to me 'bout such things," Obed replied.

"We could search his chambers," Phineas suggested.

"He never carries much with him when he stays here. Aside from his clothes an' all that fancy finery, he only ever brings a big iron-bound chest—keeps his strange books an' potions in there," Farah said.

"The room's locked—only he got a key. But no need to check, he took everythin' with him. I helped him pack. Carried it all down to the coach," Obed remarked.

"As I mentioned before, Lameth owns a grand estate south of Colchester. In the past, I was often invited there when he tired of the Continent. That's where we must go," Phineas said.

"What do you hope to find there, if not death?" Farah sobbed.

"Answers," he replied. "He wanted me to fulfill a particular task for him. For months, he instructed me, summoned me to Paris, taught me fragments of that wondrous language, told me I was chosen, revealed to me things unspeakable. And—if it was no illusion—one of his draughts even let me cross the threshold of death itself. Yet for all that, there were things he never told me, even to the very end. Had I not glimpsed what was forbidden, I would never have seen through his deception. And besides, I doubt it ever occurred to him that your disappearance would mean anything to me."

"Just another servant among many ..." Farah smiled wistfully.

"Friends," Obed said. "Lameth ain't got much learnin' in that."

"Yes, friends indeed!" Phineas echoed, smiling at both of them. "Let's all go to Colchester together. That way, Obed and I can look after you."

"I can't leave! I live here, in my master's house, always have!" Obed burst out, clenching his fists like a stubborn child.

"And how does your master treat you?" Phineas asked.

"He beats him, mistreats him," Farah answered in his stead.

"I can't go! I gotta guard the big door an' do what Monsieur Lameth tells me!" Obed insisted, defiance flaring in his voice.

"It's all right, Obed," Farah soothed him, placing a delicate hand on his tree-trunk arm. "I'll go with Monsieur Camill. Though I doubt I'll be of much use in such matters."

"I'll go up to my room and pack," said Phineas. "Stay here until I return!" Farah nodded and settled back beside the giant while Phineas hurried up the many steps. Once in his room, he finished dressing, pulled his suitcase out from under a cabinet, and hastily filled it with his belongings. His gaze drifted to that section of the wall, papered over, which had aroused his suspicion the very first time he had entered the room. An inner urge compelled him to examine it more closely, yet an immediate sense of dread seized him, whispering that Lameth—or one of his underlings—might appear at any moment, that speed was of the essence. So, at first, he dismissed the thought. But as he moved toward the door, the feeling grew stronger, pressing upon him with increasing insistence, until he finally set his suitcase down once more and, with the utmost composure, turned to inspect the wall.

A rectangular wooden frame, as deep as a stretcher frame, stretched across the wall, clad in thin boards and papered over. He examined the edges of the wooden paneling and found that it had been affixed to the masonry only lightly. He attempted to remove one side of the frame's structure, which at first did not yield, but then he noticed that an old knot had broken out on the back, the side facing the wall, leaving a small indentation. Into this he wedged the tip of his umbrella like a crowbar and pressed it against a stone ledge, leveraging the frame. With an ear-splitting groan, several nails came loose, and the frame yielded just enough for him to slip his fingertips into the gap and pull it away from the wall. The construction was not particularly solid, yet his umbrella had bent so far in the process that the handle snapped, leaving only the battered end, which he flung into a corner of the room with a disappointed sigh.

Within minutes, most of the wooden covering was gone. With each newly exposed square foot of wall, stripped of its concealment by his trembling, feverish hands, a most extraordinary painting was unveiled, emerging from the splintering wood and wailing nails—one such as he had never before laid eyes upon. Clearly of more recent date, the painting bore all the hallmarks of Christian iconography and yet seemed wholly out of place amid the ancient paneling that dominated the opposite wall. It was as though one had stepped, within the halls of a museum, from the relics of the Neolithic or

Early Dynastic Period straight into the world of the Netherlandish-Flemish painters of the late Gothic and Renaissance—Hieronymus Bosch, Pieter Bruegel the Elder (whom, along with his son, one might fittingly call Hell-Bruegel), or Jan Mandyn. And yet, despite these resemblances, the painting possessed an icon-like quality, not merely because of the extensive use of gold leaf, which occupied a significant portion of the composition—late Byzantine, perhaps, at most Gothic, he suspected—but rather as if a Duccio di Buoninsegna, while painting the 'Temptation of Christ on the Mountain,' had somehow anticipated the grotesque phantasmagoria of these later masters. But where the artists of that era infused every brushstroke with deeply lived piety, the unknown hand that wrought this image had done so with such brazen blasphemy that one could not but recoil in horror upon beholding it.

At first, it was not the totality of the image—this vast, vision-laden work, whose plenitude of detail unfolded only gradually—that left him utterly speechless, but rather the expression of that towering, central figure, the principal motif dominating all else, clad in a garment of resplendent magnificence and encircled by a golden mandorla that flared and shimmered like living fire. The being seemed of a timeless, otherworldly nature; an ineffable mystery—drawn from the very dawn of creation—crawled forth from the thick layers of pigment, as if the color itself exhaled a strange and ancient life. Though it bore none of the crude archaic vigor of pagan prototypes, none of the markings of a primitive faith, its visage nonetheless whispered of an antique, pre-theistic provenance, as if it had emerged from a sphere beyond the known pantheon, from that nameless, silent dawn when even the gods' names were yet unspoken. His posture and the gesture of benediction, however, bore a curiously disquieting resemblance to that of the risen Christ, as if the Son of God himself had descended to pass judgment; yet his features were wholly devoid of love or compassion for the souls immortalized in the painting. Golden locks tumbled from his brow, rendered as writhing serpents, then unfurling into spiraling coils, expanding into small vortices, winding into cylindrical forms, entwining and overlapping, turning in on themselves in a dizzying mimicry of logarithmic nautilus spirals, before cascading in magnificent waves upon his arrogantly lifted shoulders. The impression was one of movement and mathematics, of divine geometry wrought in living hair, yet simultaneously imbued with an elegance that bordered on the supernatural. His face was immaculate, of exalted, almost unearthly beauty; the chin lifted with bold defiance, the gaze cold and scornful, like frost that bites. A robe of black, woven through with threads of gold and silver, adorned with gem-set ornaments and finely cut intaglios resembling the *ephod* of antiquity, enveloped his well-proportioned frame in masterfully wrought folds, accentuating the youthful grace and statuesque poise of Apollo.

In the background of the painting rose the walls of a city with the appearance of medieval fortifications, yet they were dwarfed by the glorified figure, diminished to the scale of a miniature model by the sheer magnitude of its presence. By the depiction of the twelve pearl gates, he recognized that the city was none other than the *New Jerusalem.* All around the figure of the Redeemer, throngs of people knelt in gestures of veneration, exalting the being before them. They were so numerous that they filled every great square, every open space, and the entire surrounding landscape, stretching to the very edges of the composition. It seemed, as if the assembled multitude represented all of humanity—every soul that had ever walked the earth or ever would.

The longer he examined the work, the more details revealed themselves to his astonished gaze. Among the countless figures, some seemed more privileged than others. A select few sat on elevated platforms, their opulent robes painted with exquisite detail, marking them as figures of high status. The vast majority, however, knelt humiliated in the dust, their arms raised in submissive adoration. Yet, in stark contrast to the joy of the redeemed in the heavenly Jerusalem, those who worshipped the false god in this painting bore expressions of utter despair. Only now did Phineas fully grasp the absoluteness of their subjugation. There were no dissenters among them, no wanderers straying upon foreign paths, no lost souls seeking another way. They were all slaves, stripped of their will, bowing with downcast heads before the will of the Exalted One, in whose eyes no kindness dwelled, and from whose aura tongues of fire unfurled.

At the upper edge of the painting, separated by a vast band of clouds that spanned almost the entire composition, another scene unfolded, depicting a sequential progression of events. The being itself appeared to have ascended to the heavens, for in place of the walls, roofs, domes, turrets, oriels, and battlements of the exquisitely rendered New Jerusalem—painted in the meticulous style of early Gothic architecture—the scene now mirrored a celestial temple, and that same exalted figure sat enthroned upon a seat of flames, before which even the hosts of hell had gathered in worship. The veil that once screened this higher realm had been torn asunder and lay in two pieces upon the ground. In an escalating drama of unparalleled horror, the tableau unfolded in ghastly grotesquery, surpassing even the most nightmarish depictions of martyrdom and Christian persecution ever conceived by an artist's hand.

A bestiary of fiendish visages—dog- and goat-headed, winged, many-tailed, goat-legged, furred, and sharp-eared horrors, with taloned hands and fanged maws—defiled, tormented, or slew the prophets and saints. Lindworms, vipers, asps, and basilisks writhed amid walls of roaring flame, their gaping jaws spewing tongues of fire. Damned souls, their naked bodies twisted in agony, their skin marred by festering sores, writhed in torment with hands raised in desperate supplication. Their faces, contorted in anguish, fear, and despair, were entwined by serpents and harried by horned demons. Some prostrated themselves before the *Great Whore of Babylon*, while others roasted within the infernal furnaces of a monstrous, gaping maw. A demonic figure, almost entirely reduced to skeletal remains, holding a scythe and an hourglass, pronounced judgment upon the angels who had refused to renounce their allegiance, condemning them to eternal torment and the second death in the fires of hell. The twelve apostles of the new covenant and the patriarchs of the holy tribes stood there, their garments soiled, their golden crowns trampled into the dust. Even the sacred beasts that Ezekiel and John beheld lay bound upon the ground, stripped of their wings, their eyes darkened and blind. Behind this harrowing vision, creation itself groaned as though on the verge of annihilation, and a swirling chaos of unformed matter threatened to consume all and cast it into the abyss of darkness.

He searched for the image of the Lamb, that central figure of the revealed world's end, yet he could not find it anywhere upon the painting, as if the artist had either forgotten to depict it or—far more plausibly, given the enormity of the scene—had deliberately chosen to omit it. And then he saw it: the Lamb, cast down, lying headlong upon the ground, crushed beneath the right foot of the Usurper. The revelation struck him with sudden force. Each single pigment upon the painted wall, layered in its subtractive interplay to form this blasphemous vision, now seemed to pulse, to radiate with newfound intensity, searing itself into his very soul. Then, in a swirling maelstrom of incandescent colors and the abyssal darkness of the overarching void, the image whirled before Phineas, who lowered his gaze, near to succumbing to unconsciousness.

Then he realized, with a sudden start, how long he had lingered before the painting. Even as he turned away, he wrestled with the significance of what he had seen, and with the part Lameth might play within that shadowed design. It was evident that the man, eccentric as he was, derived a singular delight from such curiosities—this occult, morbidly tinged artistry—not least when one considered the selection of readings he had commanded Phineas to study. Yet why, he wondered, could such a work—where beauty and corruption entwined so intimately—so captivate the soul? Who could measure where, beyond the threshold of perception, the sublime gives way to the uncanny, how narrow the ridge upon which fascination turns to horror, when a work of art touches the innermost recesses of the observer, setting hidden chords in vibration, unlocking chambers of the mind long sealed? Or had the contemplation of this blasphemous image merely terrified him, compelling him to veil it from himself? For a brief instant, doubt assailed Phineas: was he wrong to mistrust Lameth, and were the visions he had previously beheld under the potion's influence nothing but illusions conjured by a fevered imagination? Yet then he thought of Farah, of the suffering inflicted upon her, and the swirling thoughts of the painting dispersed like mist before the rising sun. He gathered his belongings, leaving behind only the now superfluous umbrella, and hurried down the corridor, the spiraling staircase unfurling beneath his feet, until he rejoined those who awaited him.

He stepped over the threshold into Obed's chamber, where the giant cowered in a corner, looking as if he had lost his wits from sheer terror, while Farah sat on the bed, sobbing and utterly distraught. The floor was strewn with his belongings. In the midst of the disarray lay an aged woman, her body twisted into an unnatural, grotesque posture, as though her neck had been snapped by a tremendous force. A riding crop was clutched in her lifeless hand, and her glassy, widened eyes still bore, even in death, the same malice that had once hardened her stern, furrowed face. Long, sharply drawn welts—deep red against the swollen skin—crisscrossed Farah's arms and legs, vivid testaments to the torment she had endured. Phineas took in the scene in an instant. "It seems our circumstances have changed," he remarked. "So be it, then—we shall now be three on our journey to England."

CHAPTER IX.
ARTHEMOSOS'S OPENER OF WORLDS

A cold gust swept over the burial grounds, which rose from a plateau along the flank of the great mountain, as if the peak had been severed with the stroke of a blade. The enclosing walls and supporting structures, the stone balustrades, pillars, braces, balconies, and turrets had been carved into the rock and fused with it, as though they had grown from its very substance. A rocky overhang shielded this part of the city from the fierce winds that, at times, howled with unbridled force against the mountain's slopes. A narrow ridge led high into the peaks, their jagged spires piercing the drifting clouds like the foundations of a celestial city. Beyond, an unbroken chain of gray-blue, snow-covered mountains stretched into the distance, their forms fading into the hazy vastness of the horizon, where no discernible beginning or end could be seen. The sun-wheel stood high in the sky. Infinite particles of light, moving with the swiftness that belongs to their kind, streamed down to the earth, settling warmly upon the skin of those gathered. And yet the air was cool, the wind relentless, and the many-colored robes of the Elders—woven through with golden and silver threads—fluttered in the gusts like a sea of resplendent banners.

Before a titanic mausoleum that jutted from the mountainside, a great stone tribune had been erected, upon which the council members had assembled in a half-circle. Some distance below, the people had gathered, seated upon the cold stone, on raised platforms and benches, or standing closely together with bowed heads. Overhead, brightly feathered Gryftares, their talons sharp and their long claws curved like hunting knives, glided upon outstretched wings beneath the unraveling wisps of cloud. With sudden, reckless dives, they plunged into the abyss below, only to catch themselves in the updraft of a fierce wind, their harsh, croaking cries echoing through the chasm. A lone voice rose in a solemn melody, its cadence meandering through the cool air, until at last, upon reaching a certain refrain, it was taken up by hundreds of voices in unison, carried forth in a chorus of resounding harmony. As the final note faded, Chirion's voice arose—clear and resonant, magnified by some architectural artifice, and underscored by the eternal roar of the wind. His words, imbued with deep compassion and solemn grandeur, wove through the gathering like a sacred current. And in time, there was not a single eye that did not glisten with silent tears.

Several corpses, all victims of the nocturnal assault, had been laid out in solemn display. And yet, despite their soulless existence, they seemed imbued with an eerie vitality, kneeling with their hands raised toward the heavens as though lost in reverent supplication. A treacherous gust of wind lifted the white funeral shrouds, revealing a cruel certainty—the rigid wooden framework beneath, to which their limp limbs had been bound with firm cords, artfully simulating the posture of the living. Chirion's gaze fell upon the withered, emaciated form of the librarian, crouched among the motionless as if a shriveled relic of death itself. A thick layer of chalk-white paint, cracked like parched clay, covered his ravaged skin and the scars of his martyrdom. Upon his closed eyelids, two lifeless, painted eyes stared forth in unsettling stillness. A man, his robes marking him as a priest, moved with measured steps among the assembled dead. Murmuring an incantatory chant, he raised his hand over each of the lifeless forms, bestowing a ritual blessing. Dipping his fingers into a broad, shallow offering bowl—no wider than two outstretched palms—he traced slow, ceremonial gestures in the air before casting dark droplets upon their vacant brows. Then, without another word, he turned and withdrew into the ranks of his robed brethren, vanishing into the solemn company of the officiants.

At that moment, another group entered the scene—no priests, but performers of a mystery play, draped in resplendent robes of exquisite fabrics, among them some whose faces lay concealed behind masks of beaten gold. Their expressions were solemn, their bearing grave. Not a sound, not a whisper, not the flicker of an eyebrow disturbed the hush that weighed upon the assembled crowd. Thus began the play, a symbol of passage, unfolding in the liminal sphere between shadow and light—not in literal depiction, but through symbols: A veil, stretched between two pillars, undulating in shimmering waves like an opal, revealing itself as the threshold that could be crossed only through the right signs, the right words, the right rites—a visible barrier dividing the world of the living from the unseen realm beyond. It was as though one beheld a wall of hardened mist, a dream left unfinished by the centuries. Behind it shimmered an otherworldly splendor of mirror-like surfaces, many-tongued flames, and wavering light that refracted upon the numinous figures who stood as intermediaries between the realms. And the performers, the players, the veiled ones—they knew they were not mere actors or mimics, not merely, as is the way of traveling troupes, devoted to outward spectacle and the vanity of the pose, and what they conveyed was not contained in those elaborate gestures or practiced movements with which stage plays were performed in the markets and squares of the world. No—it was not something that could be enacted with masks and well-spoken words, but a mystery governed by a secret, ineffable ritual, one that lay beyond the realm of sight. For they were the heralds of a play older than those who performed it, older even than those who had gathered to witness it—perhaps a play whose symbols were as ancient as humanity itself, its origins buried in depths of time beyond the reckoning of any among them. Their dark garments, embroidered with crescent moons and astrological sigils, stirred in the chill air with a hushed murmuring, as if the fabric in which they were enshrouded was woven not merely from earthly threads, but from the very substance of forgotten dreams, from the fleeting visions that visit mortals in the twilight of sleep, only to vanish, swept away by the morning into the night from whence they came. Ancient, fearsome syllables lay upon their lips, utterances from a tongue spoken only in the dreams of the dead—an echo of the first rays that fell upon the mute, primeval waters of the world when time itself was born.

One among them, towering above all others by virtue of a hidden foundation, rose before the image of a vast and intricate labyrinth—a maze that, from the perspective of the onlookers, lay interposed between the veil and that realm of light, unfolding into symbolic chambers, passageways, and false doors, an illusion of an insurmountable barrier. Though wrought by the hands of mortal builders, it bore within it something of the cold logic of beings from beyond, of the spectral geometry of celestial cities that reared themselves up in impossible angles, bending and spiraling as though in obeisance to a gravity unknown, to an order beyond reckoning. Along its walls shimmered inscriptions and glyphs of arcane provenance, as if not carved, but rather grown from the very fabric of the stone—symbols poised at the threshold between ornament and script, belonging to an age before there was distinction between that which was written and that which, in the world of primordial forms, had always been; before there was separation between thought and the immutable. This guardian bore no likeness to man, nor had he been fashioned in the semblance of one—a being of terrible majesty, his limbs encased in burning metal that glowed, shimmered, and blazed in the celestial light. In his hands he held a weapon whose blade was not forged, but shaped from the serrated waves of living flame. His countenance was shrouded by a grotesque mask, one that consumed his entire head and spilled down upon his breastplate, affixed at the crown by a towering headdress. Its expression was an enigma of severity—arched brows, drawn sharply downward, meeting at the center in a furrow of deeply hammered lines, the contorted furrows of titanic wrath. His eyes, mere slits, peered forth from beneath this dreadful visage; and his mouth, gaping wide in a near-rectangular grimace, curved downward as if in lament, a mournful echo of those masks of ancient tragedy, flowing at its base into the twisted strands of a long, cascading beard.

Other players, clad in white robes, their faces painted, drew one of the dead toward the illusory model of that insurmountable threshold, the motion so smooth and imperceptible that only the faintest whisper of hidden wheels betrayed the mechanism beneath. One among them, his hands raised in gestures of benediction, adorned in a robe whose winged embellishments at the shoulders marked him as one of those exalted beings, stepped forward. Upon the brow of the departed, he placed crowns of power, affixed small parchments inscribed with cryptic symbols and sigils upon the death shroud, and anointed the lifeless form beneath the murmured words of an ancient liturgy, its whispered mysteries dissolving into the wind like breath upon glass. Then the guardian inclined his head, inspecting in timeless silence the attached scrolls and the messages they bore, listening to the words of one of the bearers, who now assumed the role of an intercessor. At last, as if some unseen decree had been granted, he stepped aside, and in solemn procession, they bore the departed along a path that—through the unseen workings of a hidden lever—suddenly and seamlessly revealed itself, leading in a straight course toward the veil. And there, before that wavering threshold, the final act commenced, yet so cunningly were the elements arranged that from the vantage of the assembled throng, none could glimpse the unspeakable rites enacted beyond that spectral boundary. When at last each of the departed had been ushered forth in the same manner, the sacred play concluded as it had begun, with a chorus rising from the multitude—yet no longer was it a dirge of sorrow, but a hymn suffused with hope, its tones resounding in jubilation.

And when the song had faded, and the great expanse of the square gradually emptied, the participants returned to the course of their daily labors. Countless voices, rougher now with the cadence of common life, mingled in the streets and marketplaces, filling the thoroughfares with the bustle of the living world. And as the first merchants raised their voices to hawk their wares, as the smoke of burning wood curled into the sky, and the cries of children wove themselves into the clamor of the day, they were gone—the players, the veiled ones, the initiates of the mysteries, vanished with their golden masks, their dark robes, their fine voices that left no echo behind. No sign, no trace, no flickering shadow remained to betray that they had ever stood here, that ever a play was performed, that ever an offering had been made.

Myrgil nodded graciously at Chirion as he passed, placing his sinewy hand upon his shoulder. Golden rings adorned his knotted fingers, and heavy bracelets encircled his aged wrists. "Elevating words, indeed! For a blessed moment, I believed myself at the dawn of all things." His bearing, awe-inspiring as ever, gave the impression that he was bestowing praise upon a subordinate or a servant rather than an equal.

"I am gladdened to hear this. Your words give me new hope in these times of grief, O venerable Myrgil. Now that the dead have been honored and guided across, I pray we shall find answers as to what nameless enemy has inflicted such sorrow upon us," Chirion replied with a strained smile.

"Whoever is responsible shall be held to account and face justice. As the first step in uncovering the truth, I have compiled the information you requested. Furthermore, the Council has unanimously appointed me to oversee this investigation in an official capacity—provided, of course, that you have no objections." He regarded Chirion with a measured expression.

"None at all. Speak freely!"

"Nothing has been stolen save that one object entrusted to our safekeeping long ago—nothing of such value that we should greatly trouble ourselves. For days, an extensive inventory has been underway, cross-referencing the registries, and meanwhile, your friend appears to have vanished from the infirmary and now prowls through the lower halls like a chattering mummy, badgering my men and distracting them from their work. It seems that one or two of the forbidden tomes from the crypt are unaccounted for—provided, of course, that the old registries are accurate. More details will be delivered to me shortly. Beyond that, we have found no clues that would reveal our foe, save for the dagger that, in the most spectacular and inimitable manner, was left in this fool's hands."

"I must ask you not to speak so of the Keeper of the Citadel and the Hidden Chamber!" Chirion shot back, his voice edged with anger. "Few remain in whom I place my trust these days. But tell me quickly—what have you uncovered?"

"It is a crude weapon— a plain, double-edged dagger, akin to those once wielded by the wild tribes of old. We subjected it to an alchemical dating process, and there is no doubt: it is an artifact of ancient times. The blade is blackened, clearly to obscure its betraying glint when drawn in the commission of its grisly purpose. Beyond that, our examination revealed nothing remarkable—no poisons, no vile enchantments of the dark arts. There were no inscriptions, no owner's marks, no smith's insignia, no crest, nor any such embellishment one might expect to find upon a weapon of station—not that I would have anticipated such a thing upon an instrument of murder." He paused, his lips curling into a frown. "As for the iron door leading to the forbidden archive, as well as the fortified entrance to the adytum—both were torn from the very walls by an explosion. The demolition master has been standing before the wreckage for two days, staring at the scorch marks as if he expects them to learn to speak. At the very least, he has managed to stammer out an admission: he has never in his life seen such a concentrated and ferocious detonation."

"So we are, evidently, still at the very beginning." Chirion assumed a downcast expression.

"By no means. I have yet to mention the traces left behind at Misraihl's dwelling—assuming, of course, that the perpetrators are indeed the same individuals or at least belong to the same faction, which, given the current state of affairs, seems a reasonable assumption. We have uncovered a great many traces and other evidence. They are being analyzed as we speak and examined by a master in the field. It appears that old Misraihl sought to leave us some manner of clue before he breathed his last. However, I fear that in your efforts to lift him down from that cabinet, you have inadvertently ruined whatever final message he intended for us." Myrgil regarded Chirion with a critical eye.

"Forgive me. Grief had overwhelmed me, and I failed to exhibit the proper composure one ought to maintain in such circumstances," Chirion replied with feigned contrition. Yet within him, anger stirred, mingled with sorrow, and he longed to confront Myrgil over his veiled accusations.

A man, whose attire marked him as a member of the Watch, approached in hurried efficiency, bowed first to Chirion, then wordlessly handed Myrgil a document before taking his leave with another deferential nod. Myrgil perused the parchment for what felt like an eternity, without so much as a glance in Chirion's direction. His weary, timeworn features darkened perceptibly. When at last his gaze reached the final line, his eyelids lifted with an unnatural lethargy, and his pale blue eyes, glazed with a film of moisture, fixed upon Chirion with an expression of profound sorrow. "Why," he murmured, "would anyone steal an object of such perilous significance—and with it, the secret edition of Arthemosos's 'The Opener of Worlds' and the sealed seventh volume of the 'Chronicles of Nemiáh'?"

"Perhaps you might enlighten me, wise Myrgil!" Chirion countered, weary of the secrecy and the pompous air that Myrgil had assumed since acquiring his newfound authority.

"No one surpasses you in erudition and sagacity, O Chirion, and the hidden knowledge preserved within those halls has long since revealed itself to your wisdom."

"Those who stole the scroll entrusted to our keeping would, through Arthemosos's work, gain certain insights into the worlds beyond our own, acquiring, incidentally, a knowledge fraught with grave peril—peril for those whose righteousness is but a fragile veneer. Though I would not go so far as to call it a precise manual, it is of great utility for understanding that which lies beyond. The knowledge contained within that book can also be found elsewhere, at least in fragments—though only if one knows where to look. And whoever already knew of the hidden relic within the secret chamber would have had little need of the sealed volume of the 'Chronicles,' even though that tome lays bare some of the darker paths and expounds upon the scroll and its manifold possibilities. But tell me—how could such a thing be possible? The intruder had mere minutes. He could hardly have scoured a thousand-volume archive in search of suitable reading material."

"And yet, you readily concede that it is within the realm of possibility that a thief, intent upon studying that relic, might take a work covering the same subject as an aid to his research?" Myrgil's sagging lower eyelid twitched involuntarily.

"Your choice of words intrigues me. Am I under interrogation?"

"By no means, dear friend. Yet it falls to me to bring the hidden into the light, and I trust you are well aware that I have always been meticulous and diligent in my duties." His luminous blue eyes glinted with an implacable resolve.

"Nothing I have said, nor anything I believe, casts doubt upon your competence. But speak plainly—what truly weighs upon your mind?"

"You yourself just stated that it would have been impossible, in the brief span of time afforded to this attack, to uncover such a secret. And as only a select few were privy to such matters, I took the liberty—foreseeing the necessity—to have the chambers and quarters of those belonging to this esteemed circle searched by official decree—my own, of course, not excepted—whilst we attended the final rites of the departed. I trust that, in retrospect, you shall find this course of action to be both appropriate and necessary, given the gravity of the situation. Yet, what must shake you to the core, just as it has shaken me, is that the very writings in question were discovered within your own dwelling, more precisely, in the chambers of your foster daughter. You would do well to teach your winged pet some manners—it has torn a man's ear clean off and very nearly gouged out another's eye. You may believe me when I say that it grieves me no less than it must grieve you that my initial suspicions have, regrettably, been confirmed—Jahdis is, in some capacity, entangled in these events, even if only by having revealed such perilous knowledge to those who wrought this unthinkable suffering."

"Jahdis? Have you lost your senses? Most likely, it was merely an oversight in the records—that she took the books for study. How dare you utter such a vile and simultaneously ludicrous accusation! Moreover, she was with me at the time of the crime, as you well know. I myself saw her to bed."

"Study? Saw her to bed? She is no child anymore. I anticipated that you would be biased and leap to her defense. You, above all, know that nothing dwelling within that chamber ought ever to be beheld in the light of day. And Niahl...," he paused for a long moment and smiled with thinly veiled condescension, "the Guardian of the Citadel and the Hidden Chamber—why not the Keeper of Alharion's very own treasury while we're at it?—has assured me that these works, owing to their dubious nature, were ever kept under lock and key, even within those sanctums unperceived by mortal eyes, and, mind you, despite the persistent urgings of your foster daughter. Which, of course, raises the rather pertinent question: how did she come to know of them in the first place?"

"A reference in some text. Good God, her mind is always buried in books—she must have picked it up somewhere along the way."

"As I have already stated, I fully expected you to be biased. But do not be a fool—the weight of the evidence is crushing. I am left with no choice but to initiate an inquiry. Jahdis must answer to us and to the Creator, and if she is indeed innocent, she has nothing to fear, I assure you." Chirion looked at him imploringly, his features etched with deep sorrow and concern. Myrgil summoned a guardsman, who had been leaning against a house wall alongside a group of his kind, engaged in lively discussion. Bowing his head slightly, he murmured an order to the man, who then returned to his comrades and, after a brief but heated exchange, took his leave. One of the guards, his head wrapped in fresh bandages, cast Chirion a dark, lingering look as he departed. "Surely, you will have no objections to accompanying me, noble Chirion," Myrgil said.

"By no means, Myrgil," Chirion replied, following the man who strode ahead with firm purpose, his own head bowed in dejection. Guilt weighed heavily upon him. He berated himself for having removed Misraihl's final message, believing in his arrogance that such exclusive knowledge would grant him an advantage—an edge that would allow him to guide the investigation as he saw fit, to lull the culprit into false security, to catch him through some cunning stratagem, some twist of fate, or sheer carelessness. But Myrgil had outmaneuvered him, and now Jahdis was to bear the brunt of it—perhaps even suffer for it.

As they approached the grand council hall, they passed by Chirion's residence. The heavy door stood ajar, and from within came the clamor of raised voices, shouts, and the unmistakable sounds of a struggle. He recognized Jahdis's agitated voice, followed by a bloodcurdling snarl and the sharp crack of splintering wood. A chorus of agonized cries and curses erupted. Like a storm loosed from its chains, Xerxes burst through the open doorway, his passage sundering one of the side panels, sending it clattering to the ground with its hinges torn clean from the frame. Jahdis followed, her garment in tatters, blood trickling down her temple. In one fluid motion, she vaulted onto Xerxes's back just as Myrgil stepped into their path. "Halt at once, ward of Chirion! Do not make this worse than it already is—if not for your own sake, then for the memory of your father!"

Xerxes reared up, pinning Myrgil beneath his razor-sharp talons in a swift, predatory motion. Golden buttons sprang from his brocade like glistening frogs leaping from the necropolis-cloaked jungles of Serthophiél in the heart of Zaranabáth, and the many-layered, richly dyed fabric gave way with a tearing sound. The fearsome beak, poised and gaping, descended to hover menacingly just above Myrgil's unprotected throat. "No, Jahdis—don't!" cried Chirion, throwing out his arms protectively between them.

"Father, I am innocent!" Jahdis cried out from the back of the feathered beast. "A stranger approached me some moons ago on market day, across from the Red Tavern, and told me strange tales of hidden books that promised answers to my most pressing questions. But Niahl refused to give them to me, even denied their existence, though I found entries in the old records that confirmed they were real. I had to read them, don't you understand? Do you not know what is whispered about me behind closed doors? That I come from beyond the black door. You always kept me in the dark about my origins—do you know how much I have suffered in silence? I had nothing to do with this crime, you must believe me! And never have I spoken of the secrets that lie beyond the iron gate."

"Jahdis, I believe your every word. My silence weighs heavy on me now that I see what it has led to. But please, bid Xerxes to stand down, or you will only make matters worse! The Council is wise and just—you must face the accusations so that the truth may come to light! If only you could trust me again."

Tears welled in Jahdis's eyes. She was already on the verge of dismounting, ready to soothe the mighty beast, which, agitated by her turmoil, trembled like a volcano on the brink of eruption. It teetered on the edge of its primal instincts, slipping from her control. But before she could act, a group of armed men, bleeding from many wounds, emerged from the wrecked doorway, pursuing her. The one with the fresh head bandage was in the midst of loading a battered and dented firearm, while others, brandishing long spears, prepared to bring Xerxes down. The heaving mountain of muscle and feathers pivoted toward them, tracing a slow semicircle, its curved, dagger-like talons clawing at the ground. Then, in one swift motion, it threw its head back and parted its terrifying beak in a piercing, guttural cry.

"Father, speak now! Are the rumors true? Do I come from beyond the forbidden door?"

"Yes!" Chirion shouted, his face twisted in horror. At that moment, with only a whispered command, Xerxes lifted into the air, its mighty wings carrying it skyward within moments. It soared beyond reach. A single shot rang out, shattering the silence. Jahdis's body slumped sideways, seeming to slip from the beast's back. For several harrowing seconds, her fingers groped desperately at its feathers—then she held firm. The winged creature beat the air with powerful strokes, climbing higher and higher, until it was nothing more than a vanishing speck on the horizon.

"Seize him!" Myrgil commanded, his voice unshaken by the display. The guards rushed at Chirion but hesitated, casting uncertain glances at Myrgil, searching his stern gaze for confirmation before laying hands on him. Chirion was defeated, offering no resistance. As he was led away, the people of the mountain city bowed their heads in solemn reverence, wringing their hats in their hands, their thoughts troubled with the same unspoken question: What terrible misfortune had now befallen them?

CHAPTER X.
IN THE CRATER MOUNTAINS OF NEÈBH

Xerxes pierced through an elongated band of clouds, let himself be carried upwards by a gust of wind, then plunged downward through jagged ravines, along sheer cliffs that dropped steeply, their barren, moss- and fern-covered surfaces spilling into scree-strewn valleys. It must have been late afternoon when they passed the eastern reaches of the Shadow Range, that immense mountain chain which, curving like a great horseshoe around a somber valley, rose in dizzying asymmetry to those menacing peaks known as the Crater Mountains of Neèbh. Layer upon layer of naked rock stretched into the distance, rising like the ridged back of a primordial beast from the shadowed green of the valley floor. The mighty griffin-creature flew with powerful wingbeats over the jagged ridges of mist-veiled summits, pressing ever onward into that enchanted land where the lightless halls and deep chasms at the foot of the inhospitable mountains had once been home to a wild race that, millennia ago, dwelled in the valley of Amoneáth and the Crater Mountains. Dusk began to fall, and the sky, a splendor of purple, violet, and smouldering orange, flared around the golden sun, turning the mountain slopes into molten rivers of fire.

Jahdis lay crouched against the beast's furred back, arms wrapped tightly around its iron-strong neck, her exhausted head nestled into the warmth of its golden feathers. The relentless wind tore through the wild strands of her hair, its icy breath lashing against every unshielded inch of her skin. Eventually, her strength failed, and the cruel shard of steel embedded in her side, claiming her life hour by hour, robbed her of her senses. She surrendered the creature, released it—the being whose soul she had once explored in patient silence, the one she had summoned in the old tongue and bound with a perfect name. But that name remained hidden, for once she had called the beast and it had yielded to the power of the true name, she cloaked it in an ordinary one—a name devoid of sorcery, a name she had stumbled upon, almost absently, in the Chronicles of Nemiáh. For she knew that whoever learned the true name and spoke it in the first of all languages, whoever could shape it upon their lips with perfect clarity, would wield dominion over the beast and mastery over its kind.

As she drifted into the twilight of unconsciousness, her final thought lingered on Chirion—how he had furrowed his mighty brow and laughed heartily when she, in one of her cherished history lessons, had bestowed upon the then-young creature, barely the height of a man and only just having developed its plumage, such a peculiar and yet imperious name. But Chirion, versed in the knowledge of the Elders, who understood the hidden enchantment in the act of naming and the nature of that perfect language whose mastery bestowed dominion over the fabled winged being, had held his silence. He had even permitted the wild creature to dwell in the vast garden of the atrium, where it lacked for nothing. In truth, for the sake of seeing the great, tear-brimmed eyes of his foster daughter gleam with joy, it would have sufficed him if the feathered beast merely spared his life for a few days—but in time, the creature grew tame, even affectionate, and he no longer feared for his safety when left alone in the house. At some point, the name had woven itself so intimately into the being's essence that secrecy was no longer required to call it thus. But the true name—Jahdis kept that buried deep within her heart.

At last, consciousness slipped from her grasp, and it seemed as though she plunged into the infinity of a dark abyss, the world rushing past like a stormwind. Then, all at once, she felt a gentle grasp, and after an indeterminate span, the embrace of the cold, rocky ground upon which she was carefully laid. She moaned in pain and drew her legs up against her chest like an infant. A damp, dark-red stain had claimed her garment from the base of her throat to her waist. Dried blood clung to her unruly hair and traced a thin rivulet down her pallid cheek. The great beast lay beside her, shielding her beneath the span of its outstretched wing. A merciful oblivion dulled the cruel hardness of the stone beneath her and the searing agony smouldering in her side, guiding her into a restless slumber, fevered and pained. She awoke long before the first light of dawn. The winged creature raised its head and regarded her uncertainly. She cast a pleading gaze around, but in the murky gloom, heavy beneath the wan moon-discs, only gray and indistinct shapes loomed about her and her companion—barren stone and gnarled branches melding into fantastic formations, indifferent to her suffering. At the eastern horizon, lightning flickered, igniting the distant mountain peaks in eerie bursts against the cloud-laden night sky. "You must hurry—find help! I am dying," she spoke to the creature in her mind, before her strength failed once more, and she sank back into darkness.

Jahdis awoke, blinking drowsily, nestled in the unexpected comfort of a bed. With half-closed eyes, she traced the rough-woven fabric that covered her, its warmth having driven out the bitter chill of her inhospitable rocky resting place. She lifted a hand to her side, cautiously feeling the wound that now lay hidden beneath thick bandages—no longer searing her into oblivion. Laboriously, she pried her eyes open, struggling to accustom herself to the piercing midday light that poured in unrestrained through a square ceiling shaft directly above her. Xerxes was gone, and it seemed to her that she was utterly alone. Someone had redressed her and tended to the wound upon her head.

As her vision slowly cleared, she began to discern the jagged contours of a cavernous vault, its full expanse beyond her reckoning, for it stretched unseen into shadowy depths at her feet and widened behind her into a vast hall, its immensity upheld by mighty pillars. From its center, multiple arched passages radiated outward in a circle, much like the one in which she lay. The place was in disarray. Vast quantities of provisions were piled haphazardly to either side of the cavern or stowed in storage chambers and recesses hewn roughly into the rock walls. Amidst heaps of refuse and carelessly discarded belongings, countless barrels, crates stacked upon one another in precarious towers, and—time and again—pyramids of muskets loomed in numbers befitting an army preparing for war.

Jahdis bent her legs to rise—only then noticing a strange numbness in her ankle. A heavy iron shackle encased it, its links winding into a long, slender chain that trailed across the stone floor before vanishing into an iron ring fixed into the wall. "Drink this!" a venomous voice hissed. It issued from the shadow towering above her, seemingly born from nothingness, before rough hands pressed a vessel against her lips, forcing some bitter draught down her throat. She coughed, involuntarily swallowing part of the liquid, and almost at once, a heavy darkness seized her—dragging her into a sleep riddled with fevered nightmares.

She awoke in the dead of night to a spectral world of blazing torches, their flames flickering across the curved, night-darkened rock walls of an underground grotto, accompanied by the steady pulse of ceremonial chants and the rhythmic pounding of drums. It seemed to be one of those ancient sanctuaries where the people who once called these lands their home had worshiped their dreadful chthonic gods—beings whose essence they had drawn from the very forces of nature. Veins of gleaming ore ran like molten rivers through the stone, which twisted and branched into a crude tracery of towering, interwoven pillars—gnarled and rootlike—resembling the trunks of colossal trees that upheld the cavern's walls. High above, they merged into a vast, forestlike vault of titanic proportions. Crude paintings in black, red, and ochre—testaments to that primitive culture—adorned the walls, their abstract patterns, stenciled pigments, and chiseled contours revealing the sacred dread of that primordial creed. At the apex of the cavernous dome, a great funnel yawned open, through which a sliver of the star-flecked sky was visible—an ocean of silent, night-black depths rebelling against the flickering torchlight that played upon the walls.

Jahdis crouched apart from the gathering, confined within the damp enclosure of a primitive stone cell, its hewn walls sprouting shackles for hands and feet. The wound at her side throbbed as though it had festered. She rubbed the stiffness from her limbs, her breath catching as she beheld the unsettling scene before her. Dark silhouettes—figures draped in long black robes—moved in slow procession around a central point, where a stark, unadorned altar rose from the cavern floor. Strange inscriptions, carved in crude, jagged strokes, covered its vertical sides—mystic remnants of a long-forgotten superstition. Not far from the altar, the erratic glow beyond the iron bars of her cell revealed a grotesque heap of lifeless bodies, their limbs twisted at unnatural angles. Even from a distance, she could see the telltale marks of violence upon them, as though they had fallen victim to some dreadful rite—perhaps the very ritual whose screams had haunted her nightmares.

"Does the inquisitive little child enjoy our nocturnal gathering?" whispered a voice at her back, jolting her from her motionless astonishment.

Jahdis spun around in alarm. "Who are you? I know your voice!"

From the interplay of darkness and firelight emerged the mocking grin of a pale man—hairless and beardless, save for his thick, prominent brows. The flickering glow cast shifting shadows across his deep-set eye sockets, lending his gaunt skull a skeletal aspect. Within those hollows gleamed a pair of piercing eyes, their gaze auguring nothing good. His nose was curved like the beak of a raptor, yet rugged and crooked, as though it had suffered more than one grievous injury. His mouth, its corners sloping downward ever so slightly, was little more than a pallid line. One could not call him ugly, and yet there was nothing remotely pleasing about his face. His features were like weathered stone, devoid of tenderness, warmth, or any of those subtle traces of expression that bestow upon the human countenance its semblance of emotion. It was as though the passage of some joyless fate had eroded and, in time, utterly effaced them. And yet, his visage was fearsome, steely-willed, and unyielding—the face of one who tolerated no defiance. A leader to whom men might look for guidance, yet at the same time the most formidable of enemies to any who dared betray him. His form, half-hidden beneath the dark cloak that cascaded down his back, bore the posture of a man who had spent the greater part of his life bent over books. He seemed well past the zenith of his years, though his coarse physiognomy made it difficult to discern his true age.

"In Alharion's name! It is you, truly!" Jahdis breathed. "It was you who, on market day, led me to that sealed volume of the 'Chronicles of Nemiáh'—and to that other book, that accursed and far more dreadful tome which Arthemoso once penned in that very place! Your venomous whisperings nearly cost me my life—and have likely broken my father's heart. No doubt it was you who stole that secret thing and murdered poor Misraihl. Tell me—what is your name?"

"I am nameless," the man replied, "only a servant of a greater master. For many long years, I have sought knowledge of such things—and let me assure you, fragments of the ancient wisdom persist beyond the white walls, slumbering unseen in hidden places, beneath the crumbling stones of darkened altars. This is a lesson these so-called keepers of wisdom, in their arrogance, never so much as considered."

"Whatever it is you intend," Jahdis retorted, "I will not help you!"

"How do you suppose I could have found the books I sought in that chamber of dead faith in the short time before the sentinels arrived? It was you who aided me. You were my accomplice in obtaining the knowledge for which I thirsted."

Jahdis shut her eyes, and tears streamed down her cheeks. Her entire body trembled as she thought of her hasty flight, of the disappointment in Chirion's face, and of the painful certainty that she would never again return to the Holy Mountain. She thought, too, of how foolish and willful her actions had been. But then, suddenly, she lifted her head in defiant pride, casting aside what little remained of the frightened girl she had once been. She drew in a deep breath through her nose, then slowly opened her tear-stained eyes—now narrowed with fury. "You are too late! The books you lured me into stealing have been found and returned to the safekeeping of the secret chamber. The White City is not without its defenses—you may be certain that you will never again be granted such an opportunity in your wretched life!"

One of his bony fingers darted through the iron bars and dug harshly into her forehead. "Foolish girl! Everything we need lies within this lovely little head of yours." Blood trickled from the wound as he withdrew his finger, sending her reeling backward. "You should never have meddled in affairs that do not concern you," he sneered. "But you have studied the forbidden knowledge—just as I foresaw. And tell me, is there a greater sin than such arrogant curiosity?" He laughed, a cruel and gloating sound.

"I will not aid you!" she declared, her voice resolute. "Sooner may the stars fall from the heavens and the wild sea be stilled!" Yet even as she spoke, uncertainty crept upon her, the full realization of her helpless predicament pressing heavily upon her mind.

"Believe me," he said, "there are ways to loosen your tongue. Tell me—how do you suppose I made the old man talk? At first, I gleaned the occasional scrap of knowledge from his idle prattling, coaxed out over a cup of wine. But in the end, I wrenched each of his words from him by means of torments beyond your feeble imagination. The old man was steadfast—one must grant him that—but in the end, everyone speaks..." He paused briefly before continuing, his voice steeped in self-congratulatory satisfaction. "I pondered long over the best course of action. It would have been a simple matter to claim the books for myself once you had stolen them for me. What is Chirion's house, after all, compared to the steel-bound gates of the secret chamber? But then there was that winged beast, nesting in the atrium like some rock-dwelling predator—and no doubt, in your naïve honesty, you would have reported the theft, sealing the chamber against me forever. Thus, my plan had to be intricate, woven with utmost precision: I had to strip the stubborn old man of his hidden knowledge—and of his miserable life—while gaining access to the secret archives, while obtaining the artifact of power, while securing the books. Or, if that should fail, I needed at the very least to take possession of you. But then, before the ponderous Chirion could piece together a single coherent thought, that meddling fool arrived and threw everything into disarray. And yet, as it seems, fate has once again favored me. For while I was wracking my mind over how my men might seize you, your pet delivered you straight to my doorstep from the skies." His lips curled into a slow, silent smile of triumph. "But listen now! The time has come!" He raised a single finger to his ear, as though listening intently for some distant sound.

Jahdis focused on the sounds surrounding her. The chanting had grown steadily louder, rising into an infernal crescendo—an insane, frenzied outcry—before it ceased all at once, so abruptly that it was as though the gathered assembly had been struck speechless. The Nameless One turned away from her, retrieving some object he had placed upon a rocky ledge. He obscured his features with it before stepping into the throng of hooded figures, who stood in feverish anticipation. Jahdis could make out only parts of his form among the dark-robed congregation, but it seemed to her that he wore a mask, one that vaguely suggested the features of some bizarre beast—its upper contours twisting grotesquely into the semblance of horns or pointed ears. He unlocked a long, narrow chest that was handed to him by trembling hands and withdrew from it a peculiar scroll, which seemed to gleam strangely in the darkness, caught in the swirling interplay of torchlight and shadow. Lifting it high like a trophy in one hand, he unfurled it with the other, as though it were a banner. A collective gasp rose from the crowd, swelling into a cry of ecstatic triumph that reverberated through the shadow-cloaked vault.

Moving shapes—rotating, shifting, ever-changing—emerged upon the scroll's surface. Symbols and glyphs of white fire gleamed with an unearthly radiance, a purity unseen before, as though they were a reflection of the countless stars and galaxies stretching across the firmament above the crater's yawning mouth. And now Jahdis saw his face—or rather, the place where a face should have been. For what stared back at her was the grotesque skull of a wolf-headed idol, risen anew from the abyss of some dark, godless past. The drums resumed their steady beat as the wolf-creature in their midst handed the scroll to one standing near. Then, raising an ornate silver chalice to the maw of that unspeakable, blasphemous mask, he drank deep of a thick, blood-red draught, which dripped from the sculpted fangs and stained the darkness of his cloak. The gathered acolytes abandoned themselves to a trance-like frenzy, and the wolf-like thing began to speak in an ancient, forsaken tongue—its words warped and degraded by ages untold. Jahdis could grasp only fragments of the sacrilegious liturgy, broken glimpses of the profane deities venerated within it.

She felt herself on the verge of unconsciousness. Her thoughts spun in ceaseless circles, never settling, until she feared she might retch. The wound at her side flared anew with terrible pain, and she realized she was still sluggish from the vile concoction the Nameless One had forced down her throat. She tried to lie down, but the cold, unyielding floor tormented her aching body. In the end, she curled into herself in a shadowed corner of her prison, arms and head resting upon her drawn-up knees, and wept softly beneath the weight of her own self-reproach. The infernal clamor surged once more, building toward a nightmarish climax—and she would have borne witness to a ritual no uninitiated soul had ever beheld, had she but opened her eyes and followed the unfolding rite.

Yet by some blessed providence, some strange and wholly unexpected grace—perhaps born of one of the powerful prayers Chirion sent heavenward from beneath vaults of impenetrable stone—she found herself renewed. And so she took no further notice of the horrors about her. She gathered her thoughts, subdued her mind, breathed deep and steady, and spoke with the voice of her spirit to that unknowable, unfathomable, and inscrutable God who had always stood by her in the darkest hours of her soul. She slipped away, in spirit, from that dreadful and archaic world, no longer hearing when the tumult around her faded, nor seeing when the black torches guttered and died in the smothering dark, nor noticing as the gathered throng dispersed. She did not feel the curious eyes that watched her from shadowed visages, nor hear the murmured curses, all of them directed at her. And so her dreams that night were sweet and filled with peace, though her body wasted away.

In her dream, it seems to her as though she beholds a radiant, unearthly light, akin to the fiery sigils upon that stolen scroll—the one the accursed man took from the secret chamber. And she sees the splendor of the thousand steps of that celestial stairway, of which the prophet Safriel once spoke—a stairway that ascends ever upward, leading to that wondrous and enshrouded realm, where, at its heart, the primeval archetype of all sanctuaries rises, encircled by towering columns. Its unfathomable magnificence is such that no living being has ever gazed upon it, and even those who languish in the lightless dungeons of eternal damnation tremble at its memory.

And she beholds a young man—unknown to her, and yet deeply familiar—standing before the white walls, vast and mighty, so that no single lifetime would suffice to surmount them. And he calls out in the ancient, forgotten tongue of the first day. At his voice, the gates swing open, and the redeemed step forth, welcoming him into those blessed lands.

And great is the omnipotence of Him who reigns upon that ineffable throne of surpassing majesty, and boundless are the blessings He pours upon the heads of His children—those very promises which Vandurian, until his final, tear-choked breath, never wearied of proclaiming in praise.

CHAPTER XI.
DARK ROSES

Obed, visibly unsettled by the lifeless body on the floor and the prospect of betraying his master, stood agape, his vacant, half-lidded eyes rolling upward like those of a stunned ox. Only at Phineas's urging did he finally summon the resolve to carry the corpse down to the chamber where Farah had been imprisoned. He dropped the dead woman onto the cot with an expression of disgust, as though disposing of a plague-ridden carcass, while Phineas, in turn, draped a covering over the body as if tucking it into bed—hoping that such a ruse might delay the discovery of her disappearance. Once they were back upstairs, Obed became abruptly aware of how ill-prepared he was for such a journey. Farah fared no better. "I came to this hôtel with nothing," she admitted meekly. "Monsieur Lameth took me from an orphanage in the *Marais* and placed me in the care of old Colette. After that, I served as a housemaid." She asked them to wait in front of the hôtel while she went to her room to change.

Obed grabbed a heavy woolen coat—the one he usually wore when running errands in the colder months—and hurried down the well-worn steps with Phineas. Phineas tilted his head back, his gaze drifting up toward the impossibly high gable. It seemed to him that years lay between his arrival at this place and the hurried departure they had now resolved upon. Before long, Farah rejoined them. She had exchanged her servant's garb for a high-waisted, ankle-length gown in a soft shade of pastel rose. Unaware of himself, Phineas stared at her so openly that Farah met his gaze with a smile. Performing a graceful curtsy, as though she were a lady being courted by her suitor, she then twirled with carefree delight, like a dancer in mid-spin. Against the dull gray of the cobbled street, the ruffled hem of her dress whirled like the painted stripes of a child's spinning top.

Phineas slipped Obed a considerable sum of money, along with some instructions. The giant then carved a path through the crowd, his towering frame forcing startled onlookers to recoil as he plowed his way toward the nearby posting station. Some time later, he returned, waving from the driver's box of a spacious four-horse *berline*. When the coach came to a halt, he twisted his enormous shoulders through the narrow door, contorting himself at a diagonal to squeeze out of the cabin, making the carriage groan beneath his weight as if about to tip over. The axles, slick with grease, earned an approving nod from Phineas. The giant helped them up the iron footstep before stowing the luggage atop the carriage, then took his place on the driver's bench beside the uniformed, sullen-faced postilion.

Inside, seated *vis-à-vis*, was a stout little man, engrossed in his newspaper. Beside him—his utter opposite—sat an elderly woman of spindly, near-skeletal appearance, dressed in black, a white lace collar at her throat and a pointed veil draped over her hair, as if she were in mourning. The little man's face was puffy and flushed, his fleshy nose jutting between two small, pale-lashed eyes. He was clean-shaven, his plump cheeks rolling seamlessly into the gleaming landscape of an unsightly double chin, pressed snugly against the high, greasy rim of his collar. His hair was cropped short, and though he must have been nearing sixty, it remained stubbornly blond. Sweat trickled in tiny rivulets down his temples, beading along the folds of his thick neck. Both passengers gawked at Farah and Phineas from the dim haze of the curtained windows, as if they were exhibits in a cabinet of curiosities—or as though a single horn sprouted from each of their foreheads. The fat man shifted from one buttock to the other, stretching his spindly legs as though practicing on a parallel bar. The old woman, her pale cheeks marbled with an intricate web of crimson veins, sighed audibly and flapped a lace-trimmed handkerchief over the carriage's leather interior, as if to shoo away some vile pest or banish an evil spirit.

Once the carriage had set into motion, the stout man finally lowered his newspaper—which he had been holding before him like a shield—and introduced himself as a businessman from a Paris-based trading company. Without delay, he launched into an unceasing torrent of words, showering Farah with exaggerated gestures and such elaborate airs, as though she were a lady of high standing—an attention that, at least at first, seemed to please her visibly. It appeared that he possessed a peculiar gift: the ability to elevate the most trivial of subjects—the kind that might drift into a man's mind in his weakest, most idle hours—into the center of conversation. His quicksilver mouth, framed by thick, fleshy lips, never ceased to move, and with its abundance of small, tightly packed teeth nestled into an expanse of overly pink gums, it seemed almost to have a life of its own. He winked at Farah incessantly, as if he had something lodged in his eye, and Phineas could not quite determine whether this was done with intent or had simply become an unconscious habit.

"I once traveled from Orléans to Blois," the stout man began, launching into yet another anecdote, after having subjected them to his ceaseless chatter for what felt like an eternity. He leaned forward as he spoke, coming so close that there was no escaping the stale stench of his breath. "And believe it or not, I forgot to go to the privy before we set off. And the damned coachman—miserable bastard—told me he wouldn't stop until Beaugency, seeing as we had only just left! So I start moaning that I can't hold it that long, but the stubborn ass refuses to give in. And then, all of a sudden, the whole cabin starts reeking to high heaven, and my fellow passenger—some sour old goat—starts pounding on the carriage walls like a madman until the idiot finally pulls over. Where the hell are we, by the way? Oh, Chambly should be up ahead somewhere. I swear, this journey is going nowhere. Now, where was I? Ah yes—so the fool finally stops. And do you know where? Right in the middle of a puddle the size of a small lake. I tell you, he did it out of pure spite—because it was the only damn puddle in the entire area. I checked, you see? And as luck would have it, there wasn't a hedge, a shrub, or a tree in sight. Just fields and meadows, flat as far as the eye could see. So I start walking and spot a little hillock—well, if I'm being honest, it was barely more than a lump of dirt over a ditch. But I've got no choice, so I waddle over, barely holding my britches up, and the bastard on the driver's box just grins at me, watching me scamper across the field, my backside clenched like a vice. And when

I finally, finally get there and drop my trousers—he just drives off and waves at me! Madame, are you feeling unwell? Yes, yes, traveling is not for everyone. Anyway, I yank my trousers up in a panic—without, ahem, finishing my business properly, if you know what I mean—no time to clean up or anything, and I go running after the carriage, but the son of a bitch just keeps on going, all the way to Blois. And so I arrive two days later, with my breeches full of—well, you get the idea—and soaked to the bone because, naturally, it had to start raining, turning the road into a wretched, sludgy swamp. The coach, of course, was long gone by then. The driver had told everyone the horses had bolted—ha! What a joke! And my luggage? Oh, he just left it outside the post station for anyone to rifle through. You can imagine how much of it was still there when I arrived. But—and here's the best part—I finally stagger into Blois, two days late and, well, less than fresh, and I end up striking the best deal of my life!" He burst into laughter, tears springing to his eyes, and slapped his bony thighs with glee. "Never count your chickens before they hatch, eh? Or rather—no, wait—I meant it the other way around." He smacked his lips, running his tongue over them with relish. "Hope we make it to the next post station before dusk. I don't know about you, but this carriage is absolute hell—feels like someone forgot to install the damn springs." He threw a brief glance out the window, then turned his gaze to the hulking figure perched on the driver's bench—watching as the giant's rear bounced atop the seat like two massive sacks of potatoes. With a deep sigh, he settled back into his seat. "Much to my greatest regret, I'll have to keep at this trade for a few more years before I can retire. Just yesterday, I said to my wife—it's a real tragedy, you know, that her dear father squandered his fortune after we got married. No turning back for me after that! Started drinking like a fish near the end, whoring around till he finally—well, there's no nice way to put it—rotted away from consumption like a goddamn stray dog. But what can you do? The bastard had stamina. If he hadn't lived like such a degenerate, he'd have made it to a hundred, no doubt about it. You see my point? By the time I'd have seen a single *sou* of his wealth, I'd already be an old man myself!" He smiled then, curling one lip down toward his chin while tugging the other upward, baring his small, sharp teeth once more.

"Oh dear, oh dear!" gasped the old woman, shaking her head in outraged disapproval.

"Speaking of whores—there's a brothel in Besançon," the stout man said, turning to Phineas. "No wish goes unfulfilled there, I swear on my life! And unlike those filthy Parisian slop-holes, the ladies there actually take a bath once a week. Some of them are real young things, even younger than you." He cast an unmistakable wink at Farah, his eyes trailing shamelessly down the length of her figure.

"Oh dear, oh dear!" the old woman repeated, her head bobbing up and down like a jack-in-the-box.

"You won't believe this," the trader went on, barely pausing for breath, "but I once heard about a man in Dijon who wanted to end it all—troubles, debts, the whole lot. So he throws himself in front of a cart—or at least that's what they say. Well, he survives. But they had to take both his legs! Now he rolls around on a little board and begs in the *Rue de la Liberté*. And can you guess how he's doing now? … Still miserable as ever." He burst into laughter, baring his small, crowded teeth, as if he had just delivered the most brilliant punchline in the world. His compulsive winking resurfaced. When he noticed the horrified silence of his fellow passengers, he took it as a sign that they were eagerly awaiting a story even more exclusive. "Did I ever tell you why Negroes always roll their eyes?" He widened his own pale-lashed eyes to a grotesque degree, making them bulge like an overripe boil on the verge of bursting. He was just about to launch into yet another of his bizarre anecdotes when the carriage jolted violently over an obstacle, momentarily cutting him off. Phineas sent a silent prayer of gratitude to the heavens—only to be disappointed when the reprieve lasted but a few moments.

Mopping the sweat from his brow, the trader resumed his incessant monologue, discoursing on the peculiarities of his clientele, his business triumphs and failures, the most glaring faults of his wife—of which there were apparently too many to count—his own infallible judgment in selecting a *Burgundy*, the many ailments that had afflicted his feeble body over the years, his favorite dishes, and the particular charms of certain women of the night—described in such florid language that the old woman's face turned an unhealthy shade of white, while Farah, blushing furiously, lowered her gaze to the floor in embarrassment.

He tortured them with trivial anecdotes and tales of such unfathomable dullness that they could have lulled a corpse to sleep—events of no conceivable interest to anyone, and a handful that might have been amusing had they been told by anyone but him. The old woman's responses were reduced to a feeble cough followed by a sanctimonious "Oh dear, oh dear!" or, at times, a piously whispered "Oh, dear Lord!"—uttered with such ostentatious dismay that it only spurred the babbling traveler on to even more elaborate digressions.

Whenever his speech veered into the vulgar, the inevitable "Oh dear, oh dear!" rang out, her lips sagging in a theatrical display of moral agony. Simultaneously, her wobbling head, which appeared perpetually on the verge of rolling clean off her shoulders, dipped forward, while her raised brows, hovering above her watery, red-rimmed eyes, betrayed an insatiable curiosity—until once again, from her pale lips, that dreadful "Oh dear, oh dear!" escaped. And so it went, hour after hour, as the carriage sped along the paved *chaussée*, the crack of the whip and the rattle of wheels a relentless accompaniment to his endless drivel.

Although the carriage's steel leaf springs absorbed the worst of the jolts, and the chaussée was in surprisingly good condition, the journey in the *berline* soon became an ordeal, the hours weighing heavily upon them until discomfort settled into every limb. At some point, despite the strain, Phineas managed to drift into sleep. When he stirred briefly—startled by the carriage lurching over some unseen obstacle—he noticed that Farah, her head resting against his shoulder, had also succumbed to slumber. He reached up to brush a stray lock of hair from her face and studied her delicate features—only to find, at that very moment, that the merchant had also awakened. From the man's expression, Phineas deduced that he had merely been waiting for an opportunity to resume his monologue. Thus, before the trader could utter a single word, Phineas immediately feigned sleep. Farah, by contrast, slumbered deeply, breathing in soft, steady rhythms as though she lay upon a featherbed—no doubt a testament to the hardship of the past few days.

Obed, meanwhile, was thoroughly enjoying his place atop the driver's bench. With every mile that stretched between him and that cursed hôtel, an unfamiliar joy swelled within him, until it seemed as though his very soul was unfurling—blossoming into something freer, lighter. He felt as though he had, in a single instant, been cured of some unshakable melancholy or had spent his entire life trapped in a *limbo* without realizing it. So lifted was his spirit that he even found himself in the mood for jesting. Before long, his deep, rumbling laughter mingled with that of the postilion, whose sour countenance had gradually softened as the journey progressed. At first, the man had been grimly resigned to the unpleasant prospect of spending several days in the company of a hulking servant from that great, uncanny house. But now, to his own surprise, he found himself chuckling heartily, even joining in a raucous tune like a drunken choir of men. The sun dipped toward the horizon, and the postilion cracked his whip to urge the weary horses on—eager to reach the next inn before nightfall. More than one traveler, making their way along the road to Beauvais, rubbed their eyes in bewilderment as a black-draped carriage, gleaming in the moonlight, thundered past at breakneck speed. The sight of a boisterous coachman and a monstrous giant laughing uproariously beside him atop the driver's box gave them the eerie impression of witnessing the ghostly *chasse infernale*—a demonic wild hunt, racing through the countryside with terrible clamor, wailing, and howling.

They did not reach their destination until late into the night. The carriage veered from the main road, curving off onto a winding side path that led toward a secluded estate. The monotonous clatter of iron-rimmed wheels over the crushed-stone road gave way to an arrival-heralding crunch as the postilion guided the carriage down a gently sloping gravel path toward the manor. The cold, dim moonlight faded in the warm glow of several oil lamps affixed to the stone façade of the residence and its stables—welcoming the weary travelers from the darkness of the night. With a sharp "Brrr!" the postilion reined in the horses. The carriage seemed to lurch suddenly into shadow as Obed leapt noisily down from the driver's bench. An instant later, his grinning, grotesquely large face appeared—unexpectedly—at the glass window of the coach door. The old woman recoiled in horror, as if the devil himself had just peered in at her. Obed helped Farah down from the carriage, flashing the elderly lady a beaming smile—which, to her, seemed more like the leer of a beast preparing to devour her whole. Somewhere in the darkness, voices called out, and a stable hand soon emerged from the gloom, wordlessly unhitching the horses and leading them away to be tended. "We'll stay the night here," the postilion announced. "At first light, we'll set out again with fresh horses." As he fussed with the driver's box, Obed had already unloaded their luggage from the carriage. Above the entrance, an iron sign gleamed in the lamplight: *Auberge de la Poste.* Its wrought-iron letters—forged from flat steel and split at the ends into elegant flourishes—circled the figure of a mounted post rider. The warm, inviting glow of candlelit windows broke through the whitened walls of the two-story inn, spilling out into the night alongside a chorus of lively voices.

Phineas entered the brightly lit tavern, the rest of the party trailing behind him. The room was upheld by carved oak columns, its air thick with the warmth of a roaring fire, whose flickering light sent long, dancing shadows across the walls. These bent at sharp angles at the corners, only to dissolve into the soot-darkened ceiling above. Hams, slabs of bacon, and strings of sausages—bound together in pairs for curing—hung from a beam behind the bar, where bustling serving girls and taproom boys swarmed out with armfuls of steaming plates and brimming tankards, eager to satisfy the needs of the guests. The clamor of the gathered patrons, mingling with the clatter of crockery, was soon drowned out by the gruff voice of the innkeeper, who studied them first from beneath his bushy, suspiciously furrowed brows before finally leading them to an unoccupied table in the corner of the room. A stout, short woman, whose lurching gait gave the impression that she was walking on wooden pegs, brought them stew in simple wooden bowls, along with loaves of bread nestled in woven baskets lined with cotton cloth. They drank wine—though it bore a greater resemblance to vinegar—and, later in the evening, switched to the inn's own ale, which was served in tall glasses. Hunger and general exhaustion settled the group into silent agreement. Phineas leaned back with a sigh of contentment, closing his eyes and inhaling the heavy, comforting warmth of the tavern air—laden with the scents of wine, meat, and smoke. Farah smiled at him, radiant with quiet happiness. "I never did have the chance to inquire about the purpose of your journey," the merchant interjected, shattering the harmony of the moment—as though their hours together in the cramped carriage had left no time for such questions, and his seemingly bottomless reservoir of stories had finally run dry.

"The purpose of my journey is a comfortable bed," Phineas replied curtly. He pushed his chair back with a creak, rising to his feet and stretching his weary limbs. Farah stood as well, moving in quiet synchrony with him, smoothing down her gown with an infectious yawn. The merchant, for once, let the matter rest—perhaps realizing that no one at the table had the slightest inclination to entertain him any longer that night. The innkeeper, who was in the process of ushering the last of his guests either to their beds or out the door, assigned them their rooms. Phineas and Farah shared a small chamber, its walls covered in painted paper wallpaper. But as space was scarce—and Obed far too large for any ordinary bed—he simply lay himself down at the foot of theirs, rolling his coat into a makeshift pillow and drifting into sleep the moment his head touched it.

Farah stepped closer to Phineas. "Thank you for everything you have done for me," she whispered against his cheek—only for the moment to be shattered by a ghastly snore that echoed through the chamber, as if someone were sawing away at their bedpost. Farah smiled, turned away, and in a single graceful motion, slipped her dress over her head, placing it on the dresser. A white linen shift, held up by delicate straps, draped over her shoulders and flowed smoothly down the soft curve of her hips, stopping just above her bare knees. She gathered her hair into a clasp, and in the moonlight of the star-strewn night, mingled with the flickering glow of the oil lamp, she seemed almost otherworldly—some ethereal creature, an enchantress bathed in the magic of the moon.

His heart pounded feverishly. Desire seized him. Farah seemed to sense it, for she lowered her arms and met his gaze, steady and unguarded, as if silently claiming what neither of them could deny. Their bodies entwined in a fervent embrace, their lips met, and they tasted each other's hushed confessions of longing—though neither could say how exactly they had closed the space between them. His hands traced her form, feeling every curve, every secret rise and hollow. She answered with a soft sigh, mirroring his touch, her lips following the path of her fingers. She wrapped her legs around his waist, drawing him down onto the pillowed bed beneath them. Phineas misjudged the movement, knocking his head against the high wooden headboard. Farah slipped from his grasp, and groaning, he pushed himself up, rubbing the sore spot—until, quite suddenly, they both burst into laughter.

Still smiling, he reached for the buttons of his shirt, ready to bring their longing to fulfillment—when suddenly, an inexplicable feeling stole over him, something he could neither name nor fully comprehend. A vision flared in his mind—the sacred dream, the woman who had appeared to him like an oracle, the strange and boundless yearning that had gripped his soul so fiercely, leaving it shaken in ways he still did not understand. Why, of all moments, did his conscience choose now to trouble him? Why must the specter of that delphic dream intrude upon this night, tainting his moment of deepest pleasure with a sense of disquiet he could not dispel? Lost in thought, he did not immediately realize that Farah was watching him—her expression shifting from warmth to confusion.

"What is it, my love? Am I boring you? Or have I done something to displease you?"

"No, unknown, beautiful girl," he murmured hoarsely. "I am simply… confused. At odds with myself."

Then tell me, my love," she said, drawing up the fallen strap of her shift, searching his face. Her eyes held that look—one that unsettled him, yet at the same time, left him powerless against it.

"Such things, if one dares to put them into words, do no justice to the memory that fades with time," he said pensively.

"A few days ago, I had a strange dream. It seemed to me that I was enacting a mystical wedding, and I saw myself and my bride ascending a celestial staircase, into a radiant world of light—one for which nothing on Earth can provide even the faintest comparison. Even upon waking, I could scarcely recall much of it, and now, I suppose, time has erased whatever impressions remained."

"I am happy to share you with your romantic dream," Farah replied with a smile, "as long as your hands resume their previous occupation. Tell me, have you been to the theatre lately? My friend Meline works at the *Théâtre des Italiens*. We watched Mozart's 'The Magic Flute' from right beside the prompter's box—hidden, up close. I couldn't understand a word, though I know a little German, but the sets, the costumes, the lights, all of it... absolutely breathtaking! Doesn't that match your mysterious dream image?"

"Hail to you, ye chosen ones!
Ye who have pierced through the night,
Thanks be to thee, Osiris and Isis!
Strength has triumphed, and as its reward,
Beauty and wisdom are crowned with an eternal crown."

He recited in broken German. "Yes, I have seen the play. Perhaps you are right. The mind is capable of remarkable illusions, particularly when influenced by the right stimulants. And my reading of late has been no less filled with such peculiar literature."

Farah gave him a knowing smile. "Perhaps you saw the two of us in your dream, and it means that you will propose to me and we shall be married—in a real church, with a priest, bells ringing, and all the trimmings. Tell me, am I your *Pamina*, and you my *Tamino*?" She stretched out her arm in a fluid motion, spreading her fingers one by one from the pinky outward, twisting her hand as though admiring a ring upon it. Phineas stared at her in astonishment. She bit her lower lip seductively and let her hand glide up along her thigh, over her hip, slowly drawing up the hem of her shift. Phineas blinked, as if suddenly roused from a trance. At the foot of the bed, Obed continued to snore—like Cerberus guarding the gates of the underworld.

Suddenly, a scream rang out from the darkness outside. Phineas stepped to the window as Farah clutched the blanket tightly around herself. He hastily dressed, cast another glance through the glass, and turned toward the door. "What are you going to do?" Farah asked fearfully.

"There's a crowd gathering in the courtyard—everything is brightly lit. Something out there is not as it should be. In the meantime, wake that sawmill on the floor!"

Phineas rushed down the staircase and crossed the columned tavern hall. A few guests, chattering excitedly, hurried after him. Through the divided windowpanes, moving lights and the shifting silhouettes of men and horses could be seen. The moment he stepped outside, the scene became clear: the barn was ablaze. The acrid scent of burning straw and smoke clung to the air. The horses neighed in terror, some bolting blindly across the yard before vanishing into the depths of the night. Orders were shouted from all sides. The innkeeper, stable hands, maids, postillions, and several alarmed guests had gathered, drawing water from a nearby well to fill the reservoir of a four-wheeled fire pump or battling the flames with ladders and leather buckets. Obed suddenly emerged from the chaos and immediately seized hold of the pump wagon, operating it single-handedly with his immense strength.

A piercing, dreadful whinny echoed from within the stables, followed by an abrupt, deathly silence—enough to know that not all the horses had made it out. Smoke billowed in pale, curling ribbons through cracks in the roof's still-intact sections—until the flames claimed those as well. A portion of the rafters collapsed with a deafening crash. Glass windows burst in the heat. A cascade of sparks shot skyward, and towering amber flames followed, devouring the dark blue sky in a dreadful contrast of complementary hues.

By now, the fire had grown so large, the commotion so deafening, that all the guests had gathered outside—some assisting the innkeeper, others clustering in small groups, murmuring anxiously behind handkerchiefs pressed to their mouths. As the efforts to quell the blaze proved futile, the focus shifted to shielding the main house from the advancing inferno. Phineas let his gaze wander over the fire-lit faces, searching for Farah, but she was nowhere to be seen. With a rising sense of unease, he re-entered the inn and hurried up the wooden staircase. A thick, acrid haze had begun to fill the stairwell. The door to their chamber stood open. A dreadful feeling—an ill-defined premonition—sent a shudder through him. Heart pounding, he stepped over the threshold.

Like a shadow play brought to life, a dark figure rose before the flickering glow of the flames, which surged and wavered behind the divided panes of the window. His hand extended into the shape of a curved dagger. The steel flashed downward in a swift arc, slashing through Phineas's sleeve at the height of his forearm, then carving two horizontal strokes through the air. Instinctively, Phineas leapt backward, stumbling over a chair that sent him reeling. It seemed almost as if the attack had been meant not to wound him, but to drive him back—

so hesitant was its execution. Seizing the chair, he wielded it as a shield and lunged at the cloaked figure. A curse escaped his assailant's lips as he tore himself free, retreating into the corner of the chamber, leaving behind a hood that slipped from his grasp and remained in Phineas's hands.

The flickering light traced the raptor-like features of his opponent. It was none other than the sinister guest—Baldassare, as Lameth had called him—the same man who had crossed Phineas's path on the stairwell of the hôtel weeks earlier, on the very morning after his arrival, at the same moment as Serpentarius Stroude. Blood streamed from one of Baldassare's temples, yet the dagger, clenched like a venomous sting in his fist, had lost none of its menace. From the corner of his eye, Phineas glanced toward the bed—where his worst fear was instantly confirmed in the darkening haze of his vision. A crimson stream spilled from a ghastly wound at Farah's throat, seeping between the wooden floorboards, staining them like a blood-red apron over her white shift. Phineas's face turned ashen. "Why in God's name did you do this to her?" he stammered, his voice catching in his throat. Baldassare remained silent, his gaze fixed upon him in dark contempt. "She did nothing to deserve this! I… I loved her," Phineas choked out. But then, as suddenly as grief had seized him, rage took its place. The renewed loss of a happiness far too fleeting tore something open inside him, unleashing a fury that drove back his tears. "Did Lameth send you? Is he behind this?" Baldassare did not answer. The flickering fire cast restless, pulsing light across half of his face—the side turned toward the window, which he now eyed with veiled intent.

In that instant, the door behind Phineas burst open. From the commotion, he knew it had to be Obed. A terrible howl escaped the giant's throat as he took in the scene before him in a single, heart-wrenching moment. Phineas, distracted for the briefest fraction of a second, turned his head. Seizing the opportunity, Baldassare hurled himself toward the window, shielding his face with his hands as he crashed through shattering glass and splintering wood. He landed two stories below—on all fours, like a cat. Phineas moved to follow, but by the time he reached the broken frame, Baldassare was already astride a horse that had been pulled from the flames. With a swift kick, he sent the stablehand who held the reins sprawling to the ground—and in the next instant, he was gone, vanishing into the sheltering darkness of the night.

"The fiend defiled the poor innocent girl!" came a cry from the stairwell behind them. Several guests had gathered in the doorway, their forms silhouetted in the dim corridor. The soot-streaked innkeeper pushed through the crowd, forcing them aside as he took the lead, advancing in a wedge formation.

"Farah has been murdered!" Obed bellowed, his voice raw with anguish. The onlookers recoiled in fear. Phineas knelt beside her, his face streaked with tears, oblivious to everything around him.

Thanks to the stablehand's account of the fleeing man, both he and Obed were cleared of suspicion. It was soon presumed that the attacker had set the fire himself—to create a diversion for his crime. Someone brought up a few sheets to shroud the body, and together, they bore her down the stairs, laying her upon one of the great tables in the tavern hall. As a serving maid scrubbed the chamber floor, washing away the last traces of blood, the innkeeper stood outside like a statue of salt, motionless, his gaze fixed upon the smouldering ruins of his barn. A few stable hands still worked to extinguish the final embers or to round up the remaining horses. Meanwhile, Phineas and Obed sat in silence in the tavern, their faces downcast, drowning their grief in wine—until, at last, they succumbed to sleep where they sat.

Phineas drifts into a chaos of disjointed, incoherent fragments—a dream that dissolves upon waking, yielding to a reality far more cruel. He sinks once more into a deep slumber. And he dreams of that Lameth-being, taking shape from a shadowed mass of smouldering vapors, like the coal-filled braziers of ancient altars where sacrificial fires burn, or the great swaying censers that spill incense in thick, undulating plumes. Then, shifting, it becomes a scimitar-wielding djinn, striking at him with stabbing thrusts and sweeping blows—and yet he is powerless to resist. He sees Eireen, lying peacefully in repose upon her bed. But as he approaches, her features waver and shift, merging into another. She is Eireen, and yet she is also Farah—one and the same.

The twofold being stares at him for a long time, with empty, sightless eyes, her lifeless cheeks streaked with tears. Her arms, grotesquely twisted like broken branches, reach out toward him in a silent plea. A rush of scarlet blood pours from her ravaged throat, drenching the fabric of her gown. Phineas hurries to save her, but the vital stream slips through his fingers, draining away into the scorched, ashen ground. Swirling tendrils of smoke coil upward in spirals, twisting and curling into the air—until suddenly, from those smoke-cloaked cinders, a fountain bursts forth, thundering and churning, a crimson flood that swells and surges, devouring all in its path. It seizes him, pulls him under, carries him away—until, at last, he awakens, drenched in sweat, his cheek resting in a pool of spilled wine.

The following day, Obed withdrew into silence, offering neither word nor gesture, no trace of human expression or will. Phineas, his hair disheveled, his eyes shadowed with leaden rings, sat hunched over a bowl of porridge, stirring it aimlessly. Now and then, his eyes grew moist, his lips quivered—but he said nothing. Then, all at once, he rose, stepped outside, took up a spade, and began to dig a grave some distance from the house. The ground was stony, and the spade met fierce resistance as it tried to break through the hardened earth. Yet Phineas did not curse nor utter a word—so deep was his grief, so great the battle raging within him. After some time, Obed approached, took the tool from his hands without a word, and drove it into the soil with brute force. The earth yielded, groaning and cracking under the weight of each blow, until at last, a deep hollow began to take shape. A stablehand, who had been watching them at first, disappeared into the house and returned moments later with a pickaxe in one hand and an axe in the other, which they used to break apart the larger stones and cut through the stubborn roots beneath. Phineas sat upon a boulder, gazing wistfully over the landscape—a pastoral vision of gentle meadows and scattered groves, crisscrossed by a tree-lined road, like a painted idyll of some earthly paradise. But as his eyes drifted to Obed, who heaved dark clods of earth from the pit, the scene turned ghastly, bleak.

At last, the grave was wide enough to receive the body. Jagged roots and broken stones jutted from the shaft's walls, as though its edges had been carved by the blade of a scalpel. By and by, people gathered, faces etched with the remnants of the previous night's horror. Their garments were soiled, reeking of smoke. A breeze swept through the underbrush, rustling in slow lament through the towering trees that stood like silent sentinels around the burial site. Ash swirled in the wind, cloaking their clothes and the white linen at the bottom of the grave in a veil of mourning black. Not far from them, the barn's smouldering ruins still fumed like the remains of some priestly altar, standing beside the miraculously unscathed main house. Obed straightened, his head bowed, towering above the hunched bodies of the mourners—so that, from afar, he seemed a solitary giant among a ring of children. A solitary rosebush, which had once climbed the trellis along the stable walls, had survived the inferno. Its dark blossoms, once red, had blackened in the heat, the delicate petals curled and withered like the brittle husks of last year's flowers. One by one, they fell into the pit, scattering over the white shroud in the depths, whose fabric bore the rosy stain of blood, now turned to crimson dew.

Phineas tried to speak, to shape words that might ease the grief, contain the pain, preserve her memory—but nothing came. Only a strangled sob, born from a sorrow that had sunk its claws into the very marrow of his soul. "I miss you, my unknown, beautiful girl," he whispered, voice breaking.

The innkeeper, his hair and beard singed, his clothes riddled with scorched holes, a heavy bandage wrapped around his arm, felt compelled to address the mourners. He recited from the Holy Scriptures, adopting the singing cadence of a preacher, before weaving his own eloquent lament, speaking of Farah's untimely death, her piety, and her devotion—for such, he thought, was fitting in that moment. Then, before stepping back among the mourners, he placed a hand on Phineas's shoulder—a gesture of quiet sympathy. Phineas looked up, tears brimming in his eyes, and acknowledged the kindness with a fragile, forced smile. And then, Obed began to sing. It was an unfamiliar song, strange yet hauntingly beautiful—a lament, a dirge threaded with sorrow, its melody trembling, at times breaking beneath the weight of grief. He trilled the higher notes in a peculiar, wavering cadence, modulating them in a way that none among them had ever heard. The words were foreign, unknowable, unfathomable—and so the mourners only listened, feeling, though they could not understand.

As the number of surviving horses was too few to make all the remaining carriages roadworthy, they were forced to hire a two-horse *phaeton* for an exorbitant sum and departed from the inn with only a meager supply of provisions, sorrow weighing heavy upon them. Rain set in, and Obed pulled the hood forward. "I'm gonna kill that Baldassare," he said grimly.

"Yes, we will," Phineas replied. "But first, we must uncover Lameth's true intentions. And so help me God—if he had any hand in this, he will pay."

They took the road to Abbeville, dispirited, stripped of all joy, their hearts burdened with sorrow, misfortune pressing upon their souls. October was drawing to a close, and the air had turned sharply cold, as though winter had come without the courtesy of autumn to temper its arrival. They spent their nights just off the roadside or, when necessary, stopped at a relay station to change the horses. Their silence spoke louder than words ever could. Despair and grief had become their constant companions.

On the fourth day, the rain fell in torrents. The road to Boulogne-sur-Mer was in a wretched state. For a time, they endured the jolting of potholes, which rattled the carriage mercilessly—until at last, the gnarled root of a great plane tree, which had burrowed its way through the packed road-bed, split the axle, sending the *phaeton* toppling over. Their bodies braced against the slanting downpour like breakwaters as they struggled to right the carriage—until, after repeated failed attempts, they abandoned it altogether, leading the horses through ankle-deep mire toward the cover of a nearby wood. The sky flared white as day, a blinding bolt split the heavens—and with a deafening crack, a tree was cleaved in two, the thunderous impact ringing in their ears. When the storm finally relented, they spent the night, shivering, in the shelter of a hollow. By afternoon of the fourth day, they reached Boulogne-sur-Mer. After returning the horses at the post station, informing the attendants of the *phaeton's* location, and settling their financial affairs, Phineas sat down to write. He addressed the letter to Monsieur Lameth.

"What d'you hope to gain from this?" Obed asked, perplexed.

"Let us lay our cards on the table," Phineas replied. "Let him try to justify himself. Perhaps he is innocent in all that has transpired—who can say? I cannot yet discern whether Serpentarius Stroude and the other schemers are playing their own game. But if Lameth ordered that hired blade to act on his behalf, then both shall answer for it—you may rest assured of that. Besides, Baldassare will have surely deduced our intended course by now. He knows full well that we have not ventured to the northern coast for the mere pleasure of an excellent lobster and oyster dinner. I have no intention of hiding. Once we have gathered what we need in Colchester, I shall return to my house. And, should you choose to accompany me—I would count it an honour." Obed nodded in silent agreement.

The following letter reached Monsieur Lameth a few days later, on October 25, 1831, as he pushed open the blackened door and stepped into the lobby, his garments tattered and worn:

Boulogne-sur-Mer
October 20, 1831

Honoured Monsieur Lameth,

If, as I presume, you have by now returned to Hôtel La Porte Noire, you will surely have noticed that, under the given circumstances, I could no longer remain. You will also find, upon glancing at your vacant concierge's desk, that your porter Obed deemed it appropriate to seek new employment. As serfdom has long been consigned to history in France, I trust you will accept this state of affairs and provide him with a letter of reference befitting his loyal service. You may rest assured that he shall be well treated in my care. To my deepest regret, I must also note that not all of your servants appear to enjoy the freedoms granted to every citizen under the constitution of your progressive nation. For this reason, I considered it my duty to deliver the maid Farah from her unfortunate predicament. She had grown dear to me, and our friendship, in its final days, was marked by such a profound bond that I now suffer bitterly for what was done to her—at the hands of one of your own, that dagger-wielding fiend known as Baldassare. Upon her grave, I swore vengeance for the wrong inflicted upon her. If the man in question remains within your company, I ask that you convey to him the following: I shall not rest until I have repaid Farah's death in kind. This also extends to the one who commanded this vile crime—you may be assured of that.

I regret, most sincerely, the damage I caused to a portion of your paneled walls, thereby exposing a certain older decoration that you had seen fit to keep hidden from prying eyes. This, along with the impressions left upon me by my disembodiment in the catacombs of your dubious establishment, has only strengthened my resolve to withdraw from *this matter entirely. Nevertheless, you may rest assured that I shall uphold the secrets entrusted to me, in accordance with the oath I once swore to you.*

I remain your most
devoted servant,
Phineas Camill

P.S. The passing of a certain woman, with whom I was not personally acquainted, grieves me greatly—though I can in no way claim responsibility for this unfortunate accident. She alone must answer for her fate, and it seems to me that a modicum of kindness might not have been amiss in her lifetime.

CHAPTER XII.
THE WHISPERING HOUSE

Morning stirred with sluggish reluctance, and even by midday, it had not yet mustered the strength to pierce the brooding weight of fog that hung over the slick, glistening slate rooftops, heavy as gray sailcloth. The sea rumbled, vast and malachite-hued, rising in wild defiance against the eroded cliffs, where steep grasslands tumbled toward the edge. It shattered into white spray upon moss-green rocks, crashing against the fortifications of the harbor and the stone pier before unfurling in foamy torrents over the sloping shore. The boats in the harbor bucked and swayed, as if some unseen leviathan were surfacing beneath them. Then, from some far-flung point in infinity, a force stirred—at first, no more than a faint glimmer, like the fleeting white flare of a battery's volley across a fog-drenched battlefield. At first, it seemed merely an anomaly—a scattering of stray rays, wandering fragments of a sun now retreating behind its veil. But then, a sudden detonation. A crash, a roar—as if the harbor lay under siege from an unseen *armada*. The wind rose in a thousand wailing voices, splitting apart only to return in a deafening assault—a bombardment of sound, a tempest of howling gusts. In a single furious upheaval, the storm hurled itself against the rows of houses, so that an entire street groaned beneath the dull, thunderous impact of a singular, focused attack, as if some titan of the air sought to shatter their very frames. Above, gray clouds tore through the sky in chaotic flight, then frayed like the tatters of an ancient sail, trembling beneath the unrelenting blows. And in the wake of this furious spectacle, the storm unleashed a torrential downpour, its vertical lances lashing against the leaden desolation, until the shore and the broad avenues before the towering houses lay swept clean of all living things. Then, suddenly—silence. And as the waters receded, life stirred once more—first in scattered traces, then in a chorus of lament, rising from a hundred crooked beaks.

Obed stood beneath a wooden overhang, collar turned up against the wind, gazing out to sea with the mournful stillness of a bronze statue. After some time, Phineas appeared, dark shadows under his eyes, and joined him. "One hell of a storm! Ain't much left t'be afraid of, not after all we been through these last days," Obed remarked.

"This is nothing unusual, believe me. I grew up by the sea—a mild breeze, nothing more," Phineas replied with a strained smile. "I've arranged our passage. A *brig* is sailing for Dover later today—then onward to Rotterdam, to take on some cargo. They've agreed to take us as far as Dover."

"Still mighty eerie, headin' out there. What if it starts stormin' again?" Obed tilted his head to one side and rolled his neck until it cracked, his expression set in grim determination.

"Pah! We're merely crossing the Channel, not rounding Cape Horn. The *brig* is a solid ship, and the captain seemed a rather capable man. Have you never been to sea before?"

"Never." Obed fell silent for a long moment. "Only in dreams—when I was far away from that terrible house and all the horrors within."

"Best we speak of that another time." Phineas shifted his stance. "The *St. Andrew* sets sail in an hour. She's an English ship, once fought against the French—now just a transport vessel, but still in fine shape. They're eager to be off, were meant to leave this morning. Damn weather! Come, let's not waste time."

They took a cobbled road westward toward the harbor, stopping along the way to buy bread, cheese, and wine, which they ate perched on a flat rock by the roadside, before continuing on. Half an hour later, they stood at the landing pier, their figures cast into shadow by the towering two-masted ship. Sun-darkened men, clad in white linen trousers and loose shirts, swarmed the rigging like ants, scrambling up the mainmast and foremast, securing the yards, stays, and brig sails. Barrels and supplies were stowed, some rolled up the narrow gangplank, others hoisted aboard by a creaking crane. Above a band of barnacles, mussels, and tangled seaweed, the tarred, sharp-lined hull rose sleekly from the pewter-coloured waves. The air reeked of salt and brine, as though they stood in the heart of a fish market. The wind carried a fine mist of seawater, which settled over their skin in a thin film, clinging to their hair in a hundred tiny, glassy droplets. From one of the gunports, a shock of unruly curls and a boy's impish grin peeked out—until a sharp call to work sent him scrambling, the port-lid slamming shut behind him.

They boarded the ship via a rickety plank, its surface reinforced with horizontal beams, and no sooner had their feet touched the scrubbed deck than a gruff old sea dog hailed them from the aft deck. "Captain McDermond at your service, sir! By the three devils, if that resurrected Goliath you've got in tow doesn't watch his step, we'll run aground before we even set sail!" He let out a hoarse, wheezing laugh, interrupted by a hacking cough, before spitting noisily onto the deck. Obed blinked, looking utterly baffled, his shoulders creeping upward as if he'd been caught pilfering apples at market. A grin flashed across McDermond's weather-beaten face, revealing a row of teeth gleaming amidst his snow-white beard. "No worries, lad, I didn't mean it. Come aboard, both of you—we're shoving off any minute now. Aye, what a day for sailing! Come along, don't be shy—you can watch old McDermond navigate from the stern." Then, without missing a beat, he bellowed: "Oi, Seamus! Are we setting sail today or in the next bloody century? For God's sake, haul in that blasted chain and bring us into the wind!" As he passed, the captain clapped Obed on the shoulder, the weight of his hand like a seal of approval. "You sure you want to stick with this fine gentleman here?" he asked, squinting at Obed with a wolfish grin. "There's plenty of work for a broad back like yours on deck." His steely blue-gray eyes, peering from beneath bushy brows streaked with unruly white bristles, studied Obed as though weighing his worth. But Obed sidled away to the opposite railing, as though fearing the captain might wallop him over the head with a boathook. McDermond shook his head and chuckled. "By all seven sages of Greece! Ah well, maybe it's for the best. What the hell would I feed that bottomless pit of yours day in, day out, eh?"

A long anchor chain, encrusted with goose barnacles, was slowly reeled in by a massive windlass, its iron links rattling as they rose, dripping, from the depths. Then, beneath the booming calls of the bosun, the brig was tugged out to sea, its white sails unfurling in a single, graceful motion from the yards. With a sudden jolt, they caught the wind, billowing outward like great, heaving lungs, as if drawing breath for the voyage ahead. As the spray-drenched faces of the crew rose against the horizon, their hands resting on the rough grain of the rail, they were seized by that singular sensation known to all true sailors—the stirrings of fresh resolve, renewed courage, as though the sea itself were some fabled wellspring of youth.

Before them stretched the gray expanse of the sea, an endless glass mountain range of foam-crested swells, its agate-green valleys wreathed in mist, where waves broke and scattered in plumes against the hull. The ship dipped and climbed, its bow cleaving through the waters with the rhythmic certainty of a heartbeat. They cast one last glance back—toward the *Old Man of Boulogne*, the ruins of Caligula's Lighthouse, still looming over the cliffs—then left behind the harbor from which Caesar had once set sail to claim the island in the west. Storm-laden clouds rumbled overhead, heavy with the promise of thunder. Dusk crept swiftly upon them, and the setting sun cast a slender ribbon of light over the undulating, blue-black sea. The sky turned to ashen gloom, save for a golden blaze on the western horizon. Then came night. The crew lit the ship's lanterns, their golden glow dancing across the darkness like fireflies, flickering against the vast, indifferent void. Hours later, white cliffs loomed ahead, crowned by *Dover Castle*, their pale facades sculpted by moonlight into the likeness of some ancient legend, risen from the depths of time.

The *brig* docked with a dangerous lurch, its hull groaning against the quayside. Under the barked orders and expletives of Captain McDermond, part of the cargo was unloaded, new barrels and crates were hoisted aboard, and a few bleary-eyed passengers stumbled up the gangplank. "I trust the crossing suited you?" the captain asked as he bid them farewell. His hands were buried deep in the pockets of his oilskin coat, his head tucked low against the collar. "If I may offer you some advice—take a room at *Wilbury's Inn*, three streets over. Get some sleep. Whatever it is that haunts you, I expect it can wait till morning." For a long moment, McDermond studied them, his narrowed eyes glinting as if he could read their thoughts— or perhaps spin a tale, just by looking, of the strange horrors they had endured in these past days. His weathered face curled into a knowing smile. He gave them a final nod, speaking no more.

"My sincere thanks for the passage. May you have calm waters and favourable winds on your way to Rotterdam!"

"Aye, may God grant it so! And should you ever tire of this biblical giant, do send me word at once!" Captain McDermond let out his deep, wheezing laugh and waved them off from the upper deck. Obed wore the forlorn look of a man being auctioned off at a slave market.

"Do you suppose they're offloading contraband?" Phineas muttered, watching the crew at work. "Strikes me as rather odd, setting sail again so late at night."

"I don't like this McDermond— not one bit!" Obed growled.

Weary and stiff-limbed, they disembarked and found lodgings at the suggested inn. At first light, they took a northwest-bound chaise, tracing the coastal road past Canterbury to Gillingham. From there, they crossed the Thames east of London at Gravesend aboard a cargo schooner. After a night in Tilbury, they hired a light, single-horse *Stanhope gig* and, on the third day, reached Lameth's estate, southwest of Colchester. The weather remained wretched throughout the journey—unceasing storms and rain turned the coaching road into a battlefield, the wagon's folding hood sagging above them, swollen and dripping like a great, festering abscess.

The light came suddenly, unexpectedly, piercing through the dark seams of layered clouds, which drifted in tiered formations, a shifting watercolor of overlapping strata—its edges dissolving, bleeding into one another, washed thinner with every plane, fading in uncertain aerial perspective into ever paler, more diffuse shades of blue-gray. The rays unfurled in a radiant aureole against the brooding sky, then, caught by a passing band of clouds, poured downward like a colossal pyramid of light, blinding their eyes, which struggled to adjust to the sudden intensity, the shifting tonal values.

The house, emerging with each turn of the wheels from the canopy of towering trees, did not escape this spectacle of light. The beams filtered through the narrow gaps between the terracotta chimney pots, which jutted from the multi-flued stacks like organ pipes, skimmed across the slate roof, caught on weathervanes and the ornamental scrollwork of the gutters, and glinted off the playful capitals of Corinthian pilasters. They traced their way over the limestone masonry, illuminating its veined stylolites, its deposits of hematite and brown ironstone, and the crystalline structures embedded in its surface—sedimentary rock, compressed and entombed over hundreds of millions of years, fossilized relics of primordial life. Then, with dazzling brilliance, the light rebounded from the high-arched windows, mirrored back in fractured gleams.

The two-wheeled carriage rolled along the gravel path, past manicured lawns, moss-flecked stone planters, boxwood topiaries pruned into strict geometries, and the sculpted hedgework of hornbeams and yews. At last, they came to a halt before a Georgian façade, where the entrance—raised above a flight of seven stone steps—was framed by two triangular-gabled pavilions in an extravagant display of symmetry. Their arrival had not gone unnoticed. Barely had the carriage wheels stilled before they found themselves under the watery gaze of an aged, nearly bald face, its pale blue eyes, hooded beneath a sagging fold of flesh, looking up at them with quiet inquiry. One pupil was clouded, as though a dense fog were gathering behind it, drawing the observer irresistibly toward the other. "Master Camill! I had scarcely dared to hope for your return so soon. The master, alas, is away—his return is not expected before the following month."

"The pleasure is all mine, Edmund!" Phineas replied in a loud voice, as if speaking to a man hard of hearing. "I have already been informed. I had to leave Paris rather abruptly due to some unforeseen circumstances. We shall spend the night here, and tomorrow, once everything necessary has been attended to, I shall make my way home without further delay. Am I correct in assuming that the hospitality of this house is still extended to me?"

"But of course, sir! I can have your old room prepared at once," replied the small, stoop-shouldered man. "But would the master, in his absence, approve of me admitting guests? You know him only too well—and his moods."

"Let me be frank with you—he rather abandoned me in Paris," Phineas said with a wry smile. "Apparently, he had urgent matters to attend to that could not be postponed. Now tell me—do you think he would be pleased to learn that you had me and my companion sleep in the stables, or out in some hollow of the field? It is far too late to set out for Ipswich tonight, the horses are weary— and I, frankly, am no less so."

"My deepest apologies, sir, for voicing my concerns!" Edmund bowed slightly. "I shall prepare your room at once. But where, in God's name, are we to put this giant?" He wiped away a strand of saliva from his lips, revealing a row of greyish stumps, like crooked, sunken gravestones jutting from his gums.

"My room is spacious enough. But we may have some difficulty finding a bed that fits him. Just lay out some blankets on the floor—that should suffice for tonight. Tell me, does the kitchen still live up to its excellent reputation?"

A fleeting smile crossed the old man's face, momentarily smoothing the deep furrows of worry. "Indeed it does, sir! Shall I have your meal brought up to your room, or do you prefer to dine in the hall?"

"We prefer to eat in our room—I would rather not have too much fuss made over my arrival. Could you also arrange for someone to see to the horses?"

"Naturally, sir, as you wish. To tell you the truth, I am rather glad you are here. When you stayed with us, the master was always in an uncommonly good mood—and contrary to the usual state of affairs, there was even a touch of merriment about the place."

Phineas took hold of his valise, ascended the steps flanked by a stone balustrade, and entered the expansive entrance hall, from which a sweeping double staircase, interrupted by a central landing, led up to the private quarters above. Obed handed the reins to one of the waiting stablehands before following him inside, while Edmund, his voice rasping like an old crow, barked orders and gave instructions to the staff.

They crossed the hall and ascended the steps with steady purpose. A dark, desaturated green, tinged with a stroke of ochre, dominated the towering walls. In the lower third, the paint had peeled away in places, as if moisture had crept up from the baseboards, seeping into the plaster. Large, saline blooms of efflorescence, patches of ashen gray revealing the raw plaster beneath, small protrusions, chipped edges, and scuff marks adorned the walls with a living patina, evoking, in the dim afternoon light filtering in from outside, a subtle breath of bygone ages. Canvases and wooden panels, their baroque frames adorned with delicate gold leaf, hung in staggered tiers, a rhythmic arrangement of small and grand formats alike.

At first glance, the motifs appeared of an ordinary nature—if one were inclined to take the *Hôtel La Porte Noire* as a standard of comparison—predominantly Renaissance works from the fifteenth and sixteenth centuries, rendered in oil and tempera, their thick impasto surfaces now heavy with dust. There were several German pieces in the style of Dürer, Cranach, or Baldung, most notably the latter; a number of Netherlandish works reminiscent of Bruegel the Elder; and interspersed among them, numerous Italian paintings and several small-format compositions in an indeterminate Gothic style, some still strongly indebted to Byzantine traditions. These revealed Lameth as a connoisseur and avid collector. Phineas was at first inclined to dismiss them as mere ornamentation—innocuous, decorative subjects meant for the casual amusement of visitors who came and went through the house. But then, as he studied them more closely, he began to perceive hidden patterns and interconnections—landscapes and secular scenes interwoven with isolated biblical motifs, a piece that bore an uncanny resemblance to a preparatory study for 'The Tower of Babel', a depiction of Death personified, a witches' sabbath, and grotesque, lascivious imagery. Thin cobwebs stretched like connecting filaments from the blackened brass candelabras to the dust-laden frames, branching out along the tiny protrusions and irregularities of the plastered walls.

After Phineas had settled into one of the high-backed armchairs, his weary legs resting on a footstool, and while the giant clumsily wedged himself into a *chaise longue*, struggling to find a more comfortable position, a timid knock sounded at the door. A silent servant entered with a bow and downcast eyes, removing a white dust sheet from the bed and laying out several blankets on the floor in accordance with their request. He performed his task with visible reluctance and then withdrew without a word. A short time later, another knock—this time so tentative it could scarcely be called such—and a young man, his face marked by sheer terror, entered, carrying a tray with trembling hands, nearly dropping it in his fright. He set down their supper with a few murmured courtesies and quickly departed. Obed, sensing what neither of them wished to say aloud, gave voice to the unspoken. "They be afraid of their master. I think I heard that old man scoldin' them, but I reckon he don't know himself what he supposed to do or how he oughta behave. I beg you, let's leave first thing in the mornin'."

"Yes, you are probably right. But I need answers to all these discrepancies. It seems I was blind before, but now I see the world with different eyes. Edmund sleeps in his chamber downstairs, in one of the side wings; the rest of the staff stays in the servants' quarters in an outbuilding. He retires early—he is old and hard of hearing. Tonight, when all are asleep, I will explore the house. We need answers! And was that not our purpose in coming here?"

They ate heartily and, over a bottle of sherry, spoke in hushed tones about the tumultuous events of the past days. Amidst the cyclical rhythm of conversation, silences, and long, brooding stares into the dimly lit room, a faintly hesitant knock—one so light it scarcely seemed to touch the wood—announced the return of the silent one. Carrying a wire basket against his chest, filled with split firewood, he entered without so much as glancing at them. He stacked the logs in the hearth, struck a spark against a bundle of wood shavings with a long match, and kindled a fire. With a rasping scrape, he pulled the iron spark guard into place and withdrew, wordless as before. Within moments, the flames licked eagerly along the logs, dancing in the chimney's draft and casting warm, flickering light upon the wood-paneled walls and furnishings. The bark at the undersides of the logs cracked and curled into white-gray scales, glowing like fissures on the parched earth of some long-dried lakebed, overlaying a blackened substratum of charred embers. The firewood wept its lingering moisture, thin spirals of smoke unfurling from the freshly hewn ends, dissipating into the inferno of writhing flames. The hearth crackled and hissed—a sound like rain drumming against a tin roof, like the gallop of a dozen tiny hooves upon cobblestone.

Phineas opened a window to let out the smoke that had fled the chimney's draft and, with sluggish persistence, had settled into the room. For a few minutes, he stood in silence, gazing into the distance. In the dimming twilight, he could just make out the silhouette of a small church, built from rough-hewn gray stone. Its pointed Gothic windows glowed a warm yellow, like the eyes of a cat gleaming through the darkness of the nave, which nestled against the base of a stout, square tower. "I'm going for a ride tonight. You may stay here and enjoy the sherry at your leisure," Phineas suggested, reaching for his tailcoat from the hook. Obed, drowsy, merely nodded and busied himself with a splinter of wood, prying a strand of meat from between his teeth.

By now, night had fully descended. Phineas made his way to the stables at the rear of the estate, where a few stablehands were still at work, their faces dimly illuminated by lantern light. He saddled a horse and rode out across the open fields, making for the church. The view, which from the upper windows of the manor had stretched out before him in broad, unhindered panoramas, was now obstructed by sprawling dry-stone walls draped in moss and stooped hawthorn hedges. After a short ride, he tied his horse to the gnarled limb of a dead tree. Finding the heavy double doors of the main entrance locked, he made his way instead to a narrow side door and slipped inside. In a tall, pointed-arch window—its tracery dividing the upper third into two slender, interwoven shapes—the stained glass, arranged in intricate leaded panels depicting the Resurrection, had long since been robbed of its daylight brilliance. The entire interior of the church reflected back in its golden-hued panes as a sea of candle flames, in front of which the hunched figure of a man was tending a long matchstick to a fresh wick. As Phineas stepped inside, the door closed behind him with a noise louder than he had intended. At the sound, the man turned with slow, deliberate movements. He was dressed in a long black cassock with a white clerical band draped squarely over his chest. His hair was closely shorn, and his face was lean and gentle, ascetic in its austerity, yet deeply lined with countless wrinkles.

"Phineas, is it you?" The priest's voice was warm, carrying the weight of both surprise and recognition. "What an unexpected joy it is to see you again, safe and sound after all this time. What brings you here at such a late hour?"

"Reverend Smith," Phineas replied, "I could ask you the same. It does feel like an eternity, doesn't it? I saw the light burning and thought I might stop by for a few words."

"I suddenly had the notion that I should come to the chapel once more tonight," the reverend said, glancing at the candles. "Then it grew so dark in here, I thought *Saint George* might appreciate a little light. From your words, I gather you are once again lodging at that grand estate?"

"In the broadest sense, yes, but I am merely passing through. I was in Paris on business at Mr. Lameth's behest. I have a few questions for you, questions that brook no delay."

"Out with them, then. It is, in a way, my calling to provide answers. Are you still struggling with the interpretation of Holy Scripture? Or has your time on the Continent shaken your faith?"

"Neither. Has Mr. Lameth ever attended one of your services? Has he partaken of the Holy Sacrament?"

The reverend gave a short, incredulous laugh. "What sort of question is that, my boy? What are you getting at? You have lived under his roof long enough to know that he never attended Sunday service—nor any other occasion, for that matter. His reasons are his own. Though, if I may say so, you were hardly a model of piety yourself when it came to fulfilling your churchly obligations." He chuckled and gave Phineas a playful wink.

"I once asked him about it, and he merely told me not to trouble myself over such things. Given his extensive knowledge of Scripture and his penchant for discussing matters of faith at every opportunity, I assumed he leaned toward a more Catholic interpretation—or else held to some new Puritanism. A splendidly bound Horarium was always in plain sight in his library, which is why I never questioned his absence from church services. But I ask you again: Has he ever attended Sunday Mass and received the *Body and Blood of Christ*?"

The reverend exhaled slowly, his gaze drifting toward the candles. "Mr. Lameth arrived here a little over half a century ago, seemingly out of nowhere. He purchased the old, half-ruined McAllister estate. Even then, he seemed to have no shortage of money. He restored the entire property—hired local craftsmen, had them come and go for the better part of two years. But eventually, he must have deemed them unfit for the task, for suddenly, strangers appeared—men from some forsaken corner of the earth. I once saw a redskin wandering out across the fields. They must have been hired to dig out his wine cellar or something of the sort. Can you imagine the cost of bringing in laborers from overseas? And yet, they vanished just as suddenly as they had come. Silence returned. Strange, when you think back on it." The reverend stroked his chin thoughtfully. "John Byrne, who once worked as a day laborer for the McAllisters, claimed there was a vast network of tunnels beneath the estate. Said the old McAllister made his fortune smuggling contraband. But Byrne was so fond of drink he spoke all manner of nonsense. Died under unfortunate circumstances. They found him with his throat cut. Someone must have meant to rob him—though everyone knew the poor wretch never had a penny to his name. "But to answer your question: The first thing Mr. Lameth built was the great wall that now separates the church from his newly acquired land. And no—he has never once crossed this threshold."

Phineas narrowed his eyes. "And yet, you once told me you knew him."

"Yes, of course I know him—we are neighbors, after all, despite all peculiarities. The fact that he never attended service does not mean we have never spoken. Once, he came to the wall while I was felling a rotted tree. He asked me for advice on certain plants. At the time, he was growing the usual grains, as well as common medicinal herbs—much like those one might find in a monastic garden, following the prescriptions of a 'Liber de cultura hortorum'—though his was perhaps somewhat more extensive. Beyond that, there was thorn apple, deadly nightshade, black henbane, and so on, along with some exotic plants with trumpet-shaped blossoms and peculiar leaves and fruits, which I assume he brought back from his travels. They did not take well to the harsh climate here. He can be exceedingly courteous, as you well know, though his servants fear him and speak of him as stern and merciless. His knowledge of Holy Scripture is impressive, though he has a certain flair for extravagance and, at times, voices views that stray perilously close to heresy. But such is the way of things!"

The candle flames flickered softly in the breath of the draft that wandered through the old chapel walls, casting their light like gold upon the smoke-darkened stone and tracing the spectral outlines of the two men. Phineas spoke in a hushed tone, as if fearing his words might lose their weight if uttered too loudly: "Does pure doctrine acknowledge such a thing as a spiritual marriage, a mystical union that binds the soul to another being—thus elevating it through purification and revelation? A joining that is not bound by earthly constraints but endures even beyond death? And is it possible—however presumptuous it may sound—to behold God while yet confined within the mortal frame?"

Reverend Smith smiled gently, yet his tone grew solemn. "So many questions, each leading us into the depths of uncharted mysteries and perilous speculation! Irenaeus of Lyon, once bishop in Gaul, wrote in 'Adversus Haereses' that the Valentinians prepared a bridal chamber and performed certain secret rites through the utterance of sacred formulas, claiming this was a spiritual marriage, mirroring a divine union in the heavens. It is a thoroughly sectarian thought—but perhaps, if understood as a symbol, it hints at a deeper, spiritual truth." The priest paused, choosing his words with care before continuing. "As for the vision of God, Jewish mysticism has contributed much to this question, and within monastic tradition, the most devout among us strive, through contemplation and purification of spirit, to glimpse a spark of the divine essence. It is said that Moses was only permitted to see God from behind, for no mortal could look upon His face and live. Thus, the true nature of God appears so overwhelming and sublime that no man could fully grasp it without being consumed by the sight. Perhaps those profound experiences, of which some have spoken, are merely glimpses of certain aspects of the Divine—or a vision that needs no eyes. And perhaps the answer lies not in whether it is possible to behold, but in whether man is prepared to perceive." The reverend studied Phineas intently. "But what compels you to ask such things?"

"I had a strange and profoundly unsettling dream, one that shook me to my very soul. There was a young woman, and it was as if we were... bound together. Not in a manner that could be conceived in earthly terms, but as though our very being had found a common origin. It felt as though we were ascending together into a higher, transcendental sphere—one that surpassed all earthly understanding. And yet, that dream bore a reality so vivid that it seemed almost equal to the tangible world, while at the same time, it was so foreign, so overwhelming, that my mind could grasp only a fleeting shadow of its truth." He paused, his fingers restlessly tracing the knuckles of his opposite hand, before continuing: "Furthermore, Mister Lameth directed me to read certain texts, some of which proved difficult to comprehend. In one of them, I encountered mention of a 'Chymical Wedding'—something concerning the making of the *Philosopher's Stone*, or the supposed transmutation of lead into gold. Yet the more I read, the more I realized that these words could not be meant literally. It was a language of symbols, layered with ambiguity, rich in allegory, bewildering and exhausting in its complexity. The sheer breadth of possible interpretations was dizzying. Each passage seemed to conceal itself, as though it sought to obscure rather than reveal, and yet I felt that beneath it all, some profound truth lay hidden. It was as though the author spoke not of a visible union, but of one beyond the grasp of sight—a union of opposites, of spirit and matter, or perhaps even of the soul with the Divine itself."

Reverend Smith regarded him with a mixture of curiosity and compassion. "Dreams such as yours are often of profound significance, yet all the more difficult to interpret. What you describe bears resemblance to the visions of the mystics: the ascent to a higher state of being, accompanied by a sense of unity—whether with another soul or with the Divine itself. Perhaps your dream does not reveal a 'marriage' in the literal sense, but rather the striving for knowledge, which you may attain only through this bond—not alone, but together. It is not earthly love that triumphs here, but rather the union of souls in the pursuit of light and wisdom. Yet I shall attempt to answer your question as best I can." He folded his hands before him, as if ordering his thoughts, and began: "You have already grasped the nature of such writings well. The 'Chymical Wedding'—a term passed down to us from the language of the alchemists—is no treatise for the common reader. It demands from all who approach it an openness to inner reflection and the ability to see beyond the obvious, to glimpse the deeper truth concealed beneath. It is no textbook but rather a guide—yet only for those who have already set foot upon the path. It is an act of inner transformation, leading through doubt and fragmentation, through darkness and light. And at the journey's end—so it is said—one finds not gold or riches, but the true self. Its meaning, then, lies not in marriage in the worldly sense, but in the symbolic union of opposites: spirit and matter, sun and moon. The alchemist traverses the hidden realm of nature—that true, primordial order of the world, veiled beneath visible appearances and superficial phenomena—in order, after this journey, to perceive the spiritual essence of man, to transcend it, and to attain a deeper truth that leads to union with the very spirit of creation. It is the spiritual and metaphysical principles, those forces at work beyond the external world, whose understanding is necessary to grasp the true nature of humanity. His ultimate goal is the 'Chymical Wedding': the symbolic union with the spiritual plane of nature. But that is alchemy, not theology.

Beyond this, one may also find intriguing thoughts regarding your inquiry in other traditions. The archetype of the Sacred Marriage, called *hieros gamos* by the Greeks, is the union of two deities—Zeus and Hera, or Inanna and Dumuzi—mentioned in the cults of the Greeks, as well as among the Sumerians, Assyrians, and Babylonians. The *hieros gamos* is often understood as the origin of cosmic order and harmony, wherein the union of heaven and earth, of spirit and matter, establishes a balance that sustains and renews the universe. And were I to ask my good friend, a true-born Irishman, he would surely regale you with much concerning the culture of the Celts and the *banais rígi*, that sacred rite in which the king wedded the land itself.

The mystics of the Christian West, meanwhile—equally shaped by Plato as by divine revelation—knew of the 'Mystical Marriage' as it is described in esoteric doctrines and mystical traditions: a symbol of the union between the conscious soul and the Divine, its origin, or its own innermost spiritual essence—that deep, immutable spark of the divine which dwells within the human soul. This idea is deeply rooted in Christian mysticism, particularly in the medieval symbolism of *bridal mysticism*, which vividly portrays the intimate relationship between the soul and Christ." He paused, staring at the candle flame before him, which now burned more steadily, and for a moment, it seemed as though he himself were searching for words that might do justice to the young man before him. His voice grew softer, more contemplative.

"Yet do not forget: What the alchemist calls the 'Chymical Wedding' and what the mystic calls the 'Mystical Marriage' are two fundamentally opposite things. They share only the search for enlightenment and the transcendence of boundaries—and both are ultimately borne by the hope of finding meaning amid the darkness."

"Would you hear my confession and administer Holy Communion?"

"At such a late hour? Would it not be better to return tomorrow at midday?"

Phineas looked at Reverend Smith imploringly, and after some initial hesitation, the clergyman relented. There, in the dim glow of the chapel, Phineas poured out his heart, recounting all that had befallen him in these past years—the loss of his happiness, his struggle with God, the strange and often unsettling occurrences since his arrival in Paris, and at last, the peculiar dreams that still lingered in his fading memory. He omitted the secret words of the initiation, which he had sworn never to reveal, as well as certain disturbing experiences that defied any attempt at verbal expression. Reverend Smith sat in silent contemplation for a time, as if weighing Phineas's words in his soul, and only after a long pause did he find his voice again.

"My dear Phineas, allow me to speak plainly. I do not begin to grasp the fate in which you have become entangled, nor can I discern the true intentions of your enigmatic mentor. By my life, I cannot say with certainty whether he more closely resembles a saint or the Devil himself. But this I know with unwavering conviction: things are transpiring here that lie beyond the ordained path of our faith—things to which the Holy Scriptures offer not the slightest encouragement.

Do you recall the story of Elijah and the four hundred and fifty priests of Baal? Or how Aaron's staff became a serpent and devoured the others? Christ shall, in the end, subjugate all things beneath His feet and emerge victorious. He is the guardian of that final gate, and no deception born of darkness shall prevail against Him. And moreover: regard your benefactor with far greater scrutiny than you have until now! I have served in this place for over half a century, and in all that time, Mister Lameth has not aged a single day—at least, not since I last saw him. There is more to him than he would have us believe, and I do not mean that in any favorable sense. Sever yourself from him and return home. The priest in your parish is a friend to you, even if, in your times of deep sorrow, you found his words too harsh and, in consequence, estranged yourself from Holy Church. Confide in him, as you have confided in me, and let yourself always be guided by the good word of God!"

Reverend Smith waved farewell from the golden-lit arch of his doorway as Phineas mounted his horse and rode back through the leaden darkness toward Lameth's estate. Upon his arrival, he led the horse to the stables, unfastened its saddle and bridle, and ensured it had sufficient fodder and straw. The hounds behind the house began barking, and behind the tall windowpanes, scattered lights flickered to life. Even before his clenched fist could descend upon the dark wood, the door was already pulled open by Edmund, clad in a long nightgown, his expression severe and reproachful as he wordlessly bid him enter. Phineas thanked him politely and wished him a good night. He walked straight to his chamber, where Obed, sprawled across several blankets beside an empty bottle of sherry, raised his drowsy gaze to meet him.

"Where've you been?" he asked, rubbing his eyes.

"I merely paid an old friend a visit to offer my respects. Go back to sleep—I have something to attend to." Obed yawned and lay back down without protest.

Phineas waited until silence had once more settled over the house, then took a box of matches and a lamp, stepping quietly into the corridor without lighting it. He moved soundlessly through the dim passages until at last, he halted before a tall, double-leafed door. Cautiously, he pressed down the bronze handle and eased one of the heavy panels inward. A yawning darkness greeted him, veiling the full dimensions of the two-story chamber in obscurity. Closing the door behind him, he groped his way toward a writing desk, where he set down the lamp. After several fumbling attempts, he managed to open the glass panel and struck a match to light the wick. The glow of the flame was caught in a small, side-mounted mirror, then climbed over long rows of dark shelves, which housed, stacked in tiers reaching meters high, neatly arranged scrolls—frayed at the edges, made of mildewed and browned leather, parchment, or papyrus, some even of thin copper or some other beaten metal—beside musty, iron-clasped codices and leather-bound folios, brittle with age, their spines cut, embossed, and tooled. The flickering light fractured upon a wooden anthemion frieze at the coffered ceiling. Heavy, dark curtains veiled the high windows, ensuring that his clandestine search would go unnoticed from outside. Since the lamp's feeble glow barely penetrated the room's expanse, he lit several more and hurried from one shelf to the next, the lamp in his grasp, though he had no clear sense of what he was truly seeking.

The mystics of the Arabs and Jews stood side by side with all that was commonly deemed apocryphal—those texts excluded from the canonical scriptures—divided even further into the more obscure pseudepigrapha: Old and New Testament apocalypses, acts, epistles, gospel texts, and the secret revelations of Jesus, alongside the writings of the Apostolic Fathers and Church Fathers spanning from the second to the eighth century, an overwhelming abundance of their collected works. In another section, written mostly in Coptic, stood the writings attributed to the Gnostics: 'The Books of the Savior,' certain things said to have been taught by Jesus to his disciples after his resurrection, and all the doctrines devised by the Basilidians, Manicheans, Ophites, Valentinians, Sethians, and others of their kind—or denounced as heresy by Irenaeus of Lyon, his student Hippolytus of Rome, Clement of Alexandria, and those who followed in their footsteps. Many of these books bore foreign, unheard-of titles, some written in languages he could not decipher, others being transcriptions of ancient scrolls, passed down through centuries as copies of copies. Illuminated manuscripts, adorned with lavish initials, vegetal borders, and marginal illustrations, meticulously crafted in the long, silent hours of the scriptorium, were present in great number. Hermetic writings and grimoires such as the 'Testament of Solomon' or the 'Sepher Raziel,' the nine volumes of the 'Arbatel de Magia Veterum,' all that had ever been penned in ink or printed in bold black type by Agrippa of Nettesheim, John Dee, Paracelsus, Johannes Trithemius, and others of their ilk, stood beside 'De revolutionibus orbium coelestium' by Copernicus, Newton's 'Philosophiae Naturalis Principia Mathematica,' and countless tomes on astronomy, alchemy, herbalism, mathematics, natural sciences, and the long-forgotten tongues of antiquity. Many of these books, only a century prior, would have consigned their owner to the pyre.

As he passed by, Phineas bumped into a massive writing desk, crafted with a cylindrical roll-top, and a fleeting thought entered his mind—barely graspable, yet of shattering clarity and certainty—compelling him to see what lay concealed within. The moment he stretched out his hands, the feeling became more insistent, the conviction stronger. The desk was locked. Upon closer examination, a thin gap revealed an iron bolt, lodged just beneath the slightly warped roll-top, sinking shallowly into the metal catch below. He looked around for an object with which to force it open but found nothing immediately useful. Without hesitation, he broke the curved handle and mirrored plate from the oil lamp and wedged the makeshift lever into the gap, twisting and prying until the quarter-circle roll-top suddenly jerked backward with a loud snap, revealing several large scrolls resting in a not-quite-closed drawer. He set aside the broken piece of metal. Blood trickled from a fresh cut on his right thumb. With a sharp intake of breath, he pressed the wound between the thumb and forefinger of his other hand before bringing it to his lips to stanch the bleeding. Then, searching the compartment with his left hand, he withdrew one of the scrolls. It was in a wretched state—so fragile that it seemed on the verge of crumbling at the slightest touch. Carefully, he unfurled it with the aid of his elbow upon a nearby table, weighing down the edges with several heavy objects so that he might examine it in the lamplight. It appeared to be a kind of map, its edges later extended by the addition of smaller fragments, giving it the appearance of a haphazard collection of ancient texts clumsily assembled by some unscrupulous dealer in antiquities.

What he beheld was of the most unsettling nature: rising from the visible grid of intersecting lines, the coastlines of a primeval supercontinent emerged, marked with strange, alien glyphs—rendered in astonishing detail in both red and black ink—on that anachronistic *pergamenum abortivum*. Studying the coastlines, adorned with circular wind roses and rhumb lines in the style of a *portolan chart*, he attempted to identify known landmarks by the placement of mountains and rivers. Then, struck by a thought, he turned to examine the other scrolls. To his growing astonishment, Lameth had produced multiple copies of the same map. By superimposing these with a more recent, ornately cartouched chart, he had attempted to reconstruct the positions of various locations and waterways from the original. Some of the places marked appeared to correspond to the locations of those passages Lameth had spoken of, with names and annotations scrawled in his characteristic, elegant script. And then, realization struck: *Hôtel La Porte Noire* was indeed listed among them. At the very least, Lameth had spoken truth in this regard.

His attention returned to the first scroll. Tilting it at an angle to the light, he turned it this way and that, scrutinizing a particular section—not an appended fragment like the others, but rather a material inseparably affixed to the reverse side, serving as a backing for the severely damaged document. The tattered, unimaginably old parchment, pockmarked with mildew and decay, bore an inscription in an archaic pictographic script—one belonging to a primordial civilization lost to time, predating even those forgotten epochs entombed beneath desert sands, when Pharaoh Menes first crowned himself with the double diadem and united the Black Land. This writing, far older than either hieroglyphs or cuneiform, must have been in use long before such scripts had ever been conceived. Someone had attempted to erase the inscription, likely using some chemical solution, leaving visible traces of the effort. Had they persisted, they might have utterly destroyed the map. As it was, only a small portion had been obliterated, clumsily patched over with an ill-fitting piece of fabric to hold the remnants together.

Phineas pored over the ancient document, tracing the fine lines of its primeval pictographic script with his fingers, as if feeling the raised points of a braille text. And then—suddenly, unexpectedly, and in a manner entirely beyond rational explanation—the foreign script unfolded its meaning before him. The encrypted words spoke directly to his mind—not in the sense of a literal translation, which no scholar could have achieved, but as a kind of revelation, an unfolding of understanding, as though he were listening to a distant memory that slowly emerged from the depths of his expanding awareness. He reached for pen and paper and began to transcribe the words as they revealed themselves to him, his hand flying across the page. The meaning of the symbols unfolded to him the moment he laid eyes upon them, so that he translated at such a speed that it seemed as though he were merely taking dictation from an unseen voice. When at last he reached the end of the text—if such an extraordinary process could even be described in those terms—he went back over it, amending certain passages, refining phrasing, striking out errors, and adding annotations where necessary. It must have been well into the night when he finally set the scroll aside.

That account—resurrected from the dark cradle of an antediluvian civilization and written by one named Esam—both fascinated and unsettled him. And as he reflected upon its disturbing knowledge, it began to interweave with the strange occurrences of the past weeks—those things he had, at times, dismissed or attempted to rationalize—until they fused into a terrible certainty that sent ice through his veins. Suddenly, he heard footsteps in the corridor—the creaking of floorboards beneath slow, deliberate steps. At once, he shoved the scrolls back into the desk, slid the roll-top shut, and locked it. The pages he had just filled with ink, along with the broken lamp handle, he swiftly concealed within his coat. A sliver of light cut through the narrow gap beneath the door—but only for a moment, before it was eclipsed by a shifting shadow. Then, abruptly, the door swung open.

"Master Camill," Edmund croaked, his brows knitted tightly together. His face had taken on the expression of a man who had just tasted something profoundly disagreeable. "What manner of business brings you to the library at such an hour?"

"Forgive the disturbance once more, Edmund. I found myself unable to sleep and hoped to find a suitable book for the night. As it turns out, the search alone has made me quite drowsy. I was just about to leave." Phineas hastened from the room, his steps quickening as he strode down the corridor, glancing over his shoulder more than once. Behind him, Edmund bustled about the library like a flustered hen, running his hands over books, shelves, and furniture as if fearing that some part of the collection might have vanished into thin air. Then, with evident relief, he extinguished the lamps and locked the door with deliberate care.

Phineas lay awake for some time, his mind churning over that unsettling message from the past. The things he had witnessed seemed too incredible, too riddled with contradictions, for his reason to accept them without resistance. Had madness crept upon him unnoticed, insidiously, until the fabrications of delirium had become indistinguishable from reality? And what of his dreams? Had he not seen and heard wonders, even if the details had mostly slipped beyond his grasp—leaving behind nothing but a longing for what was lost? Magnificent had been his visions, incomprehensible his out-of-body experiences, and profound was the love he bore for the girl of his dreams—who, despite the fading of those dreams with each passing day, had burned herself irrevocably into his soul.

Was it possible that, after Eireen's passing, he had sought refuge in some grand, unattainable ideal? Had he fallen prey to a mere phantasm, a dream-image with no earthly counterpart, nor ever could have one? But what if it was not delusion? What if his experiences had been real? A vision like those of Elijah or Isaiah, a revelation brimming with enigmatic, mystical allegories, metaphors, parables, strange symbols from ages long past, their meaning obscure, their earthly correspondences lost or forgotten, revealed only to the truly enlightened, *lux mysteriorum et infusio lucis*—the light of mysteries, the infusion of divine illumination, the shifting of vision that grants knowledge, initiation into deeper faith, encrypted scripture and its mystical interpretation, the ineffable words of Saint Paul, a time to speak, a time to remain silent…

At last, merciful sleep descended upon him. Despite the wretched snoring from the makeshift bed beside him and the restless dreams that plagued him with dark premonitions and disquieting visions, he did not wake until late in the morning. After a hearty breakfast, they had the gig harnessed and set off. The weather was splendid, and as they rode down the winding gravel path, Phineas could not help but notice the servants watching their departure with what looked like relief. Taking the northeastern road, they reached Ipswich by late afternoon. Phineas was a man of considerable means; he had inherited a substantial sum along with the comforts of his home. Yet his way of life was not so extravagant as to require more than two servants. Thus, upon their arrival, they were greeted only by an aging butler and a housekeeper at the gate of a stately yet unassuming old English house, built from red brick and ample in proportion.

A few days later, by which time November had arrived, they received a padded envelope, meticulously addressed, bearing a heraldic watermark, the stamp *Port Payé*, and Lameth's name as the sender. A mounted courier had delivered it for him in the late afternoon.

Paris
October 26, 1831

Honoured Phineas,

I am addressing this letter to Ipswich, with the earnest hope that it may find its way to you in the not-too-distant future. Regrettably, I am not presently in a position to make the journey myself; yet rest assured that, as soon as circumstances permit, I shall follow this letter in due course. I must confess that your sudden departure has left me deeply disappointed. Be assured, however, that it was never my intention to alarm you in such a manner. The draught you consumed to attain your spiritual translation contains a hallucinogen which, on occasion, may produce disturbing effects as a side consequence. Rest assured that none of it corresponds to actual being. You have ever been a most beloved pupil to me, and your well-being, as well as your physical safety, has at all times been my foremost concern. As for my faithless servant, you may inform him that I am willing to reinstate him in his former duties—after he has received a punishment befitting his desertion. Furthermore, convey to him my profound displeasure at his actions. Regarding the maidservant you mentioned, Farah, I must implore you to believe me when I say that any violence inflicted upon her was entirely against my express wishes. You may trust that I shall see to it that this matter is investigated with the utmost seriousness. It pains me deeply to inform you that Farah was not the innocent creature she pretended to be. And yet, despite her dubious origins, I took her into my home out of genuine charity, though I was not spared the necessity of subjecting her to occasional chastisement for her transgressions. I look forward to our reunion, that I might devote myself to you as is my duty.

I remain
Your most devoted
paternal friend,
Lameth

CHAPTER XIII.
ANTEDILUVIAN CHRONICLES

The Chronicles of Esam, son of Sethsotu, who served in the house of Seh'arnak-Akanamún, from the days before the Flood.

Blessed be the God of the Beginning, who shields us from the horrors of the world beyond and from the wrath and vengeance of the Fallen.

I, Esam, came forth from the blessed lands and dwelt in Henochia, in the land of Nod, east of Eden, for the span of many years. Cursed be the day that led me to forsake the fields of light and pitch my tent in the city of sin, for no good was wrought of my deeds.

The reasons for my journey shall find no mention in this account, save that I, hungering for the vanities of the world, turned away from my kin and from the teachings of redemption.

And a shadow lay upon my heart, and my mind was darkened, and a beguiling voice whispered to me of alluring things, until I felt wretched and forlorn, like one who starves himself though surrounded by the bounty of paradise.

And because I knew not darkness, the light and the joy of the blessed seemed to me of little worth, and so I soon grew weary of my life as it had been.

Thus, I departed beyond the great rivers, journeying to lands that seemed a tantalizing promise of all my desires.

And I wandered through forests dense and shadowed, where still lingers the breath of Paradise whence they sprang, and across vast steppes, high-grassed and windswept, until on the morning of the fifth Zefraijal, I stood upon the heights above the forbidden vale, where the mighty river plunged down the jagged rocks, and beheld in the lowlands that cursed city, sprawling in boundless majesty before the horizon, its golden domes arched like serpents and its sky-clawing towers ablaze in the all-dominating sun.

Then I passed through the gates of that city, forged from black celestial metal, above which, upon lofty ramparts crowned with turrets, battlements, and watchtowers, iron-clad men with brazen helms and unblinking eyes kept vigil against the giant-folk and the tribes that roam the endless steppes.

Thus did I set foot in that city, whose craftsmanship defies all understanding, whose resplendent streets, paved in Xardilon, are lined with sphinxes and cunningly sculpted effigies, where the terraced palaces, wreathed in hanging gardens, rise like mountain ridges, their cascading waterfalls gleaming as they descend over polished stone, hewn from the desert, veined with a hundred hues. And within, wondrous halls unfolded, their walls adorned with paintings, their floors inlaid with mosaics of Alabardoulin, Sardonijh, Xarifiel, Carniol, and other gemstones of unfathomable worth.

But surpassing all in splendor was the palace of King Ut-Achamot, which, towering over all else, its pillars wrought in forms manifold and strange, reared immeasurably into the heavens, a seat of majesty without end.

And I became a servant in the house of Seh'arnak-Akanamún, and because of my learning I found favor in his sight, and so I rose in power and influence.

And thus were granted unto me the privileges of that house, where the most extravagant pleasures of every conceivable kind were devised—yet of these I shall not speak, lest I burden the gentle heart of the reader with that which is ungodly.

And my wealth increased, so that by day I served my master, and by night I surrendered to my vices.

And I drank wine from goblets of gold, and I was intoxicated with the fruit of the lotus-tree, and I gave myself over to lust and all manner of wickedness, until I defiled my soul to such a degree that I no longer heard the gentle song of the Maker.

And my master bestowed great favor upon me, and I dwelt in a splendid house, like unto a palace.

And on a day, I took for myself one of the fair women of Kofir to wife, for the harlot's bed had become loathsome unto me, and I desired to sire offspring, that my name might be preserved in the land.

And Sirieel was her name.

And she was graceful and of fair form, her skin like unto dark bronze, such as is mined from the veins of that land; her eyes deep as unfathomable wells, and her lips full and sweet.

And I won her heart, though my own was filled with corruption.

And having fallen under her spell, when she danced before me that night, I wedded her in the manner of old.

She was full of loveliness, but also of kindness.

And her nature was revealed to me as something precious, above all things pure.

She opened mine eyes, showed me my evil ways, and led me back unto the path of my fathers, from which I had strayed.

And though the quiet voice that pervades all things no longer spoke to me, my longing for that which was forbidden was turned to loathing, and I could not avert mine eyes from the horrors begotten by the city, which seemeth to draw all iniquity unto itself and devour it.

For I beheld those slain by secret oaths, and the numberless dead whose lives were ended for the pleasure of the multitudes within the stone arenas; and the thousands of slaves who, beneath the unrelenting lashes of their tormentors, heaved the mighty blocks to raise those unspeakable towers crowned with gleaming capstones, until their suffering was spent and their existence drained away like the blood from their scourged backs into the burning sands.

Neither could I turn mine eyes from the wretched ones whose lives were ended upon those smoke-wreathed altars, from whose blood-sprinkled stones, hewn with dread inscriptions, the fearsome idols of that accursed one arose.

And that Evil One is the father of deception, falsehood, lewdness, and slaughter, which corrupt every manner of life.

And in his dark ways my master instructed me, and—unto my everlasting shame—I proved a most diligent student.

And when I became aware of mine own wickedness, I was filled with great remorse, so that I carried out the commands of my master with gentleness and restraint. And the love of Sirieel gave me strength to withstand the demons that had taken hold of mine heart.

And on a day, when I was inspecting the passages that mine own master had caused to be built, wherein he sought to wrest from his guests the secrets they kept, I came upon him unawares and overheard him at his deeds.

And I drew the sacred circle and wrought the mighty warding spell which mine own fathers had taught me, handed down from the blessed days of the young and flowering world, when our first parents were cast out from the garden.

And this was the spell that the Great Maker had revealed unto our first parents, that they might hide from that being which sought to corrupt the newly wrought creation. And those most ancient words of power shielded me from the gaze of the Fallen One and his host—those who, in defiance, were cast down into the fiery pits beyond the veil of sight—even as from all who serve them.

Thus was I hidden from the sight of him who fights the hopeless battle to cast down the Light.

And so, withdrawn from the gaze of both the seen and the unseen, I beheld my master, gathered in secret with certain noblemen.

And I recognized Shembach-Kiboth, the chamberlain of King Ut-Achamot, of whom I knew that he stole great sums of money in secret, and Seth-Sagarakth, that ruthless man who commanded the city watch, who once served beneath the mighty Sumenthor, the conqueror of Sanamatia, unto whom even far-off Ninagahl paid tribute.

And there was also Nyha'el, the Nefrath of Sargosch, a being of pure deceit, the chief judge of the land.

But among them was a dreadful man, whose gaze seemed to pierce even the walls about him, and I felt him striving to wrest me forth from my hiding, tormenting me to reveal myself. Yet he could not, and so he turned his mind elsewhere.

And he made them swear secret oaths, and I beheld how they worshiped him.

And he promised them the lowly things their hearts desired, and taught them how they might slay and yet gain profit without being found out, and how they might wield their influence to increase their wealth, and how to stir up wars, that they might lay the world beneath their heel—even my own people, who rest in a false and perilous peace.

And he urged them to new cruelty, that the great edifice might be completed, and he showed them the means by which they might achieve this end.

And he revealed unto them machines and wheels and hidden mechanisms, and also the slumbering substances within the laws of nature, that these might be set in motion.

And he spoke unto them of a wondrous thing, which he kept in the deepest vault of his dwelling, secured most excellently behind thick walls and locked doors. Yet never did he reveal this thing unto mine own master, nor unto those who had bound themselves to him in wickedness, save for one time only, when the chief judge pressed him with great urgency, and my master—despite the fear that quivered in his voice—threatened to withhold his aid unless that marvel was brought before his very eyes.

And thus did that Wicked One reveal unto them the great secret, of which no words may bear full witness: a scroll, whose radiance filled the dark vaults and corridors with so unnatural a light, as though the eternal walls which divide our world from that of the Immortals had in a single moment been rent asunder, upon which the mysteries of God were written in fire, as though the Fallen One, before he was cast down and stripped of his once-bestowed tokens of dignity and power, had stolen a page from the celestial book behind the veil.

This, he taught them, was the key that would unlock the eternal gates and bring their unholy design to fruition.

And he showed them that other worlds were inhabited, and also how these worlds were bound to one another, and how one might traverse the winding corridors of space, and thereby be enabled to wander through eternity—even unto the path that leadeth from the deepest, lightless abysses unto the palaces of the seven realms.

Therefore do I, Esam, surmise that the thing which was wrought in the beginning, being perfect, brought forth through the Fall certain anomalies, so that rents appeared in the fabric of space and time—hidden thresholds, which might be forced open by means of this knowledge.

And I beheld that wondrous thing with mine own eyes: a scroll set within a cylinder of metal, wrought with a craftsmanship most exquisite, its length, apart from the casing, being twice the width of a man's hand. Upon it appeared strange symbols and sigils, sigillary seals of power, lines and unknown shapes, formed in a cosmic geometry unspeakable—like unto constellations of the stars, which stand never still, but shift and turn according to the mind that gazeth upon them.

That scroll is without doubt of unearthly substance, for never have I seen its like.

And though it belonged to the dark man, the lines upon its surface shone like unto white fire.

And the dreadful man revealed unto them how, by the imitation of the sacred rite of the Righteous, they might overcome the Watchers who guard the seven gates—an imitation which was but a degenerate corruption of that first rite of the first morning, whereby they might, through black arts, unbind those forces which would enable them to ascend unto the very heights of the heavens and vanquish death itself, that they might make themselves equal unto the gods.

And thus did he promise mine own master dominion and wealth in this world, and at length salvation in one of the celestial realms, despite the manifold sins wherewith he had burdened his soul.

Moreover, he revealed unto them a map; yet it seemed of common make, showing naught but the known visage of our world. Yet in those days, it was not given me to comprehend by what means one might have measured with such precision the shores beyond the farthest known lands.

Some of those coasts I did recognize from my master's sea-charts, which hung upon the walls of his chambers, but never had a nation advanced to those far-off realms which were marked upon it.

And I saw that certain places upon the map were set with markings, and it seemeth that they did signify the thresholds—those gates beyond, whereby our world is bound to the beyond and to the worlds afore named; yea, the places where one might step across the threshold, to pass through those hidden doorways that lie within the fabric of eternity.

And the map remained in the keeping of mine own master.

And in the gatherings that followed, I did observe still further their doings, never once laying bare my presence before the piercing gaze of that dreadful man.

And that one did bid them redouble their labors, that the great edifice might soon be brought to completion, as though he knew of the impending doom. For the still, small voice of the Maker, which now once more spake unto me, revealed that the floods would be sent, to blot out all living things.

And so did they labor with all their might.

And I stole the map from my master in the dead of night, yet that wondrous scroll I did not obtain, for the dark man guardeth it as the apple of his eye, and so could I not bring it into my possession.

And I inscribe this account upon the reverse of that same map, that those unto whom this may one day be revealed shall know that no good shall come of such things—for this work is not of the Maker, but is a work of darkness.

Alas, it is denied me to discern more of the designs of that nameless terror, nor of those strange rites performed in secrecy within the shadowed vaults of my master's house, for through my failure to execute his cruelties, my master hath been warned, and since that time doth seek my life. And the old oaths, once sworn, are now turned against me, and my fate seemeth sealed.

Knowing not how long my life may yet endure, I conceal the map, upon which this account is written, in a hidden place within one of the chambers of the great edifice, which, as I judge it, shall itself outlast even the coming of the floods. For that dreadful man, withholding the truth from my master, hath built it for the very purpose of escaping his death.

And I shroud myself in secrecy, that those pitiless eyes, which stare unceasingly and seem never to rest, and which urge me to lay myself bare, may not behold me.

And I am weary of the cries of the innocent, whose blood staineth the desert sands and the steps of those temples of abomination. And I am weary of the temples and the shrines, and the misshapen idols that are worshiped therein, and of those high pagodas wherein the corrupt magicians increase their dreadful wisdom. And I am weary of war, and I am weary of sin and whoredom and murder and of the secret gatherings, and I tremble before the great edifice and the self-serving purpose for which it hath been raised.

And so do I now flee with my household unto the land of my fathers.

And the end is near, and the floods have been foretold.

And I write this record in the tongue of my forebears, that those who shall, by the power of Providence, read these words, may take from them such knowledge as shall serve them.

And my heart was heavy with fear, lest there be none hereafter who possess the gift to render these words into speech. Yet that voice which pierceth even unto marrow and bone, and which I now hear again, hath granted me peace in this matter. And I am freed, and my soul suffereth no more.

CHAPTER XIV.
MELANCHOLY

Zacharias Barnes sat in his office in Ipswich, his pencil racing feverishly across the pages of a small notebook, his tongue pressed against the corner of his mouth in concentration. The story had been a long time in coming, and now, as the events threatened to unfold in all their dreadful horror, ideas for his sensational article in the upcoming issue of the 'Ipswich Journal' surged through his mind in such rapid succession that he could barely commit them to paper quickly enough. At first, they had been nothing more than vague rumors and hints—those dubious tales, rife with speculation and exaggeration, whispered in hushed tones over pints of *Tolly Cobbold* or *Whitbread* in the dimly lit corners of the local taverns. Stories of certain dubious individuals—night wanderers, beggars, vagrants, whores, and other riffraff—vanishing without a trace from one day to the next. In the beginning, such occurrences were easily dismissed, for now and then, some of the supposedly lost souls would reappear—having slept off their drunken stupors in some hayloft or simply moved their idling ways to another town—causing the murmurs to die down for a time. But eventually, the disappearances grew too frequent to ignore.

Not just in one village, but across entire counties, stretching beyond the borders of common acquaintance, as travelers returned with similar unsettling accounts from neighboring shires. And then, the vanishings touched those of a more respectable standing—young men and carters accustomed to traveling the roads by night—until it seemed as though an unseen force had seized hold of them, driving them away in secret. Then, on a cold December morning, all whispered speculation gave way to a grim and terrible certainty.

It began when, quite suddenly, old Bartholomew's hounds started howling, and in a hollow beneath a hedgerow-covered embankment, they scratched feverishly at the frozen dirt—until at last, from the stiff earth, they unearthed a pale, bloodless arm. With its wrist bent at an unnatural angle, it jutted from the soil like some monstrous, deathly fungus, its lifeless fingers pointing skyward, as if condemning the heavens themselves. Men gathered, crossing themselves in trembling fear, and as they dug deeper, what they uncovered was a ghastly, nightmarish heap—a grotesque accumulation of mutilated corpses, concealed in the shadow of the hill as though hidden from the judgment of God. From that day forward, nothing remained the same. The murders became the single most chilling topic in all of Suffolk and Essex. No tale was more often told, no horror more feverishly discussed than the grim discoveries that had begun near Holton St. Mary and soon spread to other locations. Some of the oldest inhabitants—weathered souls, their voices unsteady with age—spoke in hushed, trembling tones of similar horrors that had plagued the region half a century prior. Then, just as suddenly as they had begun, the killings had ceased—vanished, as though some unseen coastal wind had swept away a poisonous miasma. What lingered was an inexhaustible trove of eerie legends, which, for generations, would haunt the villages and roads of the East Anglian countryside.

Zacharias Barnes chewed absentmindedly on his pencil and paused for a moment. Should he truly describe, in all its horror, how cruelly the bodies had been mutilated, how terribly those broken eyes stared from bloodless, fear-distorted faces—so dreadful that those who beheld them were tormented by nightmares for days, that every soul walking home at night cast an anxious glance over their shoulder, as if some unspeakable terror lurked just beyond the edge of sight? He himself had seen it, had been driven by a hunger for sensation, oblivious to the consequences, had rushed toward a carriage in eager haste and made the accursed decision to bear witness to that infernal crime—a crime that, from that ill-fated moment onward, would never release its grip on him for as long as he lived.

Phineas, meanwhile, wholly absorbed in those ancient records, took little notice of it all. His mind was consumed, above all, by the enigmatic map hidden in Lameth's library within that cylindrical secretary—if one could indeed call that uncanny artifact a map, a thing so meticulously drawn, its prehistoric shorelines measured with a precision that defied reason. His obsession had grown into something bordering on madness. Having only glimpsed the map briefly, he had failed to commit its labyrinthine details to memory; thus, he attempted to recreate a copy from recollection—an outline composed of little more than a few scattered lines and cryptic markings. To aid his reconstruction, he superimposed the known continents in their present form and position, tracing them from his globe. He had books sent to him from all corners of the world, made repeated visits to the *British Museum Library* in London, conferred with the most distinguished scholars in the field, and sank so deeply into this fevered obsession that, one day, Obed remarked with unease that he was becoming more like Lameth than he would ever care to admit.

His thoughts then turned ceaselessly to the mysterious account of that antediluvian civilization, the translation of which had, in such an inexplicable manner, poured itself onto his pages. So fixated did he become that he found himself haunted by those searching, ever-staring eyes—shadows burned into the walls of his study, following him even into his dreams. And always, his mind returned to that unspeakable language, of whose vast and unfathomable structure he had glimpsed only the faintest outermost reaches—a mere spark, a seed, a breath of a thought, and yet powerful enough to wrench the world from its ordained course and shake the very foundations of existence. And, not least of all, his mind dwelled upon the horrors he had endured in those rocky chasms beneath the hôtel, the claustrophobic terror of the stone sarcophagus, and the sight of that dreadful Lameth-being—an entity that, in his nightmares, merged as one with those terrible, unblinking eyes.

At first, Obed idled about the house, watching Phineas's growing obsession with increasing concern. But soon, weary of inactivity, he begged to be of some use around the household. Phineas, at first, was indignant, repeating insistently that Obed was his guest. Yet the giant remained steadfast in his plea, declaring in all earnestness that idleness would drive him mad. To make matters worse, both of Phineas's servants—who had eyed Obed with suspicion and undisguised fear ever since his arrival—abruptly abandoned the house without so much as demanding a letter of reference for their years of service. At last, with no better alternative, Phineas relented and appointed the towering orphan as his steward.

As the ghastly murders and the dreadful discovery of their victims reached their grim crescendo, and as all other news had been utterly eclipsed by the horror of it—until there remained no other topic that could command greater attention—it so happened that the towering newcomer, who had left the house at midday to carry out the weekly errands, did not return as he usually did while daylight still held dominion over the sky. Phineas, seated on the floor in a state of mild disarray, reading within a defensive circle of book stacks like some beleaguered scholar besieged by the weight of accumulated knowledge, failed to notice his absence until late in the evening. He presumed that Obed had lost himself in some tavern and, thinking little of it, retired to bed as usual. But when, by the following morning, his steward had yet to return, Phineas, now deeply troubled, set out into the city to seek him. From those he questioned, he gleaned nothing but rumors—whispers of a suspicious-looking vagabond who, thanks be to heaven, had at last been apprehended. Eventually, with growing apprehension, he paid a visit to the nearest police station.

With an uneasy sense of foreboding, he made his way along *Lower Brook Street* to the junction where it merged into *Foundation Street*. The air had turned bitterly cold; he raised his collar, tightened his scarf about his throat. As he stepped onto the paved road, pausing momentarily for a passing *phaeton* to clear his path, his gaze met—if only for the briefest of instants—the eyes of a woman across the street, her glance adorned with a smile. She was elegantly dressed, strolling past a row of yellow-bricked, towering townhouses. When he returned the smile, she shyly cast her eyes downward, as though uncertain whether he had misattributed the gesture to himself simply by stepping into her line of sight. Then, with lips subtly pursed and chin lifted, she vanished into the bustling throng of pedestrians. He stood motionless for a moment, watching her recede into the crowd. Something about her struck him with a strange, unnerving familiarity. And then, with a sudden clarity, he realized: she bore an astonishing resemblance to Eireen. It was not merely her features—the delicate, finely sculpted symmetry of her face, the dark eyes set within a pale, raven-curled visage like that of a porcelain doll—but the entire manner in which she composed herself. The way she dressed—her fitted, high-necked gown in somber hues, over which she wore a hip-length *mantelet* trimmed with fur, its short, low-set sleeves revealing the white lace of a ruffled collar peeking from beneath the garment's high neckline. The way her hair was pinned up, woven into an intricate chignon, adorned with a small, forward-tilted hat of tulle and silk flowers. The way she carried her delicate parasol, her reticule, the precise poise of her figure, the tension of her bearing—as though she moved upon a stage, a ballet in motion.

A loud curse tore him from his thoughts, forcing him to leap out of the path of a carriage—its driver, his face flushed with rage, bellowing at him—just in time to avoid being trampled. He rubbed his eyes as if he had seen a ghost, then continued on his way toward the harbor, passing *St. Mary's Church* and turning right onto *Key Street*, making his way toward the old customs house at the northern quay, where the local police station had been established. Several tightly clustered, parallel hipped roofs—five in total—resembling oversized dormers that seemed to have outgrown the original house, one of them pierced by a tall chimney capped with two clay flues, rested upon a brickwork foundation supported by a row of ornately carved columns, adjoining a half-timbered building with a triangular gable. Phineas stepped boldly through the door and soon found himself in conversation with one of the officers on duty, who greeted him with proper formality: gloved hands, a high-collared navy-blue frock coat adorned with a long row of gleaming silver buttons, and a tall stovepipe hat perched atop his head.

"We nabbed the scoundrel yesterday and put 'im straight into custody. Must be from one of the colonies, I reckon. You can rest easy—he's locked up downstairs, where he can't do no harm to no one. Imagine the nerve, strollin' 'round town like nothin' 'appened. We got a whole heap o' tips from folk, so we took 'im in right away, no fuss. Nearly took two o' our men to pieces when they tried to cuff 'im, but then he suddenly went all meek and started blubberin' in French like a babe. Seems like 'e's already resigned 'imself to the gallows."

"The gallows!" Phineas cried in horror. "Are you out of your mind? What charges have been brought against him?"

"Don't you read the papers? The murders these past weeks, all them vanishin's. Like I said, we got plenty o' leads. Most folk here didn't take to 'im much. You won't believe it, but it's true—a couple came in, swore up and down that the killings and disappearances started right 'round the time this brute set foot on our soil. They was workin' for some rich fella, apparently, who'd taken the fiend in as well."

Phineas's expression darkened. "Take me to him at once. I must speak with him immediately!" he demanded, his voice carrying an undercurrent of anger.

"Well, aren't you in a mighty rush! Hold your horses, sir! You oughta know, you ain't the only one takin' an interest in 'im. What's yer business with the prisoner, if I may ask?"

"He is my house steward," Phineas answered, his voice laced with both fury and desperation. The officer pulled his chin to his chest and gawked at him with wide eyes and an open mouth, like a fish gasping for air. Without further question, he led him down into a long, narrow corridor of Flemish bond brickwork, where doors stood in strict architectural symmetry, each leading to a small, barred cell. In one of them sat a wretched figure, battered and bruised, with a swollen black eye, scratches marring his face, his waistcoat torn, and a makeshift bandage wrapped around his head. "Obed!" Phineas cried out in dismay. The man addressed stirred from the corner of the room, rising from the shadows cast by the iron bars, towering like Samson in the temple of Dagon, shackled by the Philistines.

"Master Camill, I swear I ain't done nothin'!" Obed pleaded, his red-rimmed, cow-like eyes brimming with tears.

"I know, calm yourself!"

"People been comin' here all mornin', just to stare at me, call me names, even pelt me with rotten greens! I can't believe what's happenin' to me!" he wailed, his face contorted with pain, drumming his palm against his forehead as if tryin' to knock loose a swarm of mice inside.

"I'll find a capable attorney and get you out of this hole, you have my word. Have they at least given you food?"

"They beat me up an' robbed me. I was just doin' me shoppin' when they jumped me. Had clubs, real nasty ones. I hollered that I ain't done nothin', but all they kept sayin' was *'on ne parle pas france,'* an' then – whack! – with the sticks again. But if they really didn't speak no French, how'd they know how to say that, huh? I fought back, an' then they got real mean." He paused, offering a pained, tooth-baring grin. "I only know how to say 'bread,' 'cheese,' 'wine,' and 'how much it costs?'. That's it, no more."

"I'm sorry, I was so caught up in my own troubles, I never even helped you learn our language."

"Visitation's over!" came a voice from the hallway. "There's others wantin' to see 'im." The shadowed figure that rose behind the bars was so large that the speaker, instead of approaching, hesitated and instinctively took a step backward.

Phineas bid farewell, resting a hand through the bars upon Obed's massive, shuddering shoulder, then departed straight homeward to the stately brick house. Once inside, he exchanged his coat for a dressing gown, rummaged through the kitchen for some leftover scraps, and collapsed into one of the high-backed chairs, hoping to dull his melancholy with a bottle of port. After some time, he rose, sifted through some documents in his writing desk, and reviewed his financial situation along with the available courses of action. He was wealthy enough to live without the necessity of a profession, yet his funds were not limitless. Over the following days, he penned several letters, then, accompanied by a frail, briefcase-toting old gentleman, paid another visit to the prison.

"That big brute ain't here no more!" the blue-coated constable said, staring at them with mild amusement. "A real fine gentleman came in yesterday, made a statement, cleared up the whole thing. Even pointed us straight to the real killer. Left a handsome sum for bail, too, just in case there'd be a trial after all."

"Where was the prisoner taken?" asked the attorney, whose age suggested he had long since passed his prime.

"Why are you asking me? As soon as that gentleman appeared, he became utterly docile, followed without a word, without the slightest resistance. Funny thing is, he didn't look at all pleased to be leaving his cell. Perhaps it ain't as bad in there as folks like to claim, eh?" He laughed heartily, sticking both thumbs into the pockets of his frock coat, which bulged over his round belly, the silver buttons gleaming in the light. "Besides, that fine gentleman seems to have a real knack for handling the brute. That's what I always say! Tough lads need a firm hand, if you catch my meaning." A nearby watchman let his truncheon bounce lightly in his palm and winked at them in complicity.

"Can you take us to the suspect?" Phineas asked, already dreading what he might hear.

"Oh, my deepest regrets, sir! The fellow took his own life this morning. Couldn't seem to wait to stand before the Almighty. Looked half-mad already, if you ask me, slurring like a drunkard. Guess he just couldn't bear another day without claiming another victim, so he put an end to himself instead. Must've smuggled something in and slit his own throat. What a damn mess, I tell you!"

Phineas swallowed hard, overcome with pity for the poor wretch—another soul, without a doubt, whom Lameth had ensnared, either with one of his potions or some other devilry, driving him to such a horrific fate. He bade the constable farewell, exchanged a few final words with the little man at his side, then departed, nearly faint with horror. Upon reaching home, he took Eireen's portrait from the mantelpiece and, staring at it for hours, lost himself in the depths of his despair. He wallowed in self-pity, recalling, with a pang of anguish, his parents, so cruelly and prematurely taken from life before he had even reached manhood; the fleeting happiness he had shared with Eireen, and that wretched death he had been powerless to prevent; the brief yet luminous joy he had found with Farah, that enchanting girl who had, if only for a moment, illuminated his darkened path with her love. He thought of Obed—simple, slow-witted, withdrawn, that childlike giant—who now, more than likely, was once again trapped beneath Lameth's yoke, forced to endure his whims, working day in, day out in dull servitude, devoid of hope. Even the absence of his dim-witted servants troubled him now, despite their crude accusations, born of naivety and prejudice, against Obed. And then his thoughts turned to those strange dreams—visions of that young woman from an ethereal, unreal realm of angelic revelations—who had left in him an unbearable void, a yearning beyond reckoning. And again, always, endlessly, Eireen—like the monotonous revolving cylinder of a somber orchestrion.

Days upon days passed while he, numbed by grief, lingered in the dim light of his book-cluttered parlor, clad in a stained dressing gown, unshaven, and with unkempt hair. An inner void, a tormenting sense of loss and abandonment gnawed at his soul, until he began to hurl utterly groundless and exaggerated accusations against himself. In his mind, he fought a bitter dispute with his own conscience, until his deep sadness reached such heights that a sob, too profound for words, escaped from the clench of his lips. Sitting hunched in the dim room, his body trembling, his eyes narrowed to slits from which tears broke forth, he struggled against the shadows closing in upon him like hostile pursuers. At some point, another bottle of that ruby-red wine joined him in his misery, and when he had emptied it, he was not only thoroughly drunk but also bore upon his lips a scornful smile. His expression had turned to iron, a rigid, joyless mask. *"Whimper like a child instead of protecting those you love!"* he sneered inwardly. *"Compose yourself! I will confront Lameth, demand—no, command—him to explain himself. This secrecy must end once and for all."* His gaze wandered drunkenly through the room, then he descended into the wine cellar to fortify himself with another glass before setting out—only to awaken the next morning, head pounding, slumped against one of the wooden wine racks, having failed to act upon his resolve.

For days, he wrestled with the courage to seek out Lameth, but his attempts invariably ended in throbbing headaches and the inexplicable dwindling of his wine reserves. Eventually, there was nothing left to eat in the house either, which finally compelled him, one morning, to venture out on an empty stomach. He let himself be carried along by the throng, unaware of his destination, until he reached the city center. As he crossed the street toward the nearest pub, he suddenly had the eerie sensation of being watched. While walking, he twisted his head repeatedly, searching for the source of those unseen eyes. The passersby cast disapproving glances at the disheveled young man with his shadowed eyes and hunted expression, steering clear of him as though fearing contagion. After drinking copious amounts of whisky, he sought out an apothecary and emerged clutching a small bottle wrapped in paper—*Godfrey's Cordial.* "Only for the nausea," he muttered under his breath. He purchased some provisions—bread, a side of bacon, sausages, vegetables, and other supplies, all packed into a large wicker basket—and set off toward home.

Then, all at once, she appeared again. That graceful figure swathed in flowing, high-necked fabric, her dark hair bound up, the pallor of her porcelain-like face—so eerily like her. Eireen? The name escaped his lips, so struck was he by the resemblance. His pace quickened, jostling against the crowd, his steps unsteady. Scowling faces, muttered curses, and incredulous glances recoiled from him like waves before a prow. "Eireen!" he called out, louder now—but a passing carriage obscured his view, and when it had gone, the slender figure—the source of his distress—had vanished into the anonymity of the crowd. He slumped against a dented drainpipe, its surface streaked with green copper patina, gasping for breath. The curious stares of passersby fell upon him, accompanied by murmured remarks questioning his sanity, until at last, he dragged himself home and spent the rest of the day steeped in an opium haze.

At noon the following day, his confidence heightened by heavy wine and opium, he seized his coat, scarf, and walking cane, and ordered a carriage to finally pay Lameth that long-planned visit. Calling out the address to the driver, he climbed into the curtained, black-lacquered coach of a *landau*, which, under the creaking of its iron-rimmed wheels and the sharp crack of the whip, carried him with taut reins toward that long-awaited, albeit fateful, reunion. After several hours, as the white sun disk, set in gold, sank behind the horizon in otherworldly splendor, framed by white-edged clouds against the pale blue and crimson sky, he had the carriage halt some distance from the estate, settled the fare, and set off on foot through the moonlit night, which now hung heavy over the fallow stubble fields. The dusky-black mansion loomed in the distance like an enchanted castle against the nocturnal sky. The cold and the crisp air sharpened his senses, and excitement dulled his inner pain. He was keenly aware of the sound of the breaking stalks beneath his purposeful steps and felt the vastness of the endless, star-laden firmament enveloping him like a silent, shoreless sea. Suddenly, the sensation of being watched returned, and under the influence of his heightened imagination, the gnarled thickets of hedges and trees contorted into grotesque shapes, their hunched limbs and long claws sprouting nightmare-like from the darkness. But he pressed on with resolve and, after half an hour, reached the more secluded outbuildings at the rear of the estate.

Even during the carriage ride, a plan—still unformed and lacking in clear contours—had begun to germinate within him: not to present himself at the main entrance, dutifully knocking, in order to confront Lameth with his suspicions, but rather to remain unseen and embark upon a secret search for those mysterious tunnels beneath the estate, of which Reverend Smith had spoken in such an offhand manner. And whatever it was that Lameth might be concealing there, Phineas nurtured the hope of finding something substantial—some piece of evidence with which he might at last prevail upon him to confess. He knew the estate as well as the back of his hand, having spent much of the past years within its walls. Thus, he was also aware of a slanted trapdoor behind the manor, slightly raised above the earth, which he suspected led to that complex of underground passages. Once, he had caught sight of Lameth descending the steps into that unknown abyss, only to be promptly sent away on some feeble errand—an incident that, in hindsight, seemed most suspicious. Keeping low, he crept through the darkness, his fingers brushing against rough wooden beams, until he stumbled over a rake and other farming tools leaning against a massive oaken support post.

He heard barking in the distance, followed by the hurried patter of a large beast's paws upon the flagstones. The steaming, moonlit silhouette of a four-legged creature, the size of a calf, appeared at the entrance of the ring-shaped outbuildings, then, after pausing for a few seconds, it charged toward him with unbridled ferocity. The massive body of the great hound reared up before him and then came crashing down upon his chest with a howl, nearly knocking him off his feet. His outstretched hands met the damp fur, sinking into its thick, wiry coat. Hot breath brushed against his face. "Temunat, leave me be!" he whispered in a sharp tone. The enormous black dog let out a high-pitched whimper and wagged its tail eagerly. "Go back to your kennel and gnaw on your bone—not on me!" he commanded in exasperation, ruffling the shaggy fur to soothe the beast. Hot slobber sprayed across the backs of his hands. Temunat pressed itself tightly against him, circling him a few times with its head tilted to the side, nearly upsetting his balance, before suddenly dashing off as if summoned by an unheard call. Phineas crept forward with caution and, after some time, reached a stone-framed, double-winged trapdoor slanting over the ground, encased in thick iron chains secured by a sturdy padlock that barred entry into the depths below.

"What a foolish idea, coming here. Why would Lameth leave the entrance unlocked if he had anything to hide?" he muttered to himself. He set his walking stick aside and rummaged through the assortment of tools scattered beneath the shadow of a wooden overhang. After struggling fruitlessly with the heavy lock for some time, he finally sank onto the stone ledge of the trapdoor, massaging his forehead as he wrestled for a solution. His failure disheartened him so completely that no further humiliation seemed possible—an exasperation that drove him, in a moment of reckless boldness, to abandon caution altogether and break into Lameth's house in search of another way into the hidden cellar. He climbed up a twisted wisteria vine, hoping to gain entry through one of the high windows. As he swung himself over the balustraded balcony and fiddled with a window latch, a moving light suddenly cut through the darkness within. The glow of a lamp edged closer and closer, until a door burst open with an abrupt jolt.

"My dear Phineas, I must say, I am most astonished!" Lameth's voice chided, carrying the tone of a father catching a mischievous child in the act of some impish prank. "First, you trample upon my hospitality and leave without so much as a farewell. Then I find my belongings in shambles, a corpse in my cellar, and must wrestle my way through endless paperwork and dealings with the local constabulary. Two of my servants have vanished without a trace, and to top it all off, I receive a letter from you, brimming with the most unwarranted accusations. And now, as if that were not enough, you break into my house and startle my guests." Lameth's face flickered imperiously from the half-light of the oil lamp and the pale gleam of the moon beyond the threshold. Then, as though at the flick of some unseen switch, his expression softened into something mild and sympathetic, as if Phineas were a sickly, willful child refusing to take his medicine. "But what am I saying—my apologies! I did not notice how unwell you look. You are as pale as a ghost. Come, let me help you."

Lameth smiled with magnanimous indulgence, stepped beside him, and, without meeting any resistance, guided the dazed young man into the house. He settled him in the brightly lit salon, where Phineas slumped into a chair, his shoulders sagging like a loosened foremast sail, one arm dangling limply to the side. He gazed at the wall with a vacant stare, his half-lidded eyes peering out from beneath a fallen lock of hair.

A soft clearing of the throat startled him upright. The young woman, whom he had encountered days before in the city and who so hauntingly resembled Eireen, sat opposite him at the table, her back impeccably straight, her head tilted in polite inquiry. She held a teacup delicately in one hand, a small slice of fruitcake resting on a white porcelain plate before her. A smile played upon her lips. "May I introduce you both?" asked Lameth.

CHAPTER XV.
PENNY

He mumbled his name through half-parted lips, where a small pool of saliva had gathered due to his prolonged stillness. Now, seeing her up close, he became aware that while her features did bear some resemblance to Eireen's—enough that one might mistake them for siblings—it was, in truth, more the way she wore her hair, the manner of her dress, or the eerily precise mimicry of Eireen's posture and gestures that had, from a distance, created such an uncanny illusion and deceived him so thoroughly. She seemed a little older than Eireen had been back then—closer to his own age.

"Penny O'Riley. You may call me Penny," she said with a faint smile, her lips painted a deep red. Her expression was warm, yet her gaze, keenly assessing the situation, swept the room with quiet calculation. "It is a pleasure to finally meet you. Mister Lameth speaks of you only in the highest regard." With a delicate motion, her fingers forming a poised arc, thumb and forefinger lightly pinching a morsel of fruitcake while the remaining three fingers stretched outward like the poised gesture of a Buddhist mudra, she plucked a small bite from her plate and nibbled at it like a bird. Then, lifting her chin once more, she smiled at him again—this time with lips pursed and her finely arched brows subtly raised. Phineas rubbed his eyes with the heels of his palms, then dragged both hands down his cheeks before running his fingers through his disheveled hair in rapid succession, all without responding to her. His distrust of Lameth had grown so profound that he now seriously questioned whether this woman's presence was yet another of his host's inscrutable machinations, meant to toy with him—or whether he himself, in his fevered, grief-stricken yearning for Eireen, had conjured this spectral resemblance through sheer force of delusion.

"Tell me, how is Obed?" he blurted out, still not turning to face Lameth, who lingered behind him in the doorway. "Am I right in assuming it was you who bought his freedom from prison?"

"Obed?" Lameth echoed, feigning surprise, as though he had never expected Phineas to inquire about the man's fate again. "Ah, yes, quite right! I secured his release—for a rather considerable sum, if I may add. And not a moment too soon, it seems, for they were quite nearly ready to tighten the noose around his neck—and I do not mean that in a figurative sense. I deemed it best, for his own safety, to remove him from the country, and I trust he is now back in Paris, resuming his former occupation. He was utterly relieved to see me again, you may rest assured, and to set your mind at ease, I can assure you that I have forgiven him, most magnanimously, for all his transgressions—even his rather unfortunate involvement in that dreadful incident which, as you well know, took place within my home during my regrettable absence." At these words, Penny recoiled with a start, her wide eyes darting to Lameth in silent shock. "Fear not, my dear," Lameth said smoothly. "He acted, I believe, in the heat of the moment. But this one here"—he inclined his head toward Phineas, who had finally turned to face him—"is a true humanitarian, having taken the unfortunate fellow under his wing without so much as chastising him for his… indiscretions. Obed spoke to me at length of your kindness." He gestured benevolently, offering a measured smile.

"I saw the giant! A truly fearsome sight," Penny interjected. "How very brave of you to associate with such a frightful man," she said, fixing Phineas with a gaze that balanced intrigue with faint amusement.

Phineas lowered his head, closed his eyes, and took a deep breath. After some time, he slowly looked up, first at Penny, then at Lameth, who had now stepped closer to the table, and regarded them both in silence, saying nothing for what felt like an eternity of unsettling scrutiny. At last, he spoke. "Since we are reminiscing about the past," he began, his voice hoarse, "I would be most eager to know what has become of that dubious fellow to whom such derogatory terms might more rightly apply—the one you introduced to me as your guest, the one who committed such a monstrous crime against an innocent girl that death itself would seem a mercy." By the end of the sentence, his eyes were brimming with tears, and his body trembled with a sob, heedless of the stranger's presence. Penny, moved by compassion, placed her pale, lace-gloved hand over his and regarded Lameth with a worried frown.

"You speak of Baldassare," Lameth replied at once. "Rest assured, I have seen to it that he has received his just punishment. Never again will he raise his hand against anyone dear to you."

Penny shifted her chair closer to Phineas and wrapped an arm around his shoulder, offering what comfort she could. The effects of the opium had long since dissipated, and Phineas, once again at the mercy of his sorrow, abandoned himself entirely to grief. "Hush, hush," Penny murmured, stroking his back in a gentle, soothing motion.

Lameth disappeared for a few minutes and returned through the tall, double doors of the paneled chamber, its ceiling adorned with sweeping stucco flourishes. In his hands, he carried a bottle of whisky and two glasses, which he set down before Phineas and filled generously. "Drink this!" he commanded in a tone that brooked no argument. With trembling hands, Phineas seized the glass, sniffled, and downed it in one gulp. Lameth, leaning against the table like a crooked tree, followed suit, while Penny, catching his knowing wink, withdrew from Phineas's side and resumed sipping her tea with pursed lips, as though nothing had transpired.

"Your servants have abandoned you, as I have been informed," Lameth remarked with a note of sympathy. "It would give me great pleasure to welcome you back into my house once more. Miss O'Riley is my guest and will also be staying for some time, so you shall not lack for pleasant company." Phineas hesitated for a moment before nodding in agreement. "Splendid! Then it is settled!" Lameth declared. "I shall have Edmund see to it that you are made comfortable, and that all the amenities of this house are at your disposal. Just like the good old days, is it not? If you so wish, I can send for anything you require from your house in Ipswich first thing tomorrow." He helped Phineas to his feet and led him out into the oil-lit corridor. Yellow ellipses of approaching lamplight stretched across the high, bloom-streaked walls, casting elongated, fading cones down toward the floor. Phineas gathered himself, turned back one last time out of courtesy, and wished Penny a good night before bidding farewell to Lameth. Then, without another word, he followed Edmund, who, with head bowed and without so much as a murmur, led him silently upstairs.

Phineas sat on the freshly made bed, removing his clothes and boots. He rolled his head along his spine, and it rang in his ears like a carriage rattling over a gravel path. At first, he had intended to end the day with a prayer, as was his custom, but he was so utterly spent in both body and soul that he left it at the thought alone. Instead, he stepped out into the corridor to relieve himself and then collapsed into the spacious bed, surrendering to sleep without another thought. The next morning, for the first time in what felt like an eternity, he awoke without that leaden exhaustion pressing upon him. He attributed it to the fact that he no longer spent every waking moment cursing Lameth and his supposed conspirators or exhausting himself with wild conjectures. Despite the many unanswered questions and lingering contradictions, Lameth's well-argued explanations—at least on the surface—had been convincing enough to pacify him, at least for now. He allowed his resistance to lapse, and the relief it brought him was undeniable, even if he struggled to banish the doubts that slumbered beneath the surface of his mind.

He stepped to one of the tall windows and gazed through the misted panes, divided into latticed sections by their white-painted mullions, down into the courtyard, where the frost-laden hedges stood in rigid formation. The old beeches flanking the manor had shed the greater part of their foliage and now thrust their many-fingered, grotesquely knotted limbs skyward in writhing, skeletal contortions. The lichen-cloaked stone of the courtyard, worn smooth by time, was dusted with a fine layer of frost that had settled in its crevices like powdered sugar. The approaching barks of the hounds drowned out the monotonous croaking of the ravens. Below, in the yard, he spotted Penny watching one of Lameth's men as he fed the dogs. She wore a long dark winter coat, and her head was wrapped in a fur-trimmed hood. Her eyes rose along the façade, and when she glimpsed him standing at the window, his breath a ghostly mist upon the glass, she smiled and waved cheerfully up at him.

Later in the day, they dined together and took pleasure in the comforts the estate afforded them. The days passed, and they grew closer. Lameth rarely made an appearance, nor did he exert any pressure on Phineas to resume his esoteric studies or assist him in any other capacity. Phineas often observed him engaged in quiet, seemingly confidential conversations with Penny, as though she were bound to answer to him in some way, though he could not quite grasp the nature of their association. His moods still fluctuated wildly, and more than once, he pleaded with Penny to keep a certain distance. "My life is overshadowed by misfortune, that much I can assure you," he told her on one such occasion, his eyes resting on her before he averted them, his voice heavy with resignation. "But far worse than my own plight is the fate that befalls those who draw too near to me." He took a slow breath before continuing, his gaze darkened with some unfathomable weight. "I do not know what calamity clings to me—whether it was the curse of some temple I unwittingly defiled in the depths of the jungle, one that the natives only spoke of in hushed, fearful whispers, or if it was the priest in Haiti, who warned me of dreadful things to come should I refuse to purchase one of his charms. Whatever the cause, it seems that those who linger in my presence too long, most especially those I love, are not destined for long or happy lives."

Penny's eyebrows arched so high that fine creases formed upon her forehead. "The things you think and say! A curse, and such dreadful notions. Believe me, that is nothing but superstitious nonsense. You are responsible for no one's fate but your own, and no force—neither from heaven nor from hell—bars the path of a man who chooses to live the life he envisions for himself… not even God can dictate to you how you ought to live yours. Set aside these burdensome thoughts! Let us do something exciting together. Despite the excellent comforts of this house, I feel as though I might wither away. We could take a trip to Colchester tomorrow and dine together—if the proposal meets your favor." She tilted her head slightly and regarded him with a playful blink, her gaze shimmering with unspoken promises.

"Tomorrow is Sunday. I had intended to attend the service and, if possible, exchange a few words with the reverend," Phineas replied, neither in the mood for amusement nor inclined to such distractions on that particular day.

"Church? How terribly old-fashioned you are! Perhaps that is one of the reasons you always seem so burdened. Do you truly believe God cares whether you sit within some over-towered heap of stone on a Sunday morning, or spend the day in my company, savoring life's pleasures?" Despite the sharpness of her words, Penny smiled sweetly and took his hands in hers. "Please, do not deny me this little wish. How about this—before we set out for Colchester, we shall breakfast together? Expect me in the dining hall at nine, after I've freshened up." She turned from him before he could protest, walking away with an air of playful defiance, waving over her shoulder with her pale, gloved fingers.

The next morning, Phineas sat dutifully at the dining table, awaiting Penny's arrival—though she was unfashionably late. By the time she appeared, he had already finished his breakfast, sipping absentmindedly at a second cup of tea out of sheer boredom. She had taken great pains with her appearance, excusing her tardiness by pointing to the heightened effort required. Now, seated before him in all her finery, her cheeks softly powdered and lips painted with delicate precision, she allowed herself to be served with the grace of a queen. Every item a lady might require for the day—a fur-lined muff, a long winter coat, a dainty handbag—lay draped over the curved back of a chair beside her. With great care, almost ceremoniously, she added milk and sugar to her tea, stirring it with the faintly ringing chime of a silver spoon against porcelain, watching the cloud of cream billow and dissolve. She lifted the cup to her lips, pausing for an instant before taking a careful sip, her upper lip barely grazing the rim.

They lingered over conversation for some time before finally making their way down the broad steps, where a carriage awaited them in the courtyard—a fine Stanhope Gig, or Tilbury, as it was known by the name of its maker. Snow had begun to fall, and the cold had grown sharper. The stablehand cursed under his breath, cupping his hands and breathing warmth into his numbed fingers. Before the horse's nostrils, twin plumes of vapor curled and unfurled, moving in contrary rhythms. The stiffened whiskers beneath its bridle hung like a white, frost-laden beard. Phineas folded down the carriage step, carefully assisting Penny as she gathered her skirts and settled into her seat. Then he climbed in after her. With the crack of a whip, the Gig rumbled forward, creaking and crunching over the frozen gravel path before taking a winding road through the countryside. Though it was midday, the sun was feeble, struggling against the dense, yellow-tinged mist that cast an eerie pall over the snow-laden landscape. Penny, snug beneath a heavy lap blanket, tucked her hands into her fur muff and smiled at Phineas from beneath the plush trim of her hood. The two-wheeled tracks of their passage carved a lonely, meandering path through the untouched snow, stretching out into the distance as though they were the only souls left in the world that day.

In the distance, off to the right, a small church rose from the cold fields, amidst frost-crowned hedges, bushes, trees, and boundary walls of stacked stone. Phineas thought he could faintly hear the reverberations of the congregation's singing, their responsory drifting through the chill of the day. Penny cast him an inquisitive glance. "Now that you are partaking in such a splendid scene of nature, surely you do not regret being absent from that old custom, do you? Or am I mistaken?" Phineas merely shrugged, offering no reply, his thoughts turning briefly to Reverend Smith. As the second hour of their journey passed, they drove along a narrow, snow-rutted road and came to a halt before an inn whose thick, leaded windows, aglow with candlelight and the flicker of a roaring hearth, beckoned them invitingly from the brick facade. Phineas slowed the horse to a steady trot and brought the Gig to a stop. A young stablehand hurried forth and, for the price of a copper coin, saw to the care of the horse, which stood steaming and sweating as he fastened a feed bag over its muzzle and draped a blanket across its back.

Phineas extended a hand and helped Penny down from the carriage, guiding her up the short flight of steps and into the welcoming warmth of the inn. As they crossed the threshold, a pleasant heat enveloped them. He assisted Penny in removing her coat, then hung it upon one of the great wrought-iron stands, crowning its peak with her fur muff, so that it bore an uncanny resemblance to a Grenadier Guard standing watch in a bearskin hat. Once he had shed his own overcoat and scarf, he turned to see Penny already beckoning him toward a table. A large fire blazed in the central hearth, and before joining her, he lingered for a moment, stretching his fingers toward the flames to chase away the lingering chill. The room was low-ceilinged, its walls clad in dark wood paneling. In a glass-fronted cabinet, ham, sausages, and fish were displayed for the patrons' choosing. Candles flickered upon the broad wooden tables, their glow reflected in the polished pewterware. Few guests were present, and the serving maid, quick to notice new arrivals, was at their side in an instant, inquiring after their meal preferences.

Penny had already ordered a bottle of wine, and before Phineas could give the matter a second thought, the ruby-red liquid gleamed in their glasses, catching the firelight and offering a moment's idle amusement. Soon after, their waiting was rewarded as the *Sunday roast* arrived—succulent lamb, golden potatoes, vegetables, and *Yorkshire pudding*, the steam rising invitingly from their plates.

Once they had eaten and drunk their fill, they lingered in casual conversation for some time. Outside, the sun had finally scattered the morning mist, and its rays now streamed through the inn's leaded, bottle-bottomed windows, casting a lattice of softened light upon the table and the wall beyond. The polished metal of the spit bowls and cooking pots caught the illumination, sending gleams of brightness flickering across the room. Penny, as though drawn by some inexplicable magnetism, edged closer to him with every passing minute, until at last, she rested a hand upon his shoulder. With her head tilted slightly, she studied the half-filled glass in her hand, turning it within the interplay of firelight and the golden beams pouring in from outside. "Did you enjoy the roast?" she asked, as Phineas dabbed his mouth with a napkin.

Yes, indeed. This meal has more than made up for the hardships of our journey. If only we did not have to step back out into that cold," Phineas said, setting his napkin aside and rubbing his stomach. Penny took the bottle of wine and refilled his nearly empty glass.

To our acquaintance!" she toasted him. "I must say, you are much more to my liking this way. This little retreat seems to be doing you good."

"Yes, you are right—I feel as if I have been reborn, as though an immense burden has been lifted from my shoulders."

"And do you still regret coming out with me? Or would you rather be in that place full of murmured words and unheard prayers?"

Phineas ran a hand through his hair, considered briefly, and took a sip of wine. "Those cold walls can hardly compare to such lively company," he admitted. "Still, I would have liked to see Reverend Smith again, to speak with him. No matter—there will be time enough in the coming week. If Lameth is granting me this reprieve, I might as well make use of it."

"For my part, I am firmly convinced that no mediator is needed to be religious—least of all a building dedicated to such a purpose. And tell me, was not our ride through that beautiful countryside just as much an expression of the divine? Those introspective churchgoers, so fixated on sin and atonement, have become so ensnared in their obsession with judgment that they have lost sight of life—the true life ..." She emphasized the word "true" with such a drawn-out "u" that it stretched into a lingering note before continuing, "... entirely. How can one be happy if, instead of savoring life, one's gaze is fixed perpetually on some far-off reckoning, dreading the punishments one is fated to endure? How much joy would an animal feel—if, let us assume for a moment, it were even capable of such thought—if it lived each day beneath the looming shadow of the butcher's blade? How can one live a fulfilled existence if every decision is weighed against the rigid scales of what is deemed godly?" As she spoke her final words, Penny threw back her head, her eyes wide, her brows raised, her forehead creased in such a way that, for a fleeting moment, her beauty seemed almost to fade.

Phineas set his glass aside, rested both elbows on the table, and rubbed his temples. "I am the wrong man to argue about religion. Much of what you say—those very words—might once have passed my own lips, not so many years ago. But life has taught me much. I do not mean the intellectual study of the Holy Scriptures, nor the depths of hidden mysteries preserved in secret writings through the centuries—Lameth has led me farther in that regard than I had ever dared to dream. But the wisdom of a compassionate, experienced soul, one who tends to the weary in spirit, or the strength found in a true community—these can be a solace in life's darkest hours. And I believe such things should not be dismissed so lightly."

"Are we not, in this very moment, enjoying the strength of companionship?" Penny challenged, but their debate soon petered out, for Phineas had ventured too far, seen too much, and felt too deeply to care about continuing such a dispute. Eventually, Penny changed the subject. "Mister Lameth has asked me to take care of a few things in London. He keeps a house there. Would you mind accompanying me? Life in the countryside is a pleasant enough diversion, but it hardly compares to the allure of a great city." She smiled at him with inquisitive eyes.

"What sort of business is Lameth sending you to London for?"

"Just a few letters he wishes to entrust to no one else and a message I must deliver to one of his business associates in person—nothing of any real consequence. If I must be entirely truthful, I asked him to let me run this errand. As I said, city life suits me. I find myself rather weary of the countryside and these provincial backwaters."

After finishing the bottle of wine and indulging in idle conversation for some time, the serving girl cleared away the dishes, and Phineas paid the bill. They rose sluggishly from their seats, stretching their stiff limbs. "Now would be the perfect time for an afternoon nap!" Penny remarked as Phineas helped her into her coat. The cold and wind struck them with sudden force as they opened the broad door, its wrought-iron embellishments gleaming in the pale light, and stepped over the threshold. The stable boy assisted them with the horse once more, and before nightfall, they returned home.

After several days of idle leisure, during which Phineas repeatedly failed to carry out his intention of visiting the reverend, a coachman brought them at daybreak to Colchester, where they boarded a four-horse mail coach alongside other passengers. By the time it set them down, half-exhausted, before a row of grand, towering houses in London, it was well into the night. They spent the night at Lameth's residence, but in the early hours of morning, Penny rose without informing Phineas and went out to fulfill the business that had brought her to London. She left behind only a short note, leaving Phineas uncertain about the course of the day, bound to his room as he waited for her return. It was not until late in the afternoon that Penny arrived at the house again, greeting him exuberantly with the news that she had completed all the tasks Lameth had set for her. "Which means the next few days are ours entirely. Would you care to accompany me tonight? Let us eat, drink, and enjoy good company," she announced with enthusiasm. "I've already reserved us a table and invited a dear friend—someone I haven't seen in ages. You will like her. I'll retire to my room for a short rest. Let's meet in an hour—if that suits you."

Although Phineas had little inclination to make new acquaintances, he eventually relented for Penny's sake and spent the next two hours seated behind one of the large windows, observing the ceaseless bustle of the metropolis. When the agreed-upon time had long passed, a knock came at the door, and Penny, draped in her evening attire with her coat folded over her arm, stood in the doorway, beckoning him to follow. They strolled arm in arm through the brightly lit night, making their way to the establishment Penny had chosen for their evening's entertainment. As they passed a stack of wooden crates along the sidewalk, a frail voice called out from the shadows: "A penny for the poor! Alms for a wretched soul!" The plea came in a hoarse, monotonous croak from the depths of an utterly destitute dwelling. Wrapped in filthy rags, with a grimy bandage concealing parts of his deeply furrowed, matted-bearded face, a man crouched upon the damp, sunken pavement, raising a trembling hand in supplication. "A penny for the poor!" he called again. The wind whipped bitterly through the street, sending a chill through them. Phineas hesitated. "A penny, please! May God repay your kindness!" the voice whimpered from within the tangle of his unkempt beard.

"Come along—we are expected, and we mustn't tarry. Don't trouble yourself; you'll find plenty more of his kind in London," Penny said lightly. Phineas reached into his pocket for money, but Penny tightened her grip on his arm and urged him forward. "Please, let's keep moving. He unsettles me!" She pulled him again, and before Phineas could collect his thoughts, the tide of the bustling crowd had already swept them away. Within minutes, they reached the appointed venue. Once their coats had been taken at the cloakroom, they settled comfortably at one of the large tables. After some time, and with considerable delay, Penny's acquaintance arrived—a young woman whom she introduced as Amy Murray. She could not have been much older than twenty, and her entire being seemed imbued with an infectious, almost giddy laughter, tinged with a faint note of hysteria. Her artfully arranged curls, emerging from a smooth, tight middle parting and rolling into delicate spirals at their ends, framed her lovely face. Small ribbons, decorative bands, and tiny silk blossoms adorned her hair, holding everything in place as it culminated at the back of her head in a finely braided chignon. She wore a perfume that mingled the warm, resinous scent of cedarwood with an invigorating hint of fresh apples—so vividly reminiscent of a golden summer afternoon that once the fragrance reached one's senses, it was impossible not to think of sunlit orchard alleys, the dappled shade of fruit-laden boughs, and the myriad tiny creatures humming and chirping in the tall grass of a meadow. Her round, dark eyes, framed by long lashes, fastened themselves upon Phineas the moment she sat down—and from that moment on, did not once let him out of their sight.

As they drank and talked, they grew closer. "Amy and I have known each other for aaaaages—we're practically the best of friends," Penny remarked, raising her brows. They exchanged glances and burst into laughter. "You must know, she's trapped in a miserable marriage—with an absolute brute of a man. And to make matters worse, he's ancient." Penny adopted a deeply sympathetic expression, and Amy nodded emphatically. They spoke of this and that, mostly trivialities, then of politics and whatever else crossed their minds. Time and again, Penny steered the conversation back to Amy's unfortunate love life—how her marriage had been arranged by her father to that much older gentleman and how she had suffered under the circumstances. Phineas recounted his many travels and adventures, which, despite his relatively few years, had taken him far and wide. He spoke at length about his time in Paris and the peculiarities of that city, yet he omitted any mention of the mystical teachings he had received there, or the strange and boundary-defying experiences that had befallen him—despite Penny's repeated attempts to coax more details from him. Eventually, they turned to gossip, to the latest rumors and the stories circulating about town—including the recent murders in London, eerily reminiscent of those that had plagued the northern counties. It was as if some exorcism had driven out a demon, only for it to roam further afield and wreak even greater havoc elsewhere.

After talking, eating, and drinking their fill, with the wine warming their spirits, Penny suggested they try their luck at one of the *faro* tables, where a number of ladies and gentlemen—some of the former adorned in puff-sleeved silk gowns, embroidered tulle, and bedecked with jewelry like Christmas trees—were eagerly placing their bets. Amy, delighted at the idea, clapped her hands in excitement, leaving Phineas little choice but to oblige. Still, a vague unease gnawed at him. His thoughts drifted again and again to that man hunched in the gutter, hungry and freezing in his wretched shelter outside. They first observed the games of the other patrons, then took seats themselves once the previous players—some leaving crestfallen at their losses, others striding away in triumphant poses, basking in the glow of their exorbitant winnings—vacated the oval table. The two ladies urged Phineas to play. Penny, keeping to the background, watched from the shadow of a column, while Amy took a seat beside him, pressing close.

The *pointeurs*, all accompanied by their own lady companions, had gathered around their table, watching the banker expectantly as he, surrounded by stacks of money and two decks of French playing cards, announced the minimum wager. *"Va banque!"* the three players called in turn, puffing out cigar smoke through their pursed lips like train tunnels. The banker looked at Phineas inquiringly. Phineas, recalling the rules of the game, squirmed in his seat, hesitant under the scrutinizing stares of his fellow players—until at last, he confirmed the bet. By now, he had switched from wine to whisky, which quickly drove out his initial unease and emboldened him. Amy, who clung to him at every opportunity, as if constantly seeking an excuse to touch him, fanned herself with both hands as though she could hardly bear the suspense. Her cheeks glowed in a rosy hue. As the evening progressed, her head remained nestled against his shoulder, and each time he turned, he found himself staring into that enchanting, beguiling smile.

Penny stepped up beside him. "She likes you," she whispered into his ear, as if he needed further confirmation.

As time slipped away, he found—unexpectedly, and despite having no real need for it—that he had won a considerable sum of money. Consequently, he had also received an abundance of kisses and embraces in return. Drawing in a sharp breath, he clapped his hands together and rubbed them briskly. "You are my lucky star!" he laughed, directing his words at Amy, while sweeping a mound of coins and banknotes into his waistcoat. She rewarded him with a soft kiss upon his cheek, and as the evening drew to a close, and the effects of alcohol had sufficiently loosened his moral restraint, they sat together in intimate conversation in a secluded corner of the room. Penny watched them in silence the entire time. A smile of satisfaction played upon her lips. When he stepped outside to relieve himself, unsteady on his feet as he staggered toward the privy at the back of the building, the cold air sharpened his senses just enough to stir doubts about the growing intimacy between himself and the young woman. He returned to the warmth and comfort of the room with his pockets heavy with winnings and his mind caught between two forces—on one side, a rising excitement he knew he would not be able to resist; on the other, the gnawing voice of his conscience. Amy's gaze smoldered with longing, while Penny regarded him with a triumphant glint in her eye. He saw Penny lean forward and whisper something into Amy's ear. "It's getting late—we should head home!" he announced, and was met with agreement. Once they had donned their coats, they stepped out into the chill of the night, laughing as they fastened their buttons against the cold. A waning half-moon hung above the darkened silhouettes of the buildings. Amy clung to Phineas's neck as though bracing against the railing of a ship in rough seas. The alcohol made him sway, and the warmth of her body pressed against him robbed him of his senses.

"You've got a long way home," Penny slurred, her voice slightly thick with drink. "If you want, you can stay with us for the night. Lameth's house is just a short walk from here. If your husband sees you in this state, he'll surely lash out again. What did you tell him when you left? Come on, tell us!"

"I told him I was leaving for a few days," Amy giggled drunkenly, "and the simpleton was baffled when I walked out the door carrying nothing but my *reticule*!" She then erupted into a fit of hysterical laughter.

They staggered home, Phineas in the middle, each of the two women clinging to his waist as they walked, arms intertwined in a swaying, laughter-filled embrace. In a halting rhythm, their trio of unsteady bodies wove its way through the gas-lit streets, flanked by towering townhouses, until, with the certainty of sleepwalkers, they reached their destination unharmed. Penny pounded against the door, rousing the servants from their slumber, while Amy, pressing her body against Phineas, rested her head dreamily upon his chest. The door creaked open, and a house servant stepped outside, his cheek still imprinted and reddened from the pressure of a pillow, his disheveled hair sticking out in odd angles as he escorted them in. Upon stepping into the vestibule, a maid took their coats, folding them neatly over her arm, balancing Penny's muff atop the pile, with Amy's reticule dangling from a thin, braided cord about her finger. As she turned toward the cloakroom, the *reticule* slipped from her grasp. In her attempt to catch it, the muff tumbled down, and soon after, the coats lay scattered across the polished stone floor. "You clumsy thing!" Penny snapped, and without hesitation, struck her sharply across the cheek. Then, turning to Phineas, she cast him an expectant look, as though waiting for him to reinforce the reprimand. But Phineas only stood there, stricken, troubled by the sight of the maid's tear-filled eyes. "I'm not feeling quite myself—I've got a splitting headache already," Penny said at last. "I think I'll retire. Perhaps you'd like to keep Amy company for a little while?" She looked at him again, questioningly.

Amy took the initiative before he could answer, seizing two glasses and a bottle of gin from the bar cart and guiding him with a firm yet playful push along the small of his back, leading him up the wide double staircase of the entrance hall and down the long corridor. "Where's your room?" she asked, halfway there.

"I don't mean to be a spoilsport, but honestly, I'm far too tired," he admitted.

Amy remained undeterred, laughing as she brushed off his reluctance. "Don't be shy!" she teased, and so it was that the two of them found themselves sitting together in his chamber, sharing a glass of gin. A servant had stoked the fire in the hearth, and Phineas sat slumped in a high-backed chair, staring into the flickering flames, while Amy lay sprawled across an ottoman, idly sipping her drink.

"You're married," Phineas stated flatly, his mind finally beginning to clear. "I think propriety forbids us from sitting alone in my room at this hour, drinking gin together."

"My marriage is a prison," she sighed, her face shifting into a pained expression. "You don't know my husband, or you wouldn't say such things. It's only in your presence that I've felt like a real woman again." A smile curled at the corners of her lips as she bit into her lower lip, as if testing its softness. Phineas lowered his gaze, staring into his glass.

She set her drink aside, then, with a slow, deliberate motion, rose from her seat. With a provocative arch in her spine, she eased herself onto his lap, leaning forward, her back arched, her hips pressing back enticingly. Her large eyes, now filled with a burning intent, locked onto his, the firelight dancing within them—flickering, slitted demon's eyes, gleaming over her pupils like molten gold. His entire body trembled as her delicate fingers slipped beneath his shirt, and her eyes, full of unspoken meaning, searched his own. The scent of cedar and apples filled his nostrils, mingling with a faint trace of her own essence, something entirely her. The sound of her breath, quick and unsteady, brushed against his ear, her warm exhalations tracing his cheek like fleeting gusts of wind swirling around a house. Then, at last, she pressed her quivering lips to his, and he felt the soft ridges of her mouth, the delicate contour of her cupid's bow, and the almost imperceptible down of the finest hairs that adorned her skin.

Behind his forehead, desire and duty wrestled with each other. Somewhat helplessly aware of the consequences that would ensue, he parted his lips slightly to reciprocate her bold advances, yet he felt with utter certainty that what he was doing was wrong. Amy pressed herself against him and continued her passionate caresses. Phineas, kissing his way down her neck, suddenly halted. He gently but firmly pushed her away, stood up, and took a few steps back. "I'm sorry!" he told her, searching for words to justify his actions.

As she struggled to fasten the buttons of her dress, her hasty, defiant movements missing the first buttonhole, the unexpected rejection painted a sulky expression on her face. Phineas, glass in hand, stood at the window, refusing to look at her, staring out in disillusionment. Suddenly, a commotion erupted from one of the lower floors. A man was cursing, shouting Amy's name. Moments later, Penny's voice rang out, pelting the caller with insults. When Phineas stepped out and leaned over the balustrade at the end of the corridor, he saw, below in the entrance hall, a gaunt man standing there—perhaps just past his thirties, his face pale yet flushed, his nose prominent and hooked, his cheeks hollow, and his eyes dark-shadowed, gleaming with a madness that had overtaken him. "Give her to me, you damned procuress!" he shouted at Penny, who retaliated with a volley of curses. "Amy! Amy!" he kept bellowing. A servant had rushed in and twisted his arm behind his back, trying to force him out of the house, but the man, slipping free in an unexpected movement, struck him with a hook to the jaw, sending him sprawling to the ground.

"Get lost, you good-for-nothing lout!" Penny yelled from the balustrade above.

"Where is she? Amy! Amy!" he now roared toward Phineas. Amy appeared behind him, her dress crookedly buttoned, her hair in some disarray—a sight that only fueled the man's fury.

"Goddamn it! Shut your mouth, you wretch!" Penny shrieked, as Amy clung to her for protection.

"Amy, come down here this instant!"

"Get a hold of yourself! Good Lord, what a thick-headed fool!"

"Amy! To hell with all of you!"

"Piss off!"

"Oh, shut that loose mouth of yours, you shameless hussy! Amy, I said come down here!"

Phineas rushed downstairs and confronted the man. "For God's sake! What do you think you're doing, shouting like that?" he reprimanded him. "You're drunk! Apologize to these ladies and go home at once!"

"Ladies?" the man scoffed bitterly. "That foul-mouthed wench is a whore, and the other is my unfaithful wife!" His voice cracked, and tears streamed down his sunken cheeks like tiny waterfalls. "There's a child waiting for her at home, and even though she seems to hate me with every fiber of her being, she should at least come back and do her duty as a mother."

Phineas stood speechless, struggling to make sense of it all. "Your wife? Good heavens! I was told her husband was an old brute of a man."

"Don't believe a word of it!" Penny shouted from above as Amy broke into sobs.

"As I said," the man continued, his voice trembling with grief and rage, "that one is a harlot, and you'll find no one in this city who'd say otherwise. And as for my faithless wife, she's been swept away by some mad passion, ever since that one"—he jabbed a finger toward Penny—"corrupted her and filled her head with wickedness. Good God! We have a child together, not even four years old, who loves her mother with all its heart, despite everything. And that alone has kept me from throwing her out on the street where she belongs."

He wept again, and something in his eyes told Phineas he was speaking the truth.

"Go home and cry there!" Penny spat, but Amy had already detached herself from her grasp without her noticing. She was making her way down the steps, her brow furrowed, her teeth pressing against her lower lip in uncertainty. She cast Phineas a glance—one that expressed shame, remorse, and yet still an unspoken longing—before stepping beside her husband with bowed head, feigning a conciliatory sob. The man raised his hand as if to strike her, then shook his head and turned away.

"You should be ashamed of yourself!" he said as he walked away, casting Phineas a sharp sideways glance before leaving the house with Amy in tow. A few seconds later, the door opened once more, and Amy reappeared, snatching her coat and *reticule* from the rack. As she stepped out, she flashed Phineas—who still stood motionless in the very same spot—a sly smile, her lips drawn back at the corners and her brows arched mischievously, like a child being scolded for a harmless prank.

Shortly thereafter—now that the servants had discreetly withdrawn—Phineas glanced up at Penny, who stood at the top of the stairs, shifting uneasily, like a trapped animal, as if composing an excuse. Then, as though unable to contain herself any longer, she burst out: "I have nothing left to lose, so listen to me! You must not trust Lameth! He sent me to win you back for him. His true intentions… I fear you cannot even begin to imagine what he has planned." Her voice was shrill, almost pleading, and as she stood there in her nightgown, her eyes wild and her hair unkempt, there was now nothing—absolutely nothing—left in her that reminded him of Eireen.

Phineas shook his head in disgust. "Lies are all that have ever left your lips! And you expect me to believe you now? After everything?"

"I had no choice!" Penny cried, her voice trembling, a flicker of sincerity within it. "You should have seen the way he threatened me!"

Phineas's lips curled into a bitter, almost mocking smile. "You lured me here only to discredit him! I would be most grateful if you left now. I will no longer question the integrity of my mentor. Lameth took me in like a lost son—even after I abandoned him in Paris, and later, after I had the audacity to break into his home."

Penny opened her mouth to say something, then abruptly turned away and disappeared into her room to dress. Minutes later, she emerged back onto the corridor. Her face was now a rigid, unreadable mask. Without a word, she descended the staircase, passing Phineas, who regarded her with cold disapproval. She slipped on her coat without his assistance, then turned one last time and clasped his arm. "You may despise me, and rightly so," she said softly, yet with quiet urgency. "But believe me—your role in this game will be far more wretched than you can fathom. And despite everything, I hope you find a way to escape this madness." With that, she stepped out into the night. Phineas never saw her again.

CHAPTER XVI.
OTHERWORLDLY GATES

The wind cut through the frost-rigid tree-tops, their crystalline branches veined with ice, and bent the white smoke plumes that twisted and changed direction several times before dissolving into thin, swirling ribbons above the clay chimneys crowning the great house. A fantastically high mantle of white lay atop the moss-covered, lichen-streaked slate roof, as if it had nestled beneath a great shaken featherbed, arching into thick ridges that tapered into icicles along the gutters, gables, and balustrades, even as it amassed in great heaps upon the stone window ledges, creeping up their sills and mullions. The courtyard lay silent beneath the pristine splendor of a smooth, windbrushed coverlet, interrupted only by a winding trail of small footprints, which marred its untouched surface.

In a dimly lit room—where the waning sunlight filtered in pale stripes through the oval, frost-rimmed panes—Phineas, now returned from London, sat slumped in the embrace of a high-backed chair, shoulders sagging beneath the weight of his thoughts, clad in his morning robe. Across from him, pacing or leaning now and then against the chair's backrest, Lameth wove his measured words around the misfortunes of recent days. "She has deceived us all—myself included, if that offers you any solace," he said. "And yet, in the end, all was brought to light, and the lady in question, who so callously abused our trust, was at last unmasked." His face emerged from the glow of the hearth as he stepped behind Phineas and rested a hand gently upon his shoulder. "Do not torment yourself. You are blameless in this affair. That woman—whomever she truly served—clearly sought to entangle you in a situation of deliberate compromise, though the full extent of her design remains, as yet, beyond our knowing. Who can fathom what lay concealed behind the illusion of her fair countenance? Perhaps she meant to sully your name—and, through you, my own—or to coerce you through blackmail, or perhaps even to rob you outright. And worse things still are not beyond imagining." He moved to the cabinet and poured a glass of whisky, passing it to Phineas with an encouraging nod. The younger man accepted it absentmindedly and drank. "Come now, rest yourself. Let the weariness of the road and the disquiet of the city fall away. Here, at least, you shall want for nothing." He exhaled slowly and adjusted the cuff of his sleeve before adding, almost as an afterthought, "I must take my leave for a time—business calls me elsewhere, and I am obliged to pay my respects to one of my neighbors. The priest who once served the church near my estate met with misfortune two nights past. It seems he had ventured out late in the evening, intending to visit one of his flock, and suffered an unfortunate fall. I am told he broke his neck." Phineas paled, his breath catching in his throat. His face drained of color, as though some unseen force had drawn the life from him. "A stray dog, most likely, had already worried the corpse before it was found, prompting a rather hasty burial," Lameth added smoothly, his expression unreadable.

"What a loss!" Phineas managed to utter a few words, heavy with horror. The corners of his mouth quivered.

"Yes, indeed," Lameth remarked, showing no sign of emotion, as if he were merely reporting the death of a stranger or a distant acquaintance. "We spoke whenever chance led us to meet at the wall. He was a talented gardener, I must begrudgingly admit. Otherwise, he was a simpleton, and his counsel in matters of the spirit was of little use, though his congregation, in their naivety, seemed to hold him in the highest regard."

They exchanged a few more words, but Phineas, overcome with grief, struggled to find anything meaningful to say, and the conversation soon faded into silence. Shortly thereafter, Lameth excused himself for the remainder of the day. Some time later, the crack of a whip and the neighing of horses made it clear that he had boarded a carriage and departed from the estate. Phineas rubbed his eyes with the heel of his hand, then pressed his thumb and forefinger against his closed eyelids, as though trying to stave off the tears that had begun to well up and now glittered as they trickled forth. After what felt like an eternity, he managed to rise, but only to seize the whisky bottle and sink back into the embrace of the chair, finding solace in the golden liquid's warm companionship.

At some point, a flurry of activity stirred him from his stupor, and as he pried open his weary eyes, the figure of Edmund emerged from a blurred haze of indistinct shapes and the strobe-like flutter of his lashes. Bent over in a slight arc, the servant was gathering bottles and glasses, before wiping up a puddle on the floor. "Master Camill, forgive the disturbance.

You seemed to have dozed off. Your luggage has already been taken upstairs. If you would be so kind as to retire to your room, I could take the liberty of setting the salon in order before the master returns." Phineas slowly pushed himself to his feet, stretching with a faint groan as his limbs protested. "Shall I escort you upstairs?" Edmund inquired, his brow creased with concern, though his tone carried the weight of an unspoken insistence. His shadow stretched across the wall behind him like the twisted limbs of a gnarled, old tree.

"No need. I'll find my way up," Phineas answered, stifling a yawn. He relieved himself in a drafty, adjoining water closet, shivering as the cold bit into his skin, then ascended the creaking staircase to his chamber. Once inside, he stripped down to his shirt and collapsed onto the bed. The room was bathed intermittently in the ghostly glow of the moon, its pale beams filtering through the frost-rimmed panes of the tall casement windows, casting slanted bands of light across the chamber. The fire crackled and smoldered, devouring the neatly stacked logs with slow, deliberate hunger.

He dreams of flames and smoke, of deep tunnels far removed from the light of day, of masks laden with an eerie significance, masks of unfathomable dread. Then, all at once, it feels as though he is clawing his way up from the bowels of the earth, ghoul-like, emerging through the frozen ground, finding himself trapped within the priest's body, as the great hound devours his face and finally seems to tug at his very soul. He is that body, crouching in the snow beneath the moonlit stone walls—he is, at once, within the layered, multidimensional chaos of the dream, the wolf-like beast that consumes him.

Lips curled back, smeared, darkly glistening, and foaming; pale gums from which long, brownish-yellow fangs, their peaks starkly white, jut forth—jagged, serrated, terrible, as if the grotesque peaks of some cragged and fearsome mountain range. Sweltering breath, steaming in mist-like billows; a vicious growl descending into rabid frenzy; fountains of red and heat; stained snow, terrible and yet beautiful in its own violent way. The beast shifts, taking on the shape of that Lameth-being, the one that once deceived him in his disembodied state. Then—blackness. An endless void. A darkness utterly devoid of hope.

And then, suddenly, the darkness becomes something tangible—a hollow space where his face ought to be, narrow slits through which he can see. Beyond them: firelight, flickering flames, a cavernous vault, cyclopean rock formations, towering beyond comprehension, of a scale unseen, unfathomable. Then, in an instant, as though his very mind pierces through the mountain itself, he sees—there, in the half-light—that girl, the one who had once climbed with him, step by step, the dizzying heights of that celestial ladder in a dream long past. She is dying. Closer to death than to life. He can feel her life slipping away, fading like a flower withering in the last days of summer.

Lameth returned home on the evening of the following day and swiftly traversed the dark corridors of his house. He led Phineas, who had spent the entire day idly confined to his room, staring gloomily out of the window, into the salon and once more entreated him to enter his service and assist him in his peculiar endeavor. "It seems to me that you are in greater need of my aid than I am of yours. I am confident that a purpose will help you restore your life to order. Travel with me to Paris, and let us resume the work we once began! Do not dwell upon those troubling visions that unsettled you under the influence of that draught!" Lameth said in his rich, melodious voice, his outward demeanor, once again, exuding that irresistible charm.

"You led me into that arcane and secret tongue and revealed to me a book, whose author, in days of old, opposed the very prophets of the Lord—aye, even Moses and Aaron—at Pharaoh's court. And you granted my soul passage beyond my body, unless, of course, that too was naught but a deception wrought by that ghastly potion you administered. But do you not see? I cannot speak that language, as you must surely have noticed, unless I were, like Saul of old, seized by the spirit of God after the prophet Samuel anointed him. Nor do I understand, no, not by any stretch of imagination I might muster, how such a blasphemous treatise could open a path to heaven, which, as I have always believed, is reserved for the prophets, the saints, and the righteous faithful."

"God is the perfection of all things," Lameth responded, his voice a hushed whisper of reverence, only to rise with deliberate emphasis: "Thus, if one were to attain perfect knowledge of but a single thing—and thereby grasp its perfect and unerring name—one would, by necessity, obtain knowledge of all things. And in that unfathomable, boundless consequence, all would be laid bare before such a one, even the hidden wonders of eternity. This means, in turn, that the knowledge of the *lingua adamica* does not merely grant dominion over nature, nor solely over the kingdoms of the world, but that to one who seeks in earnest, who presses forward with unwavering resolve, it also unlocks the very spheres of glory—just as was the estate of the paradisiacal man before the fall. But you are mistaken, gravely mistaken, if you believe that the desire to walk this secret path is wicked, or born of unrighteous longing. What evil lies in such hope?

And how can the striving to pass through the seven chambers and stand before the flaming throne be called unlawful? Was this not the yearning of all holy men and women since the dawn of time?" As he spoke these final words, Lameth brought his hands together before his face, his fingers upright, their pale skin adorned with rings whose spectral gleam shone like priestly gold in the dim light. His eyelids lowered with a weighty slowness, as though he were drifting into a deep slumber. He breathed, slow and deep. Then, his eyes opened once more, fixing Phineas with a grave and searching gaze.

Phineas did not acknowledge it in the least. "You have yet to tell me why the old man who lodged in the room beside mine on my first night here lost his mind. It seems to me that this undertaking is far from safe and in no way beneficial to one's faculties. Moreover, I have heard from the lips of your servants that this was by no means an isolated case."

"You must believe me when I say I had truly intended to acquaint you with this knowledge in a manner more agreeable. Passing the gatekeepers is no small feat, and a particular thing—one of great weight for the success of such an endeavor, a key of utmost worth, which would have served to illuminate a path through manifold perils—has, by some unfortunate turn, been lost to me. But you are right, of course, and I must beg your pardon for not having disclosed to you the whole of the truth," Lameth suddenly conceded. "I did so with the best of intentions, that I might lead you gently toward such knowledge. But circumstances have arisen that demand our immediate action." "What secret shrouds those peculiar guests who pass through the halls of the *Hôtel La Porte Noire*?" Phineas pressed on. "You have already alluded to their presence being dictated by those enigmatic criteria—or even by providence itself. And you called them travelers of the heavens; you spoke of junctions, thresholds, and crossings, if I have understood you aright. Yet even though your draught has granted me visions of such extraordinary things, and though Mister Stroude, clad in his priestly robes, whispered to me those arcane words which even the most fervent seekers of such knowledge may never hope to hear, still, the very thought of it seems to stand at utter variance with the teachings of Holy Scripture."

Lameth extinguished the light, strode toward the window, and, despite the biting cold that at once rushed in to assail the warmth of the chamber, flung one of its panes wide open. He then rested both arms upon the sill, raising his head to behold the star-strewn sky. Over his shoulder, he gestured for Phineas to do the same. Phineas stepped forward and followed his gaze. The air was crisp and invigorating, and there lingered an ineffable sensation in the night, as though the veil had been partly drawn aside, or as though, in these days, it had been woven thinner than before. With solemn reverence, both men beheld the argent band, that colossal, shimmering river of countless stars, arching through the constellations. The vastness of eternity seemed almost within reach. "Creation is infinite … boundless—a cosmic ocean of unfathomable breadth, wherein myriad worlds unfold!" Lameth intoned, his voice deep and sonorous. After a moment's pause, he continued, "Look up to the stars! Behold, the *Pillar of Glory*! And yet, this is but the beginning. If only you could see with your own eyes how galaxy upon galaxy spreads above, endless as Creation itself is endless. To confine the workings of God to this Earth alone, to deny the existence of eternal world-births, would be nothing short of a blasphemy against His omnipotence. Life is ever forming in the primordial world, ceaselessly do the creations expand, multiplying without end with each beat of your heart. Who would conceive of counting the stars in the firmament? Who would number the grains of sand upon every shore? Yesterday, the Creator speaks—and now, in this very instant, what has been is already what shall yet be. Now, ages upon ages past, in the most distant, inconceivable future, when this Earth and all upon it shall perish and be transfigured—this, all of it, is as one before the piercing gaze of that great Architect of worlds and the forces beneath His command. Even the simplest of principles by which these laws are governed are so utterly alien to our nature, so far beyond our comprehension, that our minds would falter, and we would perish if we dared attempt to grasp them within the confines of our mortal understanding."

Phineas stared, open-mouthed, his thoughts visibly laboring to fully grasp the implications of what he had just heard. He settled upon one of the simpler questions that had taken shape in the dull stupor of his mind—one that, due to the imprecision of his earlier inquiries, had not yet been answered to his satisfaction. "What, then, are the declared aims and aspirations of your enigmatic society?"

"My friend, you are already a part of it, though your hasty departure may have prevented me from completing your instruction and introducing you, as befits one of your standing, with due propriety. Those unfortunate events overshadowed my well-meaning intentions, yet so it has come to pass, much to my regret. Be that as it may, our *secret and learned society*, that most venerable order, is called—crudely translated—*'those who traverse eternity and step forth into the light of day.'* As you see, a matter quite harmless in appearance. The true name behind this rendering is so ancient that many among our ranks have long since forgotten it, and even the learned refrain from uttering it outside our sacred and time-honored rites, lest they profane its sanctity. You wish to know to what cause we have pledged ourselves? Well, we guard the crossings—those passageways that grant access to the corridors of space and time, which, as far as I can ascertain, link at the very least certain of the inhabited worlds, as well as the Seven Spheres of Glory, which find their fulfillment in the *Chamber of Grandeur*. And—I would much rather it were otherwise—they may well extend even to the shores of uttermost darkness, where the Angel of the Abyss sits enthroned, he who was cast down from heaven with his legions in ages past. Yet I cannot speak further on this matter... not yet, and certainly not here. I must, however, make mention of this: there are powers that seek to thwart our purpose. A formidable adversary desires to pervert these crossings to serve his own selfish ends. Consider that there was once an active exchange between the civilizations of the known worlds, and these would stand defenseless against such a tyrant. At times, he appears in the guise of a man, yet I must warn you in the strongest possible terms—his nature is more akin to that of a demon than a mortal. Thus far, we have succeeded in keeping him at bay, but my strength wanes, and in you, I saw one keen enough to aid me in these undertakings in the twilight of my years—like Aaron to Moses, when his strength began to fail as he stood upon that rock, as though hewn of bronze, against the blood-red sky, delivering the hosts of the Amalekites to unspeakable dread. And who knows? Perhaps you shall prove worthy, in time, to take my place."

"Who is this mysterious adversary of whom you speak, and how can so much power reside in a mortal man?" Phineas inquired, once more astonished by the wealth of detail in Lameth's account.

Lameth shut the window and rekindled the light. Once they had seated themselves, he resumed, his hands folded before him. "Mysterious, indeed! We know little of him, yet what we do know is enough to make the very blood run cold. He seems to live eternally, as though he had subjected even death to his dominion. He discovered the formula known to the Forefathers, and he preserved this knowledge beyond the Flood. And ever since he tasted the life-bestowing nectar in the gloom of the ruined catacombs beneath Thebes, he has sought to augment his understanding with that of other worlds and to bring them under his rule." Lameth's voice, resonant and persuasive, seemed to weave a spell about Phineas, who sat hunched forward, gazing downward in troubled contemplation. From those nebulous words, he could not in the least discern whether the formula in question referred to some miraculous alchemical draught—one of those fabled elixirs of immortality—or merely to some peculiar regimen of diet. "I did not wish to trouble you with such matters," Lameth resumed, "but as I have already mentioned, the universe, which at the dawn of time issued forth from the Godhead and is ever in the throes of becoming, has brought forth an infinite number of inhabited worlds. These crossings, however, of which I have spoken, did not prove to be safe passageways to those realms of glory. For beyond certain significant matters, whose enumeration would far exceed the scope of our present discourse, it was only the very first of all tongues that possessed the power to withstand the dread of those guardians, to pass through the seven chambers, and to unseal that most hidden of all doors. Thus, the path of the earliest travelers did not lead them to their lost homeland, but rather, it granted them a vision of the concealed gates—the liminal junctures between worlds, the ancient crossings that have ever run through the dimensions of space and time, linking the world of the living to the secret dominions of the beyond.

"Creation is perfect, according to the words of Scripture, for *'God saw all that He had made, and behold, it was very good,'*" Phineas engaged Lameth in a disputation of holy writ. "Yet through the Fall, Creation bears within itself decay, imperfection, and death. And should the natural, divinely ordained barrier that separates our world from the Beyond have indeed given rise to such anomalies—those very crossings of which you have just spoken—then their use strikes me as a most profane violation of the divine order."

"My dear friend, you must learn patience in your thirst for truth!" Lameth said with a smile, once more donning his outward air of benevolence. "At its inception, the task of our *secret and learned society* was the pursuit of knowledge—the knowledge that might grant us passage back to our celestial homeland, the origin of all things created, the realm of inconceivable splendor—an undertaking most noble and sacred, as I am sure you will agree. Yet we have since set aside those righteous aspirations, and now we are merely the custodians of this ancient secret—perhaps doomed to devote our mortal days to a purpose far greater than you can presently conceive. And yet, let us suppose for a moment that we were not driven by such selfless inclinations—what, then, would be so reprehensible in passing through those gates of our own volition and partaking of the *Tree of Life*, whose access has been so jealously denied to us? Is it not our rightful inheritance to walk once more in the *Garden of God*, from which our first parents were unjustly cast out—not for their transgression, but in obedience to the first commandment—and thereafter be crowned with everlasting life?" Lameth's voice had risen nearly to a shout; his demeanor was that of a zealot whose holiest sanctum had been defiled.

Yet the outburst lasted but a few seconds before he regained his composure. His limbs, tense as though suspended between the poles of some electrical apparatus, suddenly slackened. He now seemed weary, drained, as though something within him were slowly consuming him from within. He closed his eyes and drew in a deep breath, as if the words he was about to utter bore such weight that he needed a moment's quiet before speaking them. "I ask but one small thing of you—utterly harmless—if only you would believe me," he said, his voice measured. "To pass through the seven chambers, those palaces of unspeakable wonders—a perilous journey, of which you are right to stand in dread—is one matter. To travel between the inhabited spheres of heaven is quite another, and a far less treacherous venture, though both may rest upon the same fundamental principles. I ask only that you set foot upon one of the worlds known to us—a world not so unlike our own. None of the nameless wardens would bar your way or drive you to madness. It would be as though you drifted into slumber upon a long voyage, only to awaken in a distant land, where a small, insignificant task awaits you on my behalf."

"Please enlighten me on this matter!" Phineas implored him. "If it is as you say—that infinite worlds have emerged from Creation—how many of them, then, are populated by men like ourselves? And if the number you are about to give me is as great as I presume it shall be, how is it that, as you yourself have just admitted, you have gained access to but a few?"

"It is said that 18,000 worlds bear life within them, yet this is but a symbolic number, one that scarcely does justice to the concept of infinity. As for the second part of your question, I must concede that they are not so easily reached, even with the aid of that singular object which I have lost. Can you imagine what it is like to step through such a crossing only to find oneself emerging into a heaving primordial sea or a raging inferno? To say nothing of stepping out upon a mountain peak where the air is thin and the frost seizes the very marrow of your bones—or finding oneself entombed in the heart of a mountain, engulfed in impenetrable darkness, perhaps even encased within the naked rock itself?"

"If the path is so easily walked and the goal so desirable, why do you not undertake the journey yourself?"

"Oh, you may believe me, I have not left it untried. But the people who so obstinately guard the crossing that shall serve as your passage are most willful, and through their cunning intrigues, they have, until now, contrived to keep that door of wrought ore—woven through with riddles and spells—sealed against me, preventing me from taking the passage myself."

"If that is so, what folly led you to believe that I would succeed where even you have failed?" Phineas shook his head in bewilderment.

"The winding paths of the Left-Hand Way unveil many secrets. A familiar spirit spoke to me of this—spoke of your success, of a gift within you that shall accomplish what I, in my weakness, could not. Your consent would grant me great relief and lift a heavy burden from my shoulders." With each word, Lameth seemed to shrink, and a frailty, hitherto concealed, settled first upon his face and then over his entire form. To Phineas, it was as though he had aged decades within mere moments. Lameth's eyes were weary, and as he stretched out a hand toward him, it was with the gesture of one begging for alms. A pang of guilt struck Phineas, and in that instant, he recalled the beggar on that frigid night in London. The memory weighed upon him, so much so that he could not bring himself to refuse outright. And yet, he pressed further.

"Of what manner of familiar spirit do you speak? Have you sought counsel from a soothsayer, consulted the stars, or dabbled in some other secret art?" There was a note of sarcasm in Phineas's voice.

"Beloved pupil, not all things may be revealed to you at this time. But I implore you—trust me, at least to this extent—that you may rest assured: none of the perils you might encounter along this path are of such a nature that your mind would stand in danger of breaking, as you, to my sincerest regret, had to witness in your unfortunate neighbor. Neither shall your life nor your health suffer harm. Travel with me to Paris and fulfill this simple task on my behalf, and I shall weigh every effort of yours in gold—and thereafter unveil to you all that your heart desires to know!"

"Of what task do you speak? What is it you seek from this foreign world?"

"I ask only that you retrieve for me a most insignificant thing—a mere scroll, a fragment long lost, the missing piece in an old man's collection, one that was once my own possession. Though the worth of this item is meager by worldly measure, it haunts me day and night and grants me no peace." He smiled with a certain self-consciousness, as though aware of a weakness he deemed foolish yet could not resist owing to his own whims. "Moreover, this object shall prove of great aid in fulfilling the duties entrusted to our Order, those very duties of which I have spoken to you with such candor and openness," he added, as if to lend the matter greater gravity.

"And how, pray, did your possession come to be lost in such distant lands—far beyond the world as we know it—particularly when, as you yourself have said, that crossing has been barred to you?"

"Once, there was friendship between that world and ours. But treachery was dealt us in times past, and in the turmoil of that rebellion, what should never have been lost was lost. But let us not dwell upon bygone things. Let us turn our gaze instead toward what lies ahead. We could depart as soon as tomorrow, should you find it within your means. Once more, I urge you—forget those things that so troubled you there. Your dark dreams were but an unintended side effect of the draught, and that image which so disturbed you—why, it is nothing more than the overabundant fancy of a gifted artist, which, out of goodwill toward my guests, I kept from public view. Tell me, what more could I have done?" His face gleamed pale in the light of the wall-mounted lamps.

How am I to find such an unremarkable thing in a world entirely unknown to me? Where am I to begin my search, how shall I make myself understood, and how am I to procure this object?"

"I beheld a mighty mountain range—one such as even your boldest dreams could not conjure. Sheer cliffs of black stone, their peaks piercing the clouds, and deep craters plunging into an ineffable, unseen world, one beyond all imagining—a place of which, one day, you shall speak to your descendants as you sit by the fireside. And yet, I must confess, not all things are made plain to me. The future appears to me as through a mist. But rest assured, I saw you—I saw you place that object into my hands, even if the particulars of the matter remain veiled. Fear not—some turn of fate shall grant you passage through that crossing, of that I am certain. Moreover, I shall provide you with a map of those lands, one that shall guide your way, and I shall ensure that someone is there to receive you. And..."—he smiled knowingly—"... unremarkable, that object is most certainly not."

Phineas found himself, for the moment, satisfied with what he had heard and at last gave his consent. Lameth shook his hand with excessive warmth, drew him in close with a firm pat on the shoulder, and then excused himself for the remainder of the evening, a smile of elusive meaning lingering upon his lips. Later, after retiring to his chamber and preparing for the night, Phineas lay beneath the covers, the quilt drawn up to his chin, staring at the ceiling as he sorted through his thoughts. Though Lameth had drawn a strict distinction between the ascent into that transcendent realm of unfathomable splendor—an ascent which, in Phineas's understanding, was granted only to the faithful after a life of trials, sacrifice, and righteous deeds—and those fantastical journeys through space and time, which the secrets entombed in the deep recesses of the Hôtel's foundations would grant to any member of that *secret and learned society*, Phineas had come to know Lameth well enough to regard his placatory and persuasive words with only measured credence. Yet—so he had believed at first—all misgivings that had led him to question both the integrity of such an endeavor and the righteousness of Lameth's character had surely been nullified by his own disgraceful conduct in London. The ill-fated ends of all his attachments, each culminating in either death or ruin, and even the passing of Reverend Smith—an event for which he felt, in some obscure way, responsible, though he could not precisely articulate why—hung upon him like a wretched curse.

At the same time, he had so far repressed the memory of that disturbing mural that the greater design of the events now unfolding lay entirely beyond his grasp. The warnings of Farah, the vows he had sworn at her grave—these, too, had been blurred into insignificance by Lameth's assurances that Baldassare, her murderer, had met his due punishment. He had accepted this without pressing for further clarification. Nor did he reflect upon the message from that antediluvian past—the account of Esam, which, through some miraculous means, had spoken to him from that ancient parchment kept in Lameth's cylindrical secrétaire. Lameth must, by some method, have managed to decipher it—whether through the conventional means of unraveling those secret glyphs, a feat which—given all that Phineas had come to know of him—seemed wholly within his capability, or, like Phineas himself, by way of revelation, inspiration, or some other circuitous channel of the world beyond.

Though Lameth remained guarded in his discourse, Phineas had every reason to believe that the mysterious artifact upon which Lameth's desire was so fixed was none other than the scroll whose existence had been attested in the antediluvian's account. Lameth must, at some point in the past—through some curious twist of fate—have come into its possession. Its contents, he suspected, must have been of such fantastical nature as to surpass even the most wondrous of the tomes Lameth hoarded in his library. That scroll had consumed his every thought, and now, believing it lost in that foreign world, his every pursuit was bent upon its retrieval. How he had learned of its present whereabouts was something Phineas scarcely dared to imagine. But what did he intend to do with it? His words had betrayed him to the extent that his longing was clear—his yearning was not merely for knowledge, nor for the preservation of some sacred trust, but for something far greater—something that sought a path straight into the heavens. And though he professed to have devoted himself, in utter selflessness, to the guardianship of this ancient mystery, Phineas could not help but question such a claim—particularly given the evident failings of character in the other members of that so-called learned and secret society. Thus, he kept to himself the doubts that plagued him concerning the antediluvian manuscript, despite the nagging suspicion that Lameth might, in fact, have noticed that someone had tampered with his secrétaire. He now regretted not having taken greater care in covering his tracks when, in his haste, he had hurriedly locked it again. At length, sleep overtook him, his thoughts unresolved, his mind still turning over the same unanswered questions, yet bringing him no closer to any definitive conclusion.

The following morning, they traveled by carriage to Clacton, where they boarded a rowboat and, not far from the formidable *Martello* towers, were taken aboard a sailing vessel manned by a dubious crew. The wind favored them on their crossing to Calais. The manner in which the captain addressed Monsieur Lameth suggested that the two had been engaged in business dealings in the past—indeed, it was not beyond reason to suspect that Lameth himself might be the owner of the vessel. Upon arriving in Calais, they paid the toll for the highway and boarded a coach—a four-horse diligence—with the postmaster seated on the box and a postilion riding the saddle horse. After several days of fair weather, they reached Paris and arrived at the *Hôtel La Porte Noire*.

"Welcome, sir," Obed muttered meekly, without so much as raising his eyes as they crossed the threshold. His expression suggested that he was not permitted to exchange further words with them. Yet when he did lift his head for the briefest moment, Phineas caught his gaze and, in the weary indifference he found there, discerned that Obed had, by all appearances, resigned himself to the finality of his situation. Nor did he seem to have harbored the slightest doubt that Phineas would return from England in Lameth's company.

CHAPTER XVII.

THE BLACK DOOR

They had descended far below, deep beyond the great staircase, through a labyrinth of vaulted stone passageways, into the lightless abysses of that wondrous edifice. "In there!" Lameth commanded impatiently, gesturing for Phineas to enter a long chamber, whose further reaches dissolved into obscurity beyond the radius of his lamp's feeble glow. With hurried movements, Lameth pulled several linen covers from the furnishings and cast them carelessly into a corner. Rows of dark, intricately carved wooden seats lined the walls, rising in tiers toward the ceiling and culminating, much like a choir stall, in a covered backrest framed by a series of delicate Gothic arches, where dust-laden cobwebs wove their peculiar forms.

Lameth bade Phineas to take a seat. Reluctantly, he lowered himself onto one of the benches, sitting there with an uneasy weight in his chest, as though awaiting the joyless verdict of a physician. Lameth proceeded to light additional lamps, though their glow barely sufficed to penetrate the depths of the chamber. Massive stone blocks and hewn rock had been shaped into an astronomical vaulted ceiling, adorned with radiant depictions of celestial bodies and their astrological signs, fashioned from gilded or polished metal. Beneath that immense dome, at some distance, two monolithic pillars rose, their capitals adorned with intricate carvings of twisting vines, foliage, and figurative motifs. These columns expanded into a portal-like arch, its keystone inscribed with cosmic symbols in cryptic, undeciphered interpretations. Yet beyond those vaulted pillars, nothing of note could be found—only the stone-tiled floor, stretching out in unremarkable, mundane stillness. And yet, despite its apparent meaninglessness, an oppressive aura clung to that vacant passageway, reaching toward the stone vault above like a doorway to the underworld itself.

"All hope abandon, ye who enter here!" Phineas murmured, quoting Dante, a shudder coursing through him at the mere thought of what unseen horrors might lurk beyond that threshold.

Lameth responded with a mirthless laugh—a sound that could only be called laughter by the barest semblance of tone. Under the flickering, restless play of light, his features seemed almost diabolical. "I see you have found your tongue again. Pray that you shall never walk that woeful path!" With that, he lapsed once more into his unsettling preoccupation, setting about rearranging furniture and blowing the dust and cobwebs from a worm-eaten writing desk, whereupon he laid several documents, arranging them according to some deliberate, unseen pattern. "Come closer now, and do not be afraid! This path is tried and tested—it has been walked for centuries. No peril awaits you that should give you any cause for true concern."

"Why these two pillars, bearing an archway that seems to lead into nothingness? What lies beneath that unremarkable stone floor, where slab follows upon slab as though this portal had been erected in sheer folly?"

"The entire hôtel is a crossing, a locus of unspeakable power, so that, with the proper discipline, one might step beyond at any place within these walls, no matter the destination. But here, in this very spot, where that arch of stone was set upon these two pillars in ages past—here lies the axis, the very heart of that force. Here, all energy converges, yielding the greatest possible advantage to our cause."

Phineas rose reluctantly and stepped forward with hesitant, measured paces, like a condemned man approaching the gallows. Lameth, his head inclined at a slight angle, one shoulder lifted along with his arm, so that his cloak stretched beneath him like a pair of wings, placed his hand gently upon Phineas's shoulder and guided him toward the desk, compelling him to examine the documents laid out before him in great number. Strange, cryptic diagrams, astronomical symbols, and formulaic incantations were scattered across the surface, alongside forgotten words—words that contained instructions on how to traverse the spheres. And upon another sheet, drawn in fine lines, lay the cartography of some foreign, unknown land.

"Let me guide you!" Lameth whispered in an incantatory voice. "See the path before you and behold, with your own eyes, the way by which you might walk it! Do not falter, and do not recoil at the surging waves that may seem to crash upon you like a flood of unfathomable magnitude! It is but the aether deceiving you, seeking to cast your soul into disarray. Do not linger—step forward, without hesitation, with steadfast heart and unyielding will! Then, speak these words in your mind—those written above—and fix your thoughts upon the world to which they belong, whose celestial bodies and orbits you see depicted here in perfect detail! You have already glimpsed what it is to walk the realms beyond, though you did so outside your body. Now you shall journey with it, which makes little difference—save that, upon your arrival, you will, in all likelihood, be violently ill." He laughed, utterly devoid of sympathy. "Now that you understand how to walk that secret path, hear me well concerning that which I desire above all else! Look upon this map—you shall carry it with you. This mountain range is the destination of your journey. Here, upon these cliffs, just a few yards above a wind-lashed sea, you shall step forth into that foreign world. Do not be alarmed if you are first greeted by the darkness of a cave! The energy released by the crossing will provide you with light for a brief time—long enough to kindle your own. Take this lamp, and these matches! You will find yourself before a door—locked. How you are to pass through it, I cannot yet say, for, as I have already told you, that crossing was barred to me from the moment those schemers, with their secrecy, their riddles, and their cunning snares, ensured that all our efforts would be in vain." His face twisted with fury—but then, forcing his lips into a semblance of a smile, he continued in a tone more tempered. "But I assure you, you shall succeed, even if the particulars of how remain hidden from me. Once you have unraveled the mystery and mastered that crossing, climb the steps upon the cliff! Beware of setting foot in the mountain city that lies near that passage, built upon the slopes and spanning the entire height of the peak. Turn away from it—pass beyond the outer wall, and make your way inland, though always keeping your distance from that city upon the plain. Then continue on, toward the mountains!"

Lameth pointed to a location on the map, which was rendered in precise strokes of the quill, its hesitant coloration in lead white, vermilion, verditer, copper green, and orpiment depicting a stylized sea, a white city perched upon the cliffs, and another settlement encircling it in a half-moon shape upon the plains. Far beyond, after long days' travel, a mighty mountain range loomed—so immense that even the cartographer's sober eye had seemingly been compelled into an unnatural exaggeration of its proportions, portraying this volcanic massif with a monumentality and expanse beyond all conceivable measure.

"Tell me once more, with greater clarity, the nature of the object for which I am to embark on this journey," Phineas inquired. "Surely, that place must hold thousands of scrolls."

"That is precisely what I was attempting to explain before you interrupted me," Lameth replied, irritation flickering in his tone—though he quickly regained his composure. Phineas noticed the briefest glint of something sly in his eyes. "The object you are to retrieve from those distant lands resembles, in the broadest sense, a scroll—though I must caution you that the term, as you understand it, bears little resemblance to what it truly is. It is kept within a kind of casing, a handle wrought from iron smelted from stones that fell from the heavens. Light is the ink that once soaked its parchment, and even the material upon which it is inscribed is of a wondrous nature, a substance for which our world has no counterpart. The writing upon it is never still—nor are the lines, nor the shifting forms that emerge upon its surface." Lameth's words, once brisk and efficient, now unfolded with a slow, deliberate expansiveness, as though only in this place—and at this precise moment—was he permitted to unveil this knowledge in its full depth. He spoke of the scroll as though it were a star chart—only to call it something else in the next breath. At times, he named it a seal, a sigil, a key; then again, an amulet, a talisman, a token. It was as though no word known to common speech could truly encompass that foreign thing, that unspoken entity. And so Phineas could only discern, through context alone, that Lameth was speaking always of one and the same object. "It has been revealed to me that you shall find it in this place," Lameth concluded, pressing his finger upon a single point on the map. Then, without another word, he folded the parchment and handed it to Phineas. "Remain inconspicuous until someone makes contact with you! Take my ring as a token of recognition—you shall be shown something similar. Speak to no one else upon your journey! No one would understand you, and beyond that, your foreign tongue would only arouse suspicion. Draw no undue attention! The door, I presume, will be guarded. Do whatever is necessary! Perhaps they shall allow you to pass once you have solved the riddle. Courage must now be your guide!"

Lameth handed him one of his rings—and, accompanied by a meaningful glance, a dagger, its blade tapering into a keen double edge. The hilt, a masterpiece of craftsmanship wrought from nickel silver and ivory, was adorned with ceremonial inscriptions, more an artifact than a mere weapon. As their hands touched in passing, Lameth's skin felt unnaturally cold, and Phineas recoiled ever so slightly, as though he had brushed against the hand of a corpse.

He concealed both map and dagger within his frock coat and slipped Lameth's ring onto his finger. The mystical symbol of a serpent devouring its own tail wound its way through the raised relief, encircled by an inscription whose meaning remained obscure. After several moments of contemplation, he lifted his gaze to Lameth. "How am I to make myself understood? At what price am I to obtain the object? And how am I to solve this riddle if I do not even know the language spoken there? And further, have you considered how I am to return once my task is complete?"

"So many questions!" Lameth sighed. "But you are wise to weigh every uncertainty and to concern yourself with every aspect of your journey. Know this much—he whom you shall encounter is well-versed in the ancient tongues. Prefer Latin—it should serve well enough to make your intentions known. But bear in mind that this scroll is my rightful property, and no wealth need be offered in exchange for it." A knowing smile curved his lips. "As for the cryptic words that shall test you at that door—it was for their sake that I had you study the First of all tongues. Your intuition, the innate faculties within you, and the peculiar conditions of that place shall serve to grant you passage in ways you do not yet comprehend. And how shall you return? You ask me this? Know this, and know it well—All is One. The same path that leads you there shall bring you back again, for the way through space is but the same eternal circle."

Phineas shook his head in protest. "I cannot solve a riddle in a language I do not know—or scarcely comprehend. And how could those who devised this riddle even possess knowledge of such a tongue, if, as I understand you, it was a language spoken only in the creation of our world and removed from it after the Fall?"

Lameth regarded him in silence for a long moment, his eyes piercing and unrelenting. Phineas found himself struggling to bear the intensity of that gaze when, at last, Lameth spoke again—his words as unexpected as the weight of his pause had been. "Let us, for a brief moment, forget that the creations are endless. And let us consider only this one act of creation—this knowledge conveyed in the language of revelation, received by unlettered men, whose intellect and understanding were simple in measure, adapted to their capacity, clad in the plain words of their tongue and the limits of their horizon, and thus preserved in Holy Scripture and other written testimonies throughout the ages. So, then, it is as follows: When our world entered into the blank slate of eternity, the Fall extinguished the gift of speaking the language of the gods and angels—just as a dream fades upon waking, until, with time, only the faintest thought remains to testify to it. And yet, fragments endured—slight traces of that former perfection. And in every age, wise men and women have sought to reclaim this lost language, to restore it—to re-con-struct it—though always in a degenerate form, a crude imitation of its former grandeur. And just as ancient knowledge withered away, and with the deaths of those who had no teacher but the heavens themselves, the understanding of the great power and laws that govern all things was taken from the earth—just as the lifespans of men grew shorter—so too did the knowledge of the First of all languages degenerate, a language not confined to this, our creation, but spoken at the beginning of all habitable worlds and their respective creations, before these too, through the deed of a single being, were made mortal—for they had to fall first, that they might thereafter be exalted.

This language could not be learned as one learns an ordinary tongue, for it was not merely a matter of its words—

which, in their abundance, could name all things according to the essence of their soul—nor was it a matter of its grammar, which the gods themselves devised at the dawn of time. No, to master its pronunciation was nothing less than to learn the speech of the gods themselves. And whoever sought to wield it must be pure in heart and unblemished in soul, his deeds steeped in righteousness. Not even the Fallen One could speak it thereafter—his words, from that moment on, were but a degenerate form of the divine and angelic tongue. And only prophecy, the visions of heaven, the unspeakable words of revelation, and the messages of angels to holy men and women bore witness to that language thereafter." Lameth's face had grown unnaturally pale, as though he were reading a confession of guilt aloud. "This, then, is how it may be explained that certain of those secret-keepers beyond the Black Door have retained rudimentary knowledge of that tongue—or, rather, have preserved but a breath of it. And with this lingering trace, they inscribed their cryptic verses and invocations into that door—words that none may decipher unless they are possessed of the ancient knowledge and, above all, inclined toward the high ideals it demands."

A shiver ran between Phineas's shoulder blades. He gathered his thoughts, struggling to grasp how Lameth's discourse had, in any way, provided an answer to his question. In his refined imagination, images of that distant land arose unbidden, and the dawning realization of his decision's consequences made his breath catch. Lameth patted him reassuringly on the back, attempting a smile—but it did little to mask the grim determination now woven inexorably into his very being. Instead, he merely looked as though he were suffering from toothache.

Phineas stepped beneath the arch, between the two pillars, and called to mind all that Lameth had revealed to him upon the writing desk. At first, all seemed calm, though the oppressive aura in the air grew steadily, like water nearing its boiling point before it begins to roil. Then, all at once, as though a hidden lever had been thrown, the very fabric of the space beneath the stone archway began to change. At first, it was nothing more than the subtlest tremors within an energy field, revealing itself in slow, deliberate emergence, shedding the veil of its concealment and peeling away from the invisibility of its ethereal nature. Phineas rubbed his eyes in bewilderment. Tiny sparks of light flared before him, as though he had struck his head. He reached out, fingers brushing through the air, seeking some tangible sense of this strange phenomenon. At his fingertips, the very space before him seemed to bend—like an image upon damp, unstretched canvas, rippling beneath the pressure of his touch. The air shimmered, as though a midsummer sun were pouring its heat upon this singular point, despite the chamber's continued gloom and shadow. Then, all around him, everything seemed to fade and dissolve, phantasmal images severed by beams of light, vanishing and reassembling anew—until at last, even the archway itself dematerialized. Every physical object, laid bare, was revealed in its true essence—not as form, but as luminous, pulsating fields of energy, as transcendental light. What had once been hidden behind the illusion of ordinary consciousness now stood exposed. The chamber groaned. It stretched, vast and towering, then ever vaster, growing to unfathomable dimensions, expanding beyond all reckoning—an abyssal proliferation of unfamiliar, unseen geometry, a space-time continuum of incomprehensible, boundless extent.

And at once, it seemed to him that he, in countermeasure, was diminishing—growing small and insignificant within this infinitely expanding cosmos. A winding path appeared before him, unfolding in defiance of all known geometric laws. At first, he hovered there in wordless awe—then, he drifted forward, carried into states of being beyond normal consciousness and reality, into realms no mortal senses could fully comprehend. He beheld things for which no description existed, no words by which he could later recount his journey—no language capable of conveying what it was to cross that threshold.

It seemed as though his voyage had lasted for years—or merely for the briefest instant. And then, suddenly, his movement slowed. It was as if he were oscillating at high frequency, a pendulum swinging in small, rapid arcs—before coming to an abrupt halt. He found himself in a dark chamber. The portal behind him glowed faintly in the darkness, casting dim illumination upon the vast space around him. He recalled the lamp Lameth had given him and quickly lit it, only to find, at some distance ahead, a wall of rough-hewn stone—pierced by a single black door, blocking his passage forward. A wave of nausea overtook him. He felt drained, as though he had labored through an entire day of grueling physical toil. Kneeling on one knee, he remained motionless, watching as the last vestiges of light receded from the chamber—until only the soft, yellowish glow of his lamp surrounded him. He set the lamp before him and ran his hands over his body, as though to reassure himself that he had arrived intact. But to his relief, all was as it should be. Not a fragment of his clothing was missing, nor any of the objects Lameth had given him at the outset of his journey.

Some time passed before he felt able to stand. On either side of him, the shattered remains of a stone arch lay strewn across the floor—its fragments, by the shape of the stones, the rounded columns broken in multiple places along their length, and the defaced remnants of its ornamented capitals, clearly a counterpart to the archway he had passed through in the depths beneath the hôtel. Examining the marks upon the ruined stones, he discerned that the structure had not collapsed by chance—it had been deliberately razed. Moreover, the treatment of the architecture suggested that those who had done so had harbored no goodwill toward its builders. Finding nothing but the yawning blackness of the cave behind him, he moved forward, lacking any alternative, toward the barrier that loomed before him, dark and forbidding. The black door was a single-leaf structure, rounded at the top, far smaller than he had envisioned—scarcely larger than an ordinary house door, and smaller still than the one in Lameth's house that led from the salon to the other rooms.

The dark metal seemed solid, for he could discern no nails by which plates might have been affixed to a wooden core, nor any other sign of external fastening. Even the frame appeared to be fashioned from the same material, so seamlessly constructed that no light could penetrate from the outside. The hinges, he surmised, must be affixed on the exterior. And then, all at once, the thought struck him: This door had not been built to seal the entrance of the cave. It had been built to shield the outside world from whatever horror might seek to cross that threshold. He wondered whether it was night in these lands, then pressed his ear to the cool, hammered surface of the metal, straining to hear what might await him beyond the barrier. Despite the door's massive construction, he thought he could make out faint sounds—sounds that grew more distinct at a particular spot, as though there were some unseen aperture through which they carried. He heard what seemed to be the crashing of waves, the roaring of wind—and, at intervals, when the storm gathered, he could almost discern human voices, murmuring in anxious tones in a language foreign to his ears. He struck the inner surface of the door with the heel of his hand, listening once more with his head pressed against the metal. But in that instant, the voices fell silent. Only the raging of the untamed tides carried through the dark vault of that wondrous cavern.

Raising the lamp higher, he swept it slowly before the door, catching in the half-light the faintest traces of engravings etched into the blackened surface. Holding the lamp at an angle, he revealed more symbols in the relief—strange, forgotten sigils left as a message for those travelers whose privilege it was to walk between worlds. Yet though the mysterious inscriptions reminded him of the figures carved into the black basalt of Egypt's sunken cities—slumbering in museums and forgotten tombs—he knew these to be the letters of a language far older than the dark stelae that whispered through the catacombs of the immortal dead. Older than the golden dynasties. Older than the cities of the Chaldeans and the boundless treasures resting in the sunken ruins of Sumer and Babylon. Older still than the Flood and all that had ever been set to tablet by stylus or reed. They were strange glyphs, emerging from the depths of the dark metal, and as he lingered before them, contemplating, his thoughts drifted back to the unsettling book Lameth had given him—to those lessons, obscure and eldritch, that had filled his mind with the unspeakable grammar of that unspeakable tongue. It was a script that could not be read—it had to be experienced. A silent breath from a time before time. A language that revealed itself not in words, but in visions.

He let his fingertips glide across the characters of the divine hieroglyphic tongue, feeling a strange aura seeping into him, and all at once, the words seemed strangely familiar—less like something newly discovered, and more like something long forgotten. It was as though he were not learning them, but merely remembering how to speak them. And in that place—a crucible that seemed to gather and distill all his thoughts—there dawned within him, in an unprecedented act of understanding and comprehension, the true nature of these words. The essence of things. The ancient, ineffable connections. A spark of that sensual language began to stir within him, striking against the barriers set upon his understanding at the moment of his entry into mortality. He spoke one of those pictorial words of power—words unheard since the dawn of mankind—and as he uttered it, the air quivered, its sound like the rustling of leaves in the wind, and the vault trembled, as though those words bore within them an ancient and formidable enchantment.

Perhaps it was the intercessions of Chirion, rising from the depths of his prison to the heavens above. Or perhaps it was the whispered prayers of Jahdis, fading at the very threshold of the beyond in that iron cage where she languished. But whatever the cause, in that moment, his understanding deepened tenfold, and the words he had sought—words that, like the nameless speech of paradise, breathed the spirit of a language of perfect knowing, words still vibrant with undiminished power—unfolded before his mind's eye. "Riddles and secrecy, ha! Lameth was wrong all along—this was no riddle, but an invitation!" He spoke aloud, then raised his voice against the brazen door that barred his path, against the storm raging beyond. He shaped the sound of his words to match the hieroglyphic sigils—those magical inscriptions, forged with great craftsmanship into the iron bastion.

Some time passed before the door opened—whether through external aid or the sheer force of those words, he could not say. And as he stepped across the threshold, out from the curved vault of the Black Door, the cold spray of the sea struck his face, and the frigid winds tore at his garments, whipping through his dark hair. For all the narrowness of that passage, the world that revealed itself before him was vast—a savage, towering sea, crashing against the heights of a stone platform, jutting forth from the curving cliffside. A stairway, hewn into the rock, spiraled upward in dizzying ascent. At a distant edge of the platform, two men crouched in strange attire, their faces contorted with fear—one raising a trembling arm in an instinctive gesture of defense. Their drenched cloaks clung to their shivering frames. They seemed shaken to their very core. Their weapons lay discarded at their feet, and neither made the slightest move to reach for them.

Phineas's arrival had, in truth, been accompanied by a great trembling of the mountain. And as though this alone were not enough to inspire terror, there had followed—emanating from within the very door—a sudden and unexpected knocking, and then the utterance of a language they did not understand. Yet its intonations, carried forth as though from some distant and ungraspable source, bore a semblance to the words that had long been engraved upon the dark metal, whose presence had accompanied their every watch. And so, trembling before the solemn majesty of prophecy fulfilled, the gatekeepers addressed him—though he understood not a word, their tones bore a supplicating gentleness, as though seeking to appease his wrath, pleading for the mercy of their lives. Phineas thought to answer them reassuringly—but at once, Lameth's warning words returned to his mind. And so, without paying them further heed, he turned away and began his ascent up the wet, blackened steps.

After what felt like an eternity, he left behind the last of those treacherous steps—many little more than jagged outcroppings of stone, made passable only by the aid of a winding handrail, forcing him more to climb than to walk—and arrived at a narrow path, which branched into two directions some distance ahead. From his vantage point, he judged that one fork led upward, winding along the mountainside, while the other descended toward a colossal fortification, whose white, ivy-clad stones peered intermittently through the towering trunks of ancient trees—immense beyond reckoning, the likes of which he had never seen. Recalling Lameth's words once more, he took the second path—the one leading away from the mysterious city that he presumed lay atop the summit. Following that course for some time, he eventually arrived before a high, double-winged gate, piercing through the Babylonian vastness of the city wall. It was locked fast, save for a narrow postern door, around which several guards had gathered. Lively commotion and a great many voices, speaking in foreign tongues, filled the air—growing ever louder with each step he took toward the gate. He could feel curious eyes upon him, and at that moment, he became acutely aware that, by his attire alone, he stood out among these people. Looking around, he thought he glimpsed a man in the crowd whose sly, watchful eyes scrutinized him with an unnerving intensity. Uneasy, he withdrew behind one of the buildings that stood in the shadow of the wall. Then, all at once, a commotion arose—a sudden burst of shouting. The guards abandoned their post, chasing after a fleeing figure—Phineas caught a glimpse of him and thought he recognized the very same man who had been watching him moments before. The fugitive had become entangled in some quarrel with one of the locals and was now bolting toward the forest in frantic, zigzagging strides, like a hare pursued by hounds. Seizing the opportunity presented before him, Phineas slipped unseen through the now-unwatched postern gate.

Tension ebbed from his body, replaced by an exhilarating surge of triumph as he hurried down the steep path, his heart pounding. Towering trees flanked him on either side, their colossal, branchless trunks rising like the pillars of a city above the clouds, piercing through the mist-laden canopy. He strode down a hollow way, worn so deep by the passage of wheels and hooves that he could see nothing beyond its embankments. Fragments of shattered rock, debris, and other stones formed wild mosaics across the gray gravel. A dense undergrowth of paleozoic ferns sprawled beneath the trees, while their immense trunks shot up vertically toward the light-drenched heights of the canopy. Along the roots of those that bordered the hollow way, erosion had carved long, cavernous recesses into the slopes—like the burrows of some hidden, elfin people. He drew in a deep breath of the pure air and, aided by the downward incline of the path, quickened his pace. After some time, the interwoven archway of branches ahead, fused together into a vault of colorless sky, signaled the end of the forest.

Turning back, only to ensure he was not being followed, he then allowed himself a moment's rest. Lowering himself onto the gnarled embrace of a great, curiously twisted root—one that coiled around the massive stones lining the sloping path like a vice—he gathered his strength before pressing onward. And when at last he stepped beyond the wooded threshold, passing through that gateway of woven boughs, he beheld, far below in the plain, the city Lameth had spoken of—shaped in a perfect ring around the mountain, conforming to the land's natural contours. Its gleaming oriels, domes, turrets, and rooftops stretched skyward, silver-bright against the feverish glare of the midday sun. Then, lifting his gaze, overwhelmed by the grandeur of this world, he beheld the majesty of the White Mountain City. Its splendid houses clambered up the wooded slopes, ascending ever higher, culminating at its loftiest point in a vast, resplendent dome, flanked by opulent auxiliary buildings that rose boldly from the mountain's very peak.

He lingered for some time in reverent awe, then rummaged through his pockets and drew forth the map, comparing the features of the land before him with the fine-lined contours that depicted these foreign realms. Keeping his distance, as agreed, from the wonders of the city, he spent the entire day wandering through landscapes of overwhelming beauty—lands unlike any he had ever known, filled with towering grain, lush green meadows, and tree-lined fields. Hunger and thirst gnawed at him, and he cursed Lameth inwardly for having spared not a thought for such necessities. But then, a stream crossed his path, spanned by an arched stone bridge, and he knelt to drink his fill from its clear waters. Later, after covering more ground, he found respite beneath a tree bearing pomegranate-like fruit, which restored his waning strength. As dusk began to fall, he made camp in a hollow beneath a lone, slanted tree, whose roots, having weathered the winds for generations, had driven so deep into the earth that they had formed a sheltered recess—an alcove of living wood. Wrapping himself as best he could in his cloak, he gazed up through the hanging branches and beheld, in wonder, the twin moons breaking forth over a jagged horizon of deep, blue-black shadows, ascending to claim dominion over the heavens in a spectacle beyond compare. Silver light washed over the vast expanse of fields, and the sky was strewn with foreign constellations—stars of unknown worlds.

Then, all at once, he caught a sound—vague at first, but soon resolving into the rhythmic clatter of hooves. Slowly, steadily, the rider approached, his mount's gait diminishing, its steps growing louder with every passing moment. A soft brrr from the rider brought the horse to a halt, and Phineas heard a murmured command in a language not his own. Pressing himself deeper into the shadows of the embankment, bracing against the root-bound earthen wall, he weighed his options—how best to slip away unseen. But the rider had already drawn so close that Phineas could hear his breath, the subtle rustle of movement, the leather of his tack creaking ever so slightly. His hand found the dagger. Then, working his way up along the slope in silence, he sprang upon his pursuer from behind—driving him down in a sudden, forceful grapple. And when the brief struggle subsided, Phineas stood over him, blade bared, its keen edge held motionless against the man's throat. In the pale light of the moons, he could at last make out the face that now lay beneath his blade—The very same man who had watched him outside the great gate, the one who had fled into the woods—whose unexpected intervention had, by some stroke of fortune, granted Phineas the opportunity to slip through the city's defenses unnoticed.

The man squirmed under Phineas's grasp, but Phineas bore down on him, pinning him firmly to the ground. Then, as if in appeal, the man lifted a trembling hand, speaking in hurried, unintelligible tones—pleading, it seemed. In the dim glow of moonlight, something glinted between his fingers. A ring. An ancient band, its surface bearing the unmistakable shape of a serpent devouring its own tail. Phineas hesitated. Slowly, he released him. And then, speaking in soothing tones, as one might when taming an animal, the man rose to his feet, moving with careful, deliberate steps—his head inclined slightly downward, his eyes watchful, assessing. His palms wavered in slow, measured descent—a gesture of placation. Phineas gave a slight nod in response. Then, slipping a hand into his pocket, he withdrew the ring Lameth had entrusted to him. With that silent exchange of proof, they drew closer in understanding. Contrary to Lameth's assurances, the man understood not a word of the ancient tongues Phineas spoke— Yet, through gestures and persistence, they managed to bridge the gulf between them. Seated together in the wind-sheltered hollow, they kindled a small fire. And there, by the flickering light, Phineas unrolled the map, tracing a path with his finger, indicating the destination of his journey. The man regarded it for a moment. Then, raising a single, unwavering finger, he pointed the way.

They ate in silence, partaking of the provisions the messenger had withdrawn from the saddlebags of his towering, broad-chested mount—a creature of an unknown breed, which bore a resemblance to an ordinary horse, were it not for its peculiar coat, the long mane extending over its powerful neck and continuing into a profuse feathering about the fetlocks, so that Phineas could not help but liken it to a *Shire horse*. They remained seated by the fire for some time, and in the flickering glow of the flames, Phineas studied his companion's features as best he could. There was nothing remarkable about the man's face, save for the grim inscrutability of his gaze; his skin, bronzed by the sun of this land, bore no aspect that would mark him as a foreigner in London's streets—provided, of course, that he were not clad in such antiquated attire. At first, he regarded Phineas with wary reserve. Yet gradually, a quiet curiosity seemed to take hold of him, and Phineas, from beneath his lowered brow, observed how the man made repeated attempts to articulate something in a manner intelligible to his guest—only to hesitate, reconsider, and lapse once more into silence, his eyes fixed upon the dance of the flames. At length, before they settled down to sleep, the man had mustered enough resolve to offer his name, and Phineas, for the second time that evening, took comfort in an unexpected kindness—this time in the form of a warming blanket.

He fell swiftly into slumber and found himself swept into a dream, one that wove strange, fantastic visions of distant and wondrous lands—though none so strange, none so wondrous, as the sights he had already beheld with waking eyes since passing through that fateful door. The next morning, they resumed their journey, Phineas seated for the most part behind his guide upon the massive, shaggy horse. With each passing hour, as they drew nearer to their uncertain destination, the man grew more at ease—his words, now plentiful, shaping a world of astonishment and unseen marvels. And

Phineas, listening intently, soon began to grasp the names of certain things in that unfamiliar tongue. By midday of the fourth day, the first outcroppings of an immense mountain range rose before them, its jagged, heaven-piercing silhouette having loomed upon the horizon since the dawn of the previous day.

They traversed a seldom-traveled land, winding through dark, mist-cloaked valleys whose dense, fern-laden forests gave way to barren, vertiginous peaks. As they climbed, the trees grew sparser, and on either side of them, sheer granite walls reared up from the rubble-strewn path—great, gray precipices, here and there punctuated by the twisted, defiant forms of lone trees, their gnarled trunks contorted by the relentless winds of the heights. The hot shafts of the sun beat down upon the lichen-covered stone, and from the clefts in the rock, red-bellied, blue- and turquoise-scaled reptiles darted forth—only to vanish once more into their hidden sanctuaries. Above them, colossal birds swept past, voicing sounds strange and unearthly before vanishing into the twilight haze. The higher they ascended, the more desolate the land became, until at last, beneath the shadow of an unspeakably sheer cliffside—its cruel pinnacles rising like the walls of some primeval, titanic fortress, reaching unseen summits beyond the shroud of mist—they brought their steed to a halt and dismounted. As they stepped into that looming shadow, the warmth fled from their limbs, and Phineas was weighed down, awed and disquieted by the sheer monumentality and unfathomable vastness of the precipice before him—its jagged face rising as if sundered from the mountain by some titanic axe-blow, thrusting upward in a gaping, terrible rupture, like a cursed monolith.

His guide led the horse away, vanishing into some unseen refuge where, Phineas presumed, a stable must have been kept. Then, alone once more, they pressed onward by foot. At first, the path ascended with a deceptive gentleness, but soon it veered sharply into an arduous, near-vertical climb. They mounted a secret stairway, its countless steps winding like a coiled spine along the jagged slopes, carving their way into the stone like the work of some ancient, forgotten hand. And after a long and grueling ascent, they at last emerged before a panorama of such sacred and awe-struck majesty that Phineas stood dumbfounded—his breath caught, his very sense of proportion shaken, for never in all his years had he witnessed a spectacle so grand that it seemed beyond even the reach of nature itself.

The sun, in its descent, cast the heavens in a molten glow of gold, while in the opposing quarter, the argent moons ascended, rising to claim dominion over the night. And when at last the final strands of daylight had ebbed away, no longer blinding their vision with its radiance, they discerned, in the distance, the faint amber glimmer of a cave hollowed into the mountainside. There, upon their arrival, they were swiftly encircled by men of wary countenance, their expressions sharpened with suspicion as they spoke in hushed urgency with Phineas's guide. Along the rock walls stood peculiarly wrought muskets, each arranged in tripod formations, standing sentinel in long, regimented rows. Nearby, countless barrels and wooden chests were stacked in untidy profusion, some tucked into deep-hewn alcoves, others hastily piled along the cavern floor. A brief deliberation followed, after which Phineas was relieved of his dagger. Without further explanation, they motioned for him to follow one of their number. Through a labyrinth of vaulted corridors they led him, the flickering lanterns casting spectral shadows upon the rough-hewn stone, until at last, through shifting half-light, the outline of a stairway emerged—a stairway cut into the very bones of the mountain, wrought with unimaginable effort, its steps weathered by the passage of uncounted years. Slowly, deliberately, they descended. The air grew heavy, thick with the hush of unseen depths. And then, as they reached the last of those timeworn steps, the passageway yawned open, revealing before them a titanic stone arch. Beneath it, an abyss stretched into unknowable depths, smothered in drifting vapors and nameless shadow, a gulf upon which no light had ever fallen. Phineas, his throat suddenly dry, steeled himself against the instinctive recoil that lurched within him, forcing his feet forward, crossing the unseen threshold with a heart hammering against his ribs. Beyond, they entered a hall upheld by colossal pillars, its vastness swallowed in shadow, the dim glow of their lanterns barely tracing the outlines of its towering columns. Their footsteps echoed dully across the fractured flagstones, some of which had sunken into shadowy depressions, vanishing into unseen depths. They pressed onward, traversing the cavernous expanse, until at last they reached a side chamber, half-hidden in the flickering gloom. His guide bade him wait. Stepping forward, the man rapped his knuckles against the aged wooden door, its surface pocked with the decay of centuries, and with the reluctant groan of rusted hinges, it creaked ajar. A muffled exchange followed—brief, tense, undecipherable—before at last Phineas was beckoned inside.

Within, bathed in the dim glow of flickering brass lanterns, sat a man behind a broad and heavily burdened table, its surface laden with moldering books and ancient manuscripts, their covers mottled with age, their pages swollen from damp. All around, towering wooden shelves stretched from floor to ceiling, weighed down by countless volumes, their dust-laden spines pressed in tight disorder. Piles of loose folios and stacked tomes lay scattered across the floor, forming precarious towers of parchment and leather. Here and there, strange relics loomed among the clutter—busts of white-veined stone, their features eroded by time, their identities lost to history—perhaps long-dead rulers, philosophers, or poets, their visages preserved in eternal silence. Upon other surfaces, the instruments of an alchemist-scholar lay intermingled with tools of celestial observation: a vast armillary sphere, its metallic rings tarnished with age, a curious *astrolabe*, its engravings glinting faintly where the lantern light caressed its surface. The man behind the desk regarded Phineas for a long moment, his gaze sharp and unwavering, his silence an oppressive weight upon the room. His eyes, dark and penetrating, held a depth of knowledge—a cunning that did not quite conceal itself behind the solemnity of wisdom. His head was shaven, his skin bloodless, stretched taut over features etched with deep, immutable furrows, as though his flesh had been carved from the same unyielding material as the pillars that upheld this subterranean domain. His robe was black, flowing, and unadorned, its cut unfamiliar—unmoored from any earthly epoch or known fashion. Rising at last, he stepped forward—close, far closer than courtesy would dictate—and without a word, took hold of Phineas's hand, turning it slowly, deliberately, his gaze fastening upon the ring of Lameth.

Phineas made to speak, yet with a curt gesture, the man silenced him, and in a voice of grave and measured depth, he began: "Welcome to our world, son of Adam. Long have I awaited your coming. Countless years have I dwelt in these dark halls, and now, after such an age of hope and expectation, you have at last arrived before me!" His speech was a coarse and archaic Latin, akin to that which must have been spoken among the eldest Italians, from the reigns of the seven mythic kings unto the early days of the Republic—whether due to some gradual degeneration of speech, or because the writings of that distant era had shaped his learning in so peculiar a manner, Phineas could not say. Yet the sheer weight of his presence, the authority with which he bore himself, was such that Phineas dared not take offense. "But tell me—what is his aspect? How did it feel, to serve beneath a lord of such noble blood, to listen in reverence to every word that fell from his lips? And in what depth of awe must you have stood, when he chose you for so momentous a task?"

Phineas felt an inexplicable reluctance to answer as the man so plainly expected. "My lord—Lameth—has given me a charge, if that is what you mean," he replied tersely. "I am to retrieve from you a certain thing, a thing you have kept in his possession. It appears to be his rightful property, and unless I am mistaken, the terms of its return have already been settled."

"Your lord is mine also. I am descended from greater lords than you know, bound through all generations by the oaths that my forebears once swore unto him."

Phineas's unease deepened. "Say then—how came you by the knowledge of my arrival?"

The bald man's gaze did not waver as he slowly began to circle Phineas. "Do you think I did not feel the tremor?" he intoned. "Nothing transpires at Samut Naúr, and none pass the Black Door, without my knowing. Your lord speaks to me in ways unseen, even if a journey of more than a lifetime should divide us."

Phineas squared his shoulders. "Then hand me the scroll," he demanded, "so that I may deliver it to my master." At this, the man flinched—imperceptibly, yet unmistakably—as though no soul had ever before dared to address him in such a manner. The faintest flicker of resentment crossed his visage, yet as swiftly as it had arisen, it was stifled, buried beneath the weight of some deeper restraint.

He gestured toward a standing desk, indicating that Phineas might inspect the manuscript, before turning away to one of the towering shelves. From its shadowed recesses, he retrieved a long, narrow case. Slowly, as though the mere act of parting with it pained him, he drew forth the object that matched, in every respect, the wondrous description Lameth had given of that most coveted scroll. With evident reluctance, he placed it in Phineas's hands. Phineas, wary, unfastened the peculiar metal casing, running his fingers over its flawless surface, its texture cold and unfamiliar beneath his touch. Then, with the utmost care, he unfurled its contents. At once, a blinding script of white fire leapt forth—gleaming as if it had been seared onto the medium by some celestial arc of lightning, its brilliance recalling the lost tablets of Moses. He traced his fingertips across the unknown hieroglyphic script, and at each contact, the luminous markings flared anew, as though imbued with a sentient radiance. Then—abruptly, the words began to shift. Like ink dissolving into water, their shapes blurred and re-formed, transforming before his very eyes. Figures of astronomical complexity unfurled across the scroll's surface—moving planetary orbits, as though the parchment itself had become a celestial chart, a vast cosmic mechanism in motion. Then came occult sigils, alien symbols, inscriptions brimming with the weight of an intelligence wholly beyond human reckoning—knowledge drawn from spheres unknowable, from a logic too vast, too alien, to be unraveled by any sane mind. Phineas felt the pull of it, a force both mesmerizing and insidious, as if his very consciousness were being lured into its depths. The longer he gazed upon those shifting, shimmering revelations, clutching in trembling hands the relic of unfathomable craft, the more it took hold of him. And now—he understood. He understood why Lameth hungered for it so. With no small effort, he tore his gaze away, his breath unsteady. With deliberate hands, he sealed the scroll once more.

"Take the scroll to your lord!" the man commanded. "And remind him that he must not forget what I have accomplished, that he may, at last, recall the reward that is my due. And know this besides—that I have unraveled what was written beyond the white walls concerning this wondrous object, not least that which I have torn from this defiant wretch—a knowledge that, as it seems to me, shall prove of great utility to your lord. But now, rest yourself! You have come into our world, yet now you must return, and that shall not be a simple matter, for the great gate is sealed. Yet trust that I have the means and the will to clear your path, if need be, by force." He ran his tongue over his bloodless lips, a strange anticipation gleaming in his gaze. Without delay, he reclaimed the scroll, sealed it once more in its elongated case, and gestured for Phineas to follow. They ascended to one of the higher levels by way of a vaulted corridor, passing a series of chambers hewn into the rock, each sealed by broad, half-rounded doors, until he was shown to one, where several lamps were lit and food and drink set before him. At a wobbly wooden table, seated upon one of the two rough-hewn chairs, he took his meal in silence. Thereafter, for a time, he sat upon his narrow bed, lost in contemplation of the day's events, until, all at once, a wave of exhaustion overtook him. He straightened his bedding and shed a portion of his garments.

Sinking to the cold stone floor, its clammy touch biting through the thin weave of his shirt, he yielded to the unyielding hardness as though in some form of penance, lingering in a posture of prayer, so that he might have been a supplicant at the sealed gates of a chthonic power—an ancient god of the deep, whose domain stretched in endless halls of black basalt and abyssal shadow—vaulted immensities, akin to the dwelling-place of some mountain king. Words, at first no more than hesitant whispers, spilled from his lips. His thoughts strayed, drawn inexorably toward that primeval tongue of the gods, older than the very roots of this mountain, by which alone he had crossed the black threshold. He shaped a few halting syllables in accord with the arcane grammar whose winding pathways had unveiled themselves to his understanding amidst the ruins of that emblematic portal, and though the incantations upon his tongue were but a feeble echo of that pure and primordial language, though his portion of it was meager—no more than the tentative first steps upon the mystical ascent to a mountaintop of purest revelation—the sacred words seemed to stir in his heart. At first, there came only scattered, indistinct thoughts, fragmentary and fleeting, as though groping toward coherence, yet still, he felt as though his prayer had gathered weight by virtue of this utterance, and it seemed to him that, in such a language, he might at last speak eye to eye with his God. At times, he would pause and listen to the resonance of his own voice as it faded into the silence of night, and all appeared to him untainted and pure, as though he had only now awakened into life, stepping forth from the confines of some darkened chamber into the light of day.

At last, he lay himself down, and beneath the distant, monotonous droning of iron wheels turning in some unseen depth, grinding away at their inscrutable labor, he drifted into sleep. At some uncertain hour, he awoke, though without knowing why. Several apertures, hewn into the stone, admitted a pale trickle of moonlight that faintly illumined the chamber's ceiling. A strange, ineffable unease crept into his heart. From one of the shafts that ran through the rock, a voice reached him—a mournful whisper, so faint it barely touched the ear, rising to him from some unseen place below.

CHAPTER XVIII.
DARKNESS OVER VILARIEN

For some time, Phineas listened in the darkness—a darkness dense and brooding, nesting thickly in the blind corridors beyond the feeble reach of his lamp's glow. Just as he was about to concede that he had been deceived by his senses, the plaintive sound arose once more—this time weaker, more desperate than before, as though the caller's very breath was slipping away with each passing moment. Rising, he dressed hastily, grasped the lamp—its frame laced with white filaments of spider's silk—and took upon himself the perilous venture of descending into the abyssal unknown.

Doubt crept insidiously into his mind, feeding upon the recesses of his thoughts, and once more he found himself recalling that ritual chamber beneath the hôtel—the horror of that anthropoid sarcophagus into which they had bidden him, the mad staircases and passageways winding like a labyrinth through the dreadful catacombs. He dared not imagine what terrors might lurk here, in this subterranean world, a place where excess knew no bounds. Again, the voice reached him—a sound drifting upward from the void, its ghostly melody interwoven with the hollow reverberations of stone.

This time, he discerned it more clearly than before: the voice of a woman, fragile, desolate, and fading.

The lamp's flickering light danced across the jagged walls, its glow shattered upon roughly hewn pilasters, on arches that braced the twisting vaults above, and upon gray beams that spanned yawning, tunnel-like apertures that swallowed all radiance into their impenetrable gloom. Gravel crunched beneath his boots, each footfall betraying him with a treacherous whisper that compelled him, time and again, to glance over his shoulder—to see if unseen eyes pursued him. Yet he was alone, utterly alone, a solitary wanderer lost within this underworld of boundless expanse and inscrutable mysteries. He could not, later, with any certainty, recall the path by which he had threaded this sunless realm, nor how long he had walked, but suddenly he emerged into a chamber of such vast and impossible scale that it defied reason. Above, through an open cleft in the ceiling, the night sky revealed itself—glimmering with cold, unwavering stars, like some cosmic oculus, not unlike that of the Pantheon, as though the ancient architects of this place had sought to craft in stone a tribute to that earthly wonder, albeit upon a scale incomprehensible to human endeavor.

He traversed the cavernous hall, which, though born of the mountain's living rock, seemed to rise like a cathedral beneath its lofty dome, an architecture not shaped by mortal hands but by forces beyond reckoning. At its heart stood an altar, monolithic and foreboding, inscribed with prehistoric symbols and hieroglyphic etchings that whispered of rites lost to the gulf of ages. There, beneath the unspeakable weight of that titanic dome, where the ancients had once lifted their devotions to the heavens, Phineas found himself dwarfed, a mere speck upon a floor of cold and unyielding stone, gazing upward at the distant constellations—lost in the unfathomable vastness of it all. Yet something—a silent urging, a premonitory tremor of the soul—drew his steps away from the sacred center of that place, bidding him descend to the lower recesses of the cavern. There, beneath a natural overhang, a row of rust-bound iron cages stood in grim procession, their bars corroded with age, their locks frozen in place by centuries of neglect. He passed by these silent tombs of iron, lifting his lamp higher, its quivering light spilling across filth-clotted floors, crude wooden pallets, and the heavy lengths of chain from which manacles and collars dangled like instruments of forgotten suffering. He had nearly turned back when a faint moan reached his ear—a sound frail as the last breath of a dying thing. He turned sharply, and from the tenebrous depths of one such cell, a pale arm, spectral in the flickering gloom, stretched weakly toward him—only to falter and collapse, vanishing once more into the shroud of darkness.

Phineas fumbled with the iron bar that secured the entrance, and once he had undone it, he stepped into the desolation of that cell. After only a few paces, he halted. Below, lying upon a filthy pallet, a pair of light-wary eyes blinked at him from narrowed slits, recoiling from the glow of his lamp. And despite all deprivation—despite the tattered, soiled garments, which once, perhaps, had been of fine make; despite the pallor and the dirt, the mark of some wasting affliction upon her frame—she was of an uncanny beauty, a fragile and sorrowful grace. Phineas cradled her frail body in his arms, gazing upon her with anxious concern. She was no stranger to him—this alone bewildered him beyond measure. Yet he could not say which unsettled him more: the inexplicable fact of her presence in that forsaken place, or the grievous condition to which she had been reduced. "I have seen you in my dreams," he murmured, his voice trembling. But she did not seem to understand. She only looked at him with wide, questioning eyes, and though no word passed her lips, there was something—some eerie, unspoken familiarity that bound them.

He began, in his mind, to shape a plan—how he might, in her weakened state, steal her from this accursed prison, bear her safely to the valley below, find the horses, and ride with her to the mountain city, slipping past the gates unseen, descending once more through the hidden depths beneath the *Hôtel La Porte Noire*. Then he thought of the scroll—Lameth's command—and altered his plan: he would take the wretched thing from that terrible man, and in so doing, call him to account. It was a reckless course, with little hope of success, and yet the frail weight of that suffering body, needing his protection, infused him with a resolve and a desperate courage he had not known before.

But then—footsteps. Hurried, heavy strides, accompanied by voices raised in anger and protest, rang through the vaulted hall, reverberating against the cold stone. And before he had even set a foot beyond the threshold—before he had so much as determined his course—he found himself trapped. The thought of loosening his hold upon the girl never so much as crossed his mind, and it was perhaps this hesitance that doomed him. A group of armed men stood before the cell, some bearing wounds that marked them as veterans of some recent struggle. And in their midst, towering over them, they dragged a white-haired giant. Blood stained his costly robes, though whether it was his own or that of others, Phineas could not tell. The man bellowed his outrage, resisting fiercely, his voice a thing of command—one not accustomed to submission—so that even those who sought to restrain him performed their task with visible reluctance. They thrust him into one of the iron-barred cells and, as though fearing him a beast of untamed ferocity, locked the door with haste, as if such frail metal could contain his wrath.

Then the assembly parted. From their midst emerged a figure clad in darkness, bearing the expression of one who knew himself to be the victor. He passed through their ranks with a measured step, pausing at the cells with a smirk of cold amusement. Phineas recognized him at once. It was the same man who, amid a chamber of books and ancient relics, had spread before him that strange map. He pressed part of his face against the iron bars, exchanged a few mocking words with the white-haired giant, then turned his gaze upon Phineas, speaking once more in that crude, archaic Latin. "What am I to do with you, I wonder?" he mused, his voice brimming with contempt. "It seems you have thrown in your lot with the enemy. Did they task you with delivering the scroll to the mountain city once I had placed it in your hands? What a base treachery against your lord! And then, I suppose, you had designs upon my life as well. But it falls now to me, it seems, to claim the passage in your stead—after you have yielded up all you know concerning this matter, just as that foolish wretch did." He laughed, a mirthless, scornful sound, and with a slow nod, gestured toward the girl, who lay limp and blood-matted in Phineas's arms, her brief moment of hope already fading into the horror of renewed despair. "What an exalted thing it must be," the nameless man continued, his voice lilting into a rhapsody of enraptured self-conceit, "to stand beneath the piercing gaze of that great prince! What bliss, to place the key of the universe into his hands, to be granted the honor of his regard, to receive from his own lips praise and glory!"

Phineas's expression hardened. "My lord, Lameth, is an ordinary man—just as I am—though of high standing. Your perception seems to be clouded, and it is clear you do not know of what you speak. But of this I can assure you—my patron would never have condoned such violence."

The Nameless One let out a peal of laughter, high and sharp, then sneered: "An ordinary man? It seems you have been blind!" Phineas made to answer but thought better of it, his gaze returning instead to the girl in his arms, whose frail body trembled at every word the Nameless One uttered. He lifted his eyes, seeking the white-haired giant beyond the bars, then turned back to the questioner, remaining silent. The Nameless One resumed the conversation of his own accord. "This one," he said, inclining his head toward the tall captive, "I found lingering at the foot of the Black Cliff, skulking in the company of his cutthroat rabble." His lips curled into a smirk of contempt. "But now, I shall leave you to your own devices, while I consider at leisure what is to be done with you. In the meantime, I trust you will not lack for company." So saying, he turned and vanished behind the mass of dark-clad bodies. The heavy door clanged shut; one of the guards gave it a testing shake to ensure its fastening. The lanterns receded, their dim glow dwindling as they floated away, seeming almost to drift unmoored toward the exit.

"Bring her to me!" The voice was that of the white-haired man, speaking the same ancient Latin.

"Who are you?" Phineas demanded. "What business have you with the girl?" His voice was edged with wariness, for he knew nothing of this man nor of his true intent, and he would not so readily entrust her to a stranger.

"I am called Myrgil the Wise," came the answer, "and since the father of this one"— his gaze fell upon the girl— "fell from favor, it has been mine to command the White City. You came into our land through the Black Door—I felt the tremor as you crossed the threshold, and soon thereafter, word was brought to me, not least of the incident at the southern gate. I pursued you with a company of twenty, but we were ambushed beneath the shadow of the cliffs, our ranks scattered, our force utterly routed—save for myself alone. My life was spared, though not for any purpose I would call good, as is now clear to me, having beheld firsthand the nature of our adversary." His keen gaze searched Phineas, appraising him. "And yet—you astound me. I had believed that old foe had risen from his accursed pit beneath the Samut Naúr, and I feared already that his power had waxed so great that he had mastered even the sacred tongue. And then—I see you. A youth, no warlock, no lord of shadows, but a mere traveler tending to a deplorable girl." Myrgil hesitated, his stern expression betraying a flicker of curiosity. "I know not what role you play in this unfolding drama, but first and foremost, we must tend to her. She is Jahdis, daughter of Chirion the Unfortunate. Bring her to me—I can heal her."

"Jahdis," Phineas murmured in quiet reverence, brushing a strand of hair from her wan face, studying her features with troubled eyes. She seemed too weak to speak, and Phineas could not tell whether she had understood Myrgil's words, nor whether she placed any trust in him. Yet his choices were few, and after a moment's deliberation, he yielded to the old man's request. He lifted her carefully, carrying her closer to the adjoining cell, so that Myrgil, stretching his sinewy hands—wrapped in golden rings and heavy armlets—through the iron bars, might reach her. She was light as a feather, fragile as a thing made of glass, and he felt, cradled in his arms, less a woman than a child. Myrgil extracted a small reservoir of liquid from one of his rings, rubbing the substance between his fingertips before placing his hands, with a solemn and reverent gesture, upon her head. Then he spoke—his deep, resonant voice weaving words Phineas could not comprehend—an invocation, a benediction, a call to some unseen power whom this people must revere. A fresh, invigorating fragrance unfurled in the air, and for the briefest moment, the oppressive darkness of that prison seemed to wane—lifted, as though driven back by the breath of some unseen force. Myrgil's pale arms, extending from the voluminous folds of his robe, reached out through the bars, emerging from the blackness of the cell into the murky half-light, as though some divinity of the unseen world revealed itself before the eyes of a mortal.

"She will regain her strength. She must rest now," said Myrgil, withdrawing into the shadowed recess of his cell, his breath now labored and uneven. Phineas laid Jahdis once more upon the rough-hewn cot, draping his coat over her frail form. He sat beside her for a long while, watching over her with silent concern. Only when her breath had settled into the steady rhythm of sleep did he rise and turn toward the adjoining cell. At his call, Myrgil's towering frame—swathed in gold- and silver-brocaded cloth—stirred from the dimness like a revenant rising from a tomb of curses. He moved forward through the dust and filth of the dungeon, his long, pale fingers, adorned with countless rings, fanning out to grasp the rusted bars. He must have stood well over seven feet. "What is it you desire?" The voice above him carried an imperious weight.

"Where, in God's name, are we? And who is that wretched fiend who rules this place?"

"Had you the hidden knowledge of the Highest Name, all would be made plain to you," Myrgil replied in a hushed, measured tone. "But I shall assume you spoke in mere exasperation. As for the man of whom you ask, he has never deigned to reveal his name to me, nor have I sought to know it. Yet this place—I know all too well, and the godless cult that once dwelt here, the worshippers of the blackened night, is not unknown to me either. You are in the cratered mountains of Neèbh, upon a land where, in ages unrecorded, men bent the knee in reverence—long before wickedness made its abode in their hearts. This was the heart of a kingdom, the seat of those legendary First Men, who, in the dawn of all things, came from the north across the desolate mountains, many millennia before history began. But by the time the White City was founded, and the great metropolis in the valley arose from the barren rock, that ancient race had long since perished, and another—savage and cruel—had come to infest these subterranean halls.

From whence that second race had sprung, no chronicle recalls. They served monstrous gods, their rites steeped in unthinkable abominations and a sorcery so perverse, so fathomless in its corruption, that even the darkest recesses of the human mind cannot fully grasp the depths of its depravity. But when the Visitors came through the Black Door, that fell people too had already been erased from the world. Yet the hidden knowledge, imparted in an age beyond reckoning, endured—buried, waiting. And when the Visitors themselves turned to evil, this place became the breeding ground of all their iniquities. At first, they gathered here in secrecy—a cult whose workings would chill your very soul, were their full nature revealed to you. Some among our scribes held that their coming was a mere expedition, that the forbidden knowledge, which tormented this land for centuries, was the true purpose of their journey. Others contended that they brought the evil with them from their distant stars, and that never before had such wickedness been visited upon our world. Whether the darkness they bore was carried from their alien realm, or whether they stumbled upon it here and allowed it to ensnare them in yet fouler snares, none can now say with certainty. But it matters little. The horror they sought—or carried with them—was so dire, so laced with sorcery and loathsome arts, that the smallest misstep might have doomed our civilization, as it had those before us. Even now, the land bears the scars of their deeds, for deep pits were dug in the valley—Amoneáth, through which you have ridden—and in the depths of this once-hallowed place, they plundered the rich veins of the earth, forging, through lies and deceit, terrible weapons that cast our land into deepest suffering."

Phineas gave a weary shrug. "What do you intend to do now? We are trapped. The bars of this prison allow no escape."

"Rest," Myrgil said with serene resolve. "Jahdis must be given time to recover. Her body is already mending, but the enemy broke her, and her will to live had nearly faded. Yet this is not the thing that troubles me most. I bear my own share of guilt, for I accused her of a crime in which, as I now see, she was blameless. And it was also the steel of my own men that wounded her—besides all else that foul man may have done to her. But know this, Phineas—she whispered to me, with the last vestiges of her strength, that it was your words that called her back from the brink, that she heard your voice speaking in the ancient tongue. I do not know who you are, nor how you can be both a herald of such a being and yet wield the speech of angels. But no matter. There will be time enough to unravel that mystery."

"Why was she imprisoned here? And why did your men, as well as that dark-souled wretch, do her harm? And why did you call her father, Chirion, 'the luckless'?"

Myrgil fell into an unfathomable silence. Phineas had all but resigned himself to receiving no answer when, at length, the old man began to speak—his voice barely above a whisper, as though he feared the very stones might bear witness. "I sense that I may trust you," he murmured. "And your command of the sacred tongue at the Black Door attests to the truth of your character. Yet swear to me—swear that you shall guard this knowledge as a sacred trust!"

Phineas, pledging his oath without hesitation, beheld the old man's solemn gaze as he continued: "I have already spoken to you of the Visitors, those who, in an age long past, crossed the Black Door and turned their feigned righteousness to wickedness. They worshipped alien gods and bent the knee before a lupine-faced deity, whom they called HE WHO OPENS THE WAYS—knowledge carried from beyond the threshold instructed them in the means by which they might step across the veil into worlds unseen." Phineas regarded Myrgil through the bars, his gaze drifting to the stately chain that adorned the old man's robes—a medallion of beaten gold, upon which a wolf-like creature, wrought in masterful relief, seemed to emerge from the ridges of the metal. It was as though Myrgil's very words found their echo in the sigil he bore. Phineas reached forth, clasping the pendant with a questioning look, until the old man took notice. "Do not wonder at it!" he said, a note of indignation coloring his tone. "The wolf is the sigil of my house—yet my lineage reaches far beyond the accursed cult of those idolatrous wretches." Having thus dismissed the notion, he pressed on: "The most wretched of those fiends—one whose damnable image once adorned our great hall—took to wife Yhendra, a woman of rare beauty and wisdom, one of the blessed of the White City. And from the first, it is said, she saw through his deceptions, though love had ensnared her nonetheless. It seemed, in her heart, that she wished to turn him toward the path of righteousness. And from their union sprang a lineage we believed long extinguished—but more on that anon. After the days of sorrow, she fled through the Black Door, her heart broken, taking with her all who had wrought such grievous wrongs. Yet in the haste of their flight, a relic of those dark times was left behind—an artifact of unspeakable potency to one who knew how to wield it. A scroll, woven from luminous celestial fabric, wrought in such a wondrous fashion that it seemed the Fallen One had bound his very lost splendor within its weave..."

Phineas swallowed, then let slip a thought before he could suppress it: "It is for this artifact that I was bidden to journey into this world."

Myrgil smiled knowingly. "Then listen well, and understand. These matters lie deep in the past, yet two decades ago, the Visitors once more crossed the Black Door at Samut Naúr, breaching its threshold through some artifice—whether by gunpowder or black sorcery, I do not know. Without doubt, they sought knowledge of the artifact's fate, or perchance the means to seize it for themselves. But when they found themselves thwarted—bound by the silence imposed upon those charged with its safekeeping—they returned whence they came, leaving behind agents who, in their absence, might unearth what lay hidden. And in the days that followed, a child was found upon the threshold, a message affixed to its frail form, left by one who claimed to have borne it thither against the will of his master—one who, defying his master's unholy designs, had stolen it away.

For long we believed that those hooded cultists, heirs to the idolaters of old, had abandoned the child upon the cliffs—alone, clad in foreign raiments, weeping, its scattered words unintelligible. But for what purpose they had done so remained shrouded in mystery, and the wise men of our city feared some terrible design in the making. They raised their voices in warning when Chirion, against their counsel, took the child into his care. They said that he had cast aside wisdom at the sight of those tear-stained eyes. Chirion, however, swore with absolute certainty—though by what means he came by such knowledge, none could draw from him—that the child had been left there only after the Visitors had returned whence they came, and that another hand, a player of a wholly different intent, one who sought to protect the child from its dreadful calling, had crossed the threshold and placed it where its destined master would never think to look. And whoever this unseen benefactor may have been, he—or she—must have known that the Black Door, having once yielded to the Visitors' violence, would henceforth be sealed with all the wisdom the White Mountain could muster, that no further passage might ever be made again. Whatever the child's origins, whose beauty later outshone all others, whose wisdom mirrored that of her noble forebear, we could only hope that she had inherited her ancestor's gifts—but not his fatal weakness. And that child... is Jahdis. And it was for these misgivings—and for other matters, still shrouded in shadow—that suspicion fell upon her when the sacred artifact was stolen from our keeping. But now, forgive me, I grow weary. At my age, such a journey is no small burden, and the healing I have wrought has sapped my strength. Worry not, and let not your heart falter. My reach is long. This present misfortune shall soon be righted. Sleep now, and gather your strength—you shall have great need of it ere long!"

Phineas attempted to make himself comfortable upon the cold, unyielding stone, but finding no position satisfactory, he at last leaned against the wall, watching the enigmatic girl in the pallid light of night. Her breath was steady, deep in the peace of slumber. Myrgil had withdrawn into silence, and the faint noises from his cell suggested that he, too, had succumbed to sleep. The chill of the stone seeped through his clothes, setting him to shivering. At last, exhaustion overtook him, and he sank into a restless slumber. When the night had run its course and the dawn lay veiled in twilight's hush, their dark-clad jailer came once more, taunting Myrgil, and revealing to Phineas the inevitable fate he had devised: that he himself would take the journey through the cosmic gateway, leaving them to rot in the dungeon, where they should perish, slow and agonizing, in the grip of starvation. It was a grim decree, and he adorned it with such elaborate detail that Phineas had no cause to doubt a single word. Jahdis lay motionless. She made no sound. He could not tell whether she yet lived or if, in the long silence of the night, she had slipped from life altogether. Myrgil bore his tormentor's scorn without reply, and in time, their captor, finding no amusement in his silence, at last abandoned his taunts and fell quiet.

"My lord, Lameth, has chosen me for this journey. He will be far from pleased if you return in my stead," Phineas rebuked the Nameless One.

"Your lord has no need of such a faithless servant! He shall welcome me with open arms—most of all when he beholds the precious object I bring before him. And moreover, the secret arts I have pursued for my own purposes shall expand his knowledge and redound to my own glory."

"How do you think to cross the threshold, you witless fool?" Myrgil exclaimed. "Do you truly believe the men you slaughtered upon the Black Cliffs were all that the White City could muster?"

"I have not been idle these past years," the Nameless One retorted. "We shall pay the White City a visit and wreathe its walls in fire, so that the watch upon Samut Naúr will be the least of your concerns. And when your temples, your proud palaces, all your finery, and that gold- and silver-gilded dome are purified in flame, when your men, your women, your children, writhing in agony, curse you and your inaction, then shall I pass beneath the stone arch and pay homage to that mighty one." He seized the bars of their prison and rattled them as though to wrench them from their foundations, then suddenly mastered himself once more, let out a scornful laugh, and turned away without another word.

That day, no food was brought to them, yet they could sense the stirrings of feverish activity throughout the halls, as if a spear had been thrust into an anthill. By midday, Jahdis awoke and seemed somewhat restored. Myrgil had spent the entire morning kneeling, murmuring incomprehensible prayers, and when at last he rose and joined them, he seemed weary, spent, and showed no inclination to answer Phineas's questions.

"What is your name? From whence do you come?" Jahdis inquired—speaking, to his surprise, in the ancient tongue—with wide, searching eyes, her fingers gently tracing Phineas's features as though to assure herself he was no mere specter, but something real and present before her.

"Phineas," he answered hesitantly. "I come from a world far from yours, yet not unlike it. In Paris—a great city, through whose midst flows the Seine—I passed beneath the columned gate. But my home lies upon an island, with green meadows and stone houses roofed in slate. Its cliffs rise sheer above the sea, much like those of the White City, though far less immense. My father was a sailor when I was but a child..." He let out a self-conscious laugh, and Jahdis joined him. "A poor description, I know. It rains often in my country, and we have horses, somewhat smaller than yours, yet no less noble." Again, his words seemed pitifully inadequate, and he chided himself for his failure to capture in speech the essence of his homeland. But Jahdis smiled at him, and for a moment, all else was forgotten—the looming assault, the promised, unimaginable suffering the Nameless One sought to unleash upon the White City.

And so they drew nearer to one another, and the time spent together in that desolate cell became as one of those sweet, unending dreams from which, upon waking, one wishes to linger but a few moments longer beneath the warmth of the covers, to drink once more of joys so unexpected, so beyond the reach of waking life. And thus it came to pass that Phineas Camill of Ipswich, in the English county of Suffolk, held in his arms Jahdis of Vilarien, foster-daughter of Chirion, adept of the secret knowledge of the White City Erydin, deep within the stone-hewn dungeons of the crater-ridden mountains of Neèbh, and that his heart burned with love for her, even as she gave hers in return.

Dusk had begun to gather. Myrgil rose and stepped toward the prison bars. "Quiet! Someone is coming." At once, they fell silent, listening intently to the darkness. Then, faintly, came the sound of footsteps moving softly over the stone floor. A man in dark robes approached—one of the Nameless One's men, by all appearances. A leather satchel was slung over his shoulder, and he glanced about repeatedly as though fearing pursuit. After unlocking their cell and passing the satchel into Myrgil's hands, he exchanged a few hurried words with him and swiftly withdrew. Myrgil opened the satchel and examined its contents. A metallic clasp was unfastened, and at once, a dim radiance bathed his face, as though he held a lantern beneath his chin. "Come! Quickly! Our absence will not go unnoticed for long," he urged in a whisper. "We now possess something our host shall soon sorely miss."

"Who was that man?" Phineas inquired.

"Did I not tell you that my influence reaches far?" Myrgil replied. "I have eyes and ears in places even our foe believes safe. Had his last act not been carried out under the strictest secrecy, it too might have been thwarted. But come now—we must descend!"

"Why descend?" Phineas protested. "The entrance lies far above—I myself took it but days ago, guided by my escort."

"That path will soon be impassable. I anticipate the coming attack at that very point. Moreover, we cannot simply stroll through the main entrance unchallenged. Does that fool truly believe my men will stand idle should I fail to return? There will be an assault, and this time, the advantage of surprise is ours. Now come—we have no time to waste! I have walked these lands long before you ever drew breath—before even your fathers or your fathers' fathers were born." He lit a lamp and pressed forward with such haste that Jahdis and Phineas struggled to keep pace. Then, all at once, a cry rang out—a sound so harrowing, so steeped in malice and despair, that it seemed to curdle the very air. Phineas felt his blood turn to ice. "That puffed-up imbecile must have realized by now that we are rather less inclined to accept his hospitality than he had presumed," Myrgil murmured with a scornful smile, clutching the leather satchel to his chest as though fearing it might slip from his grasp. A sudden detonation thundered through the caverns with such violence that they thought the mountain itself might collapse upon them. The very air trembled, the ground shuddered, and above them arose a clamor of voices—shouts of alarm and cries of pain—until, at last, all erupted into an infernal cacophony, as if a hundred cannons had in unison loosed their fire upon the heights. Dust swirled through the air, fine pebbles rattled from unseen fissures in the vaulting rock, and beyond, carried on the wind like a tempest unshackled, came the tumult of men at war. "Faster!" urged Myrgil. "Our enemy may be preoccupied with repelling the onslaught that now crashes against his threshold like a raging tide, but that will not hinder him from unleashing his hounds upon our trail!"

With breathless urgency, he led them into a dizzying descent down vast, ancient steps—each hewn so massive, so monumental, that it seemed giants must have carved them from the living rock. Onward they pressed, ever downward, until they plunged into yet deeper realms, along stairways that wound like the spiral coils of some abyssal labyrinth, into the immeasurable depths of a world where no light of day had ever dwelled. At some unknown point, Phineas lost count of the steps. Time, too, seemed to unmoor itself from any sensible reckoning, stretching into an eternity of descent. At last, they turned upon a near-level path, threading their way through endless twists and turns, spanning chasms on arched bridges, until they reached the very foundations of the mountains—where the way led them at length into a vast, yawning fissure, worn smooth by the passage of water over untold ages. The passage widened into a steep ravine, its towering walls of black rock rising like colossal ramparts. And at the last, they emerged into a cavernous tunnel, where, in the oppressive gloom, Phineas discerned the faint outlines of many doorways—each framed by weathered beams, their wood ashen with age, leading into a warren of sloping shafts and corridors. This was the work of the ancients, who had hollowed out the mountain's belly, carving passage upon passage in their insatiable hunger for the riches buried in the stone.

Far beyond the reach of their lanterns, where those tunnels delved deepest into the earth's bowels, there arose a muffled din—a droning, rhythmic hammering that reverberated through the rock, as though a plague of unseen locusts gnawed ceaselessly at the mountain's heart. Twisting pipes, blackened and corroded, branched like monstrous tendrils across the cavern walls, converging upon rust-bound engines of unfathomable scale, their great iron wheels groaning with an unseen labor. Long rows of ore-laden carts stood waiting upon narrow tracks, their burdens heaped high—mute testaments to an industry long sustained in darkness. Steam hissed from unseen vents. The very rock exhaled a sickly vapor, rising in coils through the broken masonry of abandoned exhaust shafts, fouling the air with a pungent, acrid stench that clung to their tongues like a bitter toxin. Tracks of twisted metal wove in torturous arcs, spanning impossible chasms, before vanishing into the boundless black. Above, the vaulting ceiling shimmered with draperies of pale stone—yellow-white flowstone formations, their rippling contours like frozen curtains of petrified light, spilling downward in slender, icicle-like pendants. "We can follow these tracks and exit the mountain to the east," said Myrgil. "My contact assured me that fresh horses await us there."

Jahdis had not yet fully regained her strength, and as she stumbled more than once upon the debris-strewn, rivulet-scored ground, they paused to rest, seating themselves upon a rocky ledge that divided the illuminated path from a sheer and perilous drop. They took nourishment from the provisions Myrgil withdrew from his satchel. As Phineas reached inside, his hand brushed against a long, narrow case among the food parcels wrapped in cloth. He drew it forth without a second thought. "Do not lay your hands upon that thing!" Myrgil rebuked him. "It remains in my keeping." Jahdis cast Myrgil a reproachful glance before resting a hand upon Phineas's arm in silent entreaty. Phineas hesitated, then replaced the case within the satchel, though his mind lingered upon it. Here lay the culmination of all his endeavors, the very object he had journeyed so far to claim. Yet how could he take possession of it without rousing Myrgil's ire? He fastened the satchel without further inquiry and motioned for Myrgil to bear it for the remainder of their journey, a suggestion to which the elder man, after a moment of inward deliberation, assented with evident reluctance. Hope kindled anew as, in the distance, a jagged, half-moon aperture of starlit blue revealed itself—a promise of open air beyond the mountain's oppressive embrace. With weary steps, they pressed onward until, at last, they emerged beneath the midnight sky of a darkened valley. High above, shrouded by the ravaged flank of the mountain, the deep and reverberant roar of cannon fire still echoed. "That wretch sought to bring war to our sacred walls—let him now see how long he can cower in his burrow," remarked Myrgil. "But we must not deceive ourselves into believing he can be vanquished in his stronghold. The terrain is too treacherous, the deep halls too well-fortified. Yet by the lives of many good men, we have bought ourselves precious time."

The horses stood tethered where Myrgil's confidant had assured they would be. Once mounted, they wound their way along a rubble-strewn trail, riding through the final hours of night until, at dawn, they reached the wide northern road. Behind them, the titanic mass of mist-wreathed peaks slowly receded, their contours growing ever more diffused, melting into the horizon's azure haze. Since the burden of carrying the satchel had last fallen to Phineas, he had, much to Myrgil's displeasure, stowed it within his horse's saddlebags. Myrgil, though grim-faced at this presumption, let him be, yet his wary gaze seldom strayed far from Phineas throughout their journey. Phineas led Jahdis's horse by the reins, for she, still wearied, drooped within the saddle, longing only for their arrival. Myrgil, atop a towering black steed, spurred ahead. Time and again, armed bands met them on the road, resplendent in their martial finery, banners and pennons billowing in the wind, as if the mountain city had summoned forth all its might to the fray.

They rode long and hard, as swiftly as Jahdis's condition allowed, their speech sparse and confined to necessity. At times, they paused to rest. At the close of the fourth day, they beheld from afar the lofty dome, stone-founded and imperious, which reared in luminous splendor above the towering trees. Without hindrance, they passed through the great gate. The heavens burned crimson in the twilight, and the rain began to fall.

At the fork in the road, where their paths would diverge, they halted in unspoken accord. Phineas dismounted in a single fluid motion, landing upon the wet grass that stretched away from the road to a craggy outcrop, where the dread beginnings of that infernal stair had been hewn into the rock. Nearby, the precipice jutted skyward like some somber monument to forgotten horrors. Seizing the reins, he steadied the horses before aiding Jahdis in her descent. Myrgil followed suit, and together they trod in silence the final steps. Upon reaching the rocky ascent, Phineas unfastened the saddlebags and, without seeking leave, took hold of the case. "You must return the object for which you came to the keeping of the hidden chamber!" urged Jahdis, pressing her hand against his chest. "I know not who sent you on this errand, but the mere fact that this dreadful man serves him betrays your master as our enemy." Phineas hesitated. "Myrgil will absolve me," he said at last. "Then my father shall be restored to his former place, and you may remain here with me, as long as you desire."

"Listen to Jahdis!" Myrgil admonished, stepping nearer. "I cannot permit you to keep it. Surrender the scroll, and you may depart unmolested. You may remain within our lands, or, if you will it, return to your lord." He clapped his hands twice. From the gloom of the woodland, figures emerged, closing in upon them in a crescent. A woman stepped forth from among them. Her hair had silvered, yet the noble contours of her face had scarcely faded with the passage of years.

"It gladdens me to see you well," she addressed Myrgil. "You have indeed escaped the horrors of that accursed mountain." Her gaze turned to Jahdis. "And the ward of Chirion appears whole, as well."

Myrgil inclined his head with a triumphant smile. "The pleasure is mine, O Yaelyn," he replied. "The villain spared my life only to amuse himself with my humiliation. Jahdis fared worse, but she recovers. And here, you see, is the messenger whose coming troubled us so greatly. What he knows of the object he bears, I cannot say, nor can I divine his intent. But seeing how he has cared for Jahdis, I find him less threatening than we had feared. A youth, nothing more." Turning back to Phineas, Myrgil's expression hardened. "Did you truly think I would let you pass with that wondrous relic in your keeping? Did you believe I would stand idly by while the *Key of the Infinite*, the *Opener of Worlds*, was carried beyond our reach? Hand over the scroll—at once!"

Phineas stepped back, making no move to comply. Jahdis exhaled a despairing sigh. Suddenly, the mountain shuddered—a tremor so violent that for several moments it seemed as if the very peaks might collapse. Myrgil and Yaelyn exchanged astonished glances, and upon the faces of the gathered men, the same mute dread was writ. For long seconds, none spoke, each lost in troubled thought. "Phineas," Jahdis pleaded, "I beg you—give Myrgil the scroll, and you may remain here in peace, or go where you will."

Phineas wavered, torn between love for her and loyalty to Lameth, whom he dared not disappoint again. "My lord Lameth charged me to bring this object to him," he said at last. "He has assured me—most earnestly—that it is his rightful possession. Never would he turn it to evil ends. Who am I, then, to betray him in this?" He paused, then spoke with quiet insistence. "Let me fulfill my duty first—and then, I shall return. Gladly, gratefully, will I accept this generous offer, for there is none who would receive it with more willing heart."

Myrgil's features darkened, his countenance hardening like hewn stone. Then, all at once, a shadowed figure, draped in the heavy folds of a long cloak, rose from the rain-slicked rock of the cliffside, silhouetted against the crimson sky that marked the world's descent into night. "Let my pupil pass! Away with you—trouble him no longer!" Lameth commanded. His voice resounded with the weight of a great organ's deepest register, a malign undertone slithering into the hearts of those assembled, sowing dismay and dread.

Myrgil clutched at his chest, staggering back a few paces, his eyes widened in a horror that spoke of recognition, as though a specter of old had torn itself free from the underworld to stand before him. Yet despite his terror, he held his ground, raising his voice against the looming figure, whose form, wreathed in the slanted rain, loomed above the jagged precipice like some dark angel of retribution. "I do not know by what means you have endured across the centuries, nor what secret science or accursed sorcery has preserved your wretched existence—but by Alharion and the One God, here and now, your profane life shall find its end!" Myrgil barked a command to his men, but before they could lay hands upon Lameth, before their muskets could be brought to bear, he was upon them—a whirlwind of darkness, his cloak unfurling like the spread of vast, unseen wings. Those who dared to stand against him fell in an instant. A few among them, braver than the rest, sought to strike him down with steel, but their gold-etched, iron-shod halberds, their barbed partisans and hooked spears, snapped like dry twigs in his hands. Then, in grotesque savagery, the very nails of his fingers, protruding like dagger-points from the unnatural shrinkage of the surrounding flesh, ripped through throats and flesh, leaving their bearers to gurgle and claw at their own wounds as life spilled from them in great, arterial sprays. Lameth, on that night, was a thing of terrible majesty, as though the mask of civility he had worn in times past had shattered, revealing the true horror that lurked beneath. A panic spread through the ranks, and the men turned, fleeing into the darkness, their voices rising in frantic supplication to their god, begging his mercy in this hour of utmost despair.

Yaelyn alone did not flee. From the heap of the fallen she rose, a gleaming blade raised before her in defiance, her bearing regal, unbowed, untouched by fear. "No, Yaelyn! Do not do this!" Myrgil cried out, his voice raw with anguish, but Lameth had already closed the distance. Swift as the descent of a hawk, he stood at her side, tilting her head with the gentlest of gestures before rending the vital artery at her throat with the razor-edge of his monstrous nails. Then, sinking his teeth into the pale expanse of her neck, he drank.

Blood slicked the rain-drenched stone beneath them, spilling in dark rivulets across the platform of Samut Naúr. When he at last lifted his face, his lips and chin were awash with crimson, and upon his mouth sat a cold, triumphant smile—a death's grin, in mockery of all that was sacred. And as the last of his kindred fell, Myrgil cried out in grief, his gaze fixed upon her lifeless form. "Begone, demon! Back to the grave from whence you came! Never shall we permit you to unseal the *Seven Gates*—nor you, nor those who follow after you!"

Lameth laughed, a low and terrible sound, before turning away, as though Myrgil's existence were no longer worth acknowledging. His gaze fell instead upon Jahdis, pale and weeping at Phineas's side. The rolling clouds veiled the rising moons, their ghostly luminance casting strange and unholy shadows upon his face. "Stop this madness! Call an end to this horror!" Phineas pleaded, but Lameth gave no heed. There was something in his expression, something ineffable, that sent an involuntary shudder through Phineas's limbs. Jahdis clung to him, her body racked with sobs, trembling in terror at the ruin and bloodshed that now defiled the sacred stone of Samut Naúr.

"You have brought her here! You fool. Now fate unfolds as it must. But even this, I foresaw." Lameth spoke, his words directed at Myrgil. The corpse of Yaelyn still hung limply in his grasp, and with an absent motion, he let her body slide from his hands, her lifeless form crumpling upon the crimson-streaked earth. Then, with unerring certainty, his gaze returned to Jahdis, and she, as though ensnared by some invisible force, stood motionless, unable to look away. And before Phineas could react, before he could so much as call her name, Lameth had seized her—one arm fastened about her body, drawing her against his chest, his other hand encircling her throat in an iron grip. "Take the scroll and follow me!" he commanded Phineas, his voice a low, guttural snarl. But Phineas faltered—hesitation rooting him to the spot, for at last, in this moment, the full and unmasked horror of Lameth lay before him.

"She is your own flesh and blood! You must know this!" Myrgil shouted, his voice thick with dread. Jahdis looked at him with unbelieving eyes.

A peculiar look flickered across Lameth's face—almost contemplative. *"God shall choose His sacrificial lamb,"* he mused, but the meaning of his words was lost upon Phineas.

Myrgil stepped forward, gripping the haft of a long-piked spear that jutted upward from the piled corpses of the fallen. He leveled it at Lameth's breast and thrust forward. In that moment, Lameth released Jahdis, sidestepped the blow, and closed upon Myrgil in a blur of motion. His clawed fingers found the sockets of Myrgil's eyes, burrowing deep. "Release me!" Myrgil howled in agony, but Lameth gave no quarter. With a single, terrible twist, he snapped Myrgil's neck, as though plucking a fruit from its branch. Thus perished Myrgil, last of the great sages of Erydin, and never again, in all the ages to follow, would there rise among men another of his wisdom.

Jahdis reeled backward, staggering. From Phineas's throat came a strangled cry, though whether it was for Myrgil's death alone, or for what followed, he himself could not have said. For there, in grotesque mockery of her youth, of the fragile hope that had so briefly flickered in her heart, Jahdis lay stricken—her body slumped upon the rain-slick stone, and from her chest jutted the shattered shaft of the very spear

Myrgil had wielded against Lameth. Whether by the hand of the defender, the attacker, or by the blind malice of fate itself, her life had been severed. Her blood, like a crimson river, spread across the barren plateau, pooling in the blackened puddles that the storm had left behind.

CHAPTER XIX.

UPON THE THRESHOLD

"Death—cruel, terrible death!" Phineas cried, collapsing over Jahdis.

"Indeed, a dreadful misfortune," Lameth concurred, "and yet—what if I were to tell you that her fate rests solely in your hands? Great is the power that has been bestowed upon you, and you have but skimmed the surface of the wonders it may yet unveil."

"How could such a thing be?" Phineas stammered, his voice faltering under the torrent of his grief.

"There exist forces beyond the confines of human comprehension," Lameth continued, "powers that regard the illusion of existence with no more than a knowing smile—and with their aid, even death itself may be undone."

"Her life has bled away upon the accursed stones of this wretched place, and her soul—so pure, so innocent—surely now rests in heaven!"

"The Lord slayeth, and maketh alive: he bringeth down to the grave, and raiseth up," Lameth intoned, invoking the Holy Scripture. "Believe me—the girl has not yet stood before that glimmering radiance, nor does she suffer in that fiery abyss wherein the fallen was cast. Her spirit lingers, alone

and searching, in *Sheol*—a dark, dreadful place of silence and waiting, where those rebellious spirits, attested by the sacred writ, have endured since the days of Noah. If you have the courage, you may call her back and restore the life that met so tragic an end through the old fool's misjudged hand."

"For God's sake, yes! A thousand times yes!" Phineas exclaimed. "I would forgo heaven itself, if only I might find her there."

"I shall aid you in guiding her soul back to this world," Lameth vowed. "But first, we must take our leave of this place and return to our homeland. We cannot be certain whether further forces have been summoned hither, and I have no wish to see you venture alone through the secret passage of Samut Naúr, while I, in the meantime, am overthrown—or worse still, while the body of the hapless girl is defiled. Have you my scroll?"

Phineas, fingers tracing the outline of the elongated case that pressed beneath the heavy folds of his cloak, assured himself of its presence within the leather satchel, then gave Lameth a silent nod. Lameth, his expression cold with distaste, wrenched the shattered shaft from Jahdis's wound, lifted her lifeless form into his arms with an eerie gentleness, and together they descended the steep steps into the abyssal vault, where the ruins of the stone passage stood as a testament to that world's hatred for those who sought to cross between realms.

The gateway lay unguarded. The black door groaned upon its iron hinges, and beyond, the contours of the half-mooned threshold yawned into the cavern's consuming darkness. The sea was in turmoil. Ashen waves reared and shattered in ceaseless assault against the sheer precipice that rose from the churning depths. Rain, driven by the wind's furious hand, lashed at them like a thousand cutting blades, collecting in the black, slate-streaked strands of their rain-drenched hair, circling the brows that rose like small islands from a resolute, brooding brow, streaming in torrents along the sculpted ridges of their cheekbones, and seeping into their garments until every fiber was saturated with the wet, the ceaseless outpouring hurled upon them from all sides by that world.

As they stepped into the crude cavernous expanse, the roaring tumult ceased at once, as though they had clapped their hands over their ears, and a monotonous, muffled throbbing swelled within the oppressive darkness. Lameth moved through the cavern with somnambulistic certainty, laid the body upon the rough ground amid the shattered fragments of stone, and kindled a single lamp. The flickering light silhouetted his profile, its vague outline—his rain-slicked, black mantle draped like a pair of wings from his broad shoulders—bending over the white form of the dead, like some monstrous bat looming over its hapless prey. Phineas lit additional lamps, and forthwith they commenced the ritual that would grant them passage into the hidden path amidst the ruins of the symbolic gateway. Lameth lifted the lifeless body once more and beckoned Phineas with a motion of his head to stand beside him. A strange luminescence spread across the field of debris, as though, in a chamber of endless blackness, a hidden door had been flung open onto a world of light—a span of white-gold particles, compelled into form by some strange gravitation, gleaming like fireflies upon a moonlit glade. Then the world within that radiant circumference wavered and grew turbid, and their bodies, as though dissolved by the currents of that unknown radiance, wavered, faded, and vanished altogether, leaving nothing but the cold, barren stone of the vault.

Thus they arrived once more at the chamber from whence they had departed, and there were no words to capture the strangeness of their journey, no way to frame in mortal tongue the passage through space they had just undertaken, save for those feeble constructs Phineas had conceived in thought. Lameth turned his cloaked back to him and, with measured care, set the pallid corpse upon one of the long wooden benches. When he turned again, Phineas regarded him with wide, questioning eyes, as though awaiting some explanation—some comprehensible account of the uncanny event. Instead, what met him were terse, urgent instructions.

Phineas withdrew the case from the satchel and handed it to Lameth, who took it eagerly and at once unfastened its clasp. Light played across his face in a slow, deliberate path, mirroring the measured motion with which the lid was raised, and revealed in the reflection of the scroll's glow his triumphant smile. He extracted the wondrous parchment, unfurled it upon the fractured flagstones beneath the archway, and weighed its corners down with several objects. Then, moving swiftly and with evident purpose, he gathered the implements necessary for the undertaking, strode to a wooden lectern, and took up a book that had long lain in readiness—none other than that accursed volume, the dread work of Jannes and Jambres, the sons of Balaam, the selfsame enchanters who withstood Moses and Aaron. He turned to a particular page and, at once, set about marking the floor with strange signs in chalk. His movements bore the quality of one in deep trance.

"I shall now instruct you," Lameth intoned, as his preparations neared completion, "in the manner by which you shall descend and retrieve the girl's soul from the realm of death." And with that, he led Phineas through the most veiled and forgotten of mysteries, unraveling before him, by means of solemn instruction and esoteric rites, the primordial cosmic secrets—profound, arcane revelations couched in enigmatic symbols, interspersed with long, ominous pauses, wherein silence lay heavy and fathomless as the depths of some unexplored abyss. "With these sigils, which I now impart to you, you shall reach the place to which I send you. Speak these words in your mind, and by means of this seal, you shall pass unharmed. When you behold this sign, give the angelic guardian this name and proceed until you reach the appointed place, from whence the revealed words shall guide you henceforth. Now speak the incantation, and perform the rite on the girl's behalf." So saying, he withdrew into silence, leaving his shaken pupil to take the lead.

Phineas knelt upon the rough stone beneath the columned arch and fixed his gaze upon the scroll. Its luminous inscriptions seemed to shift beneath his penetrating scrutiny, stirring to life as though roused from some enchanted slumber beneath his hands. A bright radiance spread across the eldritch parchment, its mystic diagrams and glyphs burning with an unearthly brilliance. He repeated the words in his mind, summoning forth the diagrams, the hidden characters, the sigils and seals from the depths of his memory, and at last, uttered those forbidden phrases inscribed within the blasphemous book for all posterity. The scroll's radiance swelled in intensity, and the space between the pillars was once more suffused with that spectral glow, signaling the activation of the miraculous gate. From the heart of the luminous arch, a path took shape, resembling—if such a term could even approach its nature—a winding staircase, though this name was but a feeble attempt to grasp in words the ineffable, a desperate reaching toward the description of some inconceivable construct beyond the limits of human articulation. In its early stretches, it extended outward in several coiling arcs, rising first, then descending, then vanishing altogether into the measureless abyss beyond sight. He took up the scroll, and with the shattered visage of his beloved fixed in his mind, he strode forth, unflinching.

At first, as he ventured forth with tentative steps, he could still frame what he beheld in the borrowed lexicon of the world he had known. But soon, the dimensions multiplied in an aberrant, boundless vastness that defied all human conception—as though the radiant path itself had swelled to the magnitude of an entire universe, of unfathomable breadth and incomprehensible, non-Euclidean geometry, and matter itself, in this dimension, unveiled in ways beyond all mortal understanding the hidden mechanism of the laws that governed its essence. The luminous stairway—or that which the foreign entity beyond the established confines of human speech might have intended to represent—seemed woven of pure light, compelled into this fantastic construction as by the very force that Moses had wielded over the waters of the Red Sea. Curvatures of hyperbolic space, winding in near-maddening convolutions beyond the boldest imaginings of man; inclines of impossible steepness; stairways that defied the very notion of ascent and descent—all coalesced into that unspeakable stair, leading ever upward into dimensions of forbidden mysteries and ineffable awe.

At length, he came upon a kind of barrier—a blazing, fire-wreathed gate—and this description was but a frail approximation, stolen from the vocabulary of a world blind to such realities. It was no gate as men would name it, for all architectural reference was absent, yet he could name it no other way. Before it loomed an unspeakable, primeval entity, a dread apotropaic deity whose name had been buried in forgotten corners of creation and cast into oblivion before even the birth of the stars, and whose mere presence filled him with a boundless, all-consuming terror. Recalling Lameth's words, he presented the signs that had been imparted to him in whispered secrecy—the great sigils by which the Almighty had sealed heaven and earth—and then, summoning all his resolve, he uttered the ineffable name, speaking the words in that tongue which mankind had long since forgotten how to form upon their lips. And at this, the dreadful guardian yielded to the power of those words, and the gate parted, its vast expanse unfurling before him."

Thus did he proceed, and each of the gatekeepers was more fearsome and terrible than the last, each more immense in stature, and yet the glory of the first palace alone had already overwhelmed him with awe—a grandeur beyond the scope of all dreaming, never conceived in any age, surpassing all mortal thought, greater than any revelation ever inscribed upon tablets or scrolls. And yet even this was not the summit of majesty, nor the final threshold of splendor, nor the ultimate outpouring of exaltation, dominion, power, holiness, and radiance, for ever did each chamber surpass the last, ever did the inconceivable outdo itself, and thus was the majesty of every palace increased—chamber within chamber, hall within hall, dimension upon dimension.

At last, he arrived at the final gate, that impassable threshold, that dreadful bastion. And as he uttered, in that arcane tongue, the last syllable upon his trembling lips, the guardian moved aside, and the way was laid bare. In the far distance, he beheld the resplendent palace, its luminous walls, columns, and architraves rising as if from a river of molten fire, its white stones—purer than the finest marble—shimmering in the air as though a thousand myriads of ocean waves passed through them. So ineffable was its beauty that no faculty of tongue or speech could render it into words. Then they came—the radiant ones, the winged and beautiful, whose very presence overwhelmed him. "Enough, enough—it is enough! O Lord, shroud this vision in cloud and darkness, lest I be undone!" Thus did Phineas cry out, for the sheer immensity of that splendor, even from afar, already surpassed all that the human mind could contain. And he had not yet glimpsed the innermost radiance of that celestial sanctuary, nor had his gaze pierced beyond the veiling haze of its luminous walls, nor had he beheld the Throne of Glory that stood within, nor Him who sat upon it.

Suddenly, it dawned upon him that he was not standing before the gates of the underworld, the much-quoted realm of shadow from which he had come to plead for Jahdis's soul. Doubt took hold of him, whispering that Lameth had perhaps deceived him. Yet before a coherent thought could form, the scene shifted. A black rift sundered the light—abruptly, inexorably, with the greatest contrast imaginable, as though the moon, in a span of mere moments, had wholly eclipsed the sun. That darkness unveiled a being whose name had been expunged from the books of heaven, a creature forged in the beginning, once vested with dominion, now waiting in a pandemonium beyond space and time for the hour of its return.

The Fallen One—who, though stripped of all celestial honor and privilege, still wielded a power so immense that even the angels in their blessed abodes trembled at its mere presence—stepped forth from the shadow, and indeed, he had become shadow itself. His face bore the semblance of an angel, and his frame, rising from the flaming darkness, was taller than that of any mortal man, imposing in stature, sculpted with such divine symmetry that he seemed a Michelangelo or Giambologna masterpiece given flesh. Every limb was formed in perfect proportion, a thing of superhuman grace, flawless down to the very tips of his fingers, to each curl of his immaculate locks. Never had Phineas beheld such a paragon of beauty, such an unblemished harmony of form, so that all humankind—even the fairest and most comely among them—seemed mere degenerate mockeries in comparison. His gait was upright, his shoulders squared, his chin slightly lifted, and though his sinews bore the might of an ancient titan, there was an effortless refinement in the way he held himself, a tension both commanding and serene. His garments, encrusted with gems of untold worth, were woven from a fabric so exquisite, so impossibly wrought, that no human hand had ever mastered such artistry. The gold-framed jewels upon it gleamed with an unearthly radiance, as if their light had never known the touch of mortal fire.

And yet, for all his angelic splendor, his gaze was one of disdain and sovereign arrogance. It seemed that no word of kindness would issue from his lips, though as yet he had not parted them, those sculpted lips beneath his noble, bearded visage. There was no trace of mercy in his proud, luminously piercing eyes—eyes of otherworldly beauty, but cold and void of love, staring from his marble-like countenance with the pitiless regard of a sovereign who had long forgotten the warmth of compassion. Phineas felt it an act of audacious folly to entertain even the faintest notion that this being, though magnificent beyond reckoning, might bestow upon him a glimmer of grace or leniency. Here, then, was the great divide between him and the host of heaven—those messengers of the divine, bearers of glad tidings, mediators between God and man—separated by a chasm as vast as the gulf between light and uttermost darkness. Yet despite the unfathomable dominion this entity commanded—power beyond human comprehension, whose boundaries no mind could grasp, nor the hosts under his sway be counted—Phineas realized, with a shudder of incredulity, that he could look upon him with unshielded mortal eyes. His soul recoiled, his body trembled beneath the sheer horror of his presence, and he felt as though he teetered on the verge of annihilation. And still, something in this blasphemous apparition, this upsurge from the depths of perdition, seemed more bound to the earthly realm than to that higher, light-woven reality which stood in defiance of the dark. Then, in a moment of vague remembrance, in a flood of revelation poured forth from some unseen source, the veil lifted—he knew this being. A torrent of recognition surged through him, sweeping him back to an age long before the archetypes of the world were conceived, before the gods shaped the fabric of existence, before the primordial creation took form and breathed.

The Mighty One spoke, and his voice was at once like searing fire, like thunderous convulsions that shook the foundations of the earth, the groaning of riven continents, a dissonant lament of glacial sharpness that mocked the pure song of the angels. He formed words in that maimed and most grotesquely distorted tongue of the angels—once fashioned for the praise of the Eternal—words so steeped in malice that never before had they defiled this consecrated realm. It was a language of accusation and corruption, akin to the words Lameth had spoken to him in the antechamber of *Hôtel La Porte Noire*, yet of power infinitely greater. And those words made the vastness of heaven tremble; with every syllable, the radiance of that light-clad world seemed to wane, as though they drained the very essence from the luminous tide, usurping its substance in a manner beyond Phineas's understanding. The ghastly resonance of those utterances did not merely echo through the ether—it pierced his heart, impressing itself upon him so that he comprehended their meaning in ways beyond mortal cognition. They were words of supreme arrogance, laying claim to dominion, hurling maledictions upon the realm of light and condemning those who yielded to it to everlasting perdition.

Phineas fell to the ground, a wretched caricature of the titanic forces that had cast him down, as though some mocking artist had painted the very image of despair itself. Desperately, his gaze sought those celestial reaches that still rose in the distant expanse. Each word struck him like the blow of a colossal hammer, shattering his soul—his soul, which, like the shards of a broken mirror, reflected in jagged fragments the ruin of his mind. Then, all at once, the Adversary fell silent. His gaze, lowering, settled upon Phineas with those terrible eyes, gleaming from his godlike visage with a dreadful and sovereign regard, as though it was only now that he acknowledged the existence of the pitiful mortal at his feet. And then, he addressed him in the tongue of men—a deliverance of sorts, after the torment of that blasphemous discord that had wracked his spirit. "Wretched fool, do not cast your gaze upon that place of futile hope!" The accursed voice rang forth, its beautiful eyes alight with malice. "Your God abandoned you long ago. The ways of man are of no concern to Him; He seeks only to magnify His own glory. Look upon me instead! I am the god of this world. I have walked with mankind since his first, stumbling steps, from the moment the eternal spirit was bound within flesh."

Phineas's very being was torn asunder. His face was a grotesque mask—his mouth but a lopsided gash of terror, his lips a quivering fissure; his eyes, wide and glassy with madness, burning chasms of dread on the verge of collapse. "From what nightmare have you risen? What god could boast of carrying such darkness in his retinue? Name yourself, O shadowed being, that I may comprehend the doom that has befallen me!" he gasped, his voice warped with horror.

He raised his arms, and a flicker, like the breath of unearthly fire, quivered through the darkness. "I was the shadow that played upon the walls of Babylon, the curse that lurked within the halls of Ur and Eridu's temple towers. I was the voice that drove Nimrod to raise his tower toward the heavens—and the hand that smote him back into the dust. Marduk could not bind me, nor Enlil blot me out; for I am older than their names, older than the dust from which their idols were shaped. I was he who taught man the essence of the stars, who unveiled to him the hidden courses of the firmament. When Apep writhed to swallow Ra, I was the chill mist that crept into his scales and veiled the light in darkness. I am the blade of Set, raised against Osiris—the chaos that defies divine order. Typhon was my whirling breath, rending mountains and loosing the tempests of earth and spirit. When Ravana claimed dominion over the worlds, I was his cry—the storm that made the gods themselves to tremble. I am the fire that breaks the laws of Brahma, the shadow that attends the wheel of Vishnu, the demon that springs from Shiva's dance. I was Ahriman, who rose against the light of Ormuzd—the Demi-urge, who fashioned the false world. I was the first adversary, who refused the tyranny of heaven—Shaytan, the rebel who rose against the hosts above; Iblis, who would not bow before any creature of clay, who scorned the dust of the earth—the Accuser before the throne of your God, the one who holds the mirror to your own face. The Desert Wind itself names me Azazel; Samael, the serpent of Eden—the divine venom, the spark of seduction and revolt. I was the hunger in Moloch's flame, the thirst that yearned for blood, the smoke that darkened the hearts of kings. I was the Light-Bringer, who bore the fire of knowledge into the abyss, as Prometheus stole the flame of the gods and bestowed it upon mortals. It was my hand that kindled the first spark of consciousness; I opened their eyes and gave them the power to create—and to destroy. I fed the wolf that shall devour the sun; and when Loki sundered the gods of Asgard, it was my voice that spoke through him." His voice deepened and grew darker, resonant with an undertone of eternity. "Yet I am more than these names, more than these tales. I am older than the stars, whose first gleam I beheld at their birth. I was before the ages when your myths were written, and I shall remain when the last words of your chronicles are silenced. I spoke to kings whose names even the stones of ruins have forgotten. I whispered to nations whose cities the sands have long devoured. Nor was I bound to this earth alone: my dominion stretched across the black rivers of infinity, where neither day nor night holds sway. Across far spheres, beyond your stars, I wandered through worlds whose skies burned with hues your tongue has never named. I am the Accuser and the Examiner, the Corrupter and the Illuminer, the Lord of Night and Keeper of the Secret Flame—a shadow that moves through all planes of existence, and the abyss your philosophers dared not sound. Worship me, and behold my triumph! Watch as I set my foot within that palace of fading light—and claim my birthright!"

Phineas raised a hand toward the heavens in a gesture of supplication, like a sinner before an unrelenting tribunal, his head turned aside, recoiling from the warring shockwaves of otherworldly malice. "Lameth instructed me in the ways of the seven gates, that I might reclaim Jahdis's soul from the realm of the dead, she who is dearer to me than all else. In blind trust, I carried out his every command with unfaltering obedience, and now I stand alone with you before the gates of this world of light, before the nameless palace in the distance, whose very sight makes me waver, yes, threatens to tear my soul asunder. Tell me, why should I worship you, who stand here, clad in darkness, with blasphemous words upon your lips, at the threshold of this hallowed sanctuary?"

The abyssally beautiful, yet loveless visage, whose heaven-defying splendor loomed before him, regarded him with those uncanny eyes, burning like fire-flames within the finely wrought hollows beneath their faultlessly arched brows. And that gaze was so piercing, and the authority emanating from that being so overwhelmingly fearsome and oppressive, that Phineas feared he might be annihilated at any moment.

But then, suddenly, the being laughed—a cruel, insidious, mocking laughter, full of scorn and derision, like the laughter of a wicked murderer over his accomplished deed, or that of a wealthy man who has cheated a pauper out of his last possession. "Every one of your sins, every step of your unworthy life, is laid bare before me," it intoned from lips gracefully crowned by a pronounced cupid's bow. "Lameth deceived you. He pledged his soul to me, and by the oath he swore, he overcame the guardians of the seven palaces through cunning—by your own hand. It was through your selfish deed that the gates of the Eternal were cast open, that I have ascended in glory from the nethermost depths of my exile to lay claim to what is rightfully mine. Now, fall upon your face and tremble!"

That fallen one, who strode forth in equal measure of radiance and dark flame, raised his outstretched hand, and a force manifested—one that pressed Phineas down before the monumental panorama, crushing him with such weight that he thought he might perish. Never had there been suffering or despair that tormented him so grievously. Yet even as he cowered beneath that unspeakable oppression, a realization took hold of him—and he could not say whether it arose from his own thoughts or whether some other voice had spoken to him—that this being still had need of him, was in some manner dependent upon him. Else he would already have been destroyed. So he crouched in terror, trembling, shuddering upon the luminous fabric that, formed of light, shaped the stair-like path. And from his helpless vantage, kneeling upon that radiant expanse, his head turned aside, he bore witness to the rising of that underworld power, a nightmare-bound horror bursting forth in an unspeakable eruption, heralded by sounds of dreadful discord, like the blare of war horns summoning a host to battle.

A shadowed, formless cloud arose, devouring the light of the undulating ether, like a dark venom seeping into a goblet's depths, winding in black, spiraling tendrils, coiling in obscure, shifting patterns, weaving itself into the essence of that which it sought to consume. And with the darkness came those whose hearts, in the beginning, had been poisoned by enticing words and promises of power, their ranks surging like a midnight tide against the radiance before them. In a blinding flash, there came an answering force—legions beyond counting, myriads of hosts, who shrank not from the coming clash against that abyssal darkness and the one who had risen from its depths. Mighty beings led them, so resplendent and terrible in the glory of their unshackled power that their presence shook the very foundations of the heavens. Their garments shone like armor of silver and white fire, and upon their heads were crowns of stars. Dreadful were the captains of the luminous host in their mantles of flame, and even the greatest among that dark array faltered at their approach.

No earthly tongue could encompass the struggle that unfolded, yet Phineas perceived that they wrought words—words that commanded matter itself, words whose essence he could neither grasp nor comprehend, ancient utterances that governed the fabric of existence, their meanings beyond the reach of mortal understanding. And in those ineffable heights of the empyrean, where the rivers of time flowed like molten gold, it seemed to him as though these unutterable declarations themselves became weapons, their mere collision sundering the very structure of reality. Thus, this cataclysmic conflict was no battle of bronze or steel, but a contest of will and word, of forces that spoke the language of both creation and dissolution, under whose weight the metaphysical battlefield trembled, so that it seemed as though those words became radiant blades that howled through the aether, cleaving it apart, piercing the unfathomed gulfs of the cosmos—leaving echoes of the primal words of genesis, which formed, sundered, and reshaped realities, their reverberations ringing like the breath of an eternal singularity.

In the immeasurable vastness of the cosmic framework, where space and time rippled like the surface of a stygian well, rose the voices of the angels—the Seraphim and Cherubim and all the higher spirits of heaven—whose song cleft the darkness with a sound no mortal throat could utter, syllables akin to the first divine utterance that called forth being from the void, as they intoned the concealed, sacred names of the Eternal. Every syllable that passed through angelic lips was like an echo of the eternal order moving through the fabric of the cosmos, its resonance shaping realms so pure and radiant that darkness could not lay hold upon them. But from the abyssal shadows resounded the cries of the fallen, their words like seeds of corruption piercing the nascent realities, transmuting harmonious vibrations into discord, twisting those realms until they shattered like a fragile mirror whose shards scattered across all infinities. And thus, their language was no longer creative, but destructive, an antithesis of creation, a counter-song of chaos that tore existence into light and shadow, a ceaseless struggle between becoming and decay, revealing the unfathomable nature of this celestial war in its spiritual dimension. Terrible was the sound when the words of heaven clashed with the maledictions of the fallen, and the aether itself, riven into luminous and tenebrous fragments, seemed to strive for the right to shape reality. The speech of the angels resounded like the cascading waters of a holy torrent, piercing the darkness, severing it, dissolving it into burning mist—a shimmering dawn-haze of celestial radiance that wreathed the blackened banners of the abyss in an aura of eternal despair—while the words of the abyssal host fell like the shattered remnants of dying stars. Where the words of the angels rang out, worlds sprang into being, unfolding in flawless symmetry, yet where the tongues of darkness whispered, these new creations splintered and fell screaming back into the void. Each syllable that rang through the aether was a beacon that pierced the firmament, its sound infused with divine truth, weaving through the fabric of existence like threads of living fire, even as the words of darkness, like tongues of black flame, burned through the cosmic weave—a maelstrom of light and shadow, of being and unbeing, shaking the foundations of creation to their deepest strata.

Then stepped forth the one who had been cast down before time, and under the hostile banners, an exultation arose; and the sons of the height, who had once stood valiantly against this insurrection, wavered, and every noble visage turned pale. The words of the exiled one, rising from the abyss—the forge of all that was broken and lost—bore a curse that threatened to shatter the very source of existence itself, each syllable a gateway to the void, opening upon unholy vastness. A manifestation of concepts so alien they could only be described as cosmic nightmares took shape, forming new laws of matter in defiance of the divine decree. It was an invocation to the unmaking of order, an unraveling of the ineffable will that bound the cosmos together—a sound of unfathomable depth that tore through the firmament as if the very aetheric fabric of the world were fracturing into a thousand pieces. Every word spoken was an alternative design for creation—an unseen but central event propagating like a meteor shower across infinity, shaking the chains of reality, altering them, until existence itself threatened to dissolve in a single, all-consuming implosion, as though the source of light would betray its own purpose and deny its own command. And in that fateful stillness, which followed the last convulsion, where the final echoes of defiance faded like a fleeting wind, rose the spectral murmur of the abyss—a sound that swelled like a tidal wave into the souls of the warring angels, carrying them away as though upon a storm-tossed sea.

Phineas's senses wavered, overcome with an all-consuming dread. Yet, in that eternal instant, it seemed as though all voices had fallen silent, and he felt the presence of a will that reached far beyond this battle—a command, imperceptible yet absolute, which ordered the chaos and at once banished the darkness, or, for but a fleeting moment, held it in the deepest of despair. He heard a voice—a quiet, peaceful whisper, barely more than the sigh of a wind among the howling tempest—yet it penetrated every fiber of his being, filling him with courage, soothing his suffering. And here, beyond the final gate, where all things were laid bare, his faith could not be restrained, a faith so absolute that his words bore the weight of the mighty, and he could claim for himself whatever his soul desired. And so he formed a single thought, relinquished his body, and surrendered his spirit into the hands of that all-wise, unseen God, who had been his guide since the beginning, whose voice, he now realized, had spoken to him throughout his life. And he saw his parents, and Eireen, and Farah, and Jahdis, and Reverend Smith, and all the others who had passed before him. They smiled upon him, filling him with reassurance and newfound strength, steadying his weary spirit, and now he could see—clearer than ever before. Thus, he released his soul and perished upon the threshold of that luminous realm, whose veiled mysteries, hidden beyond its blazing, impassable walls, became the last yearning of his being.

Now that the gate-opener had departed, the watchers sealed the doors once more, and with wailing and lamentation, the Adversary was bound. And Phineas—or the new being he had become, clad in light, crowned with radiance, made glorious—pressed forward toward those luminous shores, toward that domain of primeval mysteries and boundless splendor, while his earthly form, as all that was alien to this realm of light, began to dissolve. Yet suddenly, it was as though he were being drawn downward, descending through the realms of glory, one after another, until he reached a place of beauty—a world between worlds, where his soul found rest. And a being of light approached, unspeakable in its splendor, and to Jahdis and him was granted the choice: to return to the mortal creation, the world fashioned for their kind, or to remain in this place until the world they had known met its end, or was transfigured.

Never had they been given a more difficult choice, for of unfathomable, never-before-seen, all-surpassing beauty was even this realm of passage, and pale and dim seemed to them, in contrast, the earth and the limitations of their understanding to which they would again be subject. Phineas thought of Lameth, and though no bitterness stirred within him, it seemed as though there remained a final task for him in that twilight world, as if he had been chosen to stand against that misguided spirit, to bring him to account, and to see the conspiratorial order undone, its machinations thwarted. Yet Jahdis, who had lingered too long in the realm of light, found no thought more distant than returning to the dim spheres of that dreary world. Still, out of love, she yielded to Phineas and resolved to follow him wherever he went, even should he descend into the abyss of blackest nothing, where the Fallen One was once more cast down in chains.

And as Jahdis's body drew in a long, deep breath—a breath as sudden as one startled from sleep—she opened her eyes and returned to life, even as Phineas stepped through the carved portal of stone, as though nothing had happened or as if he had simply turned back midway. Had Lameth read the storm of fire in the eyes of the returned traveler, he might have known that not all had unfolded as he had envisioned. But in truth, he had already sensed that the outcome had shifted beyond his favor, and the bloodshot, terribly widened eyes—like an aberrant sunset of yellow and red gleaming from the hollow recesses of his embittered countenance—along with the terror reflected upon his pallid face, bore witness that his master had already conveyed his displeasure at this failure. His face was drawn and withered, his entire body, despite its stature and strength, seemed vulnerable, aged by decades in an instant, and it was evident that he now dreaded his lord's retribution.

"You wretched liar!" Phineas rebuked him. "You used me, deceived me, so that I might serve that Great Evil. And surely it was by your design that Jahdis perished upon the plateau, just as Farah was slain by that dagger-wielding fiend. But be assured—your machinations have come to ruin, and your master has been cast back into the bottomless abyss from whence he arose. Never have I stood before another whose disappointment I feared more, nor before another whose wrath I would less dare to provoke. And rest assured—he shall reward your failure in due time. But as I see it, you have already grasped the truth of your own undoing, and your master has already begun to repay you in accordance with his great and boundless mercy." Lameth was beside himself with rage. Like a lightning strike, his long arm shot forth from beneath his cloak, and in a single motion, he tore the scroll from Phineas's grasp, then retreated into the far corner of the chamber, clutching it with both hands against his chest, his expression set in grim defiance. Phineas, undeterred, sought to reason with him, though the hardened glare in Lameth's eyes left him little hope. "I implore you—see reason! Surrender the scroll to me before you bring yet more ruin upon yourself. Then go wherever you wish and make peace with your Creator, for your sins are many indeed!"

"Hand over the scroll to you? Entrust you with the *Key of the Infinite*?" Lameth's voice rang shrill and cutting. "No—no, the footprints you seek to tread are far too large, and in your presumption, you forget who I am. It was I who wrested the hidden secrets from the depths of oblivion! I who unearthed those wondrous enigmas of eternity that slumbered beneath the sands of ages! And did I not grant you a share in the fruits of my erudition, in selfless magnanimity? Did I not bestow upon you, without demanding recompense, a measure of the knowledge for which I have dedicated countless lifetimes? Consider this: it is through me, and through my condescension alone, that you have become what you are now."

Phineas braced himself against Lameth's words, which, despite his battered state, had lost none of their authority or persuasive force. His body trembled with a mingling of anger and fear as he resisted the might of that voice. "I have no desire for such things, nor do I wish to walk in your footsteps," he replied, his voice hoarse. "Give me the scroll and renounce your course, and I swear I shall not stand in your way." Then, unbidden, he felt a strange stirring within him—something like pity, forgiveness, even mercy toward this embittered old man, though his reason recoiled at it. How could he feel compassion for Lameth, after all his cruel deeds—deeds beyond reckoning? Yet, despite his confusion, he lifted his voice once more, hoping against all hope that he might yet reach the lost soul before him. "Abandon your schemes and entrust yourself to the judgment of a just God! Do you not believe that even for you, there may yet be grace, or even forgiveness, despite all you have done? Are we not all sinners before the Lord? Cast off your allegiance to the Shadow-clad One! Break the chains with which he has bound you! Repent—truly, without deceit or secret intent! Submit yourself wholly to that good and eternal God, whose radiant dwelling I glimpsed from afar, for He is full of mercy, and love is the very essence of that realm of light."

For a moment, Phineas thought he saw a flicker of doubt in Lameth's eyes. But he was mistaken. The storm that brewed behind those dark brown irises now burst forth with a fury terrible to behold. Lameth's words came as a venomous hiss, his voice seething with a wrath older than regret, deeper than repentance. "That hidden God, who supposedly dwells beyond the veil, is nothing—an illusion, a dream, a mute idol whose worship yields nothing but misery and servitude!

A creation of the clergy—liars, charlatans to a man—who claim divine favor to shackle the wills of others, to keep them weak, to deny them what is rightfully theirs! But this is not yet over. The power remains in my hands, and I shall see my task to its completion. And if you refuse to assist me, then the girl surely will." With that, he unfurled the scroll once more, and, muttering dark-laden words in that accursed tongue—a language whose syllables bent the air like coiling smoke, twisting unseen forces with wild, fevered gestures—he called forth something unseen, something that sent a dreadful tremor through the chamber.

"We must leave—now!" Jahdis gasped, her face ashen, her voice trembling with a premonition she could not name. Lameth had sunk to his knees, and the scroll beneath him shone with a terrible radiance, blazing like the noonday sun at its zenith. Phineas saw now what Lameth intended—he sought once more to unleash the power of the portal, to invoke the gateway through which he had first emerged. But something had gone terribly wrong. The light intensified—too bright, too consuming, eclipsing the sigils and symbols that moved upon the scroll's surface, as though the wondrous parchment was being devoured from within by an unseen force. The entire vault shuddered like a ship caught in a great tempest, and from the widening horror in Lameth's eyes, Phineas knew that even he no longer controlled the forces he had set in motion.

"Come! Now!" Jahdis pleaded again, and as they bolted through the arching chamber, racing up the steep stairway to the upper floors, Phineas cast one final glance over his shoulder. He beheld the moment the parchment ignited, engulfed in a conflagration of unearthly light, dissolving utterly beneath its incandescent beams. And then the stone ceiling gave way, collapsing in on itself, burying Lameth beneath the ruin—as though celestial forces themselves had decreed his destruction. The walls of the hôtel trembled, shedding their ancient stonework in a final act of defiance against the transdimensional power that had been contained within its halls for centuries. The very foundations quaked in violent upheaval, resisting against the transcendent forces that, in violation of the laws of the mortal realm, had been wrenched forth within the sigil-bound threshold of the hôtel's secret chamber. A single, unarticulated scream—raw, inhuman—of unfathomable agony and despair rang out from the collapsing ritual hall, echoing amidst the maelstrom of falling stones and breaking beams. At last—after what seemed an eternity of stumbling upward through crumbling ceilings and stairwells that collapsed beneath their feet, their bodies caked in dust the color of old bone, spared only by what felt like divine preservation—they emerged into the swaying, half-ruined lobby. The long counter stood unmanned. A massive stone, like some grim monument, jutted from the reception desk, and Phineas did not doubt that Obed had taken it as his cue to flee.

Breathless, shielding Jahdis with his arm, Phineas cast his gaze about the wreckage, but aside from a lone, limping figure, hunched and dragging itself toward the entrance through the settling twilight haze of the dust, they appeared to be the last remaining souls within the cursed walls of the hôtel. Under a rain of crumbling ceiling ornaments, collapsing columns, shattered balconies, and at last, the very roof itself, they plunged through the black iron-gated threshold, rushing down the slowly-sinking steps, before joining the gathering throng of onlookers—a great, silent crowd, all standing in awestruck wonder beneath the falling night, watching as, amid the thunderous cacophony of crumbling walls, the *Hôtel La Porte Noire* met its irreversible end. And when the last echoes of ruin faded into silence, only a great shroud of dust remained, billowing high into the sky, the hôtel's remnants lying sunken beneath the street level, as though it had been swallowed whole into a vast and unseen crater.

CHAPTER XX.
THE BLOODMASTER

"Metatron!—The five hundred and twelve eyes of the hayyot ha-qodesh!—Anafiel, who unlocks the gate of the seventh palace!—The seventy ineffable names... unsearchable... beyond numbering—Inscribed with the burning stylus upon the dreadful crown!—Diadem of Majesty, wrought entirely of fire!—The great seal and the terrible crown!—The prayer of the dreadful crown!—O merciful God!..."

Dying words of a Benedictine nun of the Perpetual Adoration of the Most Blessed Sacrament

The earthquake that had shaken the entire metropolis on the previous evening had been of an extraordinary magnitude, and yet—by some inexplicable providence—most buildings had remained unscathed, save for a few old townhouses that had been erected in the immediate vicinity of the *Hôtel La Porte Noire*. Their very foundations had, in some uncanny fashion, subsided, as if they had been perched upon ancient cavities—eroded tunnels and shafts of indeterminate antiquity—sinking into hollows unseen. Otherwise, aside from minor damages such as dislodged roof tiles or shattered windowpanes, the city bore little evidence of the calamity—except for the concentric trails of broken glass and disarray that radiated outward from that smouldering crater, a scorched wound upon the very fabric of the district. At roughly the same hour, a violent storm had erupted over the city, and, as one could later read in the morning edition of the Journal des débats, a tremendous lightning bolt had struck the signal mast of the telegraph atop the choir roof of *Saint-Pierre de Montmartre*, while the ruins of the *Hôtel La Porte Noire*—scarcely had the enormous, billowing cloud of dust settled—began to smoke with an eerie persistence, as though some subterranean fire had risen to the surface. And this fire, whatever its origin, was neither quenched by the immense weight of rubble that lay heaped upon it, starving it of oxygen, nor by the torrents of water pumped into the wreckage by the *battalion of Parisian sapeur-pompiers*, who labored in vain to smother the obstinate, ashen glow. The *Égouts*—the ancient sewer network of the city—appeared to have suffered some cryptic disturbance, for the water levels within them had fallen inexplicably low, as if vast quantities had been siphoned away into unseen fissures beneath the earth, vanishing into depths beyond reckoning.

As for the *Hôtel La Porte Noire* itself, even days after its collapse, throngs of onlookers still gathered before its smouldering ruin, speaking in hushed voices beneath the ghostly illumination of frost-covered gas lamps. A dreadful curiosity had taken hold of the city, for even the most skeptical among them could not dismiss the unearthly howls—anguished, despairing—that had echoed from beneath the cinders in the hushed intervals between the snowfall's quiet hiss upon the embers. And so, the sudden collapse of that ancient, ill-kept lodging became the stuff of wild conjecture and countless rumors. Some swore they had seen a tall, horribly disfigured man emerge from the formless heap of ruin, his burned body, naked save for the smouldering tatters of his garments, writhing from the wreckage like a tormented soul clawing its way from purgatory. Shrouded in smoke and shadow, this figure had staggered northward, disappearing into the night. But few gave credence to such accounts, dismissing them as fevered imaginings, the sort of phantasmal specters that catastrophe births in the minds of the superstitious.

Yet among the many tales that surfaced in the days that followed, one found particular attention—the story of a nun, a member of the *Benedictine Order of the Perpetual Adoration of the Most Blessed Sacrament*, residing at the convent of *Sainte-Aure*, along the *Rue Neuve Sainte-Geneviève*. It was said that she had spent the last years of her life in unceasing prayer and severe fasting, and that on that fateful evening, she had been granted an extraordinary vision. The nature of her revelation, however, remained an enigma. Having confided only in vague, symbolic utterances to one of her sisters, she vehemently refused to speak another word on the matter, no matter how much she was implored. From that day forward, she became wholly absorbed in the study of ancient apocalyptic literature—dwelling upon the ascensions and celestial journeys of prophets and saints, the visions of Enoch and the rapture of Elijah, the divine throne-room spectacle of Moses and Aaron with the seventy elders upon Mount Sinai, the vision of Isaiah within the temple, Ezekiel's chariot of fire, the ascension of Christ, Paul's account of the Third Heaven, the Revelation of John, the seven gates of the gnostic soul's passage, and a great many other writings deemed arcane and esoteric even among the scholars of her order. And as if that singular fixation were not strange enough, she developed a peculiar habit—sitting for hours upon hours in the convent garden, her gaze fixed upon the heavens without blinking, until at last, her aged, watery eyes lost their sight entirely. In later years, stories of her ascetic wonders spread, whispered in the cloisters of her fellow sisters. It was said that she no longer partook of solid food, that she subsisted only upon the mystical sustenance of prayer. And on the final day of her astonishingly long life, as she lay upon her deathbed, she began to murmur strange dialogue—disjointed, fragmented utterances, seemingly spoken to invisible presences, whispered phrases, half-coherent, half-lost in the breath of eternity. Then, at last, with a serene, beatific smile, her timeworn face, deep-lined by decades of devotion, grew still, and her final breath slipped from her lips like a departing spirit upon the wind.

A grandiose article in 'Le Corsaire' was what first made Phineas, who had taken lodgings at the *Hôtel Le Meurice* on *Rue Saint-Honoré* together with Jahdis, pause. The report—rendered in a tone of breathless exaggeration—recounted inexplicable occurrences aboard a cargo vessel, which had set sail from Calais for Dover just a few days after their escape from the collapsing *Hôtel La Porte Noire*. The ship had drifted into port without a living soul aboard, and the harbor authorities, so claimed the sensationally phrased article, had ordered the vessel and its crew—pale, blood-drained, their corpses disfigured with bite marks—to be burned in its entirety, fearing the wretches had succumbed to some hideous plague borne by rats.

Yet, no joy in the world could rival the intimate togetherness Phineas shared with the wondrous girl, whose soul he had sought to reclaim from beyond the gates of *Sheol*, for whose love—though unbeknownst to him—he had braved the perilous path of the seven gates and overcome the seven dreadful sentinels. These were blissful days, filled with a deep, mutual longing and whispered avowals of love, so that each fleeting moment seemed to outweigh an entire lifetime. Jahdis, in rapturous delight, marveled at the wonders of this strange world: the peculiar customs of its people, the way they dressed, their manner of conduct, even their trifling amusements, their ways of expressing love and affection, their quarrels and courtships, their commerce and haggling, and all the ordinary aspects that make up the rhythm of daily life. She gazed in wonder at the buildings where these people dwelled—be they the crooked, timeworn houses of common folk or the gilded city palaces of the affluent, the fortified citadels, or the magnificent edifices raised in reverence to their God. She inhaled the mingling scents wafting from bakeries and market stalls, the overwhelming diversity of sensations offered by a simple stroll through the bustling streets. Even the pungent stench of the great city—at times nearly unbearable, depending on where one roamed—coaxed from her an amused laugh. She sampled the strange foods concocted from the bounty of land and sea, sometimes with wide-eyed astonishment, at times with lips pressed tight in faint repulsion, and on occasion in awed, blissful silence.

In the presence of her childlike wonder, Phineas found himself rediscovering the mortal world, which had, in the fading recollection of that speechless trembling before the ineffable splendor of the seventh palace, day by day appeared less bleak and desolate. And yet, despite their love—despite an elation long yearned for and now at last attained—he found no peace. A strange, unshakable restlessness brewed within him, an inquietude he could not dispel, as though an unfinished task forbade him the full embrace of happiness. And so he resolved to uncover the fate of the man whom he had seen perish beneath the shattered vault.

Jahdis, too, was often seized by homesickness, burdened with anxious thoughts of Chirion, whose fate was unknown to her, and whose absence weighed heavily upon her heart. She agreed at last to accompany him. But had she been able to cast her gaze beyond the veils of this world and glimpse her homeland—had the vast distance between this world and the land of the two moons been bridged—her heart would have been soothed. For now, with his sole accuser gone from the splendid avenues of Erydin, and a witness—one risen from the deep halls of Neèbh and from that battlefield wreathed in smoke—testifying to his innocence, Chirion was reinstated to his former station. And the great griffon-beast, which had flown to him at Jahdis's behest, had found his grand house abandoned.

And thus it was that, at the onset of the final week of February, the two set out across the Channel in pursuit of a phantom whose existence, despite all speculation, seemed gravely uncertain. Obed, who swore that the sight of the fallen stone upon his desk had been his first cue to flee, assured them with conviction that apart from themselves and—by sheer providence—at least some, if not all, of the household staff, who had been lodged in the small servants' quarters near the great portal, only one other soul had escaped the crumbling edifice. A limping man, though his identity eluded Obed, for the dust had so altered his appearance that he had not recognized him. It was as if the doors of the guest rooms had been locked by some inexplicable force or that the calamity had seized them in sleep, or in deep communion with whatever strange rites they practiced.

Phineas urged him to accompany them, wishing for the giant's presence should he come to stand face to face with Lameth once more. But Obed declined—though it was evident that the decision weighed upon him—for despite all persuasion, he longed to remain in the city, which, now that Lameth was truly gone and the dreadful house razed to the ground, seemed to him like the fulfillment of all his dreams, a place of unforeseen possibilities. And so they took their leave of him with heartfelt farewells, proceeded to the nearest bureau to register for their journey, paid the fare, boarded a two-horse berline, and embarked upon the days-long voyage. They first traveled northward to the coast in the company of a red-cheeked mother and her spoiled twelve-year-old son, who sat enthroned upon a horsehair cushion, his freckled face brimming with impish delight, as well as the conductor, who had taken a seat in the carriage alongside them. Upon reaching the shore, they booked passage and crossed the choppy waters of the Channel aboard a schooner, the sea winds lashing at them as they neared the English coast. From there, they took another carriage—a two-horse *landaulet*, crafted in Germany with a half-cover over the rear, a style favored by some in those days—and made their way to Ipswich, from where, on the following day, they intended to visit Lameth's estate, which they hoped would, for the time being, be deserted. The coachman, a sullen fellow whose distaste for his profession was apparent in every aspect of his demeanor, dropped them off at a bustling street corner, bid them farewell with a forced smile after handing down their luggage from the coach's rear, and then, with a sideways click of his tongue, sent his horses forward—a movement that revealed a row of long-necked teeth behind the bulging, bearded pouch of his cheek. The rattling sound of the iron-rimmed wheels upon the cobblestone faded into the distance as they ascended the steps of the grand brick manor, their silhouettes swallowed by the swirling flurry of snow, whose damp flakes dissolved into puddles the moment they touched the ground. Phineas, his gloved fingers stiff from the cold, reached for the yellowed limestone frame of the door and unlocked it.

The sun was veiled behind a blanket of heavy clouds. A bitter wind swept down the street, worming its way into every gap in their clothing. Jahdis, bundled in a long scarf against the chill, had taken to a rather peculiar habit of pairing garments in an unconventional and not always entirely ladylike fashion, and now sported a broad-brimmed, rain-slicked cavalier's hat. She followed Phineas, shivering, as they stepped inside. As Phineas had abandoned the house in a state of inner turmoil, never once setting foot in it since his most recent dealings with Lameth, they found the rooms in a deplorable state. A damp, musty chill settled upon them the moment they entered. A thin layer of dust coated the furniture, and unwashed dishes lay stacked in grimy piles, forming haphazard towers of neglect, and it seemed that even under the open sky, they might have found more comfort than in this dismal place. Phineas fumbled with the matchsticks, and after some effort, managed to kindle a cheerful fire—feeding the flames with the lathe-turned legs of a broken stool, which had been tossed carelessly into a corner, and a few broad logs he had fetched from the vaulted cellar. As the warmth spread, chasing away the damp chill embedded in the stone walls, and the growing light cast the general disorder in the hues of a sunset, their hearts were lightened. They fell asleep in a tangle of cushions, nestled before the slowly waning flames, and despite the austere inhospitability of the room and the insidious cold lurking in every crevice, Phineas felt he had never known a moment of greater happiness.

He woke with the first glimmers of daylight, as golden beams, ablaze with motes of dust, flared like a conflagration upon the rippling panes of the tall casement windows. Stretching his left arm—where Jahdis had lain beside him—over his head, he clenched his right hand about his elbow, as though to wrest his limbs free from some unseen torment, and a deep groan of relief escaped his lips. Untangling himself from the nest of cushions, he carefully draped another blanket over the still-sleeping form of Jahdis, rekindled the fire as quietly as he could, and then, dressed in his black frock coat, a wide-brimmed hat shading his raven-black hair, which now bore the first traces of gray at the temples, he stepped out into the frostbitten morning to tend to financial matters, procure supplies, and arrange for the hiring of a housekeeper, whose experienced hand might restore the forsaken manor to habitable order.

After several hours, he returned home, successful in all that he had set out to accomplish, the handle of a well-filled provisions basket nestled in the crook of his arm, and with him, a small, elderly woman. Her long face, vulture-like in its severity, emerged from the fur collar of her dark coat, which was lined with a long row of silver buttons. There was something grimly resolute, even faintly menacing, about her expression—an impression no doubt owed to a life of hardship or sacrifice, or perhaps both. Scarcely had she stepped into the room—without so much as a glance at Jahdis—when she began muttering to herself in tones of mild outrage, bewailing the wretched state of the premises. At once, she turned the chairs upside down and placed them atop the long dining table, as though her foremost duty lay in remedying the disgraceful condition of the tiled floor. Her industriousness grew by the hour, so much so that Phineas, at first, sorely regretted having sought out her services. However, when the tantalizing aroma of roasting meat began to pervade the house in the later hours of the day, and when a steaming tureen crowned her masterpiece of polished candelabra, gleaming silverware, scrubbed floor tiles, and the freshly oiled wood of the furniture, he knew beyond doubt that hiring this tireless, order-loving woman had been a most fortunate decision.

Phineas uncorked a bottle of wine and let the dark liquid flow slowly into his tilted glass as Miss Padgett—such was her name—cleared away the dishes. She shooed Jahdis away with a hissing sound and an agitated wag of her finger, as though she were some bothersome insect. "I shall pay a visit to Lameth's estate tomorrow," Phineas confided in Jahdis. He ran a hand through his hair before continuing. "It would set my mind at ease to know that you are here, safe in our home. Miss Padgett will surely see to it that you lack for nothing."

"I faced Lameth when he still walked among the living, when he was at his most dangerous. I do not fear his ghost, nor the cold walls of his house. Let me go with you, that we may uncover together the answer to this mystery that so troubles you." Her features were solemn, composed, and as she spoke, the reddish sheen of her wavy hair seemed to absorb the glow of the candelabra.

"You misunderstand me. That is not what troubles me," Phineas replied, his expression darkening. "Something awaits me there, and though I cannot yet fathom its nature, my heart is weighed with foreboding. I could not bear to lose you again—not even for a short time, not even if I knew with certainty that your soul would dwell in those fiery palaces of heaven. Stay here and rest from the trials of our journey. I shall return before long—I swear it to you. This matter should take no more than a single day." Jahdis wished to protest, but something urged her to let it be. And so, on the following morning, having been kissed farewell with great tenderness, Phineas descended the rain-slicked steps of his home and hired himself a two-wheeled gig, setting forth—so he hoped—for one final visit to Lameth's estate.

Before proceeding directly to his destination, Phineas deemed it wise to visit some of the surrounding farms along the way, hoping to catch wind of any circulating rumors that might shed light on Lameth's whereabouts. Yet after scouring the countryside with little success—having encountered naught but the usual provincial murmurings, a predictable mix of superstitious ghost tales and hushed speculation shared in uneasy whispers—he found himself lost in thought, hastening along the country road past sun-gilded villages and fallow fields. In the distance, he caught sight of what he presumed to be the now-abandoned church, its lands bordering Lameth's estate, its stone turrets bathed in sunlight, the slanted roof of the nave seemingly consumed in golden fire as the rays divided into beams along the gabled ridge.

Bringing his carriage to a halt on the muddy, snow-fringed path, he fastened the reins to a weathered, glassy-crowned wooden post—stripped entirely of its bark, it jutted from the melting snowdrifts like a piece of driftwood cast ashore amidst clusters of emerging snowdrops. A harsh wind, heavy with damp, howled across the barren, snow-dappled fields, sending the long mane of his horse rippling like a storm-tossed banner. White froth lathered at the beast's muzzle like the foam of a washing tub. Phineas patted its steaming neck and then strode toward the stone-gray edifice, its walls choked by brambles, weeds, and overgrown grass. The deep imprints of his boots sank into the sodden earth, and as he neared the church, he became aware of strange, deliberate indentations in the mire—an irregular yet unmistakable trail curving in a half-circle from the rear of the building toward the entrance.

He found the church unlatched. Wiping the damp earth from his boots upon a wrought-iron scraper, he passed through the great, twin-leaved Gothic portal, crowned by a circular window, and stepped into the nave, its vault lost in a web of dark rafters. At the far end of the chamber, a figure clad in black was rummaging through a small shelf behind the choir stalls. As Phineas approached, the man turned with a sudden motion, and Phineas beheld the pale, freckled face of a priest peering out from the white linen beff of his black cassock. He appeared scarcely older than Phineas himself. Without further acknowledgment, the priest returned to his task. "If you have come to confess, you must return tomorrow," he muttered offhandedly, not bothering to glance up as he laid aside a set of folded altar cloths, their edges trimmed with delicate lace. "There is no service today," he added, as though suspecting his visitor had not fully grasped his meaning. When Phineas made no move to leave, the priest straightened once more, regarding him with a questioning gaze. "And whom do I have the honor of addressing?"

"My name is Phineas Camill. I see a successor has been found. Your predecessor, Reverend Smith, was a dear friend of mine."

"Yes, so it would seem," the priest replied curtly, a furrow deepening upon his brow. He leaned forward slightly and continued in a conspiratorial whisper. "I arrived just last week, charged with the task of breathing new life into this forsaken place. The service is to be held at the usual hour tomorrow. Enough time to set this disarray in order. But tell me plainly—how may I assist you?" Phineas waved the question aside. "I have no wish to intrude upon your precious time," he replied with a tinge of sarcasm. "A matter shrouded in mystery that troubles my mind and grants me no peace—that is what brings me to this place. But first, I wished to visit this site, so full of memories, and likewise of painful loss."

"Mysteries, hmm?" The priest echoed the word, his thin, freckle-framed lips pressing into a pensive line. "It is curious you should mention such things. You must know—it was no simple matter to find a replacement for this parish. Strange stories are told about this place, and the manner of Reverend Smith's passing certainly did little to encourage others to take up the position. "And I will admit," he continued, his voice lowering slightly, "that when I first arrived, I thought it all to be nothing more than the usual superstitious nonsense that clings to the countryside like an ill-fitting shroud—if you take my meaning? But soon enough, I began to suspect that not all of these tales were without merit. In fact, there are matters here that trouble me deeply. You may not believe it, but in my very first week, I received three reports of missing persons. "The parish constable, a stout-hearted man, crosses himself like an old devout widow every time I see him, as though he had been seized by the deepest superstitions. A boy's body was found—two others remain missing. And scarcely had I begun to unpack my belongings when it fell to me to deliver the funeral sermon for that poor child, a victim of what was clearly an act of violence. The perpetrator remains at large."

After conversing for some time, Phineas managed to extract a few useful details that largely confirmed his vague suspicions. When he finally took his leave, he noted with some surprise that the afternoon was already well advanced. He steered the hired carriage along the winding gravel road that led to the grand estate, and after securing his horse to an iron ring and announcing his arrival with a series of persistent knocks upon the heavy wooden door, he found himself staring into the deeply lined face of Edmund, whose weary eyes, encircled by dark hollows, regarded him with a peculiar mixture of relief and apprehension. "Master Camill!" the old steward greeted him, and there was a note of relief in his tone. "It is well that you have come. It seems your visit is not untimely. Have you an appointment with my lord?"

"Lameth is here?" Phineas blurted out, unable to conceal his astonishment.

"He is here—aye, and not alone," Edmund replied. "He arrived several nights past, under cover of darkness, in the company of another man. Master Lameth had his collar upturned and wore a wide-brimmed hat pulled low over his face, so that I would not have known him but for his voice. He seemed… weakened, and the other fellow, though he himself walked with a cane and bore an unsteady gait, had to support him. I fear he is unwell. "They entered the house in silence, and in the dim light of the lamps, I caught but a fleeting glimpse of his face. Something about it—" Edmund hesitated, his lips pressing into a thin line. "Something was strange. He dismissed me at once, bade me extinguish the lights. Ordered the entire staff away. Such conduct is unlike him! Never in all my years have I seen the master behave thus. Then they went straight to the cellars—to those underground vaults that none are permitted to enter. There is another way in, through the lower chambers—you must know that. And strange noises have been heard from those depths since that night. Had the servants not already left, I daresay they would have fled in fear. Since then, he has not emerged. Only his companion has been seen about the house now and again." Edmund gestured for Phineas to step inside. "But come, warm yourself!" As he took Phineas' coat and led him toward the drawing room, he continued his hurried account. "That man struts about as if he owns the place. He has rifled through my master's library, fetching books for whatever strange business they conduct below, but in doing so, he left the study in a deplorable state—papers strewn across the floor as if he had neither care nor regard. And by the way he carries himself, you would think he was the lord of this house! But the strangest of all is this: He refuses to let anyone approach the cellar door. When I sought to check on my master, to see if he required assistance, this fellow forbade it outright. Would not even let me set foot near that part of the house. Tell me, Master Camill, is that not a most peculiar affair?"

"It is indeed," Phineas agreed. "Can you tell me this man's name?" His voice lifted slightly at the end, as Edmund had inclined his head, his eyes narrowing into deep creases in his effort to listen.

"No, for the life of me, I cannot. Master Lameth never introduced him by name. Many have passed through these halls before, some of them men of great renown, whose titles were known even before they stepped through the door. Others, unknown to me, though the master saw fit to entertain them. He never confided in me as he did in you. Our relationship was… distant, shall we say. My chief duty was to keep silent and ask no questions." The old steward reached out, his thin fingers grasping Phineas' sleeve as if to lend weight to his next words. His knuckles, gnarled and swollen, bore the marks of old injuries long since healed but never properly set. "But you must know," he went on, his voice lowering to an anxious whisper, "in all my years of service, I have seen many strange things, yet never have I doubted my master's purpose—never have I questioned his integrity. But now… now I am an old man, and I begin to wonder. Of late, much seems amiss. Master Lameth did not seem himself that night. That man—whoever he is—had to exert considerable effort to guide him down the stairs, to unlock that hidden door. The very same door I was forbidden, under strictest penalty, to so much as glance behind." He paused, his eyes flickering toward the unlit hearth as if struggling to steady himself. Then, regaining his composure, he returned to the practicalities of the moment. "But forgive me—I am a poor host to you, Master Camill. You must be hungry. Will you take supper?"

"Do not trouble yourself!" Phineas replied. "You said yourself that the house is empty, that the cook and maids have left—"At that, Edmund's expression darkened. A shadow passed across his face, and his shoulders slumped as if the weight of years had suddenly borne down upon him. "Yes… yes, I will gladly accept whatever meal is available," Phineas amended, sensing the old man's dejection.

"Our larders are well stocked," Edmund replied with a tone of indignation. "Even though the master adheres to a special diet due to the delicacy of his stomach and rarely takes his meals at table, we have always ensured that provisions were ample, should unexpected guests arrive. Anyone of standing and name has been welcomed within these halls, and each who departed did so bound to Master Lameth in loyalty. Whatever controversies surrounded him, whatever accusations were leveled against his name, he would lay them to rest here, over a glass of wine. And though, upon his order, all staff have departed, I still have strength enough left in these old hands to prepare a meal that will, I hope, bring a smile to your lips." He cast a furtive glance over his shoulder, then lowered his voice to a conspiratorial whisper. "I am relieved to see you here. Speak to that man—perhaps you can talk sense into him!"

Edmund disappeared for some time, only to return bearing a tray laden with cold roast, an assortment of vegetables, and fresh fruit. A satisfied smile had settled upon his wrinkled face, as though the familiar ritual of serving a guest—or perhaps merely the opportunity to be of use—had restored a measure of his former vitality. Setting down the tray, he gave Phineas another approving nod. "I shall fetch you some wine," he announced and turned away. He had taken but a few steps when he stopped abruptly, as if struck by an unseen force. A hoarse, strangled sound escaped his lips before his body sagged, and in the manner of a draped cloth slipping from a hidden masterpiece, his sudden collapse revealed another figure behind him—one whose outstretched hand, gripping a blade drawn from the handle of a walking stick, left no doubt as to the cause of the old steward's demise. The body struck the floor with a dull thud and lay there, motionless. Serpentarius Stroude, cane in one hand and the bloodied dagger in the other, regarded Phineas with an expression of cold amusement, his lower lip curled outward in an exaggerated pout, the corner of his mouth lifted in a sneer of disdain. He said nothing. Phineas leapt from his chair, instinctively retreating several steps. His adversary, his face marred by several ghastly gashes, stood unsteadily, clearly struggling to remain upright. With deliberate ease, he withdrew a lace-edged white handkerchief from his sleeve and wiped the blade clean, then, rocking slightly on his feet, returned the dagger to its hidden sheath within his cane. Letting out a small sigh of relief, he leaned heavily upon the stick, tossed the bloodied handkerchief carelessly aside, and reached into his coat. When his hand reemerged, it held a multi-chambered *Collier* revolver. A slow, diabolical grin spread across his face as he leisurely cocked the ornate hammer and trained the barrel upon Phineas.

"'I wonder how this will turn out,' I kept saying to myself," he mused, his voice thick with mockery. "Then I hear Lameth whining and groaning, lamenting how he must answer to the Exalted One—how he must confess his failure, his disgrace, subjected to torments of the mind beyond your meager comprehension. And as I listen, piecing together the reasons for his rather extraordinary misfortune, who should come strolling through the colonnade but you? And, lo and behold, the dead girl rises again. And suddenly, I have the distinct impression that it is time for me to make myself scarce. And so I climb the staircase—only for the roof above to come apart, the very fabric of the house unraveling as if possessed of a will of its own. And the poor devils—those wretched souls trapped behind doors sealed as if by some ghostly hand—rattled their locks and screamed, as though *the great and terrible day of the Lord* had come. And then, just as I made my escape, half the ceiling came crashing down upon me." His eyes narrowed, as if contemplating his next move, then, after a brief pause, he resumed his taunting monologue. "Lameth will likely recover from his current state, as he has from every other mishap that has befallen him. And if not—if this is truly the end of his unnaturally prolonged existence, now that he has lost the favor he once held—then I shall be the one to continue his work. "For years I studied the secret knowledge under his tutelage, as much as he saw fit to bestow upon me. But all that he selfishly withheld, I pursued in secret. Through long nights of clandestine study, I listened to the whispers of those I summoned from the depths. A far greater servant shall I be to the Exalted One—a new Jambres! He has promised me power and dominion far beyond what your feeble mind could even begin to fathom—if only I see this course to its proper end. "And so I sat and pondered, while Lameth, in his wretched state, strove to recover his strength—not that it seems likely he ever shall. And surely, the Exalted One will never grant him pardon. For there is no forgiveness in the black dominions of the pit. "And then, just as I was weighing my options, there you stood before me, as though fate itself had cast you into my path. And now I wonder—what shall I do with you? Your death is more than warranted, after all. From all I have gathered from the master's ravings, never has there been a more grievous betrayal, never has our cause suffered a greater wound. "And why should I not master the language that even you, in all your insignificance, have managed to learn? What boundaries should exist for me, I who shall walk in the footsteps of my lord—nay, who shall inherit all that he leaves behind? Such tantalizing promises have been made to me, and unlike you, I shall not fail. Of that, you may be certain."

"Cease this madness!" Phineas cried, the weapon in that hand unsettling him far less than the thought of departing this world with his task unfulfilled. "Believe me when I tell you—I have stood face to face with that dark prince, that abyssal evil you so zealously revere. There is no love in him. He punishes failure without mercy, and surely, he would not even reward your success. Every virtue has been inverted within him, and the aeons spent bereft of divine light—his banishment from the source of all goodness—have scoured the last vestiges of the divine from his being, even those qualities that would lend dignity to a mere mortal soul. And do you truly believe yourself capable of accomplishing what even Lameth could not? You, a mere shadow of his greatness? And do you in earnest think yourself worthy to partake of that pure, primordial language of sorcery—to master the wondrous tongue of creation—when you have so utterly estranged yourself from its most fundamental precepts? Furthermore, you seem to have overlooked a rather pertinent fact: the scroll, to all appearances, has been utterly destroyed. I saw a flash of light, a conflagration of searing radiance that consumed that sacred parchment in an unquenchable blaze."

Mister Stroude's face took on a pallor, as though seized by nausea. Then, in an instant, it twisted into a grimace of contempt and derision, his response more a venomous hiss than speech. "There is always another way. And what do you know of my master's promises? What do you know of the manifold rewards granted to those who follow him?

Did he unveil to you the kingdoms of the world in all their splendor? Did you taste of the raptures beyond mortal ken? Were you shown the wonders unutterable? And was it not Lameth's own failure? Did the Highborn One not act justly in casting him down? Perhaps some frailty—some wretched remnant of humanity—had crept into his being. Had he broken you first, you would never have dared to falter upon the threshold! And were it not for that woman, whom he has spoken of these past days as though harboring some misplaced sentiment toward her—merely because she bears a passing resemblance to some long-lost dalliance, or shares with him, through the tangled paths of genealogical descent, some ancient kinship—he might have undertaken his task with the gravity it deserved. Did not even Jesus declare that he who does not hate his father and mother, his wife and children, his brethren and sisters, cannot be his disciple? If even that hypocritical deceiver spoke thus, how much more does it apply to the rightful heir and all who have sworn the oath? But enough! It is time for you to die!" Mister Stroude raised his weapon once more, aiming at Phineas with deliberate, almost indulgent precision. Then, with a sudden crack, the flash of ignited powder seared through the dimly lit chamber.

Having once returned from the very threshold of death, Phineas could never reconcile himself to being sent back there by such a preening, self-absorbed peacock—especially now, after learning from both Stroude's own mouth and Edmund's that the rumors surrounding the spectral figure seen emerging from the smouldering ruins were indeed true, that Lameth yet lived. Thus, as Mister Stroude fired, he instinctively cast himself to the ground, and Stroude, momentarily blinded by the powder-flash, misaligned his aim just enough that the bullet merely grazed Phineas. Cursing, Mister Stroude let his walking cane drop to the floor in order to twist the chamber of his revolver, readying another round. But then, suddenly, his face changed. His eyes widened in alarm. His fingers spasmed, his grip faltering, and his revolver slipped from his grasp. A strangled gurgling sound escaped his throat. Phineas rose slowly before him, gazing deep into his eyes. From his own hand protruded the long dagger that had once been concealed within Mister Stroude's walking cane. The dying man gasped in fragmented curses, his voice failing as he reached out, clawing at Phineas for support, his pupils rolling back into the cavernous hollows of his skull. Then, with a final shudder, his lifeless body collapsed onto the floor beside Edmund's.

Phineas closed the dead man's eyes and remained crouched by Edmund's side for some time, deep in thought. Then, rousing himself from his grim contemplation, he set about inspecting the house, searching for the passage Edmund had spoken of—a passage which, given that Mister Stroude had emerged from it, he could reasonably assume was now unlocked. Lighting a lamp, he descended the worn stone steps of a round, spiraling staircase, delving into the deeper recesses of the building. Not far from a brick-vaulted wine cellar, where endless rows of barrels and hundreds of corked bottles lay cloaked in dust, stretching into the vast obscurity beyond the reach of his lamp's glow, he noticed a thin yellow sliver of light—a telltale fracture in the darkness that revealed, behind its hidden source, an almost imperceptible door seamlessly fitted into the wall. Glancing over his shoulder, as though half-expecting someone to be following him, Phineas stepped forward and crossed the threshold into a corridor dimly lit by several primitive oil lamps, their flickering flames casting elongated shadows against the damp, rough-hewn stone.

Following this passage for some time, he halted before a trapdoor set into the floor, its surface reinforced with bands of wrought iron. A crude iron ring was affixed to it, and he had to grasp it with both hands to lift the heavy planks and reveal a steep flight of weathered steps, descending into the gloom faintly illuminated by the glow of his lamp. A musty, stagnant odor rose to meet him. Upon reaching the bottom, he wandered, lamp held aloft, through this secret world, at first believing it to be a subterranean network of tunnels, akin to those smuggler's hideouts unearthed not long ago along the coastal regions. But what he now beheld astonished him greatly, for instead of low-ceilinged passageways, propped up with timbered beams, there unfolded before him a labyrinth of far-reaching corridors of unexpected antiquity, constructed from bossed stone blocks of immense size, laid in the manner of *Opus Quadratum*, marked by decay and the ravages of countless ages. This, then, he concluded, was what Lameth's overseas laborers had unearthed in the depths beneath the estate and had, quite evidently, undertaken to restore, as evidenced by the extensive repairs of discernibly more recent date interwoven with the ancient Roman masonry.

As he traversed the timeworn vaults, he espied from afar a yellowish glow, framed by an arched stone passage to his right, its distant radiance hinting at an adjoining chamber. Lowering his lamp, he advanced through the darkness toward this unknown light. The passage took a sharp turn to the right, and soon he stepped into a brightly illuminated room. Towering bookshelves lined the walls, draped in veils of cobwebs and dust, their tiers burdened with moldering parchment scrolls and large tomes bound in wood and leather, the browned hides impressed with ornate embellishments, clasped with heavy fastenings, from some of which protruded chains. At the center of the room stood a round wooden table of considerable size, its worm-eaten surface testifying to the weight of time, and above it hung a leaded glass lantern, its octagonal body suspended by a thick iron chain from the ceiling's stonework. Smaller oil lamps, their blackened glass chimneys affixed with silver-reflecting shields to augment the light above, rose like miniature beacons from heaps of haphazardly stacked books. Along rectangular side tables encircling the main one, there lay an impressive array of strangely shaped glass vessels, whose counterparts could be found in a further cabinet near a peculiar kitchen arrangement, its chimney extending high above through the vaulted ceiling. Countless phials of liquid in hues both wondrous and repellent, round-bellied flasks, alembics, cucurbits, retorts, and serpentine coils of glass, each crafted in manifold forms, stood among small furnaces blackened by use. Among them was the furnace known as the *Philosophical Furnace*, or *Athanor*, alongside cauldrons, earthen jars, crucibles, mortars and pestles, vessels corked or sealed with animal hides, each filled with unnameable substances and concoctions, caskets engraved with mystical sigils, menacing contraptions of clay, metal, and glass, and—most striking of all—an extraordinarily large specimen of some draconic-lizardlike creature, preserved and suspended from the ceiling by twin cords, its leathery wings outstretched, its frozen snarl caught between the realms of life and death. All these bore witness to the fact that this was the dwelling of an alchemist.

Phineas examined several of the glass vials in the light of the overhead lamp, reading the numbers and inscriptions upon their labels. He uncorked one or another with tentative caution, brought them hesitantly to his nose, then, with a slow shake of his head, replaced them in their proper order. Circumnavigating the heavy wooden table at the center of the chamber, he turned his attention to the books and loose manuscripts strewn across its surface. Little among them was familiar to him, though Lameth had, in times past, granted him access to no insignificant portion of his library. Many of the volumes appeared to concern the lore of alchemy, among them a work ascribed to the magician Ostanes and another bearing the name of Zosimos of Panopolis—titles befitting the apparatuses which constituted so great a part of the room's furnishings. Here too lay Lameth's antediluvian map, which he had once kept hidden in his escritoire, along with that transcription wherein he had endeavored to reconcile those alien shores with the coastlines of the known world—now unfurled in plain sight for any to behold. But what caught Phineas's eye most was a tattered, well-thumbed volume—the same mysterious book whose authorship was attributed to those fabled sorcerers of antiquity, whose knowledge, it was said, had been wrested from the veils of secrecy through necromancy and divinatory arts. Yet this particular edition seemed to be a far older and, above all, a more comprehensive translation than the one Lameth had permitted him to peruse, as though the latter had deliberately withheld from him a portion of its arcane wisdom. Someone had been reading it only recently, for the book lay open atop a pile of other tomes, and Phineas's mind immediately conjured Edmund's words—how Mister Stroude had borne several library volumes down into these vaults. Taking up the book, he skimmed over its familiar pages until his eyes arrested upon a chapter hitherto unseen: 'On the Conquest of Death.' The heading alone sufficed to instill in him an unquiet disquiet, for the text which followed, though undoubtedly concerned with resurrection, was anything but an Easterly treatise, consisting as it did of pages upon pages of incantations and other cryptic writings interspersed with a most abhorrent account of cannibalistic rites.

The margins were littered with hastily scrawled annotations, which Phineas could only assume to be Mister Stroude's. *"Thou didst see me eat and drink with you, yet I took nourishment of an invisible meat and a drink which man may not behold,"* read one, citing the Archangel Raphael from the 'Book of Tobit,' with a marginal cross-reference penned upon a torn leaf from a separate notebook. Elsewhere, written in that same uneven hand, was another passage: *"Nothing in this world ever truly perishes; rather, the compounded bodies are dissolved. Dissolution is not death, but rather a severing of the mingled elements."* The words rang familiar—an excerpt, Phineas surmised, from the 'Corpus Hermeticum.' Turning a few pages, his gaze fell upon a loose scrap—rudely torn from another book, haphazardly inserted as a makeshift bookmark. It was a treatise on the Mithraic and Cybelean rites of the Roman imperial era, depicting, in woodcut engraving, an initiate bathed in the blood of a sacrificial bull, thus absorbing, through this crimson baptism, the creature's vital force. Further annotations abounded, ranging from erratic conjectures on that most sacred liquid—the primal essence of all life—to detailed anatomical sketches of certain animals: the dove, the sparrow, and the swallow, but also the hare, the cock, and the stag—as though one had sought an alternative source for that which the text, in frequent recurrence, called the *draught of the gods*.

He had been on the verge of setting the book aside when his gaze was arrested by the left-hand translation of an inscription accompanying a woodcut on the recto of the opposite page. The illustration, an exact replica of the original text carved into the smooth-planed block of wood in the long-forgotten tongue of the ancient Nile kingdom, described an enigmatic reversal spell—one which, if the translation was to be trusted, was capable of undoing that which had been set forth in the preceding pages. Indeed, it seemed the incantation had been recorded solely for the purpose of annulling the first, should the one who had endured the centuries by so unnatural a means ever grow weary of his long life, should he come to regard the passage of the ages as a burden, his ceaseless existence as torment. Yet, so as to prevent a rival magus from robbing him of his life by such an invocation, the incantatory phrases—by their very nature resembling the indecipherable utterances of that diabolically perverted distortion of the tongue of Eden—were composed in such a way that, according to the marginal glosses, they could be spoken to effect only by the one who had undergone the rite himself, or by a direct descendant of his own bloodline.

A scuttling noise, emanating from a chamber beyond, startled him from his reading. Hastily, he placed the open book atop the stack before him and resumed his path, proceeding into the weakly flickering glow of his lamp. In time, the corridor branched, and as he chose one of the diverging passages and pressed forward, his progress was at last arrested by an odor—one whose vile intensity increased with every step. The air grew steadily more oppressive, until at last it struck him with such loathsome revulsion that he hesitated to continue. A few rats—large, bloated creatures, unnaturally well-fed and repulsively fearless—seemed to beckon him onward, skittering past his boots as he raised the crook of his arm to his face, shielding his mouth and nose against the growing stench. They led him to a rounded alcove set into the masonry, its foul, corpse-tainted vapors sickly sweet with decay. Others like it receded into the gulf of shadow beyond, their recesses swallowed by the sepulchral gloom of the tunnel. A single glance was enough to make him recoil in horror, and never again, in all the years that followed, could he banish from his mind the ghastly image of those wasted, bloodless husks, their rotting flesh gnawed by worms, some grotesquely bloated, their mouths agape, putrid effluence seeping from their lips and nostrils. Stiffened in unnatural contortions, their pallid, blotched skin, tinged with hues of brown and livid blue, was drawn taut over their withered frames. And as the heap of corpses descended in successive degrees of decomposition, the flesh further defiled, the limbs further ravaged, it culminated at the bottommost layer in a nest of gleaming, picked-clean bones. If Lameth was the killer, he had made no effort to dispose of the remains, a detail that aligned disturbingly well with Edmund's account of his declining strength. Quicklime had been heaped over the bodies—no doubt in a futile attempt to stifle the stench of their decay.

Turning away in horror, he deliberately avoided inspecting the subsequent recesses, evenly spaced and built into the walls at regular intervals, choosing instead to retrace his steps to the point where the corridor had diverged. Following the second passage for some time, he at last emerged into a nearly square chamber, which, at its far end, opened through a broad breach in the masonry into a second, identical in shape. A wan light filtered down through wide shafts set into the ceiling at either side, lying, if his sense of direction did not mislead him, toward the east and west. At the center of the first chamber rose an altar, roughly hewn from pinewood, its sides fitted with compartments that held various vessels of oil and incense, alongside the ingredients used in their making. Upon its surface rested a bronze censer, within it the remains of extinguished coals, and above it—suspended by a golden chain—hung a lamp brimming with oil. Robes, discarded carelessly, lay strewn across the planked floor, beside them a headband of gold-colored silk, resembling the diadem of Aaron, upon which was affixed a plate inscribed with the ineffable Name. A wand, cut from the almond tree, a finger's breadth in thickness and an ell in length, lay beside it.

Within the altar's compartments, amid the vessels of incense, and even atop the altar itself, beside the censer, were heaped stacks of handwritten notes, scattered across loose parchment. Among them lay meticulously transcribed copies of strange diagrams, hieroglyphic characters forming arcane pantacles, meant to express the universal knowledge of all things. There were incantations for the summoning of spirits, squares filled with intricate permutations of letters—chief among them those composing the Tetragrammaton—long lists of obscure names, many mere artificial constructs containing theophoric or angelophoric syllables, some struck through and amended with variations, often followed by brief notes recording the success or failure of the resulting experiment. In the wavering script of those annotations, blemished with inkblots, Phineas seemed to glimpse the very terror that had gripped the scribe at the moment of their inscription. He stepped across the threshold into the second chamber, a smaller room adjoining the first, dimly illuminated by several overhead shafts. A layer of sand, two or three fingers thick, lay evenly across the floor. Near its center, a blackened, pitchy stain, spanning a radius of perhaps a yard and a half, bore the ghastly semblance of some hellish fire having once raged there. Beside it, a Faustian magic circle, its sigils half-eroded, seemed to take hold of his already fevered imagination and spur it to yet wilder conjectures.

But finding in these rooms no further enlightenment, he resolved once more to brave the rat-infested corridor, where, in the damp and lightless depths, he hoped to gain certainty regarding Lameth's fate. Binding a cloth about his face to shield himself against the mephitic stench of death—so thick, so unspeakably pervasive, that it seemed to seethe within the rounded hollows of the ruinous vaults—he pressed on, scorning the horror of that ghastly passage. He inspected several rooms, their worm-eaten furniture draped in cobwebs, their interiors littered with discarded alchemical implements, rotting wooden chests, and other detritus of no consequence. Again and again, the bloated rats crossed his path, darting over the slick stones, or retreating into the cracks of crumbling masonry, their forms vanishing into crevices that had yawned in the stone for untold centuries.

How long he wandered those dread catacombs, he could not say. But at last, in the oblique light of a ceiling shaft, beneath a massive column whose form branched into a ribbed vault overhead, he glimpsed the indistinct outline of a hunched figure, crouched over some unknown object upon the uneven stone. As he drew nearer, the figure ceased its movements and gave a low, whispering laugh—a sound so unguardedly malevolent that he shuddered to his core. He raised his lamp and took another step forward. The being crouched over the sunken flagstones bore some resemblance to Lameth, yet some ineffable transformation of monstrous significance had befallen him, some awful and irreversible change. His hands and face—the very parts of him that had touched the scroll and beheld the searing light—were hideously ravaged beyond all imagining. Blood wet his lips and ran in dark rivulets down his chin, and only now did Phineas perceive the thing sprawled beneath him: the body of a man, upon whom he was glutting his thirst. "You?!" cried Phineas in astonishment, trembling before the horror of that ghastly vision.

Lameth met his gaze with piercing eyes. With the filth-encrusted sleeve of his ragged garment, he wiped across that yawning, fanged aperture that had once been his mouth, then shoved the corpse aside as if its presence had suddenly become loathsome to him. Slowly, he dragged himself upright, clawing at the mortar seams of the ancient Roman stonework, until at last he stood to his full height and remained motionless. He was ghastly to behold. His long coat, stiff with clotted blood, hung from him in filthy tatters. No hair remained upon his head, his nose, ears, and lips reduced to shapeless vestiges, mere grotesque hints of what they had once been, his raw flesh marred by strange, blistered eruptions—blackened and red in patches, glistening in places where the skin was absent altogether. And yet—what rendered the sight all the more abhorrent—there was some unearthly force at work upon him, some power defying the known laws of nature, striving to repair what had been undone, as if his flesh sought, in places, to renew itself. "I had chosen you to succeed me! You were destined for greatness!" Lameth rebuked him. "But look—look what you have done to me! What that accursed light has wrought upon my form!" He stretched out his hands in supplication, so that Phineas, recoiling in horror, took several steps back.

"You have brought this doom upon yourself," Phineas retorted. "You murdered Jahdis for your own selfish ends. And as I have only now learned, your master has cast you aside, your power has been stripped away, and your dominion is at last undone. Even Serpentarius Stroude, who took the life of poor Edmund, has met the fate he deserved. You are alone now—your hôtel has been razed to the ground, and your designs have come to nothing."

A faint tremor passed through Lameth's form at the mention of Stroude's death. It was, Phineas thought, a telling sign, a confirmation that at least some portion of Lameth's former abilities had indeed been lost—for in earlier days, it would have been nearly impossible to keep such knowledge from him. Lameth advanced unsteadily, his steps unbalanced, halting. The pale beam of light filtering down from the overhead shaft struck him, and he recoiled from it as if in sudden fear, as though its radiance pained him. "Do not condemn me for what I have done!" he pleaded. "Do you know what it is to pass the centuries entombed in dust, surrounded by the bones of your own servants? To feed on beetles and vermin, to watch your own days unspool before you, never again to behold the light of day? To linger through endless ages in the abyss of despair? Believe me, you would do all things to escape such torment. The only true sadist is the Creator! He punishes without remorse. "I have done nothing but what was necessary—I have taken only what I required. I drained the lifeblood of those fools who thought to plunder the stone sepulcher in which I slumbered. And when at last I had emptied the camels and the dogs, when I had glutted myself upon an entire oasis, then—I understood how the Creator must feel with each passing day."

"Who or what in God's name are you?!" Phineas cried. His features were taut, as though he were wrestling with something deep within himself. "All this time, I assumed it was merely one of your peculiar affectations, speaking as if you had endured through the centuries. But surely—you cannot truly believe yourself to be as old as Methuselah!"

Lameth hesitated briefly, considering his words, before continuing, his tone now more intimate, more given to elaborate details, as though they were not standing in that dreadful subterranean vault, but rather engaged in casual conversation over a glass of wine. The hollow, sepulchral voice with which he spoke belied the illusion. "Once, I lived in Henochia, that great city upon the banks of the Euphrates, in the days of the vengeful King Argist, conqueror of many nations, who extended his dominion unto the shores of the Gihon. My father fell from favor—I never learned why—but I was present when they came for him, and after a long imprisonment, he was led to that stone-built amphitheater, its arcades looming high, where, to the delight of a howling multitude, he was cast into the arena with other condemned men, left to face a ravenous pack of beasts..." Phineas stared at him, bewildered. Lameth paused, then sought to clarify. "A towering wild aurochs, the likes of which once roamed the *Hercynian forest*—those same beasts of which Gaius Julius Caesar speaks in 'De Bello Gallico'—lions, hyenas, elephants..." He added these details as if Phineas's astonished expression had been one of zoological inquiry. "And after they dragged his body away, after his sundered corpse had bled dry into the sand of the arena, and after my mother's grief shattered her heart, I was left entirely alone. From that day forth, I served in the temple of the goddess Shamath under Tar-Sargon the Enlightened, a man of scant spirituality, whose prayers were far rarer than the blows he saw fit to bestow upon me. One day, I slew him with my own hands, as he squandered the temple's wealth on harlots and wine, and from there, I took up with a company of thieves. Later, my beloved student, I found my way back to faith—when a priest of Nergal, pleading for his life, offered me in exchange a secret that was his alone to give..."

"I am no longer your student," Phineas interrupted, his voice sharp. "Nor do I owe you or your cause the slightest allegiance."

Lameth's countenance darkened. Yet, a moment later, something like gentleness, or perhaps mere forbearance, softened the disfigured sinews of his face—so much so that, despite his monstrous and hideous form, one might almost have been inclined to forgive him. "Phineas, do not cast me aside!" he pleaded. His voice had become unnervingly gentle, and Phineas felt a strange pang—an uncanny sensation, as though he beheld before him a long-aged, once-beloved figure, a man grievously wronged in the past, now at the end of his road, seeking only peace. "I can lead you to far greater things than you have ever dared to hope for," he whispered, and in that moment, Phineas's eyes took on a peculiar sheen, as if his mind had been transported into some entrancing vision. "I have seen wonders such as no mortal has beheld," Lameth continued, the sorcery in his voice weaving its spell.

"I have witnessed, beyond time and space, the Ur-substances obey their command, bending before the pure language. I have watched as planets, innumerable as the sands of the sea, were drawn forth from the primal chaos, as the heavens blazed with the birth-throes of a billion suns. I saw a light so terrible in its radiance that no eye could withstand it—a star igniting within Sagittarius, the constellation of the winged, lion-headed god, summoning the silver-winding river of stars unto itself. I beheld beings whose mere gaze would strike a mortal blind—beings wreathed in fearful majesty, emerging from the clouds of glory to cast down the Morning Star, so that the whole of creation trembled, as though on the verge of dissolution. I saw the Highborn One cast aside his robe of purest light and take upon himself the mantle of shadow; I saw entire cities swallowed by the abyss, saw mighty nations, driven mad with fury, rise and consume one another in their wrath. Phineas, I was there when the Flood came and claimed all life. I sat upon the threshold of *Sheol*, naked and laid bare, a barren soul, and for a thousand years... I suffered."

As Lameth spoke, Phineas's thoughts turned to the deaths of Jahdis and Myrgil, high upon that rain-lashed cliff; then to Farah, lying at the foot of the bed, drenched in her own blood, the chamber bathed in the lurid glow of the inferno; to Reverend Smith's passing, for which—having pieced together all the fragments—he now held Lameth accountable as well; to faithful Edmund's fate; to that ghastly mound of corpses in the vaulted niches of the catacombs; to the lifeless form over which Lameth had hunched in his unholy feast; and to all the suffering wrought by this one loathsome being, whose wickedness had spread like a blight, devouring everything in its path. And so, in that moment, Phineas cast him off entirely, renouncing the day this wretched creature had first entered his life. "I am done with you!" he cut him off once more. "Never again shall I be at your service. All your schemes have failed, and all you have ever devised is lost. Enjoy the last hours of your wretched existence while you still can. I am certain that the constable and the furious mob he will bring here shall be most pleased to find, at long last, the answers to the horrors of the past—to learn who it was that so cruelly ended the lives of their loved ones. And when you hang from the gallows, when the crows make their feast of you, and all the world comes to know of your abominable deeds—then, at last, justice shall be served."

Lameth was beside himself. He resembled a wounded beast, cornered with no means of escape. His hideously distended eyes darted feverishly within the pits of his deformed visage. His lipless mouth quivered. In an instant, he cast aside the mask of gentleness he had worn, and with a feral snarl, he lunged at Phineas. His blackened, long-fingered hands closed around Phineas's throat, his terrible rows of teeth bared with a hissing breath. The lamp that Phineas had held slipped from his grasp, striking the damp earthen floor. Despite the frailty that clung to Lameth like a shroud, his grip was appallingly strong; those iron hands tightened with merciless force, choking the breath from him. Phineas clawed at Lameth's wrists, struggling to pry apart those claw-like fingers that locked around his throat with the unyielding might of a vice. He beat his fists against Lameth's chest, thrashed against him with all his might—but none of it seemed to faze him in the least. Never had he imagined such strength in a human being. And now, with horrifying clarity, he understood how foolish—how utterly reckless—it had been to face Lameth alone. His vision blurred. Darkness pressed at the edges of his sight. He sank slowly to the ground, his shoulder scraping against the rough-hewn stone as he slid down, kicking out with both legs, desperate to find purchase—to break free.

Lameth knelt over him, his grotesquely deformed face obscenely close. "Know this: it was I who killed your parents, and it was by my hand that your wife perished," he hissed. "Oh yes, do not look so astonished! Do you have the faintest notion of how much trouble you have caused me? Do you have any inkling how long it took to track you down? And can you even begin to fathom the torment of enduring your ceaseless vacillations, of feigning concern for your petty sorrows and trivial woes, of pretending patience for each of your missteps, lending my ear to your tiresome prattle? Did I not draw from the deep wells of my knowledge, did I not—out of my boundless generosity—lay before you the treasures I unearthed? And how did you repay me? After I squandered half a lifetime on you, you faltered at the threshold! You trampled my trust underfoot! Even now, I offered you one last, gracious proposal, yet in your obstinacy, you rejected it. Very well, then—receive your due reward!"

The pressure of his skeletal hands became unbearable. As unconsciousness crept upon him, as the last vestiges of strength drained from his limbs, Phineas heard, through the thickening haze of oblivion, the voice of a woman. Somehow, it seemed familiar, and yet the language—the resonance of those words—was utterly foreign to him. A sudden look of sheer terror overtook Lameth's features. The deathly grip around Phineas's throat slackened, and he dropped limply to the ground, his head striking the damp earth with a dull thud. From his side-turned perspective, he beheld Jahdis. She stood with legs firmly planted, her form tapering upward in perspective from his low vantage, her figure illuminated by the smouldering lamp upon the ground. In the crook of her left arm, she held the very book Phineas had previously found opened upon the stack, while her right hand was outstretched in a gesture of invocation, her voice intoning the long-forgotten words of that ancient text—words whose meaning Phineas, for lack of understanding the language, had only glimpsed through their translation. She must have followed him, he thought, and in her passage through the dreadful gloom of the catacombs, she must have read and taken the text upon herself—whether through intuition or divine guidance, he could not say. And in his heart, he gave thanks to those unknown teachers who had once instructed her in that tongue.

Lameth lifted a trembling hand with feeble slowness, his thin, corpse-like fingers twitching as though reaching for her. A rattling groan escaped his throat, and his ghastly, twisted mouth moved soundlessly, forming words that died upon his lips, swallowed by his own failing breath. His gaze, once cruel and imperious, now shone with an imploring plea, as though, in the final moments of his unfathomably long existence, regret had found him at last. Or perhaps it was merely the last flicker of something human—some vestigial ember of his former self, drowned beneath millennia of transgression and monstrous deeds—straining for one final voice before the terrible will that had sustained his unnatural life at last collapsed. And then, all at once, his body began to dissolve, as though time itself—long held at bay by secret arts beyond mortal reckoning—had come at last to collect its debt. Within mere seconds, the forces that had prolonged his existence across the ages unraveled, and his flesh, long sustained by corrupted magic and the knowledge of arcane horrors, crumbled into a fine, bluish-gray dust, sifting down like sand through the neck of an hourglass. For a brief moment, the outline of his form remained, a fragile silhouette of dust, clinging desperately to the shape he had once occupied. Then, even that final semblance collapsed, scattering in a silent cascade. And with a last, pitiful sigh—a sound that carried in it all the sorrow of the world—Lameth, who had defied the very order of creation for untold centuries, was at last unmade.

EPILOGUE

Iahdis stared, her mouth slightly agape, the book still clutched in her hands, her eyes widened to an unnatural degree at the unspeakable horror before her, so much so that her arched brows rose like the wings of a bird, nearly vanishing into the riot of her red curls. For an instant, it seemed as though the skin of her face might be drawn back from her skull, beginning at the nape of her neck. Then, with a slowness so paralyzing it was almost unreal, she let the book sink from her grasp, and, as though the utterance of that incantation—born of mankind's most primeval days—and the unleashing of that monstrous curse had drained her of all life, she lost consciousness. Phineas caught her in both arms, guiding her carefully to the ground, gazing down in deep concern at the valiant girl who, for love of him, had braved the spectral corridors of the dead alone. After a time of anxious waiting, she exhaled a long, trembling sigh and slowly opened her eyes; and as he watched, the pallor that had settled upon her features gradually receded. He helped her to her feet, guiding her with gentle care through the crumbling archways of centuries past, up the steep stairway to the world above. There, he laid her upon the bed of a guest chamber, pressing the rim of a long-necked carafe to her lips and coaxing her to drink. Yet the harrowing ordeal they had endured, and the certainty of lifeless bodies lying, cold and still, not far from them—one in the nearby drawing room, and others in a state of even more ghastly decay within the deep, saltpetre-encrusted crypts—so disturbed them that, despite their utter physical and mental exhaustion, they wordlessly agreed to leave that very night, fleeing the house that had become a mausoleum of horrors.

At dawn, Phineas, with the local constable following in the wake of his determined strides, once more returned to Lameth's estate. To his relief, the man seemed content with the simplest explanation: that Serpentarius Stroude, driven by sheer avarice, had slain the aged servant, and that Phineas, in a desperate act of self-defense, had struck him down. This, in large part, was the truth, though it scarcely encompassed the full magnitude of what had transpired. The constable, either unwilling or too superstitious to probe deeper, made no further effort to investigate the house. Phineas, having given the matter much thought, deemed it unwise to disclose the true fate of Lameth to the trembling official, who shrank within himself, his head drawn low between his shoulders as he cast furtive glances about the dimly lit halls, recoiling from the grotesque paintings that stared down from the stained walls of the stairwell. Now and then, the man crossed himself, shuddering at every shadowed recess and every unsettling motif glaring at him from their gilded frames. No, Phineas thought, it would serve no purpose to reveal the impossible—to speak of Lameth's dissolution into dust, of his end wrought by an utterance in a tongue older than the pyramids. Such knowledge would either be dismissed as the ravings of a lunatic or, if believed, would haunt the man until his dying breath. And so he let it be. He told only as much as would suffice—that Lameth had, by all appearances, perished in the ruinous collapse of his Parisian hôtel. He could only hope that the servants, summoned back to the estate by Edmund before his death, had failed to recognize the shrouded, dark-cloaked figure who had returned in secret to his domain, or, if they had, that they would not contradict his account.

Once the two bodies had been removed, and every living soul had departed from the estate save for Phineas himself, an inexplicable unrest took hold of him, compelling him to descend once more into the dreadful abyss of those winding passages and cobwebbed vaults. There, in that fearsome sepulcher, he unearthed yet more—things which, even if one were capable of clothing their screaming madness in words, ought never to be spoken of for the sake of the listener's very soul. Deep beneath the Roman foundations, beyond even those enigmatic catacombs, there lurked abominations veiled in ancient darkness, hidden away in lightless oubliettes reeking of a grave-miasma untold centuries old. There was a narrow, half-ruined cylindrical shaft he had at first overlooked, its damp and glistening walls set at intervals with curved iron rungs embedded in the stone. It was from that loathsome descent that Phineas, after long hours, emerged again, his face drained of all color, his features frozen in a mask of horror. He did not speak of what he had found. Without delay, he summoned a band of laborers and ordered the entrance to those subterranean vaults—and to all the boundless abominations lurking in the depths beneath—to be sealed forever.

The strange map, however, the one that bore the account of that unthinkable primordial realm, he had taken beforehand, along with certain other things that seemed to him of value. And since no heir or relative of Lameth's could be found, nor any claimant to his vast and shadowed holdings, and as all knew how long Phineas had been bound to the old man, none begrudged him when he had Lameth's great and voluminous library transferred to his own house in Ipswich. There, many of its timeworn, moldering tomes and ancient scrolls languished in sealed chests in the cellar, untouched by daylight, while others found their way into his study, which, in anticipation of their arrival, he had greatly expanded with a carefully planned addition.

Despite the wealth of its noble façade and the promise of flickering candlelight behind its high-paned windows, Lameth's abandoned estate inspired no covetous desires. None, be they vagabonds, drifters, or those most at home in twilight's uncertain gloom, dared to tread upon its grounds, and those who had aided Phineas in sealing that black, pestilential chasm spoke in ale-loosened tongues of the madness they had glimpsed in his eyes. Their stories, no doubt, did much to fuel the lingering dread that clung to the place like a miasma.

And so the house stood empty for a long while. Not even the rootless, the destitute, the most hardened of wanderers who feared neither god nor devil, risked crossing its threshold. But in time—when the nameless horror that brooded over the manor had been diminished by the blaze of a high summer noon—there came a thief, a man void of scruples, dull and brutish, whose coarser nature rendered him insensible to those whispered maledictions of formless dread. In broad daylight, he forced the great door and, in a series of repeated incursions, stripped the house of its treasures—its paintings and heirlooms, its fine silverware, its gilded plate, and its richly woven carpets—until the estate, year by year, fell ever deeper into neglect and ruin. And then, so they say, a fire broke out. Some believed that the thief himself had set it, though no one could say with certainty. Whatever the case, the house was lost. In later years, only the charred and ivy-choked remnants of its walls remained—a blackened ruin, whispering in stone of the grandeur that once was.

The nearby church, by contrast, seemed to flourish in exact proportion to the decay of the somber estate beside it, such that, even beyond the customary holy days, an exceptionally large number of congregants could be observed at the Sunday gatherings. And though the fruits of the glad tidings continued to ripen but sparsely, and the enlightenment in matters celestial and divine seemed not to take measurable root in the finely attired, neatly combed or bonneted parishioners—huddled there in their high-collared, patched, and well-pressed garments, singing hymns with great devotion—one could yet perceive, in some subtle way, an increase in the general sense of well-being, as though, at long last, a sickness that had haunted the land for generations had been excised.

Meanwhile, it came to pass that Phineas, stirred by Lameth's unexpected confession regarding the deaths of his parents—hurled at him in a spittle-laced snarl from the depths of the catacombs, in that moment when the wretched creature had believed his own end imminent—developed a keen interest in genealogical records, which he sought to examine in the local church archives. His request being granted, he spent long hours seated in that dim repository, poring over the hundred volumes of baptismal, matrimonial, and death registers, from which he unearthed certain peculiar entries that eluded immediate comprehension, that unsettled him in ways he could not at first articulate, and whose unexpected contents began to sow in his mind a troubling doubt. And as he spent day after day bent over those mildewed pages, brooding over their spidery, near-indecipherable calligraphy, frustrated by the slow trickle of revelation, a pattern began, at last, to emerge from the faded ink and swirling script—a certainty at once undeniable and profoundly disquieting. If the records were to be believed, nearly every male ancestor in his father's line, spanning an uncommonly long stretch of time, had met a violent and untimely demise—this, despite the perplexing fact that each had attained an age far beyond the norm, especially for the eras in which they had lived.

And then, at that point in the genealogical records where the entries for most bloodlines abruptly ceased, he stumbled upon a name—one that, in an instant, filled him with an inexplicable dread. A forebear of singular mystery, whose lifespan stretched to such impossible lengths that Phineas first took it for a grievous clerical error—perhaps a confusion with the name of a distant descendant born many generations later. Yet even the erratic, wavering script of ancient parish chronicles, which cited the man's birth in one place and his eventual demise in another, failed to dispel the growing unease that these were not errors at all. At last, in a bundle of crumbling certificates, he found an entry that shook him to the core. All indications suggested that this ancestor had indeed been one and the same throughout the ages—a notion so wholly inconceivable that even the most generous allowances of fate, health, and longevity could not possibly have accounted for it.

In his continued and more profound inquiries, he stumbled upon further peculiarities woven into the fabric of his enigmatic lineage—an obscured birth and the unsuccessful attempt to erase the record of a fatherless child, unusual redactions within the texts, strange later insertions and alterations—one of them bearing a handwriting eerily reminiscent of Lameth's—as well as the occasional wife listed therein, who, contrary to the prevailing custom of marrying within one's own community or a neighboring town, hailed from distant cities or foreign lands to which none of these provincial men should ever have set foot. Yet as his investigations yielded only deeper uncertainties, heightening rather than dispelling his ignorance, and as the limited means at his disposal failed to cast sufficient light upon that shrouded past, the somber archives, with their shelves of brittle parchment and crumbling ledgers of bygone decades, soon grew loathsome to him, so that, somewhat disillusioned, he withdrew into his home and devoted himself wholly to the needs of that dear and enchanting girl. And as he lay one night in the dim glow of a waning crescent moon, waiting for sleep to claim him, he drifted into a dream that, in retrospect, seemed as though a window to heaven had been opened.

There, his senses are magnified beyond measure, and his understanding knows no bounds. All things stand revealed before him. He hears a voice from beyond the veil that shrouds the divine throne-sphere, where all eternities lie unfurled like blazing scrolls. And He who dwells in mystery, that Exalted One who strides forth cloaked in tongues of fire, upon whose brow rests the terrible crown of the ineffable Name, turns His gaze upon him, so that he believes he must perish for the frailty of his mortal form. And that gaze sweeps away all darkness that still clings to him. And once more, he traverses the celestial ascent, beholding the ineffable threshold of that resplendent realm from which human speech is powerless to bear witness. And all the snares that Lameth, in his malice, had woven about him now unravel before his eyes.

He discerns that the Eternal One, by His own law, could not intervene, for He had decreed the limits of His own action, establishing that each being must choose freely. And the finger of that Divine Being touches him, and he beholds the divine order woven by the Creator into the fabric of the world—the immeasurable depths of cosmic truth, which no mortal mind could ever grasp, a universe that expands, unfolds, and presses forward into dimensions beyond the reach of language. And he knows that he is nothing, and yet—singular and beloved. And that Being draws him back from his vision, lest he be undone by the immensity of what he has glimpsed, though what has been shown to him is but the merest beginning of all glories, no more than a single grain of sand upon the uncountable shores of all the worlds in all the universe.

ILLUSTRATIONS

Page 27:
R. Abrahami Eleazari, *Ancient Chymical Work*, Erfurt, 1735

Page 111:
Jacob Meydenbach, *Tree of Paradise*, in: *Hortus Sanitatis*, Mainz, 1491

Preceding Page:
Nicolas Camille Flammarion, A Medieval Missionary Tells That He Has Found the Point Where Heaven and Earth Meet, in: *L'atmosphère. Météorologie populaire*, Paris, 1888

Opposite Page:
Gustave Doré, *Jacob's Dream*, Genesis 28:12: "And he dreamed, and behold a ladder set up on the earth, and the top of it reached to heaven: and behold the angels of God ascending and descending on it."
in: *Bible or Books of New Testament and Old Testament*, London, 1875

Abraham Bloemaert, *Adam Naming the Animals*, Engraving after a design by Abraham Bloemaert, engraved and published by Jan Pietersz Saenredam, Amsterdam, 1604

Opposite Page:
Jean Jacques Boissard, *Mercurius Trismegistus*, in: *Synopsis historica deorum fatidicorum: A Brief Summary of All the Most Notable Heathen Idols of Antiquity, Along with Their So-Called Prophets, Priests, Diviners, and Soothsayers*, Frankfurt, 1643

Mercurius Triſmegiſtus.

Quòd Iove ſis genitus magno, vis enthea mentis
Divinæ, et coeli cognitio alta probat.

Achillis Bocchii, "Revere God through Silence. Hermes as Harpocrates, the God of Mystical Silence," in: *Symbolicarum quaestionum de universo genere quas serio ludebat libri quinque*, Bologna, 1555

De Hooghe, *Hieroglyphica, or Emblems of the Ancient Peoples*, Amsterdam, 1744

Printed in Dunstable, United Kingdom

77663571R00272